I0593626

Hellion Chained is intended for mature readers, 18+, and contains multiple love interests, graphic intimacy, graphic violence, past parental neglect, and strong themes of drug addiction. It also contains explicit MM romance within the harem, and as the first in a trilogy ends on a cliffhanger. Read responsibly.

JADE BONES

HELL'S FIRE REBORN I

HELLION
CHAINED

For those who are fighting demons.

BLURB

I'm an angel barred from Heaven, and so who else but the Devil would take me in?

Through no fault of my own, let's just say I've been away for a while. But when my return to the Pearly Gates is blocked by a fiery, destructive power that shoots from my fingertips, I can tell you, no one is less surprised than me that the angels do not play nice.

That's when Lucifer steps in.

At first, I think he's on my side. But soon, I realize he's holding secrets, and he doesn't care enough about me to let me into the Brains Trust and share them. In fact, he enlists his two most trusted men to guard me and keep me locked in his castle so my power doesn't destroy Hell—a trickster demon called Tobias, and a jaguar shifter named Logan.

Now, all three of them are calling up feelings I'd long since locked away. When it's revealed that the blue cords connecting us mean they're my soulmates, it's yet another problem added to the pile of crap my life has become. Only, I can't solve this problem with fire.

Should I let myself fall for the men guarding me against my

will? Sure, they're kind to me and give me everything I could want, but they're still the ones holding the key.

They're captivating, but I don't want to be a captive.

I don't know the answers, but I'm beginning to think my romantic problems are the least of our concerns, because there's this voice in the castle that only I can hear.

And it's screaming.

This is a SEQUEL TRILOGY to Hell's Fire Burning (book one, Hellcat Escaping) with a new heroine and a new harem. You can read it on its own and it will make sense, but there are spoilers for the first trilogy's cliffhangers from the FIRST PAGE. So make your choice now.

Hellion Chained is intended for mature readers, 18+, and contains multiple love interests, graphic intimacy, graphic violence, past parental neglect, and strong themes of drug addiction. It also contains explicit MM romance within the harem, and as the first in a trilogy ends on a cliffhanger. Read responsibly.

1

HELENA

WHEN THE METAL DETECTOR GATES GO OFF AT THE AIRPORT, I FEEL like there's a grace period of about three seconds before people get nasty. When the metal detector gates—for lack of a better term—go off at the entry to Heaven, there's no grace period.

The angels tend to get a bit unreasonable, actually.

"What are you doing?" I yell, struggling in the grip of the angel that's holding me. His hands drive in far too tightly to my skin; I'm going to have bruises for days. "We've been through this! I was *stolen*. I've been in Hell for years. Of course the gates are going to bloody beep."

Beeping might be an understatement. Currently, the air is on fire.

When every other stolen angel had walked through the portal between Earth and Heaven, it had glowed with a glittering, golden light. So, naturally, as soon as I stepped up, the damn thing turned orange and started to spit sparks.

I'm feeling a bit that way, myself. Funny that.

"She must be an interloper," the angel hisses to his partner, ignoring me completely. "She saw the stolen angels coming through and thought she'd try her luck sneaking in."

"Excuse me?" I snap, incredulous. "You seriously think I'm not even an angel? I've got your wings!"

To emphasize the point, I give my shoulders a little shimmy so that the feathery wings of an angel burst free. They're a little clunky from disuse, I'll admit. They've had a few years of being permanently locked away, after all. But they're still there. Just as fluffy and pristine as the rest of them.

Sure, I've never really *felt* like an angel, but they've let me in once so they can let me in again.

The angels fall silent, staring at my wings with mutinous expressions. Then the other angel—the one who isn't holding me—pokes them roughly with his finger.

"Who'd you steal them from?" he snarls, and just like that, I realize I'm never going to convince them of the truth.

"Stop struggling," the angel snarls. "You're just making it worse for yourself."

"No, *you're* making it worse. You're *choosing* to make it worse. Stop treating me like a naughty demon, and we can work this out civilly."

A howling wind whips up around our feet, kicking the strange purple dirt into my eyes.

"Shit!" I hiss, squeezing them shut and fighting back the enormous urge to knee the nearest angel in the balls. It won't help, but for a few shining seconds there, it will really feel like it.

I'm not typically a fighter, but all those late night infomercials teaching women's self defense really leave an impression on a girl, I can tell you.

"Shut the portal off!" someone yells.

"Something's blocking it!" another voice yells back. "I can't touch it."

"Get an officer!"

The angel behind me shoves me to my knees, his hand around the back of my neck as he hisses in my ear. "Whatever you're doing, stop it. That's an order!"

"I'm not doing a bloody thing," I hiss, bristling at the unfairness of it. "This is the portal to Heaven, mate! If I could screw with it, why would I have waited until now, when you were letting me through?"

"I don't know how a demon's mind works," he spits, shoving me closer to the ground.

On the bright side, the wind isn't quite as strong down here, and I can see a little better. On the less bright side, that means I can see his face—the flaring width of his nostrils, the self-right-eous glint in his eye.

The hatred.

He isn't going to believe me, no matter what I say.

So I guess I'd better become someone he will believe. Or, at least, someone who can get me out of this mess.

I hang my head as if I'm ashamed, as if the mortification is just beating me up inside.

Behind me, the angel laughs. His voice sounds all twisted—far more like the demons I've been hiding among for years. I wonder if he'd love the torture, too, even though they're meant to be above it. *We're* meant to be above it.

But then, it's all in the name of righteousness, isn't it? It's all in the same goddamn name?

"You want me to stop what I'm doing?" I ask in a whisper, making him lean even closer to hear me.

He shakes me, rattling my head back and forth. "Hurry up about it!" He almost sounds afraid now. "The portal's about to blow."

"Come closer," I breathe.

The shouting in the background is getting nearer—angels

are coming down from their guard post to fix the portal. I wonder how many are on the other side right now, doing the same.

He leans closer, the harsh pant of his breath scraping against my neck. He's almost salivating. For a second, I swear he breathes in deeper, tasting the scent of me.

I crack my head back into his nose, shattering it.

I'm not typically a fighter, but against my will, I've learned how to be.

"I'm not doing anything, so let me go, you utter moron!" I snap, breaking free and punching him in the throat when he comes for me again. It's quite an angle. This guy is tall, and I'm barely rocking five feet on a good day.

He coughs, chokes, and lunges for me with an incomprehensible snarl. I dodge him and punch again.

Fuck, there goes a nail. Don't know why I even bothered getting dressed up for this mess. Try looking glam with a broken nail; it can't be done.

"You already checked me—I'm clean!" I remind him, yelling now. "There's nothing on me that set this thing off! You're just so shit at your jobs that you panicked and tackled me to the ground so it looked like you were proactive. Sorry, mate, but I'm not here to be your scapegoat."

He yells for backup and rushes at me, making me whirl aside again. The new angle gives me my first real look at the portal since it spat me back out.

Holy hell. That thing looks gnarly...

Grimacing, I duck below his attempted jabs and uppercut him to the chin. He howls, stumbling backward.

"Didn't they tell you?" I crow. "I've been working for Ronin for years now." The name hurts me, like a physical wound, but I don't let it show. "Don't you think he trained me up right?

What the hell does a glorified doorstop like you have that I don't?"

I flip over him, catching his shoulders with my knees and twisting so we land with me on top. I straddle his chest, disarming his knife and holding it to his neck.

My vision flickers, and suddenly I'm looking at a different scene—the same position, but the man below me isn't an angel. He isn't a demon, either. He's just a man.

Gibbering in fear, the whites of his eyes flash in the eerie fluorescent lights above us. Something drips—a broken tap. There's an echo to the room that sets my teeth on edge, and the acrid smell of abandoned bathrooms assaults my nose.

"I swear I don't know anything," the man whimpers.

Worthless, my brain decides, the assessment oddly disconnected from what I've come to think of as my personal thoughts.

I slit his throat, the taste of blood overwhelming the stench of old toilet as the droplets land on my lips.

I blink the memory away, returning to my real life at the portal to Heaven. The angel stares up at me, shock making his eyes wide. I readjust my knife at the angel's throat.

"Ronin took on the Devil," I whisper to the angel, relishing the sudden fear that sparks in his eyes, despite how that asshole's name chokes me. "Or didn't you hear?"

He whimpers, and the flashback hits me again. I close my eyes, delivering the last words into the darkness there so I can't see the other man's face. The man from my memory.

"Don't you think I learned a thing or two under him?" I force myself to smile, because if I have to live with what that piece of shit did with me, I'll at least turn it into a strength. Into power.

"Just... leave the portal alone," the angel whimpers.

"They're innocent. New souls. They're not even angels on the other side! Not even warriors."

What?

Realization hits like bile in my throat. He thinks I'm trying to start some kind of rebellion. I shove myself backward, holding the knife in front of me. "I don't want the portal, you idiot," I hiss. "I just want to leave! Fine, Heaven's spat me out; it's cool. I'll go back to Hell. Just quit bloody manhandling me!"

I don't even *like* fighting. Can't they see I'm only doing this because they started it?

I'm beginning to wonder if I actually want to go back to Heaven. Those idiots didn't even know I was missing. They needed Ciera to tell them.

My heart twinges. If I can't get through the portal, I can't get to Ciera. But it's not like she won't visit; she already visits Catrina, the angel who freed us all and lanced that disgusting parasite Ronin from my brain.

I stand up tall, backing away slowly toward where the demons led us up from Hell. I'll ask Catrina to call Ciera and tell her what happened. Anything that gets me away from this fritzing portal right the hell now.

I don't know how much more of this I can take. Something in me has been threatening to explode ever since the gate rejected me.

Maybe longer.

The angel scrambles to his feet, the fear in his expression fading a little now that he isn't pinned beneath me.

"Easy now," he says, jerking his chin out like he wasn't just ten seconds away from crying for his mom. Embers from the portal skim across the air in front of him, and kudos to the prick, he doesn't flinch. "Give me back my knife. We can deal with this like adults. Innocent until proven guilty—that's what you want, right?"

I hesitate. Not because he's convincing me with his logic; I don't trust this prick as far as I can throw him.

No, I hesitate because I don't especially feel like becoming a wanted felon today. And if I run away from a Heaven gate that's on the fritz, its magic swirling in a terrible, chaotic bonfire around us, with three angels unconscious—I hope—at our feet, and twenty more pointing the finger my way...

Well. I don't like my chances of surviving that one, no matter how many sympathy cards they give me for what Ronin did.

"You promise to be cool until Cat gets here?" I demand, bringing my arm across me in case he's been watching too many action movies and wants to be a hero.

I need someone high up on my side, over here. Someone who can de-escalate this situation and defend my honor without me having to beg for the privilege. Someone with a nickname I can drop in to make myself look even more important.

Since I doubt Lucifer is going to come to my defense any time soon, I'll take my Fellow Angel Turned Hell Queen, Catrina, thanks. Even if I don't know her super well yet, I know she'd be on my side; she just has that kind of vibe.

Something flashes in the angel's eyes, but he nods and backs up another step. I don't trust him, but it's good enough for now. I just need to keep a safe distance away so he can't surprise me.

The portal makes a noise.

"Is it meant to sound like that?" I ask, my lip curling into a grimace.

The noise is like what I would imagine ten thousand bees would sound like if they were caught in a hurricane and were also undead.

A new voice starts screaming, and the shouting is even

closer now. I think the angels have given up trying to fix the portal and they're coming to us.

This doesn't sound good for me.

"I'm not doing anything!" I say warningly, brandishing my stolen knife. "Don't even think about grabbing me!"

The angels come into view, and the sheer amount of armor they're wearing makes my breakfast threaten to come up.

"Come on," I hiss, rolling my eyes to the sky and praying to the harpies that someone comes to save me soon. "First you let me get *stolen out of Heaven,* and then you blame me when your portal breaks? You're not even trying to look like the good guys now."

Man, maybe I should stop trying too, you know? Take a leaf out of their book. It's not like I don't have family down in Hell; I'm the only one out of my nearest and dearest who made it to Heaven. Maybe I should just trot down the stairs myself and set up a reunion.

I always felt a little guilty about that fact, if I'm honest.

The undead bee noise kicks up several decibels, and the portal starts to... oh, God. It starts to shrink.

"Don't lock us out of Heaven," I whisper under my breath. "Don't lock us out of Heaven. I can't bounce back from that PR. I'm already on thin ice."

The fear swirls inside me, screaming to get out. The sensation is familiar. I see the man's face again on the bathroom floor, but I think it could be anyone's face right now—there are so many. So many memories to choose from, where I'm trapped inside my own head watching my body become commandeered for the most awful acts I can imagine.

The fear escapes.

Something explodes, and suddenly more than the air is on fire. There's screaming, horrible screaming, and the angel I've been caught in a stalemate with stumbles into view, clutching at his face. Oh God, does he still have a face?

He does. It's okay. It's just burnt, everything is burnt, and the portal...

It's not there anymore.

"We've got her!" The voice comes from behind me, and then pain erupts in my skull as the world goes black.

The last thing I remember thinking is: *that one was definitely my fault.*

I just don't know how.

"Where are you taking me?" I mumble, struggling against the chains around my wrists.

Someone shoves me, and I go flying, crashing straight down onto my face.

So much for everyone going so very gently around the stolen angels. I knew it wouldn't last. First chance they got, they blamed me for something, just like they always do.

The memory of my energy unleashing into destruction rattles me, but I shove the thought away. I put it where my personal thoughts used to hide when Ronin controlled me.

I've always been good at that. Probably a little too good for someone who's meant to be all sunbeams and goodness, or whatever, but everyone's got secrets, right? Point is, I got better at it under Ronin's thumb. Way better.

Shaking with pain, I rise to my knees and then back up to my feet. Rough hands grab me by the neck and march me down the corridor, which I notice is made of a mixture of marble and rock.

We're in the Devil's palace.

It's changed since my time here under Ronin's spell, though.

When I was here, it was mostly modern. The rooms of state, or whatever, were older. Fancier. But Lucifer seems to like his creature comforts, and who can really blame the man? So penthouse suites and elevators were the norm for the rest of the place.

Now, it's a curious mix of both.

I know that Lucifer re-jigged the power currents when he came back last, after fighting Hell's rebellion up above. And with that shuffle, Hell did its thing and terraformed into something new. But this is like he terraformed the palace into... well, a proper palace.

No, a castle.

The walls are lined with flickering sconces that do nothing to light the ominous stone corridor. The artwork on the walls is still a mix of old tapestries and more modern paintings, but I can't shake the knowledge that I'm in a castle. Looming ceilings, narrow window slits, and the candles all give me the impression that I'm Belle being led to her prison in the dungeon.

We enter an enormous room, and then everything goes spinning again as I'm shoved unceremoniously to the ground.

"Why do you keep *hurting me?*" I hiss, finding that, actually, I still have a few reserves of energy left. They're based on rage.

"You have to stop throwing stolen angels at my feet like this," a dry voice interrupts before I can really get going. "People will talk."

I stiffen. I'd recognize that smooth, low voice anywhere.

Lucifer.

Well, strap me down and call me Candy. Can't say I love the raging ego, but maybe top dog is just the man I need right now.

"You sent us a demon," the angel rasps, voice catching.

His throat must still feel raw from where I punched it. Good.

"I sent you an angel," Lucifer replies, still in that calm, icy voice. "Would you care to tell me why that angel is cowering in pain before me?"

Look, I wouldn't say I'm cowering. The fetal position is circumstantial. Carefully, I make a point of straightening up and kneeling so I can look the Devil in the eye.

Well, slightly to the left of the eye. He's an intimidating figure. I've never been able to figure out where I stand with him, even when I wasn't two feet in front and the sole recipient of his attention. He always seemed nice enough when he was attending to the angels in the temporary healing shelter they put up for us halfway to Heaven. But... he's the Devil.

And there's something about him. Something cold and impenetrable that makes you wonder what, exactly, lurks beneath the surface.

"She destroyed the portal!" the angel insists.

There's a scuffle of movement behind me, and I wonder if he was about to kick me again. The soft slink of metal tells me Lucifer's guards stopped him.

"Impossible," Lucifer hisses, and he's standing now.

I didn't even notice the moment he stood. It's like he was seated one moment, and the next had simply uncoiled—a cat striking down its prey. I lean back a little, unable to keep myself from staring up into his wrathful gaze. His eyes are strikingly blue.

They cut to mine, and it's like a jolt of electricity runs through me. More than just desire—which, hell yes, I am absolutely feeling at the worst possible moment, thank you very much—this is something else. It's like power.

"I— I don't—" The angel seems to abruptly realize that he's yelling at the Devil.

Lucifer's eyes slide back to his, and the corner of his mouth curves into the slightest smile.

Up close, he's even more beautiful than I'd realized, and it's not like I hadn't realized... Golden skin, thick black curls. The thin sliver of silver in his hair looks out of place, like an affectation put there with dye. But his eyes tell a different story. He's thousands of years old. How did I ever forget?

"Allow me to get this incredible story straight," Lucifer says, still in that icy, still voice. "You were tasked to guide a number of your own warriors—who had been stolen and abused in Hell—back to Heaven. All but one made it through before the portal... did what? Went up in smoke? Flashed red and produced a big black sign on it saying 'no entry'?"

The angel blusters, but it's this weird kind of silent bluster. Like he's got no more air in him.

"And then," Lucifer continues, his voice now a low purr, "you decide that the culprit must be one of those victims."

The word 'victim' jolts me from my trance, and yet, it doesn't have the effect it usually does. Normally, it fills me with rage when I remember what Ronin turned me into. When I think of all the things I watched through my own eyes as someone else controlled me, brainwashed me.

From Lucifer's lips, the word 'victim' sounds like an oath, as though he's a witness standing before the jury in my defense. He makes it sound like the tree that grows from scorched earth. Like the strength of metal once it's been tempered through violence.

Lucifer makes the word sound like a strength, and I feel that little surge of electric power once more. Except, this time, I see it, too. It stretches between my body and his—a flickering blue cord. And then it vanishes.

"The power surrounded her!" the angel says, visibly shrinking now.

Clever boy. He's caught up to the danger.

"Surrounded her," Lucifer repeats. "Do explain."

"Like electricity," he stammers, and my heart skips a beat.

The electricity between me and Lucifer sparks again, lighting up his face in an icy blue light, and I see it for what it is now—danger. Intoxicating danger.

"It leaped from her to the portal and everything... caught fire," the angel continues.

I think there's smoke in the air. Am I imagining it?

"Not again," I whisper.

The sound is so quiet, there's no chance of being heard, but Lucifer turns to me all the same. His eyes seem to bear into me as he watches. And waits. No one else notices the flickering blue light, the pulse of power connecting us.

The angel jabbers in the background, describing the embers and all the ways they knew it was me. The white light that shone in my eyes. The way the portal spat me back out as it darkened like a storm. The lines of power that connected me to the portal right before each line shattered.

I don't think Lucifer is listening.

It's like the world has narrowed to the two of us. I'm pretty sure my life depends on what he's about to say next, and I can't read his expression at all.

His gaze flicks to the blue line between us, but it's so quick I'm not sure if I imagined it.

"Perhaps your angel has been chasing Heaven for too long, and she's forgotten who she is," Lucifer says distantly.

The angel stutters to a halt. "Why would that make her forget who she is?"

"That tends to happen when one chases a love that is undeserving." The angel flinches, as if Lucifer struck him. Lucifer's eyes flash with cruel delight, and he finally turns away from me. "After all, if you deserved her, you would have found her, would you not?"

There's a pause, and this time when Lucifer speaks, his voice is harsh. Final. It snaps me straight out of my daze.

"Thank you for your diligence," he says, somehow making the words an insult. "I'll take it from here."

"What will you do with her?" the angel asks, as if he can't stop himself.

Lucifer pauses, and a roll of thunder crashes through the room. Or maybe it's just through my body—starting at my head and swooping all the way down to my toes.

"For now, she'll stay here with me."

2

LUCIFER

"THIS IS BAD FUCKING NEWS," I SAY, GRIPPING THE EDGE OF THE bathroom sink. "Tell me you didn't feel what I felt in there."

"If I could feel it, you'd have a far bigger problem on your hands, buckaroo." Catrina's chirpy voice comes from behind me. I look up into the mirror to find her examining my shampoo bottles with interest, her legs delicately crossed as she perches on the edge of my bathtub. "Because *I* am a package deal, in case you had forgotten."

"If only I could," I mutter.

She ignores me.

I'm not sure how I found myself in my ensuite after that meeting with the angel Helena, but here I am. I'm even less sure how Cat found me. She managed to witness the tail end of my altercation with the dickhead of an angel restraining Helena, but everything after that remains a blur.

There's something soothing about the carefully decorated walls in here, at least. If I'm going to utterly lose the plot, it's a good place to do it. It's the one part of the palace that didn't shift when the rest of the world did.

I resurrected too much of the old Hell, I think, though I'll never admit it to anyone. There are wings in the palace now that haven't seen the light of day for centuries.

It's become a castle again. Worse—even the parts that aren't ancient, like my penthouse suite, *feel* ancient. Because I can sense the weight of the rock beneath them. I can feel Hell calling to me, like the bones of the Earth.

And when I walk the ancient halls that I did unearth, it's like I'm alive in those centuries once more.

I even dragged up Tobias' wing, somehow, for fuck's sake. I'm working on blocking it up again, but the castle won't let me so far.

Cat laughs as she looks up and catches my eye, her own dancing with amusement. "So if I could feel the start of your soulbond with Helena, then I'm afraid that would mean *you*, my dear Devil, were also bonded to Dax, Marek, and Colton."

She grins brightly, dropping my shampoo back into the caddy with a clatter while I briefly contemplate the horror of that statement.

"I don't *share*," I snarl, my eyes flashing golden.

And I definitely don't share those men or with them. There would be casualties.

"Of course you don't." She laughs. "So, no, I couldn't feel it. And that's precisely how we know it's real."

"Fuck."

"Mmm," she hums joyfully. "By the way, why did you say Helena had forgotten who she was?"

I flinch, recalling what Cat went through—her own experiences with amnesia. "I didn't mean like that. I'm sorry, my dear."

Her expression softens. "I'm not hurt; I just had to check."

I swallow, searching for the words. "It was only a sense I got; I'm not completely sure why I said it." Other than the fact that Heaven really doesn't deserve her. "Perhaps I was hoping it was true, because if she had simply forgotten herself and the portal was confused, that is something one can easily fix."

"Is it?"

I blink up at Catrina once more, noticing the calm, steady certainty in her gaze. The steel.

When Ronin—one of my kings in the Devil's Court—rose up against me, he played a long game. For years, he captured angels from Heaven and brainwashed them until they became his spies. Catrina was the only one he couldn't break to his will, but there was a price for that resistance.

The torture he put her through broke her mind, and she spent years down here, forgotten, fractured, until she rose up again.

It was for her that I rebuilt Hell at all. That I took Hell's power currents, its rivers, back into the jewel that funnels them and reset it all, shifting the lands all at once instead of drop by drop. Ronin's actions proved to me that the Hell I ruled was no longer balanced, and the sadistic hellborn among my ranks had outweighed the kind ones while my back was turned. While I...

Well. Let us say I was asleep, and now I am awake.

Ronin's rebellion continues—under the worst name I've ever heard, the *Rising Snakes*, for fuck's sake—and I intend to squash them into the dirt.

Sometimes, I forget I'm not the only one Ronin hurt. I'd do best to remember from now on, especially if Helena is staying for a while.

She, after all, is one that he did break.

I watch Cat carefully, waiting to see if this steel becomes something more. But then she smiles—as she always does—and climbs from the edge of the bath. The atmosphere shifts, easing back into friendly camaraderie.

Cat hooks her arm through mine and leads me from the room.

"You know, I didn't invite you in here," I tell her, one eyebrow raised.

"You'll have to do more than that to kick me out," she says. "Don't you know I don't take hints?"

"It wasn't a hint," I say flatly. "I'm telling you to leave."

She sighs. "There you go with those mixed messages again."

An odd swirl of emotions flickers in my chest. Irritation, affection... anger. "Cat," I say, my voice even quieter than before. "You know I like you, but a man has limits."

Her eyes flash, her own anger flickering just below the surface. "And even the Devil can be an idiot," she says.

My teeth clench together. "Catrina, this is a warning."

"And who will warn you, Lucifer?" she snaps, and suddenly it isn't two people circling in anger, but two fallen Seraphim clashing in righteousness. "Who will you trust to warn you when danger comes knocking?" She steps away, holding her hands up in easy defense. "I'm worried about you. That's all. And you won't even give me that privilege."

Her sadness takes over then.

"I don't mind, Lucifer," she says carefully. "It shouldn't be me you're coming to, anyway. But you need someone, and I've been here long enough to see what they all just accepted. There is no one. Why is there no one?"

I grow very still, a familiar ice overtaking my veins. "I think you should leave," I say finally.

If possible, Cat's sadness grows even stronger, and the ice hardens.

"You're always on the other side of the room," she says quietly, looking down at the scant few inches separating us. "We're here whenever you want to join us."

She sighs, dropping the subject finally as she switches to the slightly less terrifying issue at hand.

"Whatever is happening between you and Helena, she definitely destroyed that portal. But I can't figure out what power she used to do it. Colton will look into answers and let you know what he finds."

Cat watches me silently, and for a moment I'm sure she knows what I'm thinking. I'm sure she knows the small but significant details of this situation that I haven't told her.

But she can't, and I won't tell her, because this problem is my burden to bear.

If I'm even right about what I suspect, which, logically, I can't be.

Her jaw tightens, but she doesn't call me on the things I won't say. She can't read my thoughts; only one demon can do that.

"Alright, then," she says, straightening. "We're heading into Death for a few weeks. Got a soul blinking in somewhere near the Distant Orchards. Try not to burn everything down while we're gone." She taps her hand twice on the back of the sofa and leaves me to my thoughts.

I blink at her retreating figure. It's a gesture she's picked up from Colton, sort of. Two raps of the knuckles on a table as he stands up. But with Catrina, it's different. I get the impression she would have liked to pat my hand instead, or my shoulder, and I'm not sure how that makes me feel.

I'm not sure how I feel about seeing these four demons meld together to become something new, something both greater and gentler than they were alone.

I grit my teeth and turn away. My fingers twitch, my hands begging to reach for the vase or the ornamental statue by the door and smash them against the wall. But I don't.

There's ice in my veins, and if I can keep it there, I can prove to them all that they're wrong. They're wrong about me, about this bond... about Hell.

I bring my hands up in front of my face, studying them. Long, pale fingers, covered in scars. I used to wear rings, but they remind me too much of Tobias, and after what Ronin did to me... I don't want to think about Tobias. I wait until the trembling stops, until I'm back in control.

"So, Cat thinks it's a bond," I say out loud, running my hand through my hair. Dark curls fall in front of my eyes, and I realize I'm gripping the hair too tightly. Fuck's sake. "It's just a Ludus bond," I snarl in agitation. "Blue is Ludus. Means nothing. Isn't even through the neck."

Except it might have been through the neck. I couldn't quite tell. The entry point was... vague.

It has to be the shoulder. A Ludus bond through the shoulder means nothing—a connection based on flirting and fun. We have a thousand of them in a lifetime. Well... humans, perhaps fewer. Five. Ten.

Two, typically.

It's a connection we carry to our death bed, but as far as soulbonds go, they're the least committed of the lot.

I can ignore it.

Decision made, I allow the ice to thaw a little. Now that I know what's beneath it, it's safe to let it go. I only have to make sure there's nothing but steel and fire below the ice.

Just to be certain, though, I call in a little hellfire and turn to the mirror in the corner of the room.

A demon's face stares out of it. Twisted sinew coats bleached bone, my own skull leering at me as if this terrifying face knows something I don't. I reach for the carafe and pour myself a glass. Then I turn to the mirror, holding my own gaze and tilting my head from side to side.

It isn't just bone and sinew; there's golden metal bolted into the skull. Armor that never fails me. Armor that even God can't penetrate, although he'd love to try.

Even this face, though, isn't the Devil's face. This is just a demon face. My demon face—my soul, made visible from the hellfire.

Oh, my soul and the Devil's face are similar, for sure, but for two key details: the shape of the skull... and the horns of the beast.

It's difficult to comprehend until you actually see the Devil's face and see how much *more* those features can become. Until you see that my demon soul is only a pale imitation of the real thing.

I've seen the Devil's face.

I wore it for centuries, while ice coated my body and the souls of the worst sinners kept me alive.

I never want to see that face again, and looking at my soul now, I can finally relax with the knowledge that I don't have to. Not today. He might be close to the surface, but I am still in control.

Banishing the hellfire, I turn away from the mirror and smile into the amber liquid, stability finally restored.

As I sip my drink, I even form a plan to deal with Helena. First item that needs addressing—her comfort. I'll send Logan with a few things to help make her settled while she waits. And then, to solve the actual problem...

Something has clearly gone wrong after she's spent so long in Hell, which means I simply need to correct the error. I thought I had identified the power rolling off her in the throne room, but given time to think about it... no. It's impossible.

Helena is just giving off invalid readings because of how long she's been in Hell when she shouldn't have been.

It's incredible to think she's been in Hell for so many years. She's just so... angelic.

I wince, covering the grimace with another sip. It's not how I typically describe people—and if I do, it isn't usually a compliment, like it is now—but in Helena's case, it happens to be true. She's barely scraping five feet tall, with her thick, wavy hair wound in a perfect braid down her back, and bright, curious eyes that seem to see far more than she notes out loud. Not to mention her lilting, curious accent that makes me want to say anything just to hear how she responds.

Not a bad person to be soulbound to, for sure. In another life, maybe...

But I can't handle that complication right now, so it's best to resolve this quickly.

Thanks to Ronin, the system doesn't know where to put her. Since she obviously belongs in Heaven, it simply means the system needs to be reset.

So, I'll pass her through Judgment.

Even once souls have gone through the initial Judgment—Heaven or Hell—there are more layers we pass them through, down here. We need to know where they belong, in Hell. We need to know how to treat them.

With Helena, I'll pass her through it all, starting right back at a soul's first Judgment.

We'll clear whatever is mistakenly blocking this angel from returning to Heaven, and then I'll send her on her way. Back to where she belongs. And after that's taken care of, I can go back to dealing with the shit Ronin left behind him.

In other words, I can go back to dealing with what really matters.

The angels will be out of my hair, Catrina will quit psycho-analyzing me, and Helena will be back where she belongs.

We'll all be where we belong.

I down the glass and drop it back onto the tray.

3

HELENA

THE DEVIL WASTES NO TIME IN PROVIDING ME AN ESCORT TO MY rooms. The guard who leads me there is silent and stoic, which suits me just fine because the adrenalin that got me through the portal situation has long since pissed off. All I feel now is shaky and alone, and the last thing I need is a chatterbox.

And yet... it niggles at me that Lucifer didn't take me there himself.

Everything I'd heard about the big guy from Catrina made it sound like he was reasonable. Logical. Sure, you didn't want to get on his bad side, but it was at least possible to be on his good side. At least, that's how I'd understood it.

But the casual way he dismissed me from the throne room after the angel left told a slightly different story.

Maybe it was just Cat. Maybe there's something special about her that made even the Devil soft on her. Something that I don't possess.

I curl up on the soft cushions of the window seat in my room and stare blankly out the window.

What am I meant to do now?

Without the adrenaline to see me through, I'm left with the unpleasant realization that everything has gone tits up. I'm stuck here. I mean, it's not like I really wanted to get back to Heaven. I mean, I did, of course. It's Heaven; who wouldn't want to go there? It's a twilight world of ethereal purple... purpleness. It's beautiful.

But part of me thinks I was just kind of going through the motions, or—

You know what? I don't want to talk about it.

But I don't want to be here anymore, that's for sure. I don't want to be in Hell. I'm ready to put all of that behind me. Everything that Ronin did to me... I'm ready to forget it and move on. And now it's like I'm stuck in a cage of my own making.

So what do I do?

Do I wait patiently until Lucifer sorts out the problem of my paperwork and sends me on my way?

Or do I get myself out of here?

I think the answer is pretty clear, but I'll probably need to use some of my angel powers to do it. And I'll need to have a proper plan before I pull those out, because once I start manipulating demons, I'm on a time limit to get out the front door.

Angels have powers of influence. With a little nudge and a little twist, we can move someone down the path of righteousness... or otherwise.

I haven't needed to use them in a while, but I've always got them waiting in the wings. They're my little trump card, ready to save me when I don't have enough time to attempt something more discreet.

So, what's my plan?

A knock at the door startles me out of a thought loop that's slowly becoming all-consuming.

"Come—" I begin to answer, but the door opens immediately.

I lift one eyebrow. Why bother knocking if you're just going to charge through?

I don't say anything out loud, though—not until I can see who it is, and therefore how they might react.

A sheepish face appears through the gap in the door. A grinning, sheepish face that shoves all protests from my mind.

Shit, this man is good looking.

He grins, hazel eyes sparkling as he shakes his long red hair out of his face. Actually, red might be the wrong word. There's definitely red *in* it, but... it changes with the light. From some angles it's brown, from others it's auburn. It's... it's mesmerizing, actually. Already, I just want to run my fingers through it.

And if that weren't enough, he has broad shoulders that are covered in delicious motorbike leather, and a black shirt that stretches tight across his chest.

Boy howdy, what is he doing here?

"Sorry, I wasn't sure you'd heard me," the man says cheerfully, giving me a once over of his own that ends with a little flicker of heat in his eyes. "I've knocked a couple of times."

Oh.

A flush creeps onto my cheeks, reminding me yet again that the adrenalin of my fight with the angels has long faded. I'm all on my own now, with only my usual skills to get me through.

My skills are a little different, and they typically rely on me having more of a head start than this. I don't like being surprised.

The guy apparently takes pity on me and holds up a large box from the corridor, as if it's an answer.

I frown at him. "What's that?"

"Lucifer wanted something sent up to your room, and I'm the bell boy."

Okay, he's so not the fucking bell boy. But something about

the way he says it so cheerfully makes me think that this isn't his first time running errands for Lucifer.

Maybe he's the Devil's messenger boy. Does the Devil have a messenger boy? Oh my God, is he a PA? Am I looking at the personal assistant to the most powerful demon in Hell?

I take him in again from head to toe: the long flowing hair, the motorcycle leather, the pointy black boots... He's certainly bringing a new look to PAs everywhere.

Then, reluctantly, I pull my attention away. If he *is* Lucifer's assistant—or his right-hand man, which would make more sense from his attitude and clothing—then I shouldn't get too attached. He's not a distraction I can afford.

Given the little flicker of interest in his eyes, I should make that clear.

"Well, if that's what the Devil wants," I say through gritted teeth, gesturing vaguely with my hand as I turn away. "Do what you need to."

I hear the guy make a soft sound behind me, like he wants to protest, but since I've already turned away, he doesn't say anything.

After a minute, I hear the soft sounds of someone lugging in heavy furniture.

I stick to my perch on the window seat and gaze down onto the vista of Hell below us, waiting for him to finish. It's remarkably green down there, with lush gardens and forests, although still kind of... spooky.

The sun is clearly fake—something I never noticed when I was under Ronin's command—and it shines an eerie orange light onto everything.

After five minutes of this, where my agitation is slowly growing, I have to turn around again.

The box has become ten boxes, and they're all piled high in the center of the room.

"What the hell is this?" I splutter.

This isn't just sending something up to my room; this a whole new room's worth of stuff.

"Well," the guy says, and it occurs to me that he hasn't given me his name. Which is, you know, pretty rude if we think about it, and I'm not going to be the one to prompt him. "As far as I understand it, Lucifer thought you could do with some things to occupy your time, and so..." He gestures broadly. "Books. And clothes. And some of those funny little perfume bottles, too."

Clothes. Perfume. Books.

Books!

My eyes widen with interest, and already I'm standing and walking across the room before I know what I'm doing.

This might just be the first good thing to happen today. I crack open the nearest box, while the man who won't give me his name chuckles softly and turns away, retrieving more boxes from the crowded hallway.

Wow, this selection is... It's quite something. With shaking hands, I pull out a first edition of Lord of the Rings.

Then I remember that I'm not alone.

Glancing over my shoulder, I see the man has his back turned to me. I shift my body so that it's hiding the cover, and I very carefully crack it open.

It's in pristine condition. I pull open the drawer beside my bed and shove the book inside, slamming it shut just as the man turns around.

He quirks a brow, glancing from the drawer to me again.

And then he winks.

"Don't worry, I never look in a lady's bedside drawer unless I'm invited."

A shiver of heat runs through me, and for a second I consider inviting him.

What can I say? It's been a long day. Besides, I haven't had my body back for very long at all, and I'm pretty keen to take it for a test drive.

There have to be some perks to being stuck in Hell's palace for an unknown amount of time, right?

But, like I said, this man is not a distraction I can afford.

So, instead, I turn back to the books, because an idea is forming in my mind. No one knows why the portal shot me out, right? Well, from the quick glance I had of the first box of books, it isn't just a wonderful array of fiction that Lucifer has sent me. He's sent me nonfiction, too.

I flip the lid and take in the titles on the top of the pile, making sure I'm not getting ahead of myself. I can do that sometimes, getting too excited about an idea and charging madly down the path only to make an idiot of myself at the end.

But no... I think I'm onto something.

Several of the titles seem to focus on Hell in the general sense—kind of like a Funk & Wagnalls of the realm's history and power. And since Hell is inevitably tied to Heaven, there'll surely be something I can piece together about Heaven from these books, too.

Maybe I can find an answer to what's blocking me this way. And if I can't find an answer, I should at least learn something that will help me steal a key so I can get in another way.

If anyone knows how to sneak through a back door into Heaven, it'll be someone from Hell, right?

Knowledge is power.

Reaching back into the box, I carefully flip through the selections, piling the books from one side to the other, making my choice of the top five nonfiction titles which seem to give some sort of history of Hell.

The man finishes carrying in the last box and leans one elbow on top of it, studying me with a quirked lip. But he doesn't say anything. He just watches as I carry the books over to the small desk by the window seat, pile them on, and curl up in the corner.

"Do you want me to unpack these for you?"

"Nah, I'm good," I tell him, barely glancing up from the first title.

There's a pause for several seconds, then:

"You know, the bookcases are over there. Are you sure you—"

"No, I'm good," I interrupt him.

A soft chuckle breaks through my concentration for the third time, and I drop the book into my lap with irritation.

"What is it?" I ask him.

Actually, I'm more irritated with myself than with him. I forgot where I was for a moment—forgot I wasn't alone.

"I'm just saying, normally people put the books away before they start reading them."

"Deliver personal libraries to prisoners often, do you?" I throw at him, because he looks like the kind of person who enjoys a bit of sass.

Bingo—he looks even more amused.

"You're not a prisoner," he says lightly. "Trust me, you don't want to see where Lucifer keeps his prisoners."

Hell yeah—there's a hint of a threat in that. Now I've got something I can work with.

"Aah, so you do make deliveries to prisoners," I push, watching carefully for signs I've gone a bit too far. It's risky pushing someone new like this, with his kind of authority. But after so many years, I've got the instinct for it. Some open up better when you praise them... others prefer to be insulted. And I have a hunch about this guy. "Sounds like you rank a bit lower than a bell boy, to me."

His lip twitches. Bingo.

I lean forward, elbows propped on my knees, casual and open. "Not that it's any of your business, but I think Lucifer might have sent me these titles because they hold a solution to a problem we're both having."

Finally, the smile falls off his face. I've got him—he's intrigued. The man takes a step closer and then, presumably when I don't yell at him, crosses the room to perch on the other end of the window seat. He picks up the top book on my stack and studies it.

"You're working on a history project with the Devil?" he asks slowly, affecting a confused expression that's clearly a joke.

I have to bite down on my lip not to laugh at his terrible sense of humor. It's irritating how some people are just like that. You want to be mad at them, but you can't because they're just so... real.

His attention flicks to where my teeth bite into my lip, and his eyes flash gold.

He's a shifter, I realize. *I wonder what kind.*

A low rumble comes from his chest; I don't think he meant to make it. Strangely, I can't tell if he's an alpha or a beta. He'd have to be alpha, surely... but he isn't acting like it. And I can't sense it, like I usually can.

My core tightens, and I feel the atmosphere shift between us to something closer to interest. Maybe I could invite him into my bed after all. There's always a chance he could be a helpful distraction, if he's in the Devil's inner circle.

Bizarrely, an image of Lucifer flashes into my mind then, and it isn't because this dude is his right-hand man.

I hesitate.

"It's not a history project," I say finally, getting my head screwed on right again. "I've been locked out of the Pearly Gates."

His eyes widen. "You're one of the angels."

Something strange starts fluttering in my chest—something I don't want to examine too closely. I lock it away. I've probably always been a little too good at locking things away.

"Yes," I say shortly. "But the portal closed on me and now there's some kind of weird power thing going on, so I'm trying to get some answers." I hold up the book I'm reading and tap on the cover. "I'm guessing Lucifer sent me these because they might give me information about what sort of power would be doing this."

The man frowns. "Don't you think the Devil would already know the answer to that?"

That makes me pause. You know, I would have thought he would.

Is what's happening to me really so strange?

That thought is kind of alarming, if I'm honest.

I give him a shining smile, aiming both to soothe and distract. "I don't know and I don't care, I just... Look I've gotta keep busy somehow, right?"

I shrug, keeping the gesture inoffensive, like I'm just a girl who's down on her luck and keeping busy. Nothing to see here.

Then I flip to a random page in the book and drop my attention pointedly back to it.

A little thrill runs through my body despite my attempts to shut this thing down before it starts. What can I say? There's a gorgeous man in my room and he's watching me.

But the hum of desire is slow—distant—and it isn't difficult to ignore. It's just my body doing its thing. Ultimately, I'm the one who's in control of it, not the other way around.

Sense memory hits me—blood. Screams. A voice in my head that isn't mine. A time when I wasn't in control of my body at all.

I clench my jaw, and the memory fades.

"So, I don't know," I say casually, since he hasn't taken the hint. "Go run another errand for the Devil, if that's what you do, messenger boy."

"It is what I do," he agrees, and there's a low simmer of heat in his voice that makes me look up again, quite by accident.

His eyes flash gold once more, and when the light fades, they're even darker than before—dark with desire.

But instead of acting on it, he stands, nods to me, and then retreats into the hallway before I can stop him.

What a strange man. And I still don't know his damn name.

4

HELENA

In the end, I do two things at once. I shelve the books with my right hand while holding another open with my left and reading through the pages. I'm not immersing myself, not like I want to, but I'm not reading for pleasure right now.

I'm reading for answers, mate.

My brain picks out the keywords, and I spin through the pages as quickly as I can absorb them. Right now, I'm hunting. When I see something I need, I'll read it properly.

I skim over summaries of Hell's ever shifting geography— the way it syncs up to the excess power in the land and undulates at a whim. I flick through lineages of royalty through Hell's history, cataloging these basic systems away in case I need to draw on them in the future.

There are thirteen rivers of power in Hell, each one based on emotion. Thirteen hell currents. These rivers rise up from the energy generated by tortured hellsouls—aka, their agonized screams—and they're invisible to all but the kings and queen, who filter that power back into the earth so that Hell itself shifts shape on an almost daily basis. Otherwise, the whole place would explode.

It's all a bit gnarly, really.

But since I'm not a hellborn—who can access some parts of the raw power, even if they can't see the rivers—and I'm not a queen with a power current of my own to command, I don't bother doing more than basic revision on the thirteen hell currents. I keep searching... searching.

My attention snags on a line. It's some dry bit of history about the guards at the palace. Uniform changes, and the meaning behind their pips and insignias.

It's perfect. I'll definitely need it later.

I finally pull myself away from the bookshelves, surprised to see the sun has disappeared from the sky, and search for a bookmark.

Ever the boy scout, it seems, Lucifer has provided me with a selection of ornate metal bookmarks that fold over the pages. I give a surprised nod to it as it slides into place, weirdly impressed.

I should probably thank him.

In fact, I should definitely thank him, and take the opportunity to butter him up a bit and find out what the hell happens next.

I leave the room in search of the boxes of clothing that the man had also dropped off for me. Since I'm trying to get on Lucifer's good side, it doesn't do any harm to appear appreciative of all the gifts he's given me. Words can be taken as lies; if I'm literally wearing the clothing, it should ruffle his ego in just the right way.

When I see how much clothing he's left me, I almost lose my nerve.

God, does he really think I'm staying here that long?

Apparently, when Lucifer wants to provide you with a

wardrobe, he means more clothing than you've ever owned before. I pull out a couple of pieces from their boxes, wincing when I realize that Lucifer has impeccable taste.

It would be too much to ask that the man has one flaw, wouldn't it?

I throw the clothing on the bed quickly, one by one, mostly just wanting to find something that isn't covered in burn marks and angel blood. Then I pause, my hands freezing above an outfit that breaks through my practical need for blood-free clothing.

I shouldn't. I really shouldn't.

But Lucifer *has* given me these clothes...

Oh, I want to wear this at least once. And what if he's already worked out an answer to getting me home, and I'm on my way out of Hell the second I see him? I'll only be able to bring the clothing on my back when I leave, I'm sure.

It's not like he'd let me leave here with an entire library, so, I mean, that settles it, right?

A black silk blouse lies on the bed. Tiny silver stars are embroidered into the collar, so fine you can barely see them. I've never been able to afford anything like this in my life, but I've stared at enough beautiful things to know that this is high end. And even the lace bodysuit that I want to pair with it isn't a cheap off-the-rack kind of thing.

If I didn't know any better, I'd say these are couture. But how, precisely, Lucifer has gotten hold of haute couture fitted to my measurements, I couldn't tell you.

Either way, I've had one shit of a day, and I want to feel put together, sexy, and powerful in one.

So I throw off my filthy clothing, take a quick wash in the shower, and then slip into the softest lace bodysuit I've ever worn.

As the silk settles over my shoulders, I finally feel like I can relax.

I pair it quickly with some simple jeans, and grab some boots that seem sturdy enough that I can fight in them if I have to again—but sexy enough that I feel like I'm only wearing them for the look of it.

And then I slip down the hallway to find the Devil.

I'm hesitant at first, since the corridors are filled with guards. I didn't think I was a prisoner here, but now I'm not so sure.

But they don't come after me, and in the end I relax into my body—it's the best way to stay unnoticed after all—and stride through the halls of Hell.

As I near the throne room, where I'd last seen Lucifer, I pass by a wing of the castle that feels colder than the rest. I pause, glancing down the dark, empty hallway. The wall sconces aren't lit here, and the whole thing has a musty, old smell. Like it's been buried for centuries.

It probably has. I swear Lucifer has recently redecorated by means of just digging up ancient ruins like some kind of archeologist. But I mean, to each their own. I don't judge, mate.

But even ignoring the ancient feel of the corridor, it's eerie in another sense. Like there's something forgotten about it.

Someone forgotten.

And like, maybe they're still in there, waiting to come out.

My eyes land on a passage a quarter of the way down the wing. Its stones are crumbling, the opening scuffed and tenuous, like a cave-in waiting to happen.

With an odd sort of certainty, I register that the coldness—the icy wind that sweeps from this wing—is coming from that passage. It must lead outside the castle.

But there's power attached to it, too. Ancient, terrifying

power that tells me in no uncertain terms that taking this passageway is forbidden.

Taking it means death.

Shuddering, I turn back to the comparably warm, modern hallways of the palace, and keep walking.

I can hear Lucifer's voice in the distance, so I hurry down the corridors, following the sound until it takes me into a tiny alcove that turns out to be a mezzanine for a floor below.

I'm partially hidden by vines up here, and I feel a bit sneaky about it, but I'm not one to turn down an opportunity for information.

So when I glance over the banister and see Lucifer talking with Cat, I stay silent.

"We'll be back before you've even had a chance to miss us," Cat says cheerfully.

I notice her three men standing behind her; they must be off to trace another soul.

"Don't wait up," the sandy blond-haired one drawls. "And don't get distracted."

The amusement on his face is nowhere near as harmless as it had been on the man who brought me my books. This guy is all harsh angles. Sharp points. Lucifer seems unbothered by the insult, and when my eyes land on him, a shiver of heat races through me.

I know exactly why the image of him had popped into my head earlier when I thought of wasting a few hours with his errand boy.

Lucifer's arms are folded casually before him, and it's only by this act alone that he isn't completely bare chested. His shirt is unbuttoned to the navel, the fabric falling to the side to reveal smooth, tanned skin. He leans against the marble pillar, casual as anything, his eyes fierce as he looks across his most trusted kings and queen.

One eyebrow quirks as he turns on the sandy blond man who I think is King Marek. "And what, precisely, will I be getting distracted by?"

Marek's lip curls in delight, and he opens his mouth to answer, but Cat smacks him on the shoulder.

"Leave it," she hisses.

Shockingly, he does.

Lucifer's eyes darken. It shifts the air slightly, like a scent of apprehension on the breeze, but none of the four of them seem concerned.

"I assure you, one pesky little angel won't be a distraction."

My chest jolts; he's talking about me.

Lucifer's gaze flicks to Cat and turns unexpectedly warm. "She wasn't before."

"Oh, come off it," Cat says. "You know I completely derailed you."

The brunet says something under his breath, and he and King Marek snicker while Cat shoots them a glare.

Lucifer sighs, although it looks at least seventy percent put on.

"I don't intend to see much of Helena at all, for your information," he says sharply.

The surprise becomes a sinking feeling in my stomach. I know it never does any good to eavesdrop, but still, that was pretty clear cut, right? He doesn't want anything to do with me.

"She has been appropriately catered for," he continues, "and I intend to stay far, far away while I pursue an immediate answer to the problem she poses."

"Ouch," the other blond says under his breath. "You're not even going to try to help her?"

"Of course I'll help her," Lucifer argues. "Getting her out of here will help her. It's what she wants; it's what I want."

Cat reprimands him, "Yes, but you could be a bit nicer about it."

I agree, Cat, he could be a bit bloody nicer about it.

Lucifer snorts. "There's nothing to be nice about," he says. "Now get out of here before you miss your coach."

I don't hear any more of it as they say their goodbyes. My body is buzzing, filled with the unpleasant sensation of over-hearing things about yourself you didn't want to overhear.

So, he doesn't want to work with me, does he? Do I even bother suggesting it, or will he just say it's another problem for him to have to deal with?

I get my answer sooner than I would like.

The sensation of someone watching me makes me shiver, and I turn to find blazing eyes fixed upon me.

"Hiding in shadowed corners is frowned upon around here," Lucifer says casually, looking up at me. His voice carries, low but strong, up to the balcony. "I trust you have settled into your suite."

I grip the edge of the mezzanine tightly and study him. Am I mistaken, or do I see a flicker of something else in his expression?

I swear there was something other than distaste there... But maybe I'm imagining it. I'm only a problem to solve, after all.

"I wanted to thank you for the books," I tell him, my voice carrying easily down to the floor.

There's a pause as we study each other. I've never met anyone I could read less than him. I don't know what he wants from me. I don't know how best to lead this conversation.

Will he be impressed by my ingenuity?

Or does he want to look after a damsel in distress?

I take a punt, feeling unusually slimy and uncomfortable as I tell him the truth. "I thought we could use them together to find some answers. To get me home."

Nothing. Absolutely no response that I can interpret.

He hasn't moved from the pillar, the seeming picture of arrogance and laziness. If I'm honest, it's hot as fuck.

But it also makes me feel like I'm not worth moving for. Like he's not even threatened enough to come up to equal ground.

"Did you?" he finally asks.

"Yes."

Keep it simple until you know how he's reacting. Don't fill the silence.

He watches me quietly for another long pause, but then he shakes his head. "That won't be necessary. I believe I have a course of action for us."

Finally, he pushes away from the pillar, unraveling one long leg and gracefully stepping into the shadows. "Follow me."

5

HELENA

Call me crazy, but I thought that when the Devil got all macho and had my back in front of the angels, it might mean he was on my side. I thought being given a whole guest suite and a freaking *library* might mean he was going to help me.

Looks like I was wrong, because today is apparently my Judgment Day.

I stand before his throne, the empty hall looming over me, and try insanely hard not to quiver in my little booties. I usually pride myself on having a stiff upper lip no matter the situation, but I'd dare anyone to stand in my shoes and not discover it was brown trousers time.

Lucifer rests his palm upon the hilt of his sword, his knees braced wide on the edge of his throne to accommodate for the length.

Of the sword.

Not his junk.

But the whole knee bracing thing is making it difficult to remember that.

He lifts one eyebrow, as if he can read my thoughts. I swallow thickly.

"Are you ready?" he asks, the words carrying through the hall.

They almost make me jump, I'd been so lost in my own thoughts. Was he waiting for me this whole time? Is that what the whole staring contest was about?

"Sure thing, boss," I say, straightening up to my full—tiny—height and, in my nervousness, failing to cover my old Essex accent.

I thought I'd butchered the thing out of me after a lifetime of working as a showgirl and running cons in Vegas, but this whole demon-angel mess has been a rebirth in more ways than one.

Lucifer nods and mutters something under his breath; it sounds like a spell.

My gaze shifts nervously to the other side of the throne, landing on an ornately framed mirror. It doesn't seem like Lucifer's style. Even with the resurrection of Hell's castle, he seems to prefer more modern touches.

Don't think I don't see that cushion under your bum, mate.

But this is clearly very old, and it would so easily be removed from the throne room, so maybe it has another purpose.

The surface shimmers, and my eyes widen in realization. It's probably some kind of portal, like demonic FaceTime.

I wonder if I could reach Ciera with it? I don't exactly have a phone.

She spent so long searching for me, and she probably doesn't even know I'm stuck here. Is she still waiting for me on the other side of the portal to Heaven?

Lucifer finishes his quiet chanting, stands, and draws his sword.

My eyes widen, and I take a step backward, holding up a hand. "Oi, what are you doing with that, then?"

Lucifer's face does something complicated, and then—so quick I almost think I've made it up—he winks at me.

The Devil winks at me.

And when he lowers the sword to the crown of my head, it's slow enough that I don't flinch this time.

"This will only take a minute, Helena," he says gently.

Embarrassment burns from my head down to my toes. But just as quickly, it's followed by desire. What can I say? I am not immune to the most powerful demon in Hell showing me his softer side. Even if it is because I wigged out like a first rate idiot.

Maybe he is on my side after all. He just has a funny way of showing it.

I close my eyes, feeling an unexpected sensation of power running from the blade and into my skull. The power is warm, like a soothing current of water rippling through a hot spring.

I kind of want to bathe in it.

My body preens without my conscious say-so, rising up toward the power. If this is what Hell's Judgment is like, maybe I don't have anything to fear, after all. Maybe it really was the portal that went wonky, not me. I'll be back up the golden stairs in no time.

The thought should fill me with relief, but it doesn't. It fills me with something twisted and mean. I tuck that detail away deep inside me, where I can ignore it for another millennia or so.

I'd much rather spend these moments enjoying the delicious power coursing down my spine.

So, of course, that's when the pain starts.

Ripples of agony course through my skull, so shockingly

quick, I can't even scream at first. The air escapes me in a rushed gasp, catching in my throat, and my eyes snap open.

All I can see is Lucifer's face, his own expression torn open in shock.

And fear.

Oh, hell no. This isn't what I wanted. I open my mouth to ask him what the hell is going on, but no words come out—only a dry sort of wheeze as I fall to my knees, bones slamming into the tiled floor.

Lucifer wrenches the sword free and falls back against the throne. His eyes widen, the whites terrifyingly distinct against the darkness of his pupils. His shirt falls open almost to the waist, and from this angle, he looks divine in the most biblical sense.

Flowing fabric, golden light emanating from the sword, and eyes blazing with a fury I can't comprehend.

Then the light snaps out, leaving the room in stark silence.

I wait for my Judgment to fall, and any warm feelings I had about that power and what it would mean for me are far, far away.

"There is no Judgment," Lucifer says, voice low.

The words don't sink in for a moment. I frown. "What do you—"

"None." He straightens, the sword hanging limp in his hand. "Nada. Zip."

His lips pop the 'p', and I stare in utter confusion, feeling like I've maybe slipped into another dimension where the Devil has lost the plot.

"No Judgment." I repeat slowly.

"No Judgment," he agrees. "According to Hell, you are not required to be here." His head tilts to the side. "And according to Heaven, you are not welcome. Which means, for now... you will stay with me."

I thought I was already staying with him?

Lucifer's eyes narrow. "By my side," he corrects. "No further than a handful of meters."

Unease sinks low in my stomach. "You mean I'm a prisoner again?"

Something flashes in his expression, but he doesn't acknowledge it. "You are my guest," he says tightly.

"But I can't go more than a few meters," I protest.

I'm not sure what I'm doing here. Arguing with the Devil is clearly not the way to get what I want. Every part of me knows that instinctively—I don't need to research him. But I can't stop the words from coming out. I think I'm in shock.

"Correct," he says, the word even more clipped than before. He's getting pissy.

My brain still hasn't turned off the idiot function; I keep arguing. "But that makes me a prisoner," I spit out. "You can't do that. I've just been a prisoner for years! How can you do that to me?"

This time, Lucifer visibly winces. After a second, he smoothes out his expression, but there's something a little fragile about the way he's holding himself. It's shocking enough that I finally manage to shut my mouth up and focus on reading the situation properly.

"Fine," he says tightly. "We shall forget the distance requirement, but you cannot leave the palace. Castle." He pauses, and I swear I can hear him think the word 'thing'. Like even he isn't sure what he's turned Hell's Palace into.

"I can't leave," I repeat slowly, far more in control than before.

That's the definition of a prisoner. But I don't argue this time; I assess, like I should have from the start. He still looks a little frayed around the edges.

Why did he wince when I accused him of holding me prisoner?

He pauses. On anyone else, I'd call it a hesitation, but on him, it's calculated. Everything is calculated, except for that wince.

"It's for your safety," he says in a gentle tone that is nonetheless clearly not up for discussion. "You're not a hellsoul, but you are no longer marked by Heaven. There will be places in Hell that do not know what to do with you."

I guess that makes sense. Regrettably. "All right, then," I nod slowly. "What about visitation rights?"

"I must insist that you have no contact with Heaven until this matter is resolved."

I blink at him. That's not exactly what I meant. Heaven wants no contact with me, either. Consider it a mutual...

My eyes widen. Ciera is an angel. "But Ciera—"

"Ciera is a part of Heaven," he says gently but firmly. "Until this is issue resolved, you cannot have contact with Heaven at all, and you cannot have free contact with Hell."

This issue. Me. I'm the issue, just bloody say it.

"What about that mirror thing?" I ask, pointing at the ornate frame. "Can I talk with her via that?"

A flicker of surprise crosses his face, like he hadn't expected me to work out what it was.

"No," he says, still in that calm, measured voice. "Not for now."

My blood boils, just for a second. So, I really am a prisoner. I can't take this; I need to convince him.

And I need more than a few minutes of studying him to work out how to do that. Fortunately, I have the necessary skills to get around that. They couldn't help me at the portal, because I was dealing with other angels who would have smacked it down in a second. But Lucifer is no longer an angel, so I reckon I've got a shot.

I can send Lucifer gently down the path of righteousness— or, in this case, down the path of not being a dick to someone who really doesn't deserve to be punished any longer.

It's time to call in my angel powers and get the fuck out the front door.

I take a slow breath, gather my strength like I used to as an angel, and let it infuse my words. "I need to speak with Ciera," I say calmly and gently. "I'll stay here without trouble, but I need to have contact with someone other than—" I break off before I say 'other than you'.

Or your dreamy personal assistant.

And when I reach out to Ciera, she can bust me out of here somehow.

I even turn to the mirror, speaking a little louder, wondering if it operates on a verbal command. The surface swirls, and for a moment I swear I see her face. My heart leaps; I can do this. I can get through to someone who actually cares and bust out of here.

I wait for the power to drift from my words to the air, to Lucifer's ears, but something jolts. Like a road block. No—like an empty well.

My eyes widen, panic stirring as I look inward for the first time since I took my body back from Ronin.

There are no powers there.

I have no angelic powers of suggestion. In a desperate bid for freedom, I try to launch my wings free. Wings that I saw only hours ago.

Nothing happens.

My body is mine, but it's... changed. Wrong. I clench my hands by my sides, and they don't feel like mine at all. I feel off. Like I'm wearing a coat that doesn't fit.

"No contact," Lucifer snarls, unaware of my internal freak-out, and there's something... wrong... about his voice.

My eyes slide up reflexively, drawn to that voice, fear burning my throat, and for a moment I see a whisper of the Devil.

Not Lucifer, but Satan. The Ruler of Hell, Lord of all Demons. Bringer of Judgment.

I smell sulfur burning and feel a rage that's thousands of years old.

"No contact," I repeat, the words no more than a faint whisper.

Lucifer sheathes his sword, and it brings a strange sense of finality to it, like a low thunderclap on a cloudless day.

The hint of the Devil has vanished, and I realize with an odd queasiness that it isn't Lucifer's Devil face that scares me. It's the kind one. It's the fact that he clearly knows I hate being a prisoner, and he's trying to ease that.

It's the books and the clothing. The luxurious suite.

I don't think his kindness is faked. He's respectful, even gentle, but I know there's a beast inside him.

Of course I know; I just saw it. The Devil lives inside him, and what is the Devil if not a beast?

The kindness of a beast terrifies me.

"Where do I go?" I ask, reeling and uncertain.

Lucifer shrugs. "I don't care," he says flatly. "And Helena, that tunnel you peeked at on your way here..." He smiles coldly. "It's forbidden. Don't forget that."

Before I can read his expression, he turns away—I'm dismissed.

I flinch, hurt and yet somehow relieved. It makes it easier now, seeing him act like a dick. Scrambling to my feet, I back away, moving faster when he doesn't turn. I make it all the way to the door, and still he won't look at me.

My resolve hardens.

Fine. Fuck him, then.

If the Devil won't tell me why I'm trapped down here, I'll figure it out myself. And I'm not going to sit around under his watchful, arrogant eye while I do.

6

LOGAN

I THINK I LIVE FOR THE MOMENT THAT I SEE THE PALACE IN MY rearview mirror. Not because I never want to come back, but because you just can't beat the feeling of leaving. Of the wind rushing through your hair and the freedom of being on a motorbike, tearing through the highways of Hell.

You just can't top that kind of shit.

And knowing that I not only have the Devil's approval to do so, but that I'm doing it *for* him. That the most powerful man in Hell trusts me enough to send me on these missions for him...

If I'm honest, it makes my dick a bit hard.

I'm not a fool. I know there's a lot that he isn't telling me and will never tell me. But I also don't give a shit about that. I have no interest in politics; I have no interest in running this place.

Maybe that's exactly why he trusts me enough to be his right-hand man, as much as the Devil ever has one of them. Because he knows I'll never fight him for the position of top dog.

The gravel drive that leads up into the palace shifts into

cobblestones. My back rattles along with the bike at the change. I grip the bars and rise just a little on my feet, letting my body absorb the shock while I pull the throttle and tear even faster down the highway.

For some reason, Hell never really took to cars or bikes.

Oh, there are tons of them down here, but they're bombs. There are little car graveyards sprinkled around the place from young demons who've stolen them from Earth and brought them down for a joyride.

Hell prefers carriages and coaches, driven by odd little hell beasties and commanded by skeletons or other hellborn.

Miss me with that shit.

I need to be in charge of my transport, and I reckon you'd know it just by looking at me. Can't wipe the damn grin off my face.

I tear down the shadowed highway, eyes flicking among the ghostly, spindly trees that line it. They creep up into a kind of tunnel, hundreds of meters above me, where even Hell's orange burning sun can't penetrate. You never know what might come at you from the shadows.

But I pass through unscathed, and it's not long before I'm at the bar Lucifer directed me to, holding a pint and settling into my favorite corner by the window.

"Looking for some company?" a succubus asks me, bending over the back of the chair before me so that her breasts are on ample display.

I smile openly, giving her casual interest and appreciation but nothing more. "Not tonight, love."

"You sure about that?" she asks.

Her eyes turn a little hazy, the way that succubi do when they're assessing your aura. Studying your dreams.

"There's something you want very badly," she says, her

words taking on a curious tone. "I could give you her, you know."

I laugh softly. "No, you couldn't," I tell her, not really arguing, just chatting.

I'm not threatened by the offer, and she knows that. I can see it in the way that she relaxes, realizing that while I might not be a potential customer, I am a passing friend.

"Well," she says, the corner of her lips quirking. "I could give you something close to her. We all feel the same in the dark, Red."

My eyebrow flicks upward. "I don't know if I'd agree," I say, taking a sip of my beer and studying her over the top.

She laughs, the sound a silver tinkle that carries across the bar. Several heads turn our way, and I might not be an incubus but even I can sense the desire that floats in the air at the sight of her.

"Well, are you sure you won't trade me your dream for a little cash?" she asks. "I could make money off the things you want to do to her."

My eyes flash—I can see it in the reflection of golden light off my glass—and this time there's an edge to the amusement that colors my voice. Fortunately, I'm sure she won't need more than a warning.

"I think you should go now," I tell her.

She sighs, straightening and turning away. "Don't say I didn't offer."

Her eyes land on a promising demon by the bar and she winks at him, straightens, and strolls toward him.

I turned my attention back to the sights around me.

I picked this spot not only because it's out of the way and I don't usually get bothered in it, but because the acoustics of the place tend to funnel toward this corner.

If you bother to listen, you can hear a lot of the conversations around you, and that's what I'm here for. Because Lucifer is looking for someone. An old friend, he said.

Although, in my experience, you don't track friends down this way. And this person doesn't sound like someone you'd really want to call a friend.

"Listen out for any mention of unexpected rage currents," Lucifer had told me. *"Any surges in the rivers that we should know about. Obviously, I should hear about those anyway, but more importantly, my old friend tends to be drawn to that particular current."*

So, Lucifer is after someone who likes to bask in the warm glow of people's unbridled fury. Sounds like a charmer.

He can keep that one all to himself, when he finds her.

I'm just the messenger boy.

I smile softly into my glass as I think of Helena calling me that. It's not what I usually go by, but the name tickles me. Especially when it's said by someone like her.

I'd asked Lucifer for her name the second I left her suite. The glare he'd given me before offering it in a pained voice had made the answer even more worth it. Pissing off Lucifer and getting that angel's name in one go? Bargain.

And now I can't stop thinking about her. Her unassuming braid and short stature made her look almost mouselike—until I realized that was exactly what she wanted me to think. Somehow, she's trained herself to sit in just the right way that she looks meek, unnoticeable.

Until you look straight at her and see the fire burning at the center.

Those deep brown, serious eyes drove right through me... I could sink into those eyes and get lost in them. Just looking at her makes me think of that Creedence Clearwater song.

A girl like that would be just what I need. She'd never want more than a man who cruised in and out of her life when he was in town. She's far too independent for that.

She'd never take offense at me riding off onto the highway, with her standing in my rearview mirror.

And the fun we could have when I was in town...

As my mind drifts through pleasant thoughts, I notice a faint blue light shimmering in front of me. Frowning, I reach out, my hand passing straight through it. Definitely light, but it's very piercing... like a thread.

It moves like a thread, too.

What the hell is this?

Wait—what am I doing? I've never become distracted on a mission before.

The light disappears with a snap. I drop my beer down on the table with a loud thump and force myself to pay attention, but I don't appear to have missed anything. It's easy enough to tell—I have the added advantage of my shifter senses, my cat-like hearing that makes the conversations sound as though they were right next to me.

I think I'm in for a long night. From the chatter I can hear, it sounds like we're past the political discussion and small talk part of the evening, and well onto the drama and gossip. No one's talking about rage currents right now, and definitely no one gives a shit about the weather anymore.

While that might be more interesting for me, sadly, it's not what he's paying me for.

Then a voice catches my attention.

I tilt my head so that my ears turn subtly toward the voice. It's three of them in the back corner, huddled together, speaking in low whispers.

Even I can barely catch the words; they really don't want to be heard. Which is precisely what drew my attention. Amateurs.

"What did she say?" the first demon whispers, his voice obscured by what sounds like a mouthful of sharp teeth. "Has she found it yet?"

"Nothing yet," another answers. "We've tried the north. Tomorrow we'll move to the west."

It could be nothing, but Lucifer's attention right now is fixed on the small pockets of Ronin's rebellion that have survived his death, and I'd bet cash that's exactly what these three are.

There were far more pockets of rebellion than Lucifer anticipated, when he came back here. Cutting off the head of the snake hadn't taken care of the problem, and instead seems to have given rise to an even deeper issue.

Not to mention this new group call themselves the *Rising Snakes*. Can you get any lamer?

The thing they're discussing might not be the information Lucifer sent me out for, but I think it might be useful anyway. Because it seems that Lucifer isn't the only person looking for something—or someone. If I can find out what they're looking for, maybe Lucifer can get a step ahead.

I take a sip of my drink, making it look as though I'm studying the bartender with interest.

The third demon speaks up in a low husky voice, "S'no point checking down here. You know it's not where we'll find it."

"We don't know shit," the sharp-toothed demon snaps. "All we know is that it exists. We can feel it."

"It's like a dam," the other demon mumbles, "blocking all the rivers at once." He shudders in what feels alarmingly like ecstasy. I feel like I'm witnessing a private moment. "Can you feel it?"

All three of them begin to cackle. "Oh, we can feel it."

And that's when one of them makes a small sign on the

table. It's just small enough that no one should notice. No one except me.

It's definitely them.

The *Rising Snakes.*

That little vee motion is the gesture they use to recognize each other, and since these demons obviously all know each other already, they're just doing it for the aesthetic.

I slam my beer down on the table and rise to my feet.

There's nothing I hate more than a poseur.

I cross the room and grin down at the three demons. God, they're tiny.

"Hello, gents."

"Wadda you want?" the sharp-toothed demon sneers, and I was right. He's got about three layers of sharp teeth in that face.

A shiver of interest floods me at the thought.

God, sometimes I don't know what the fuck's wrong with me. But it does make things pretty hot.

I smile slowly at him, letting my lips curve into a seductive, arrogant grin.

"I want to know what you're looking for in the west."

Their eyes widen into something like fear, and they go very, very still.

It's gratifying. Almost as gratifying as the very clear trouble they're having determining whether I'm an alpha or beta.

At least they know I'm not an omega.

But no one can tell the rest these days, and that's how I like it.

"Who's asking?" the middle one wants to know.

It's a very thinly veiled attempt to discover if I'm on their side or not. If I made their little vee on the table, I'd probably get the information.

But where's the fun in that?

"The Devil's messenger boy," I say with a grin, thinking of Helena.

And then I shift into a jaguar.

All hell breaks loose.

The demons scramble for the door, recognizing me instantly the second I change. They've all seen me prowling at Lucifer's side. They've seen the big, spotted jaguar that roams the palace gardens.

I'm delighted to be able to introduce myself.

I pin one of them to the ground—the sharp-toothed one, I find to my delight. But he holds me back with remarkable strength.

Strength that I could imagine put to far better use.

He snarls, "Fucking kiss-ass."

I roar, snapping my teeth close to his neck.

Behind us, the bar has fallen into chaos. Chairs are flying, demons taking the opportunity to pick a fight—or to jump in on an existing one. It gives me a heady rush, this kind of shit.

When it's no one I know and no one I care about, there's nothing better than a barroom brawl.

The demon flips me, getting his own teeth in my neck, and I take a delicious second to imagine how they'd feel somewhere else.

Probably not worth discovering. Besides, now that my thoughts are entirely filled with a five-foot angel with the fiercest scowl I've ever seen, it's difficult to get a rise from anything else.

I flip him again, and just as I've got my jaw around his throat, strong hands haul me off. I look up into blazing hellfire.

Two Summoning Demons—the bouncers—hold me like a lost little kitten in their arms.

Without ceremony, they march me to the door and throw me out.

I shift back, naked as a babe, and brace myself on the ground in the filthy alleyway, laughing.

From this angle, I can see the twisting tattoos that line my arms, and they only make me grit my teeth, anger burning even brighter. Memories of my failure. Of who I failed.

I should charge back in there and finish the job.

Not now, I tell myself. *Let it ride.*

"You're not gonna kick any of them out?" I prompt the bouncers, eyes blazing.

"They didn't start shit by listening where they weren't invited," the second one says.

Ah, of course, I've broken the unwritten code: places like these are neutral. No politics.

No reconnaissance allowed.

Lucifer warned me about that one, and I didn't care.

Standing slowly, I catch my clothing as he throws them at me and step, unhurried, into my jeans.

Well, that puts paid to that idea. But I did get something for Lucifer, even if it isn't what he wanted. And even if it's ultimately more trouble.

Trouble that he's been desperately hoping would be over by now.

Shaking my head, I walk out of the alley and back around to the front of the bar where I left my bike.

My eyes catch on a bookstore that I hadn't noticed before.

Rows of dusty, well-loved books line the window, faded in the sunlight. Before I know what I'm doing, I'm heading over to it.

I stand in the shadow of the awning for ages, scanning the titles before finally deciding to go in.

I pluck one of the titles from the shelf—one that I've seen in Helena's room, right before she shoved it into her bedside table —and find a place to sit down and read.

After a few minutes, the shop keeper approaches me and grunts, "Are you gonna buy that?"

I smile slowly, widely. "Not today," I tell him. "But I will keep reading, thank you."

"Jackass," he mutters as he disappears.

So, nursing bruises that feel like medallions, I settle in to find out what this book might be about.

And why exactly it made her face light up like the sun when she saw it.

7

HELENA

Sleeping in the guest bed of Lucifer's palace is an unparalleled experience, which is absolutely infuriating. It's the best night's sleep I think I've ever had, and even in my dreams I'm rolling in luxury. Silk sheets and fluffy pillows. Literal clouds. I think there was even a meadow of heathery flowers in there.

Disgusting.

As soon as morning arrives, I decide I really do have to get out of here, or I'm in danger of Stockholm Syndrome. A well rested body was an important part of the escape strategy and all, well done me, but that's all I can afford. It's go time.

All I keep thinking about is that look of understanding on Lucifer's face. Like he was sorry. Like he cared.

Right before the Devil appeared.

I take a cold shower, gasping as the freezing water saps every inch of comfort from my bones.

"Not today, Satan," I mutter, glaring at the beautiful little bottles of perfumed shower gel and lotion and leaving them untouched.

When I get out, I don't even bother toweling dry. I just

shiver on the bath mat with the hair dryer on full blast until I'm confident about my ability to make decisions again.

I try reaching for my angel powers one more time—and for my wings—but nothing happens. At least, nothing wing-like.

My whole upper body begins to feel slightly off, though, like I have a fever. And when I look down, I keep seeing blue flashes of light. Little threads coming out of my chest, like the electrifying cord that linked me to Lucifer in his throne room.

I think there are three of them, this time.

So, first I get electrifying, terrifying, raw power thrumming through my veins that likes to explode things. Then I get freaky blue threads leading from my body to God knows where.

Third step, profit?

Swallowing thickly, I briefly acknowledge that, whatever these threads are, I'd trade them for my wings any day. But it doesn't matter, because I can't. Experiment over; I have no wings.

Then, I force the memory of flying from my mind. Lock it away. Pretend it was never there.

In a few minutes, I've basically forgotten it.

"Okay," I tell myself. "It's time for a plan."

My best chance of getting out from under Lucifer's thumb has to be that tunnel in the forgotten wing.

It was clearly off limits. No one was guarding it because the entire wing gave off creepy 'get out' vibes, and Lucifer is exactly the kind of prick who would think I was too timid to run down the death tunnel in search of freedom.

Never underestimate people, big guy. It'll be your downfall. And given the choice between sitting here like a good little inmate while you tell me what to do, versus taking my chances against an unknown beastie in the hopes that I can hole up somewhere quiet on my own while I work this problem out my way... it's a no brainer.

Besides, something tells me I don't have much time left before escaping isn't even an option. I'm already a glorified prisoner, up here in my little suite full of books, and Lucifer's a smart man. He'll know I'm not happy with how my Judgment went, but he won't want to upset the abused angel by putting bars on the window while I watch.

The bars will go up slowly, before I've even noticed.

I get dressed and then give my room a quick once over to make sure I haven't left anything important. Then, I swing my bag over my shoulder and leave.

It isn't a perfect bag for the situation. It's a designer handbag with fancy zips and funny little tassels. But if I'm seen carrying a duffel bag out of here, it's not exactly going to be a clean getaway, you know what I mean? I managed to squeeze the two most important books into it, and I tore out a bunch of useful chapters from the others. I can start my research, even without his library at my beck and call.

It hurt to tear the book, but now isn't the time to wig out over the little things.

The hallways are quiet when I move through them. Every few corridors, I pass a guard, but they don't give me more than a glance.

Their eyes always, without fail, flick to the handbag before they move on.

It's like an invisibility shield. People on the run either have a huge, practical bag full of stuff, or they have nothing. They don't carry little Gucci looking things that attract attention, barely hold shit, and get in the way whenever you move your arms.

So, clearly I'm on my way to an important, Lucifer-approved event.

I force myself to walk slowly, admiring the hallways like an awed little demon. The decor is shifting into that older style.

The meticulously plastered walls with their modern art have become stone and tapestries. Candles flicker in their sconces, and even the guards I pass now look unsettled. Like this entire wing isn't meant to be here.

Why did Lucifer resurrect something that clearly no one likes?

Even the shadows feel wrong here.

Two more corners to go. One more.

I come to a halt, eyes wide.

"What the fuck?" I breathe, staring up at the wall in front of me.

The corridor that leads to the tunnel is no longer there. It's been bricked up. I reach out cautiously, poking the brick to see if it's an illusion, but no—real.

The mortar is still wet.

So is this one of those moments where Hell shifts its geography as the power currents settle? Or has Lucifer literally bricked up one of his own hallways to stop me escaping?

I poke it again, frowning.

"This can't be happening," I mutter under my breath, giving the wall a proper shove.

I know that amateur demolition isn't exactly the subtle escape I had planned, but there's a fluttery, panicky feeling starting up in my chest. I thought I was in control, but now the walls are literally closing in and I don't even have my fallback of angel powers to fight it.

Lucifer's kindness, even as he slammed the door and turned the metaphorical key, floods my mind until I can think of nothing else. It isn't right. None of this is right.

I'm on my own, with no real power at all.

I back away and move quickly down the corridor, searching for another way through. Maybe there's an entrance to this section that hasn't been bricked up yet.

I start flicking tapestries aside, searching for secrets. A castle wing like this has got to have secrets. Roses under glass domes, that sort of shit. There'll be something. Maybe if I go back out to the modern corridor, I can find a way to come back in from the other side.

I step back onto lush carpet and glance around. There are guards down one end, and doors lining the hall all the way to the stairs. One of them might have a back entrance.

Casting a glance at the guards out of the corner of my eye, I lean down and squint through the keyhole of the nearest door, holding my body loosely like I'm a nosy tourist instead of an escapee.

Colored flashes dart across my vision, and I barely hold back a gasp.

Whoa, it's like showgirl heaven in there. Glitzy guests roam through a magnificent ballroom. Champagne towers line the center, and trailing ivy drifts from the lights above like some kind of trendy interior designer's wet dream.

And the walls of the room are nothing but stars.

No, I mean that. Real, actual stars. Galaxies swim through the edges of my vision, surrounding the ballroom in the fierce colors of a nebula. And instead of screaming in horror, the guests reach their hands out into those heavens and bask in the glow.

An unexpected ache starts up in my chest. Whatever world this is, I know it isn't Heaven. That would be impossible. And still, it reminds me of that twilight place.

I should be back there, with Ciera, fighting against the Leviathan that claw their way upward in an eternal battle against the light. I don't even *like* fighting, goddammit, and I miss it all. The galas. The ceremonies.

Now the angels won't even look me in the eye.

A hand on my shoulder startles me, and I turn to find a guard watching me shrewdly.

"Not in there," he says.

Why? I think to myself. *Is that only for extra special prisoners?*

But out loud, I only smile sweetly—a slightly adoring expression of awe on my face, like I just love a man in uniform. The guard softens immediately, his ego soothed, and the hand falls away.

A soft snort catches my attention. When I turn to look down the corridor, back toward the castle wing, there's a man laughing at me.

Well I'm certainly not going to appeal to his ego. Arrogant lean, sharp eyes, white teeth; this is the type of man who needles at someone until he gets what he wants, and smiling at him will only make him go harder.

Irritation spikes in my chest, not just because he's clearly a prick, but because of what he's standing in front of.

A servant's passage. Ten bucks says it takes me straight to where I need to go.

Checking the guard is back at his post, I switch directions.

Men like this one want an easy target, so I won't give him one. He'll call some nasty shit after me to assert his dominance when I challenge him, but he won't do anything more with the guards watching. And more importantly, he'll leave me the hell alone instead of going through with whatever bored plan he's concocted.

"Mind your own business," I tell the man sharply as I approach him, trying to get a good look at the door as I pretend to move past.

It's smaller than the others, discreet, and with a well-worn handle. Definitely the servant's passage.

I wait for the anger to rise from him as he takes the bait, but it doesn't come, and as we draw level, he says in a quiet, measured voice, "This *is* my business."

That stops me.

Does he know something I don't?

"Then where's your guard uniform?"

"I'm not a guard, sweetheart," the mystery man tells me.

He's well over six feet tall. Tanned skin and rich, dark eyes place him as somewhere in the Mediterranean in appearance, but that could mean anything down here, with so many centuries of history still living and breathing. The open linen shirt and smooth silver rings on his fingers definitely sell the story, though.

Fortunately, the beautiful, soft waves of his mid-length brown hair—falling in an utterly dreamy way across his face—piss me off just enough to snap me out of my daze before I fall too hard for an asshole.

He reminds me of Lucifer, actually.

"What are you talking about then?" I ask him sharply.

He smiles, like I've just fallen into his trap.

"This is my wing," he says, waving a hand to encompass the ancient castle walls just around the corner.

Shit. Busted.

"Then maybe you can tell me why it's half bricked up."

No point trying to hide my motives now. Something tells me I'll get further with this man by being honest.

Well, semi honest.

The man's smile deepens. "I was hoping you could tell me the same thing, as Lucifer's pet."

My jaw drops. All the carefully formed plans and pathways to navigate this conversation and get what I need from him vanish as I bluster silently. "Excuse me?" I finally spit out. "I'm no one's pet."

"Why not?" he says airily. "Anyone would kill to be the Devil's pet. I know I would."

Something flashes in his eyes, but I can't pinpoint the emotion.

We don't all have your kinks, I think but manage not to say.

Bizarrely, his lips quirk, like he heard me anyway. But then his eyes dart to the guards down the end of the hall.

"You really haven't noticed, have you?" Something about his words chills me, but before I can argue, he points over my shoulder. "Look at the walls," he says.

I look at the walls.

My mouth drops open. "Oops," I murmur.

The guard's eyes widen, and he spins. Then, all chaos breaks loose. The magic fire creeping along the side of the corridor is just like the one at the portal. Whatever it is, it's followed me here.

Or... No, scratch that. The alternative is too bogus to consider.

I can't really be doing all this, can I?

Who am I even kidding anymore? I know I am.

"Now's your chance to run," the new guy whispers in my ear, surprisingly close.

I startle, eyes flicking to the guard who's still yelling into the little tech device on his wrist and approaching the flame with his sword out, like a knob.

I swallow down the urge to pick on him for attacking fire with a sword, and run.

The man even steps aside for me, clearing the way to the passage. I don't question it. My time has officially run out, and speed is more important than stealth right now.

I charge down the corridor, its plain stone walls covered in cobwebs and burnt out sconces. I can tell by the scent that I'm back in the ancient ward—musty fabric and the faint touch of dampness linger too close. Now I just need to find a door that comes out behind the bricks.

Around another corner, the guy reappears. His arms are folded, and he leans back casually against the wall.

"Don't you have something to ask me?" he queries as I hurtle toward him.

"Mate, I don't even know who you fucking are," I pant, breezing past just in time to see his eyebrows rocket up in surprise.

"Well that's interesting," I hear him mutter. "Then why am I here?"

A door creaks open in the wall beside me, almost invisible except for the ripples of flame that have caused it to burst at the seams. I only hesitate for a second, then I take it before it becomes a fire hazard.

I'm behind the brickwork; its oppressive blockage towers over me about three meters back. To my left is the dark, whistling passageway that leads beyond the castle.

To my right are two stony-faced guards eyeing me through concealed visors, because Lucifer doesn't miss a damn trick.

"Bollocks," I mutter.

I wonder if idle chit chat will get me through here. You know, for old time's sake. Probably not.

Magic fritzes along the walls, crackling like lightning. I'm not sure the guards can see it yet, because they don't flinch, but then maybe they're just really good at playing chicken.

"You've met your match," the new guy says, appearing beside me again.

He's fast becoming the longest-running companion I've had down here, and don't even get me started on how sad that is.

I round on him, ready to lash out, but then I realize he isn't talking to me.

He's talking to them.

Open-mouthed, I watch him continue. "Can't you see the light?" He points to the walls.

No longer made of stone, apparently, the guards follow his direction. I do, too, and I see that within the lightning that's now sending scorch marks down the paint, there are tiny, dazzling lights. Thousands of them.

The guards begin to move, now, exchanging orders in low, inaudible voices. Their hands find their swords, and they square off against the dazzling lights that are beginning to turn—like everything in my life lately—to a great big raging inferno.

My mystery side-kick holds up a hand, head bowed in thought as he steps forward. "Just before you do charge in head-first like the decorated heroes I know you're dying to be..."

"Get out of the way," the nearest guard growls, gesturing roughly with his sword.

The second guard, I realize with sudden alarm, isn't wearing a helmet like I'd thought. The hard ridge of bone encasing his head is simply shaped like a helmet; he's in full Summoning form, and with the power pooling at his feet, I'd guess he has a witch in the wings.

My man smiles, once more like he has everyone exactly where he wants them. It's the eeriest goddamn thing I've ever seen, and I'm overcome with the urge to run far, far away.

"Then by all means." He steps back, waving his hand graciously in an obnoxious gesture of permission.

"They'll run you through for that, alone," I tell him, eyebrows right up in my hairline as the guards snarl and shove past us. "You wanna be careful."

"I'm touched, Helena," he says, something odd in his tone—like anticipation. "But I'm quite alright."

How does he know my name?

I'm prevented from asking when the raging fire suddenly explodes. For a moment, all I can see are those dazzling lights, cascading around us while the heat singes my skin. The power echoes in my own body, stretching beyond what I can see, and I just know it's tearing holes somewhere else in the castle.

In the midst of all the light, I see the guards—or what's left of them.

Their bodies are crisped, skin flayed from their bones as the fire consumes them. There's an eerie sense of prophecy to it— my man had told them they'd met their match, and now there they are. The only pieces left of them are the frayed pips on their uniform—each one so mangled, it looks like there are more stripes than there should have been.

Decorated heroes, indeed.

I don't stay to comprehend what my body witnesses. I move on autopilot, charging for the passageway and tumbling inside.

The man doesn't follow me this time, and it's like all sound cuts off as I cross the threshold. Darkness encloses me, and the scent of ancient earth coats the walls.

"Fuck," I whisper, the sound echoing strangely. When I glance over my shoulder, there's no sign of the strange man who helped me.

There's no sign of anyone.

And there's no light.

Swallowing thickly, I step further into the passage, and further still. There's a stale, cold breeze flickering over my hair, tickling my nostrils with its icy touch. I begin to walk faster, shuffling at something like a run further into the darkness.

And then... there's a voice.

It sounds like wind at first. Like the low, moaning whistle that haunts caves and mountains, making tourists shiver in fear. But unlike the wind, this voice speaks words.

It speaks my fucking name, man.

"Helena," the cavernous voice murmurs. "Tell... him..."

"Tell him?" I whisper back, my voice way higher than it should be. "Tell who what?"

The darkness is all-encompassing now; I can only feel my way further down the passage by touching the walls. But I can't turn back.

Back there lies Lucifer and his gilded cage. Back there lie angels and demons, all of them out for my blood.

I don't want any of that. I don't care about Heaven or Hell and all their little secrets anymore, not now, not after that power exploded *again*.

I just want to be me. Safe. Alone. No fire at my fingertips. No guards breathing down my neck, or people pretending to be my friend but still holding keys to a locked and bolted front door.

Ciera can come too, but that's it.

"What do you want me to tell him?" I hiss, louder now.

The voice begins to moan, and not the sexy kind. I flinch, covering my ears as the sound gets louder. And louder.

It's screaming now.

Crying—howling.

"Fuck!" I cry, clutching my hands over my ears and stumbling to my knees.

"Helena!" the voice screams. "Come *here*."

My weirdass power flares, bursting the corridor into light. Flame ripples down the walls, and one by one, the burnt, destroyed torches catch alight, revealing what I hadn't noticed.

The corridor leads down.

Down, down, down, those flames flickering smaller and smaller as the impossible distance continues.

The voice screeches, and fear rips through me. I silently beg that strange man to appear again, but he doesn't. No one does, and my fear is distorting everything, tearing it apart. Lighting it on fire.

A blue thread appears before me—it's the thread I saw in

Lucifer's throne room, when we first met. But it's stronger this time, like a rope.

I grab hold of it, and as I do so, the darkness shatters.

Strong arms engulf me around the waist, and I catch a glimpse of dark curls broken by a single thread of white.

Lucifer.

"I told you not to come here," he snarls.

For a moment he looks panicked. Not angry but afraid. But then his hold on me tightens and we're hurtling through darkness.

I gasp as the world rematerializes; the first thing I see is the light.

It's brighter than it should be, and yet I can't work out where it's coming from. Or why no one else is paying attention to it.

Granted, there's a lot of shouting going on, and I can't properly work out what's happening so I guess they've got their hands full, but this light—it's beautiful.

It's like starlight brought down to Earth.

I lift my hand unconsciously, reaching for it as if I could touch it. For a moment, it looks like I can. Silver sparkles cluster around my hand, and a shining blue cord stretches from my fingers to the very center of the light, then through it, out the other side to something else.

It's that same blue cord that brought Lucifer to me, down in the passageway. There are three of them; I didn't imagine it.

"Logan!" Lucifer roars from behind me, making me spin around.

When I see him, my heart stops.

I thought he was intimidating before, but in kind of like... a CEO sort of way. Like he had the money to buy out an entire city just to destroy you if you cut in front of him in line for coffee, kind of intimidating.

The way he looks now is a very different sort of intimidating.

We must be in his dining room, because he stands behind me with one foot on a chair and the other on the table itself. The shifter who brought me my books—Logan—has appeared at his side and thrown Lucifer a spear, which he's now wielding above his head before shoving it straight through a man's chest.

I realize slowly that the ground is littered with bodies, all of which are lined with piercing wounds. For a moment, it looks all too normal. My brain catalogs the bodies as numbers, assessing the scene for threats rather than the sheer fucking horror of it.

Then feeling hits me, and I reel backward, gagging on the stench of blood. When I was working for Ronin, I couldn't *feel*. That's the difference.

Now, I can feel again.

I mean, that's the problem isn't it? That's what this power is feeding off when it explodes things?

It takes a second, the gears crunching poorly in my head, but I look around properly and see the room as it is now, untainted by my memories. I realize for the first time that we've jumped into pure fucking chaos.

My power definitely tore holes somewhere else in the castle; it tore them here, and there were apparently people waiting to climb through those holes. How is that even possible? I destroy one portal, and then spontaneously create another? And what kind of assholes immediately tumble through a random portal and attack the palace?

This must be the rebellion. I thought it was destroyed with Ronin, but obviously not.

Lucifer's shirt has been torn open during this fight—the fight he was clearly having before he whipped out to grab me. His chest is lined with blood, but I can't quite tell whose blood it is. And most importantly, his eyes shine a golden light—a light that is nothing like the yellow of a shifter. A shifter's light is very clearly a transformation, some kind of animalistic power.

This is pure power. Energy. And it's animalistic only in the truest sense—that I think Lucifer would cut me down like a lion cuts down a gazelle if I so much as breathed wrong right now.

He looks around the room, chest heaving, appearing to count the bodies silently. When he reaches the end, he relaxes a little, satisfied.

Then he turns to face me.

"I have to bind you, Helena," Lucifer says in a strangely quiet voice—strange, because it carries straight to me as if he'd whispered in my ear. He pulls a glass orb from within his shirt and holds it aloft. My eyes track the movement, confused and afraid.

Bind me? What?!

Why does he look so apologetic?

"What is this light?" someone murmurs, distracting me.

I turn to see Logan standing beside me, looking just as amused and casually sinful as he did before. Blood covers his knuckles, and his golden alpha claws are free, even though he hasn't shifted.

But he sounds nervous.

And then a new voice sounds from the doorway—a drawling, wicked sound like laughter and wine. The voice of my mystery man, who owns the forbidden wing of the castle. "Lucifer, what fish have you reeled in today?"

"Tobias," Lucifer growls, the sound shocked and broken all in one.

I never thought to hear the Devil sound like that.

I never thought for anything like this crazy afternoon to happen at all. What the hell is going on? Why does it feel like I just ran in a giant circle, and I've only now arrived back at the beginning?

But it's a beginning that's all twisted, changed. Wrong.

Lucifer lets go of the glass ball.

It falls, falls, falls. The orb shatters on the ground, and the flame licks out along the tiles. The blue cord that seemed to link me to Lucifer bursts into light.

Along with two others. One connects me to Logan, and the other to this stranger behind me—the tall, dark-haired man with rings on his fingers and a wicked smile on his face.

The room falls silent.

"Well," the stranger—Tobias, apparently—says brightly, seemingly undeterred by the rage on Lucifer's face. "Is anybody going to fill me in on what I've missed?"

8

HELENA

"I'm sorry, you what?" I can't quite believe what I'm hearing. "You were worried I'd go running off, so you bound me to you?"

"Now, did I say that?" Lucifer asks calmly, propping one elbow on the arm of his throne and resting his chin there.

I'm finding it hard to see him as Lucifer right now. Right now he's Satan, and I'm ready to kick Satan's ass, throne or no throne. I don't even care that fighting is usually a last resort for me, it's just going to feel so damn good.

I'm pretty sure he's using the throne as a power play, and that's just pissing me off more.

My hair falls in front of my face, loose from its plait and tangled after the scuffle in the passageway. I blow it out of the way, grabbing the strands and shoving them back into the curls of the plait as I pull it over my shoulder.

"Yes, you did say that." You arrogant asswipe. "You said you bound me to you and your friends as guards until you can trust me."

Satan's eyes flash, the gold reminding me of how he looked

standing on that table, spear aimed at a demon's heart. I swallow.

"I said the power that is running through you is unhinged," he says flatly. "It tore open a portal straight into my dining room, unleashing demons from Mystic's Peak into the middle of my lunch."

He closes his eyes for a moment, as if the image is too painful. It takes me a full three seconds of willpower not to laugh at how strange and domestic that image is.

Lucifer continues, "So for everyone's safety, while you are in Hell, I need to bind that power to *me* so that I can control it. Since that power runs through you, for fuck knows what reason, that means binding you."

"That's what I said," I mutter under my breath, throwing my plait back over my shoulder. Speaking louder now, I add, "And I'm sure your assault on me in the passage had nothing to do with it."

This time, he doesn't need the golden flash to remind me of his power. He just has to look at me. I have to admit I'm a little scared.

"Your attempts to flee had everything to do with it," he says quietly.

"Why do you think I was fleeing?" I throw at him. "You said I could explore the castle—that was just part of the castle, right?"

One of the men—the one I found in the rooms near the passage—shifts on his feet and stares at me intently.

Lucifer leans forward on the throne, propping his elbows on his knees. "You were attempting to flee, Helena," he says, still in that terrifyingly quiet voice. "And on the surface level, I don't care. I even understand. But your power cannot be allowed to roam beyond the gates—not with the destruction it has already caused. And since you are attached to your power, and you are unwilling to do as I requested"—I snort; *requested*—"and remain here, then I will *bind you.*"

I jump at the last two words, thrown into the cavernous throne room with enough power to sound like a yell, even though they weren't. They were even quieter than the rest. I shiver, hugging my arms around my body and wishing that someone would turn the thermostat up, like, pronto.

Not a thought one often has in Hell.

"And what about that voice?" I force the words out, fear still lingering in every cell of my body. "What was that thing?"

A strange frown appears on Lucifer's face. "What voice?"

"In the passageway. It was like a... rumbling... thing. The voice! You heard it." I trail off. "Right?"

After a very long pause, Lucifer shakes his head. "There was no voice."

Well. What exactly do I say to that?

"Fine," I finally throw out, my brain whirring as I try to process more information than any one person should have to deal with in a lifetime. I can barely think in general, and certainly not while those words still echo in my head.

Not Lucifer's words—the *thing's.*

I know it was real. I heard it, even if Lucifer denies it like the bastard he is.

Unless he really couldn't hear it...

I don't know what's worse. Maybe it isn't such a bad thing to have Lucifer attached to me, if there's something down here that's got him running. Or if there's a beastie in Hell that's reaching out to me and only me.

I need more info. I can't work out a plan when there's so much I don't know.

My eyes flick to the side of the throne room, where the only two other occupants lounge against the wall.

Speaking louder this time in an attempt to cover up my

quavering little knees, I say, "Binding my power to you doesn't explain your beefed up guard squad."

Lucifer's face gives an odd twitch, like he's clenching his jaw. "Three points to the triangle will make the holding spell stronger."

Somehow, then, I just know.

"Holy shit," I gasp, eyes wide. "You didn't mean to bind us all!"

The newcomer with the rings straightens, his foot sliding down the wall so he's standing straight finally instead of lounging. Beside him, Logan doesn't even twitch, but I can tell he's listening intently.

They definitely weren't clued into this binding spell, like Lucifer has spent ten minutes trying to imply.

I'm willing to bet if we weren't all physically bound together with a spell that doesn't seem to want us out of each other's sight, at least while it's settling, Lucifer would have run to the other side of Hell rather than have this conversation.

It's kind of funny when you put it like that.

"So... what kind of binding is it?" I ask, going for a neutral sort of peace offering. But judging by Lucifer's expression, it doesn't land.

The air begins to chill a little at the edges. When I breathe, it frosts.

"That doesn't concern you," Lucifer says, and there's something about his voice that tells me not to argue this time.

The newcomer didn't get the memo, apparently.

He steps forward, ignoring the warning rumble in Lucifer's chest. "I think the girl should be allowed to ask some questions," he says with a predatory smile as he stares Lucifer down. "As should we. If we are all bound together, do we not deserve the truth?" The last words are spoken in an affected tone, like he's on stage and we're his audience.

"Tobias, now is not the time." Lucifer snarls, rising and stepping off the dais. "I will answer your question in due time, but for now—"

"No, Lucy," Tobias says pointedly. "I want to know why I was compelled to step foot in this vile place well before you shattered that orb. What called me here? You know I'd never come here willingly."

"Oh yes." Lucifer laughs, his tone bitter. "Believe me, I know. How many centuries, and you couldn't even step foot on the *outskirts* of a rebellion to help me."

"You're always on the outskirts of a rebellion," Tobias snaps back, the two of them almost forehead to forehead now. "Let's call a spade a spade—you fucking love it there. You're in your element right now, with all of Hell rising against you."

"How dare you—"

The sound of two quick claps breaks the two of them mid-stride. We all turn to find Logan grinning lazily, his hands pressed together. "Have you ever seen two chained dogs fight?" he asks casually. "Let's not tear each other apart when no one has the privilege to run away."

For a moment, the two of them simply stare at him, chests rising and falling. Then, reluctantly, they drop the fight.

"We have questions, Lucifer," Tobias says carefully, turning back to Lucifer. "And we deserve answers. When will you give them?"

"When it is safe to give them," Lucifer says, his eyes sending a message I can't read as he stares Tobias down. "For now... the rift to Mystic's Peak is still open."

Tobias sucks in a breath, his eyes widening briefly. Lucifer's lip curls just barely.

"Now you understand."

A flash of anger crosses Tobias's face, but he steps back. "I will guard the girl until you return."

Lucifer nods. "It's an unexpected blessing, to have the two of you caught up in this," he says, sounding almost distracted as he glances from Tobias to Logan and back again. "I'd intended for the binding to keep Helena and I within thirty meters of each other, but with you here, I believe I can stretch my own position on the binding without breaking it."

I puff up, indignant, and just manage to bite down on my tongue before I speak. Oh, so he can stretch it, can he? What a *blessing*. Meanwhile I'm stuck here with two extra guards, presumably unable to move beyond thirty meters from them.

And they're stuck to me, too.

So the only person who's hashtag blessed here is Lucifer himself. How convenient.

"If she..." Lucifer pauses, his eyes cutting to me and back. "If she shows any sign of power, contain it."

Tobias's eyebrows lift, but he nods.

"And keep Logan with you. You never know when you'll need a cat on your side." The smile he sends in Logan's direction is equally as shrewd as it is unexpectedly genuine. These two know each other well.

Maybe he is Lucifer's right-hand man after all. Quite an upgrade from messenger boy.

I shake my head, dismissing the mental compliment. Fine, so he got caught up in the spell accidentally somehow, but he's still in the Devil's power and I still need to watch him.

I need to watch all of them, since apparently they're my guards.

"As soon as the mystics are appeased, I'll be back to sort this out," Lucifer strides toward the door, leaving us with that parting note as he pauses in the arch. He doesn't turn around as he says, "This is a bump in the road. Nothing more."

Then he's gone, leaving me with two nursemaids and a rising fury that can't be contained.

Light and fire flicker in my memory, and I know I have to get out of here before I blow. No matter what Lucifer says about this binding making the power controllable, or whatever, I can *feel* it waiting.

There's a truth to Lucifer's fear, I can admit that much, even if I care more about my freedom than his precious damage control. The second my emotions get out of line, this power is going to reach through me and zap the nearest thing it can.

And somehow, these two men, plus the one who's just gone charging off without me, make me more irritated than anyone has for years. Even Ronin.

It's getting harder and harder to think up a clever plan, even though I know I should. I'm starting to *react*.

I never react. I'm always careful.

What the hell are these men doing to me?

"Well, sweetheart," Tobias says, running his thumb over his chin as he studies the door Lucifer disappeared through. "Perhaps we should get to know each other since it seems we're stuck together for now."

An unexpected flash of heat runs through me at the low rumble of his voice. It isn't the sensuality of his suggestion—though I'd be an idiot to miss that. It's the curiosity. The interest.

For someone who's been ignored her whole life, and then trapped inside her own mind for years, that invitation is... tempting.

But these men are my guards, and when we're all together like this, we're a ticking time bomb duct taped to the back of a missile. I need a breather. I need a bloody plan.

It's a good thing I've been outrunning teachers and wardens all my life.

By the time Tobias and Logan have turned around, I've already slipped back to my room.

9
HELENA

I LOSE MYSELF IN MY BOOKS FOR THE REST OF THE AFTERNOON, CURLED up in the beautiful window seat which is fast becoming my favorite place in Hell. Tiny vines are etched into the wooden backing, and the cushions, while modern, are that kind of rich, blue-green velvet that makes you think of big old rooms and hidden libraries.

Time fades into the background in a way I only allow it to do when I'm alone and no one is watching. Well, usually, anyway. I'll admit I've slipped a bit lately.

Only in front of Logan, though, when he first brought me all these books yesterday. What can I say? It was a rough day, and I still wasn't used to having my body back under my control. I let him see how I am when I'm not several moves ahead of the situation—when I'm just me.

It's dangerous to let people see that. It won't happen again.

Especially now that my body is feeling more and more like my own again, and I can remember how to use it to get what I need. How to move in the subtle ways that will turn me into someone else.

Right now, I reckon I'd benefit from being a guard—someone with access to keys and the ability to stand in the corner of a room and eavesdrop while no one gave them a second look.

I tuck my ankles under me and pull the blanket up higher. Outside the window, little figures run around in the castle grounds, doing some kind of training routine. Wooden swords clash together, and it all feels very medieval.

It's not so bad being here, I suppose. I just can't stand being locked up. Controlled. I know Lucifer believes he has very good reasons to do so while he works out how to fix me, but it doesn't mean I have to sit here and wait for him.

I turn the page and find I've exhausted my chapter on the history of guards. I didn't find much that was helpful, sadly, but I could whip up a uniform with my eyes closed, so that's something.

Flicking through idly, now, I stop when something on the page stands out. I frown, flipping back until I find it. Something about a stuck ghost...

I read the passage aloud.

The soul was eventually discovered on the fringes of the Black Mountains, near one of the forgotten portals into Death. It became quickly apparent that their unfinished business belonged with someone who had also died and been taken down into the seventh circle of Hell for their punishment. This unresolved conflict presented a conundrum. Given the timing of both their deaths—almost simultaneous—the ghost had become stuck between one place and the next. Unable to move forward, as their soul's longing had been registered a split second before resolution became impossible, the ghost was in neither Death nor Hell, and could only wait until someone found them.

Lost souls.

Those are what Cat tracks down, if I've remembered right.

This book is talking about a soul that became lost here because his unfinished business couldn't be resolved.

What if kicking Ronin out of my head was like a second death? I mean, it must have done something to my soul, right? Was my soul even recognizable anymore, after all that? And so what if I now have unfinished business? And what if that unfinished business is here in Hell?

I know exactly what it would be.

And if I'm right, the first thing I'll need is a key, just as I'd planned—but not for myself, this time.

I snap the book shut, straightening and staring around the room in a slight daze. Lucifer still isn't back from wherever he's run off to, I can tell by the faint tugging on one of the threads in my chest. And while the sun here is artificial, it still follows the passage of time.

It's been several hours since he left.

I turn to look out the window again, studying the little figures going through their drills. It doesn't seem fair that Lucifer can go wherever he wants, but I'm stuck with two bonded guards while he vanishes. This bond was meant to inconvenience him as well as me. He doesn't bloody seem inconvenienced.

Unless...

I frown, my heart thumping in my chest. Maybe the bond didn't work at all. Maybe he's just making me think it does. I mean, what kind of bond is this, anyway? He was curiously silent on the details...

Oh, that bastard.

Before I know it, I'm marching down the corridor and toward the castle gates, off to test a theory.

Sure, it's probably like a rope, and if I go too far something will break—and my money's on me breaking, not the bond. But even just getting these guys off my case for a few hours will be an improvement. If they're not breathing down my neck, maybe I can think.

Maybe I can do a bit of digging outside the castle and see if I'm right about this unfinished business of mine.

The gates of the palace rise in the distance, and they look different to my memory. They're huge, wrought iron monstrosities with little gargoyles sitting on top the pillars. I swore the gates to Hell's palace were lighter than this, more modern...

I'm closer now. Ten meters. Five. Three.

Then... snap!

Okay, so it's not like a rope; it's like a freaking bungee cord.

I launch back into the air, shrieking and scrabbling like a mad thing, and then plummet to the ground.

Something soft cushions my landing. Something soft and loud, that grunts *oof* in a vaguely familiar, deep, sexy way.

Strong hands steady me at the waist as we stagger backward the last few steps and collapse into a spiky, uncomfortable bush.

I stare up at the sky. "Ouch," I wheeze, too nervous to turn and see which one I've just crushed.

"Indeed," a dry, pained voice comes from beneath me.

Tobias. Great. Because he really looks like the kind of man who likes to be knocked flying and covered in dirt—it was the expensive linen shirt and tailored trousers that sold me on that.

He laughs from beneath me, and it sounds just as pained as the word. "Can you get off me now, please?"

I scramble to my feet, helped by his guiding hands behind me.

By the time I turn around, he's already up, smoothing down his trousers and eyeing me with deep suspicion.

"Did you plan that?" he asks.

"Did I plan launching myself into the sky like a fucking

rocket?" I shoot back, too incredulous to stop myself. "No, not particularly."

He hums, straightening the final button and sticking his hands in his pockets.

Well, one hand. The other plays distractedly with his collar, and my gaze is drawn to the slender arch of his fingers, covered in silver rings.

"Well, it proved a theory, at least," he says after a moment, studying the gate. "Only Lucifer can extend the bond past thirty meters. The rest of us have to stick together."

So, he was curious about the limits, too.

"What about Logan?" I ask, looking around. "How far away is he?"

Tobias smiles. "Not thirty meters."

Great, there's two of them.

But then Tobias relaxes further, something I never see Lucifer do, no matter how similar they are. "But since we're all together now, we can take this beyond the gates if you'd like. You must be feeling stir crazy by now."

I stiffen, watching him out of the corner of my eye. Is he serious? Or is this a trap?

"Lucifer said not to go out there," I remind him, waiting to see what he'll do.

"No," Tobias says, smiling very differently this time, "he said to watch you and contain your wayward power."

Ah. I relax minutely as he begins to make sense—he's a loophole guy. I can work with that. In some ways, they're the easiest. I love loopholes.

"Well then," I tell him, scanning the grounds for Logan and still not seeing him. "Where will we go?"

"Do you like Starbucks?"

I blink around me in surprise. Hell is officially far weirder than I ever noticed before.

I duck behind a modern-looking building, not because I need to hide, but because I need to take a second to quietly mouth *what the fuck*, because... what the fuck?

These buildings are so bizarre. Currently, I'm perched on the curb of a cobblestone alleyway, staring up at a Starbucks. However, before I can properly take that in, I need to give a special shout out to the building over the road, which looks like it's been taken straight out of a book illustrating a medieval apothecary.

I suppose it makes sense. Hell isn't going to live in stagnation, especially not with the hell currents running through the whole place, twisting the geography and creating new buildings and landscapes in literal seconds. But it also isn't going to relinquish the past so easily. Not when it's still within living memory.

I wonder... if I slipped among the smoke pouring from the apothecary, would I be able to lose Tobias?

"Lucifer didn't explain the details of the binding, did he?" a pleasant enough voice murmurs in my ear, but it still makes me jolt in fright.

"Stop doing that!" I hiss, whirling around to see Tobias leaning his shoulder against the dumpster beside me, arms folded and amusement dancing in his gaze.

"Sorry," he says, not sounding sorry at all. "The coast is clear, by the way. We can go inside." Tobias gestures grandly toward the busy street and the entrance opposite.

He'd been checking to make sure my power wasn't likely to ignite a vat of gasoline, real or metaphorical. I suppose I should thank him.

But I think he prefers a bit of sass, actually.

"What do you mean, the details of the binding?" I ask

him, injecting just enough irritation into my voice that, if he really does like the confrontation, he'll be provoked into responding.

Tobias lips curve upward—bingo. "We can track you."

I groan, shutting my eyes and covering my face with my hand, tipping my head back to the sky. "Of course you can."

No wonder he found me so quickly, by the gate. And I guess that's a big old 'no' on the escape plan.

"I thought it was just to lock the power away," I snap defensively, dropping my hands to glare at him. "Not to spy on my every move."

I would have realized he could track me via the bond if I'd thought about it. I just assumed Lucifer wouldn't be so devious.

I believed him when he said he didn't want to do this.

Tobias hasn't moved, but something about his stance has definitely shifted. "Yes, the power," he says.

He steps forward, moving through the shadow into the light. The burning red of the strange sun above us glints in his eyes, even though his smile is as bright as ever.

"What are you doing?"

"Guarding you," he says, like it's obvious. "Or am I guarding the rest of us? I'm not quite sure. Tell me about this power that has dear Lucy in such a snit."

"Who the hell are you that you can call the Devil 'Lucy'?" I ask without thinking.

He laughs. His teeth are startlingly white. "Anyone can call him Lucy behind his back. Give it a try."

"Is this some kind of 'speak of the Devil' trick?" I whisper, backing up and finding my heels hit brick.

"I never trick," he says quietly. "I only ever tell the truth. Whether you hear it is up to you."

I open my mouth to throw something back, anything, drawn by the way his casual demeanor doesn't match his argumentative words. Then I hear it—what he's really said, even though he pretended to say something else.

"You didn't just say it behind his back, though," I counter, holding his gaze. I think I see a flicker of surprise there. "You said it to his face."

"You may have noticed we were having something of a disagreement at the time," Tobias says, his smile widening like a threat. "I'm struggling to see your point."

"No you're not. The Devil hates you, but I've seen him with enemies before. He isn't fire; he's ice." Tobias's eyes definitely flash with surprise then, his mouth even softening. "You're not an enemy, not quite." I swallow. "You were a friend."

He stills, the thumb of his right hand twisting the ring on his pointer. It's a casual movement I'm probably not meant to notice, but it's kind of what I do. I notice things. "Very good," he finally says. "What else have you noticed?"

"I want a coffee," I say suddenly, jerking my chin at the Starbucks beside us. "Will you get them for us, and we can trade answers?"

This time, his eyebrows fly up in surprise. "Trade," he repeats. "Well, that's a first." He glances at the watch on his wrist and shrugs. "We probably have a couple of minutes before the cat joins us. He decided to patrol the suburb fences to check for new rifts while I caught you."

"Charming." I wrinkle my nose. "Did you decide which one would slap me in irons, or are you leaving that up to fate?"

Tobias gives me a slow, wicked smile. The soft fall of his brown fringe shadows his eyes just enough that they appear to glint. My cheeks heat, and I turn away at the low chuckle he gives in response.

"Calm down, little angel. No one is slapping you in irons."

He rests a hand just over the dip of my lower back and gestures for me to go back out onto the street. Annoyed at the fake gallantry, I move quickly, ignoring the second chuckle that sounds even more amused this time.

The sun above us flickers an unnatural, orange light. It isn't the first time I've been distracted by Hell's sun, but it's the first time I might be able to get some answers about it.

"Is there some kind of story behind the flaming sun?" I ask as I step through the door to Starbucks.

The bell above the entrance chimes eerily. This is too bizarre. Thank the Devil that Ronin never let us assimilate down here; I would have dissociated my way into a full-blown meltdown just from how weird this all is.

"We're in Hell," Tobias says lightly. "Everything has a story."

"And do you know this one?" I ask drily. "Or are you pretending to be mysterious to avoid the fact that you don't know."

The corner of Tobias's lip twitches. "Since I put that sun there, I think I know."

Well. Isn't that a conversation stopper?

Tobias leans against the counter, ignoring the queue of people winding between the tables. Somehow, no one seems to notice, and I watch curiously as the server drops her customer mid sentence and switches to Tobias.

"Welcome to Starbucks," she says, a deadened look to her eyes. "What can I get you?"

"An Apple Crisp Macchiato and a Caramel Frappuccino," he says, rattling off the exact order I'd been craving.

I narrow my eyes at him as he returns. He spreads his hands and smiles innocently. "You look like a frappuccino woman. Did I get it right?"

"You know you did," I say carefully, the gears in my head turning slower than they should have. But surely not...

Moving on—for now—I jerk my chin toward the server. "What kind of demons voluntarily work at Starbucks?"

Tobias laughs, the sound so abrupt I swear I've taken him by surprise. He blinks at me, a furrow in his brow, and then he leans forward. "Look again," he whispers.

I turn around.

This time, I barely manage to suck in a gasp of horror. Chains stretch from the woman's wrists to the walls—walls that are dripping with blood and fire.

This isn't a job; it's a punishment.

When I turn back to Tobias, I find him smiling in this unnerving way, all teeth but with darkness in his eyes. In this moment, he's a predator, but he's not hiding it behind false seduction, like so many men in his position would in a moment like this.

He reminds me of the fae, with his dark hair falling across deep, enchanting eyes. What promises is he hoping to extract from me, in return for my everlasting soul?

"No promises," he says softly, a huff of laughter dropping when I gasp. "Only information."

"You can read my thoughts," I breathe, finally admitting that the coincidences add up to one too many.

I pull myself up tall, twisting my focus into a sharp point and locking up my thoughts behind a brick wall in my head. It works for my day-to-day functioning; surely it will work for a mind reader as well.

His smile softens. "Perhaps. Or perhaps you are very easy to read."

I narrow my eyes. "I'm sure others fall for that, but I don't. What kind of demon are you, exactly?"

He leans back, glancing at the menu above the counter with bored disinterest. "The original kind."

"What, the kind that collects souls and possesses bodies?"

Still looking at the board, his mouth twitches. "Are you saying you want me to possess your body?"

I roll my eyes. I'm pretty sure he uses seduction as a distraction, by now. But I'll let him think I've fallen for it if it will make things easier. I need him amenable if we're going to trade answers, after all.

"Why do you want to know about my power?"

He levels me with a flat stare. "Seriously? You're going to waste your turn on the obvious?"

"I need to know what you already know about it," I return.

Something like approval crosses his face. "I know that it created a rift to Mystic's Peak, and an opportunistic gang of cutthroat morons decided to attack the palace through it. If they had known it came out in the Devil's dining room, I doubt they would have been so eager. The idiots probably thought it was a back entrance to the kitchens."

He waves the waitress back over, orders a lemon tart, and turns back to me. "You already know why I want to know about your power. Learn to ask the questions you really mean."

I bristle, but he's already moved on. Our drinks appear, and we take them along with the cakes and sit down at a table.

"Did you know it had created the rift?" he asks me. "Could you feel the moment it tore, or were you ignorant?"

Reluctantly, I admit: "Ignorant. Sort of. I felt something tear, but I didn't know where or what. Do you know what that might mean?"

He pulls a thoughtful grimace. "Could mean a few things. Someone is using you as a conduit—the most likely answer. You're untrained and unskilled—also possible, but it's a strong power to appear out of nowhere."

"You're telling me." I pause. Tobias is unlikely to answer this question, but I have to ask. I don't know where else to start, and

I have to start somewhere. "Do you know where the prison keys are kept?"

I mean, I'm sure there are like fifty thousand of them, but any key is in the right direction. Because one key will lead me to a key holder... and they'll know where the rest are.

Tobias studies me, unreadable.

Dammit. I knew it was useless to ask. But my unfinished business... I need this.

The door jingles, and we look up to see Logan loping in. His eyes scan the room quickly and efficiently, and then he drops into a chair beside our table, facing the door. "No sign of Lucifer," he murmurs.

I frown, looking between the two of them. "I thought you were checking for more rifts."

"I was," Logan agrees easily, eyeing off the remaining piece of lemon tart and wrinkling his nose. "But I was also looking for a clue to where Lucifer might have gone."

"Didn't he say he was going to that mystics' place?" I can't follow the twists in this plan, and I don't like being left in the dark.

They aren't telling me everything.

Tobias glances at me sharply; I think that thought might have slipped out, even with my control.

"You're right," he says, his words coming out slow and thoughtful. "We are looking for Lucifer and we were hoping that there were other obvious rifts in the area that could explain his disappearance."

"So he didn't go to Mystic's Peak after all?" I'm not sure how that makes me feel.

An odd twinge of discomfort hits me, though I don't know why. It's familiar.

I haven't felt it in a long time.

Tobias reaches for the tart, popping it into his mouth with a defiant look at Logan, who's still watching it suspiciously. "It isn't so much that he didn't go there—we haven't checked yet," he says when he's finished chewing. I wonder if the food was to make us wait or to give him time to think how best to answer. Maybe both. "It's that, when he bound us all, the rift sealed. I thought I was mistaken, so I went back to check after you ran. But no. The rifts you create are like tears—wild and broken. This was a slice, created with very deliberate power drawn from the hell currents. Which means that Lucifer created it after the bond, most likely as an excuse for why he had to run and why we had to stay."

The feeling curdles in my stomach, bringing an aching sharpness with it. My jaw stiffens, and I turn away. "It doesn't just mean that," I say softly. "It means he lied."

Despite my desire not to look at either of them right now, something draws me back. I turn to find Tobias watching me intently, his own jaw just as tense as mine. "Yes," he says quietly. "And the Lucifer I knew never bothered with this sort of deception. He would have ordered us to stay and removed limbs if we disobeyed him. So why did he choose this course of action?"

He leans forward slowly, elbows propped on the table and dark eyes piercing. "What do you say we make a deal, Helena?" He holds up one hand before I can respond. "I am a man of my word, so I will guard you and manage your power where I can. I will also not allow you to leave the castle on your own, and, I suspect once Lucifer cottons on to his poor choice of wording, at all."

Drat. No more loopholes.

"But I am interested in uncovering Lucifer's secrets, since he's insisted on uprooting my life and throwing me in the middle of them." Something flashes in his eyes. It's a reminder that these two are enemies, technically. "I think it might be in both our interests to make sure dear Lucy doesn't get away with complete autonomy here. And if it's keys you're after, in return, I will help you get the best of them all." He grins broadly. "Lucifer's skeleton key."

My stomach swoops, and a longing I can't define appears within me. A skeleton key—a key that opens all locked doors. Of course Lucifer has one.

And it's exactly what I need, because if I truly do have unfinished business down here, there's only one thing it could be.

I always felt guilty for being the only one of my family to make it to Heaven. I remember seeing my parents' names in Hell's ledgers when I was under Ronin's spell; it was almost enough to break me out of it, the shock of seeing them there. Seeing their torture listed: spiral torture. That's all I remember, whatever the fuck it means. That's all I know.

But knowing that should have been enough to do something about it, and yet I never did. I got my body back, and I did nothing. This is my chance.

I need to track down this spiral torture, find my parents, and bust them out of Hell.

I drain the last of my coffee, standing abruptly, and hold out my hand. "Deal," I tell him.

With a lazy unfolding of limbs, Logan follows, eyes darting between me and Tobias as he rises.

After a beat, Tobias follows and takes my hand in his. His palm is warm and softer than expected. He squeezes harder than most men do for a woman, nods, and drops his hand to his side.

Is it my imagination, or did his touch linger more than it needed to?

Do I want it to?

Tobias gives me no answers, simply waiting for me to speak.

It's unnerving having so much attention, after so long without a voice of my own.

"And for my final question," I say flatly, thinking of the possible reasons why Lucifer might have recreated the rift and pretended he hadn't. "What's at Mystic's Peak? Is it misdirection, or a trap?"

Tobias grins. "Shall we go together to find out?"

10

HELENA

Mystic's Peak is aptly named.

"Well, there's the peak," I say, pointing up to a craggy rock face above us. "And there's the mystic, I presume."

A giant statue stretches from the base of the mountain thirty feet up toward the unnerving orange sun. In her hand, she cradles what looks like hellfire, although there's something mixing with the flames that I can't identify from down here. Maybe a skull? With her other hand, she holds her robes back from the ground, as if she's standing in mud.

Behind her, the mountain itself seems to have been carved with the faint outlines of people stooped over, or buried in huddled conferences. They're all robed, like she is. It's obviously some record of an ancient people or something.

Either way—very mystical.

"She is the mystic guide," Tobias agrees, "but the mystics themselves are hidden in the rocks."

"They're hiding from us?" I ask, leaning up on my toes to see if I can see someone crouched there, watching.

Logan chuckles. "No, Hel." He reaches out and raps the rock with his knuckles. "*In* the rocks."

It's the first time Logan's called me by my name, and it sends strange tingles down my back to hear him do it so casually.

"Oh."

Oh.

The rock gives a little shimmy, and the jagged points of its carving suddenly shift away from the rest of it to become... a person.

The man blinks, tiny rocks falling from his eyes as he looks around at us and squints. "What day is it?"

"Friday," Tobias says pleasantly.

The man appears to make some mental calculations. "Still March?"

"Still March."

The man straightens up and grins. "Then what can I do for you? The name's Eldon."

Tobias glances up at the rock face, lips pursed. "We heard word you were under attack. Cutthroats, we thought, but you seem to be quite... peaceful."

Eldon shudders. "No skirmishes here, not for months. You know how volatile it gets when those break out." He gestures around at the still earth.

The carvings in the rock, now that I look closely, are very slowly moving. A hand lifts to point; another takes a full five minutes to write a note.

"Yes," Tobias says flatly. "That was my estimate, too. Thank you, then."

Eldon nods, and without asking if that was all, he simply steps back into the rock.

"So what does that mean?" I ask.

"When Mystic's Peak is attacked, the statue comes to life,"

Tobias says thoughtfully, spinning in a slow circle and looking around as he does. "Hellfire takes over the mountain, and—if left long enough—burns through any rifts connecting it."

"Ah. So that's why Lucifer had to deal with the rift urgently."

"It is why he had a good excuse to hurry off, yes."

I don't miss the dry tone to his words. Sighing, I sit down on a rock and drop my elbows on my knees. "So where the hell is he?"

"Couldn't tell you," Tobias says, glancing suddenly at Logan as if it's the first time he's actually seen him. He turns to me, the same narrow-eyed expression on his face. "And I think we've reached the limits on what we can achieve," he says abruptly. "I'll be back when Lucifer decides to show his lying face again."

Then, the bastard disappears.

Logan startles. "What the hell?"

"Well he can't be more than thirty meters," I snap. "Or he'd bungee back into us immediately."

Logan leans forward, hands in his pockets and checks behind a rock. "Got a point, there. Looks like it's only Lucifer who can go as far as he wants."

Don't remind me, I think bitterly.

So why has Tobias taken off if he can't really go anywhere?

We don't have time to wallow in abandonment, though, because the ground begins to shake.

"Oh shit," I yell, pointing to the statue.

The arm is raising, the fire in its palm cracking free from the stone. It's definitely a skull at the base of the flames, and the skull is coming alive.

Fiery red eyes turn our way, and it spits a glowing glob of embers straight at our feet.

"Fucking Tobias," Logan yells, hooking his arm around my

waist and pulling me back into the stone, toward the rift. "He must have set off the intruder alarm."

"He probably didn't know," I say, ducking under the rock and steadying myself against Logan's shoulder. I'm just as annoyed as he is, actually, but I'm trying to stay cool.

Otherwise I might actually deck him when I see him again.

Logan snorts, pulling me down into a narrow crevasse where we can run at a crouch. "He's a trickster demon, Hel. He knew."

Oh, Christ in a bucket. That explains a lot.

The rift we all came through surges before us, rippling back from the heat that rages toward it. It senses danger and pain, but it's ultimately a mindless hole in Hell's geography, so it can't actually do anything about it.

Anything except close, that is, if the people on the other side of the rift sense the danger in time.

"Nearly there," Logan grunts, his jaw clenched as the statue howls behind us.

The walls are coming to life, too, the carvings moving faster and growing smaller, as if they're hurrying further into the wall.

Neat trick. I want in.

"Come on," I spit out through gritted teeth. "A few more feet."

A demon from the palace pokes his head through the rift, his eyes widening when he sees the hellfire. He garbles something behind him, his guard helmet nearly falling off as he hastens to drag his head back through.

"No, wait!" I yell, reaching for the rift.

He doesn't see us.

The rift snaps shut with an elastic wriggle, blinding us for a second. Then, the statue roars louder, and two more waves of hellfire come rushing toward us.

"Keep running!" Logan yells.

I turn to see his eyes glowing yellow, his reddish hair turning bright like flames. When he yells again, it comes out like a snarl, his vicious mouth twisting into teeth and an elongated jaw.

"I didn't catch that, but I'm going to assume you said climb aboard," I yell back, reaching out for a handful of fur and swinging onto his back just as he finishes the transformation.

It might even have worked—our strides immediately lengthen, and the air grows cooler as the hellfire falls behind.

But then the ground caves beneath our feet and everything turns black.

I wake slowly, groaning as my eyes adjust to the dim light. It isn't complete darkness down here, even though it seems that way at first. Glowing bugs line the roof of what seems to be a cave, its little crevasses and nooks lit up with stars.

Reaching out, I feel carefully around me, looking for a sign of something other than stone. My fingers find soft fur, and I shrink away until I remember Logan. He hasn't shifted back, obviously.

An animalistic growl comes from my left, the fur rumbling beneath my touch.

Whatever his shifter vitality is, it doesn't sound like a wolf.

I'm sure I saw spots, and Lucifer called him a cat...

Is he a jaguar? Or a leopard?

I pull my hand back, squinting into the low light, but the body is already shifting into a naked man. He props himself up on his elbows and groans, tilting his head back so his long, reddish brown hair falls away from his face.

"Fuck, that hurt." He grimaces.

Yeah, yeah... sure. Pain. We're in pain. That's totally what I'm thinking about.

Christ, he's well built...

I try to look away, but my eyes flick up to his and I find him grinning at me.

"Look away if you don't want to see," he says simply. "It'll take me a minute to recharge. Then I can get my spare set."

I turn immediately, flushing that I was caught staring. But then... he didn't say *he* wanted me to look away. I glance back. He's still grinning, and it only gets wider when he sees me peeking. My lips twitch, and I hold his gaze.

"If you insist," I tell him.

With his eyes fixed to me, hunger in his expression, I let my attention roam over his upper body. Lean, strong muscles flex in the darkness, the broad expanse of golden skin only broken in one place.

Unthinking, I reach for his shoulder, running my fingers over the dark ink. "I can't tell what the pattern is."

His expression hardens, but when he reaches up with his other hand to cover mine, it's a gentle rebuke. Almost apologetic. His fingers close around my hand, squeezing gently before he brings it to the middle of his chest.

"It's a long story," he says. "You wouldn't recognize the pattern."

I shrug. "You've got your secrets. I get it."

Suddenly, a light over his shoulder catches my attention. I lean forward, trying to make sense of it.

"It's moving," I say, not making any sense at all.

Logan twists his hand in the air, and a pile of clothing drops into it. He quickly dresses in gray jeans and a tight, white shirt, and then he leans into the spot in the wall that's caught my attention.

"Ah, it's the gems," he says, straightening. He sticks his

hands in his pockets, looking bored. "This is what the mystics are all chasing."

"Gems don't move," I say flatly.

"These are no ordinary gems." He grins, but there's a hardened edge to it. "Lots of prestige in owning one of these things. You'd be the envy of all your friends."

"What friends?" I mutter, leaning in to examine it. "I'm dead."

The gem moves again and I freeze. There are things *living* inside there. I can't see them clearly, but I swear I can make out tiny forests... lakes.

People.

"What the hell am I looking at?"

"Worlds."

I jump a little when his voice comes from right beside my ear. I hadn't realized how close he'd come. There's something odd in his expression, but I can't work out why. I'm too preoccupied by what he just said.

"*Worlds?!* How do they fit whole worlds in there?"

"I'm told that, to them, we're the ones inside the gem." He shrugs. "If you want answers, become a mystic for the next few thousand years."

The strange look is still there. It sends shivers racing down my spine.

I lean back from the wall, but when I turn, I find myself trapped between two strong arms. The cave wall is jagged and freezing cold against my back, but the heat in Logan's gaze floods me with warmth.

"Is that what the demons told you?"

"What?" What on earth is he talking about?

"That you're dead."

Oh.

I wet my lips, shivering as his gaze drops to the movement.

"Well... I am. I remember living, dying, and then the choosing ceremony for the angels. I remember my afterlife, and committing to become a warrior of Heaven, and I remember being stolen... I remember coming down here. I remember it all, Logan. This is my afterlife. I'm dead."

His breath hits my cheek, hot as he slowly purses his lips and blows. I shiver, my eyes falling shut as my head tips back against the rock.

He doesn't stop. He trails the hot line of his breath over my neck, across my collar bone, and then pauses right over my cleavage. There's no deliberate current of air anymore, but after a pause, he laughs, and the huff of hot breath is just as intoxicating, if not more so.

"Do you feel dead?" he asks, his voice lower than before.

No. I feel alive, so fucking alive, it makes me wonder if I was dead every moment before this.

"You know I don't," I whisper.

He rises slowly, his lips tracing my ear before he pushes off from the wall and takes a step back. "You aren't dead, Hel. This is your afterlife, sure, but it's a *life*. Only hellsouls, spirits, and heaven dwellers are dead. And trust me, you'd know if that were you."

He holds my gaze, and even in the dim light I can see the intensity of it. Feel it.

I can feel him, and it's like this binding Lucifer put on us means something else entirely. Like I can sense Logan's emotions in the same way I can feel my own, and like he's...

Important.

To me.

I blink, looking down as movement appears between us: a thin blue cord, stretching from my body to his.

Logan reaches out, wrapping it around his finger and

tugging lightly. I have to bite my lip to keep from making a very inappropriate sound.

He must sense it anyway, because he looks up, his eyes full of heat. "Is this Lucifer's bond?" he asks, his voice lower than before.

"No, this was already there," I answer faintly, wondering what it means.

What it all means.

Before I can ask, something crashes into the other side of the rock I'm leaning on. I jump, stumbling away and covering my head in case there's another cave-in. But Logan steadies me and points to an odd little window of quartz in the rock.

Through it, I can see Lucifer and Tobias.

Tobias didn't abandon us after all. Why on earth would he make us think he had?

Then I realize they seem to be fighting... Tobias throws Lucifer back by the shoulders, but even when he slams into the rock and the entire cave shudders, no sound comes through. It's like they're caught in one of those tiny worlds, themselves.

I pound my fist on the clear crystal, but they don't hear me.

Then, Tobias kicks the rock at his feet, stepping back into a strange stance, and a whirl of dust and crystals rises before him. The crystals glitter, trapped hellfire caught within them, like the sentinel rock above ground.

He shouts something at Lucifer, his eyes blazing with fury, and Lucifer shouts back.

His face flickers, and my eyes widen as the hellfire in the crystals reveals a hint of Lucifer's demonic soul. Bone flickers in the light, crystals slicing across his whitened skull and peeling flesh as the whirlwind rises. But there's gold there, too—golden metal bolted into his jaw and across his temple, disappearing into his dark curls.

The crystals fly back in the wind, and his soul disappears.

A second later, the wind hits the crystal separating us, and it shatters. Sound assaults my ears, their shouting mixing with the howling wind, and I double over in pain.

Not from the sound or the wind; I can't tell what it is that hurts me. I can't work out what's happening at all.

It goes dark, and the shouting stops. The wind cuts out. Suddenly, it's too quiet. Ragged breathing fills the tunnel, but it's too close to gasping for my liking.

Is there enough oxygen down here?

"Helena?" Lucifer's voice cuts through the gloom.

"Finally, you can hear us," I say, unable to keep the bitterness from my voice. "Are you finished with your little fight?"

An insulted silence follows. Good. We need to get out of this place, not settle grievances here.

"We will resolve it later," Tobias says, his voice smooth and certain. "For now, can someone bring the lights back?"

Lucifer claps his hands together. Nothing happens. There's a slow pause, followed by the thoughtful scratching of nails over skin.

"That should have worked, I take it," Tobias says drily.

Lucifer snarls. "The mystics have done something," he mutters. "Must have felt us down in their catacombs, and they're locking us in before we ruin any worlds."

"Even you?!" I spit out, shocked at the ruthlessness.

"They don't care for authority," he says wryly. "I have a feeling you have that in common."

I grin. "Gotta respect that," I say under my breath.

There isn't much of it; the air is getting tighter. My grin falls away.

"So what do we do?" I ask.

"We need light," Lucifer murmurs. "Without light, there is no power."

I frown, feeling for the wall and steadying myself against it.

Not that I'm getting woozy. Definitely not. "I'm sure I've seen people drawing on hell currents in the darkness before."

"Darkness, yes, but not without light." Lucifer makes a rustling sound, as though he's leaning back against the wall. "There is always light above ground in Hell, even if you can't see it. The sun shines in all cracks and crevasses. Whether it is the flicker of a dust mote or the shimmer of a reflection through a crack, there is light." He pauses, swallowing. "Down here, there is nothing. And..." The next words sound like they cost him. "I am drained of power."

All that fighting did him in. Literally anyone could have told you that.

Unfortunately, no one did, and it doesn't help anything because here we are.

Beside me, Logan breathes, "Fuck," and drops back against the wall.

It's starting to feel seriously stifling in here.

"What are you even doing down here?" I snap.

Agitation and guilt flicker along our bindings, and I realize suddenly that's what he and Tobias were fighting about.

"Oh my God," I mutter, sinking down the wall and dropping my head onto my knees. "Forget it."

"Ask him again when we're out of here," Tobias says, a smile in his voice. "It's quite the workout."

"Are we even getting out of here? Why can't you do anything?"

The smile falls from his voice. "The mystics have thousands of years of spells guarding this place. And..." He pauses. "I'm out of power, too."

Great.

"Hold on," Logan starts up. "Can you make another rift, Hel?"

There's a thoughtful silence.

"Worth a try," I say.

The words come out softer than they should. Drained of life and breath. Swallowing, I close my eyes and try to summon up the strength of emotion that seems to come before everything goes shittastic.

It's hard, when I can hardly find the energy to be angry.

"Someone piss me off," I mutter, swaying a little as I stand up.

"Excuse me?" Lucifer asks in that stiffly polite and incredulous voice he has.

My annoyance immediately spikes. "Yeah, that'll do it," I say, turning in the direction of his voice. "Do more of that."

"More of what?" he asks, his own anger rising. "I'm simply existing."

"And you do it so offensively," Tobias purrs.

"You're not being helpful," Lucifer snaps.

"On the contrary." Tobias shuffles against the wall. "All you need to do is tell the truth. It's uniquely infuriating when you reveal what little undercurrents you've been hiding."

"Oh?" Lucifer snarls, and there's an echo of power in it.

Unfortunately, it's nothing like it should be, and while this conversation is definitely up there with Irritating 101, it's not exactly bringing me to boiling point.

"Try harder," I hiss. Then it hits me. I grow still. "Tell us what the bond really is, Lucifer."

He goes silent. All of us do. I can barely hear the others breathing, as we all hold our breath in anticipation of his answer.

"No," Lucifer finally says.

My anger spikes again. We're getting warmer.

"Yes," I insist, shuffling toward him and reaching out into the darkness. My hands meet a warm, hard chest, and I grab a handful of his shirt and drag him in close.

"A little to the left," Tobias's low voice murmurs in front of my face, rich with laughter.

Grunting, I shove him back and snatch for Lucifer. He barely moves when I grab him, and I can feel the irritation rolling off him in waves.

"Tell us what you—"

"It's a soulbond," he snarls. "A Ludus bond, to be specific. It was there already. I just used it to hold you to me. I didn't realize you had two others ready to go."

A soulbond.

It's a soulbond. As he says it, I can see it in my mind—the same as it was in the dining room when Lucifer ignited it. Three blue strings, emerging from each of our bodies. The entry point is vague, somewhere around the chest or collar, but the threads themselves are distinct. One for each of us, like a strange little spiderweb linking us all together.

"Ludus?" I ask faintly, desperately searching for solid ground.

Lucifer sighs, ever so faintly. "There are seven kinds of soul-bonds, named after the divisions with which the ancient Greeks defined various kinds of love. Eros—you can guess that kind, I'm sure." And then, in case I can't, he adds, "Passion. Obsession. Desire."

Heat runs through me, and for one aching moment I wish it were that kind of bond. Instead, I'm forever cursed to know what Lucifer's voice sounds like when he says those three words.

"Philia," Lucifer continues. "Or the bonds of deep, enduring friendship. Storge, which is similar to Philia and speaks of the love between children and their family."

My heart twinges unexpectedly.

"Ludus is the playful bond of first lovers, flirtatious and vibrant. Agape is a... universal bond of true altruism, you could say. Love that is unconditional—the truest of all, in many senses."

His tone sounds almost bored now, but I know Lucifer a bit more than I did a day ago, and my body tenses up in anticipation. No—in apprehension.

"Philautia is the soulbond one forms with oneself, in times of need and expansion. And finally, Pragma. The enduring love of two people who were, in every way, made for each other. Love that comes with maturity and the ability to respect, grow, and change with each other over time."

He says it too casually. Too light.

A spark runs through me, although I can't explain why. I only know that Pragma bonds mean something to Lucifer.

"But Ludus," he says finally, something unreadable in his tone. "We have a Ludus bond."

We sit in silence for a while, absorbing, reeling... and then the reality hits me.

He knew.

He *knew*, and he didn't tell us; he just used it to trap us. And then he ran off and left us stewing all alone.

Who the fuck does that to their soulmates?

"How dare you keep that from me!" I snarl. "This is my *life*, mate, and you're just—just—playing with it!"

Rage floods me, and the cavern explodes. It isn't a rift though; instead, it's a swirl of light, like the starlight in the dining room. We fall back, gasping in lungfuls of air as the light brings with it power, and with the power, a link to the surface.

Starlight dances across our faces, glowing a gentle blue, and for a moment we're all mesmerized. Silent and still.

In the flickering waves, I study each of them. They feel unexpectedly familiar to me. Known, like I just...

Like my soul knows them.

My breath catches, and instead of feeling joy, I feel the most horrendous sadness.

These men are locked to me, not just while Lucifer works out my issues, but forever. For eternity.

What the hell do I have to offer them?

I know what I am—I'm a thief. A con artist. A liar. And that's fine, mate, that's just fine, because I never owed anyone anything more than that.

But now I'm hit by the horrible thought that I do, and I can never possibly measure up.

The blue starlight flares, and there's a ripping sound. Suddenly, I'm gasping in lungfuls of oxygen, and then there's a hand in mine, pulling me forward, and we tumble through onto the castle floor.

11

LUCIFER

WELL, I THINK TO MYSELF AS I SLOWLY DESCEND THE STAIRS TO THE
First Circle of Hell. *The cat's out of the bag now.*

There's nothing quite like a soulbond to shake things up,
although I do find myself wishing I could have watched this one
from the outside as well. At least it's only a Ludus bond.

The name causes something inside me to constrict, of
course, but that's nothing new.

The First Circle doorway passes on my left, and I keep going,
rubbing my chest absently. The proximity aspect of the bond
hurts a little, stretched as it is, but it's bearable.

I wasn't entirely honest with Tobias. It isn't their presence
in the bond that allows me to leave; it's the fact that I hold the
Grave: the bright red jewel that funnels Hell's power currents
into my command and asserts my role as Hell's master.

The Grave bears more resemblance to the gems the mystics
pursue than it does to any diamond. Through a trick of its
magic, when I hold this gem, I hold all of Hell in my palm.
Helena is never more than thirty meters from me; she is never
more than a foot from me.

I could have left her alone when the bond was only the two of us, but if I'd let her know that, she would have run immediately. Again. I was relying on her belief in the bond—after a practical demonstration or two, without the Grave in hand—and the tracking aspects to control her.

This way is better, and while it aches a little—especially when one of those three, and my money is on Tobias, happens to be playing the cord between us like a fucking violin—it is bearable.

Tiny beasts scurry past me on the stairs, freezing in terror as they realize who just passed them by. The hell current of fear coils down the staircase, overwhelming me with each new demon and monster I witness.

One little beastie squeals and curls in on itself in fright, tumbling back down the stairs like an armadillo. My lip quirks, and since it can't see me while it's tucked into its shell, I gently stop its descent with the toe of my Testoni. Then I move on, hiding my smile at the confused squeaking that starts up behind me.

The creature's fear—now floating in Hell's rivers of power—is delicious, but I would rather the creature itself remained safe.

I shook up the power currents when I rebuilt Hell and made Cat a queen. Made it a point that Hell would change, although I'm not convinced it has. It's less of a shitshow of torment now, at least, and the rivers are far more pleasant to bathe in, but there are certain currents that couldn't be removed.

There's far too much fear in Hell, especially as you descend lower into the circles instead of staying on the ever-shifting surface.

Far too much fear.

It would be stupid not to use it, for one thing, and secondly, the entire place would probably implode if I didn't.

I shudder, reaching out to wrap a tendril of that terrified power around my finger. It glows bright white, like fear always does, and as I touch it, tiny, jagged points emerge.

It fades into me, into the Grave at my hilt. I don't feed the power into any of the shifting geography above; I'm too far below the surface for it to do any good. No, for now I take it into myself as comfort.

I let it soothe the shaking edges that have been threatening to come apart ever since Mystic's Peak.

None of that was as I planned it.

Not the two extra people I bound to me without realizing, or the shitstorm that had erupted immediately after.

Or the near-cataclysmic event that happened right before.

When Helena ran down here, into this passage, it was the first time in years I'd felt true fear. Real, bone-chilling terror. Not only because of how she might betray me, if she mastered these stairs.

But for what might happen to her if she didn't.

Even now, I shudder at the thought.

Best to focus on the positives. There was one small benefit that came from it all: the rift that Helena had opened into Mystic's Peak had been sealed immediately, but I'd felt something through the other side. A familiar scent—an old friend.

She was hiding in the mountains, I'm sure of it. But by the time I got there, she was gone.

And I was left with three soulmates demanding answers.

Helena—who carries the stench of Heaven on her but looks like everything I've ever hungered for. A temptation stronger than anything I've felt.

A jaguar shifter who I've wanted to take to bed for a while, though I never allowed myself to admit it because a repressed alpha like him would surely mean only one of us left that bed alive.

And fucking Tobias.

A bright red tendril of power drifts in front of me, and through it I can feel the entire river.

Rage. Anger.

It's easy to connect with that power current whenever I think of Tobias. After centuries of friendship, we've spent decades avoiding one another.

To the point where, when he was called to my aid when all Hell turned against me, he didn't come.

You really learn who your true friends are when you're being usurped.

Walking these stairs is taking too long. The trail I'm chasing ends far deeper than this, and if I don't speed up, I'll lose it. Today, I'm not chasing the spirit of my old friend. Today, I am chasing a thread of Helena's wayward power, searching for answers.

I return to the power current of anger and let my hand drop into the river.

The power floods me.

The kings and queen of Hell can't do this, and the hellborn with innate power certainly can't. I wouldn't let them even if they could.

This is mine and mine alone.

So much of Hell is mine alone.

I step into the river, close my eyes against the surge of souls that clutch at me with drowning, desperate hands.

The wrathful. The violent.

Two circles of Hell call this river their home; the fifth and the seventh.

I step into the river, close my eyes, and let it take me down into the depths.

Bones rattle against my body. Forgotten souls, forgotten

bodies, long dead and buried. When at last I open my eyes, there isn't even the warmth of hellfire.

Not in this circle. Not in the eight.

So close to the one below it.

I look around, expecting to see an answer. To see why my trailing of Helena's wayward power led me here.

But there's nothing, and I can't for the life of me think why an angel would have a power that seemed rooted in the eighth circle of Hell where the con artists go. Those who lived a life of fraud and trickery.

Perhaps I should investigate Helena's history on Earth. It might prove illuminating.

Reaching out, I grab hold of the shoulder of a passing demon who hasn't yet seem to realized that the Devil has appeared in the midst of his workplace.

He glances at me, horned face grimacing in sudden terror.

"Your majesty," he says. "It's an honor."

"Is it?" I drawl.

"Of— of course," the demon stutters.

I take a second to count to three—I can never make it to ten —and smile.

"I'm looking for something. Can you help me?"

The demon appears to shrink a good foot lower as he obsequiously bows and snivels, "Whatever you need, Your Majesty."

I've never actually gone by that title. I've never gone by any title at all. I just let them make up whatever they feel like calling me and watch them squirm, wondering if they've got it right.

Everyone needs a hobby.

"I'm looking for power that shouldn't be here," I say, lifting my hand from his shoulder and glancing around the tenth ring.

The eighth circle of Hell is the only one of the circles to be so detailed in its construction. Every other one is more of a flat plane, but this one—just like the cons they constructed on earth—this contains spirals within spirals.

Large walls of hedges, twisted and now full of thorns, and a rocky outcropping divide this ring from the next so that it looks as though it has its own stretch of geography.

Just like the surface.

Sometimes I suspect a number of demons have snuck down the staircase and decided to live here, feeling more at home among the devious and wily than they do among the relatively well-behaved society on the surface.

But I don't bother interfering with that.

I know how it feels for a man to need a home of his own.

"Power that doesn't belong," the demon says, his entire face crumpling into a frown. "Is there a new power current? A new river?"

"Not as yet," I say, although the thought is intriguing.

Could she be doing that? No, certainly not.

"No, it's more than that." And, here, I hesitate, holding back the bone-weary sigh I long to give.

I haven't admitted this out loud yet, and doing so feels like it's admitting something else.

"It's an unknown power that seems to be attracting the Joker."

The demon's eyes widen.

There, I've admitted it—what I discovered in the hall when Helena's judgment refused to pass.

Well, part of what I discovered. The rest is well above this demon's pay grade, hence the white lie.

Her power isn't unknown. I knew what it was the second I laid eyes on her, and despite my hopes that the reading was invalid, it doesn't appear to have been. The impossible has occurred.

And no one else must ever know. Not even Helena.

Part of me regrets keeping it a secret, especially after her outburst about the soulbond. It's clear that she needs to be in control of her life. She needs to know things, and I can even respect that. Just as I respect how furious she would be with me if she ever understood just how much I was keeping from her.

It doesn't change what I have to do. I'll bear the weight of her anger, if it comes to that.

Besides, the Joker is a big enough problem without going into the extra details.

There are thirteen rivers that make up the powers of Hell. Thirteen currents of emotion fanned by the souls in their tortured states below the surface. Happiness, Sadness, Disgust, Fear, Surprise and Anger on the lower layer of the rivers. And then the upper, the deeper emotions: Euphoria, Depression, Shame, Panic, Shock, and Rage.

And then the Joker. The wild card.

When I reshuffled things I took out shock and brought in love for Cat, because she could never command any of the others.

And secretly I'd begun to wonder if it was Ronin's command of the wild card that had sent him so deeply into the edge of madness. I don't want that happening to another king, and I definitely don't want it happening to Cat, who, despite every-thing, I do adore.

It's the wild card that is the most drawn to Helena's explo-sions, and that makes her more dangerous than any of us can imagine. Because the wild card is the power that's left over.

Any emotion that is unnamed and untamed—the dirty, contaminated feelings rooted in trauma and suffering as opposed to the clean pain of a wound.

"The Joker," the demon breathes, and somehow he's shrunk even smaller. I think he may be doing it deliberately.

I narrow my eyes at him suspiciously, trying to gauge his

height against my torso, but he turns and scurries off, so all I can do is follow.

"There was one thing, my lord."

I should keep tally marks. Two for 'your majesty', one for 'my lord'. It doesn't even make sense, logistically.

"The other day, when we were lowering the prisoners into the sheep dip..."

Well, that's a new one.

"The sheep dip is poisoned, you understand," the demon adds.

I raise my eyebrows politely and nod, as if impressed by his ingenuity.

"And as we were lowering them in, this kind of... It wasn't euphoria, and it wasn't lust. It was something in between," the demon says, his low voice rasping in a kind of thwarted rapture.

"It was ecstasy," he hisses. "And pleasure."

Which I guess explains his response.

"It rose up out of the sheep dip, coated the prisoners and—" His face twists in a horrified grimace. "For a solid five minutes, they were happy."

More than happy, I imagine. I imagine they were positively perverse if they were coated in that kind of sensation.

"Yes, that's definitely the wild card," I mutter.

And it should not be down here at all, and certainly not with power bordering on euphoria. Euphoria never makes it below the third circle, where the torturers get the most glee.

The prisoners never have euphoria of their own. There's nothing to find down here.

"Take me to the—" I pause, holding back a sigh. "To the sheep dip."

Grinning broadly, the demon leads me through a winding mess of hard, rusty metal. Like a junkyard turned into a maze. And finally we arrive at a very large vat.

Well. That's what it said on the tin, I think.

I nod to him. "That will be all."

Suddenly reluctant to leave, the demon shuffles from foot to foot, tilting his head like a bird as he looks up at me.

"Do you know what the power is?"

"I said it was unknown, didn't I?" I say icily. "If I knew what it was, it wouldn't be unknown."

The demon's eyes widen and he lets out a little squeak. Without even a hint of 'your majesty' or 'my lord' or even a 'ma'am'—which I haven't been called for at least a century, and didn't mind in the least—he scurries off.

At last.

I stare into the poisonous depths of one of the oddest torture devices I've seen in at least the last year and think.

How did Helena's power get down here?

And why has it attracted the Joker?

My brow furrows, and I think of all that Ronin did with his crown linked to the wild card and his madness in control of the body mill.

He turned himself into a rotting corpse. Body dripping with pieces as he tried to contain the power that he couldn't possibly hold.

He became a leviathan—the slimy beasts that claw their way up to Heaven for all eternity. Beasts that formed from the tainted, rotten power that...

I turn away, rubbing my temples and willing the thought back into the darkest recesses of my mind. Fancy that; even now, I can't consider it without shame coursing through me.

Moving on.

Perhaps it's Helena's link to Ronin that has attracted the Joker. Does the power remember her through him?

Does it remember him through her? That's the bigger question.

He can't be resurrected, at least. I made sure of that. He's down in the Ninth Circle and that's where he'll stay.

Sticking my hands on my pockets, I begin to make a slow circle of the vat, looking for any signs of power.

Whatever it was doing here, it appears to have finished. There's nothing left. I'd know Helena's flavor of power anywhere. It has an energy to it that I haven't felt in a very long time and I can't quite place, even though I know what it is.

It's light, where the power in Hell isn't light.

Hell's power is strong; it's deep; it's vicious; it's cruel; it's brilliant.

But never light.

Helena's power is light.

I stop, my eyes landing on a tiny sparkle in the midst of depravity.

"Let there be light," I mutter.

I step closer and notice another and then another. A tiny trail leads off into the distance, and ice coats my heart as I realize where it's heading.

The staircase to the Ninth Circle awaits me.

I pause for what feels like an eternity. I've only descended those steps once since I crawled out of it. When I cast Ronin in and ensured his chains would hold.

I vowed never to descend them again, but now it seems Fate would make a liar of me.

Footstep by footstep, I descend the stairs. Halfway down, the frost creeps along the wall.

My breath chills the air, sending crystals of ice dropping to the floor and shattering before me. It's the only sound apart from my own footsteps.

Not even the drip of water lingers down here. The cold is too deep.

Taking a slow, deep breath, and not even bothering to count

this time, I descend the final step and look out upon the lakes of ice where God cast me for eternity.

There is no movement.

There is no light.

Except that there is. One single bright spark rests on the very edge of the water.

I stare at it for a long time. How could it possibly be here? Nothing is here.

A strange sensation uncurls in my chest. It's warm, when nothing in this circle should be warm. Staring at the light though, I feel it. I feel curiosity and unmistakable affection for the woman who has defied everything and brought light to Hell's deepest, darkest cage.

My cage.

She's nothing like I expected her to be. When the angels cast her at my feet, I didn't think twice. She was just another angel when we'd already sent so many home; what was one minor setback?

And then she spoke, and that unexpected accent came free. A hint of London or something similar. Something she'd obviously spent years trying to hide, but that crept out in times of stress.

This five foot nothing girl, with a wild, barely tamed plait, and fierce burning eyes with an energy to match.

She is the one to bring light where light never existed.

The light in question glints.

I frown, realizing that its location isn't random. It's stuck to something below the ice.

Apprehension surges. Something inside me tells me I do not want to know what the light has stuck to. But I can't turn away now.

There is no one in all of Hell who I can trust with this. Not even Logan, my right-hand man, who has proven himself over and again. Proven that he won't ask questions and will simply do as I bid him.

Even he is useless to me now, given how deep I have to dive to get the answers I need.

No, there is only me, if I want to solve this puzzle. If I want to reclaim Hell before the beautiful angel with the quirky accent accidentally destroys it.

Before my enemies take it from me.

And so I kneel by the lake and I touch the frozen water that I vowed never to touch again.

The warmth from my palm melts it instantly, but I can still feel the ice beneath it.

I can still feel the centuries of aching cold that I spent in here before I wrenched myself free of God's punishment and claimed the land that he had exiled me to as my own.

And that's when I realize what the light is stuck to.

I freeze and jerk back reflexively, but it's too late.

The chains spring from the water. Even after so long, they still wait for their prisoner. They still wait for their purpose to reignite.

And now they've found it.

Cold metal clasps around my wrists, and for just a single moment I freeze in abject terror as I remember how it felt to be bound by this.

To be stuck down here.

My thrashing begins to crack the ice, sending shards flying into the air, giant chunks surging. A low, distinct sound of laughter comes from the other side of the lake, where Ronin lies. But he's practically bodiless now. He only has enough of a body to keep him chained here, and so I don't bother with him.

I tug at the chains, searching for the power that allowed me to break them once before, but I can't reach it.

True terror fills me now. How can I not reach it? The power

is mine; over the centuries it has only grown. The chains are already bent, already shattered. They shouldn't be able to hold me here, and yet—

Frantic now, my clothing in shreds around me, I search for anything that I can latch onto as the chains begin to drag me deeper into the center of the lake. Anything that might set me free.

My hands find a cord.

A blue, solid cord that stretches to my chest and fills me with warmth as I touch it.

I don't think. I don't question it. I latch hold and begin to pull myself free.

Agony tears through me, as it should. As much as I can stretch the limits of the proximity bond I've given us all, I can't push them like this. Nobody can. It already hurts to be so distant from them.

Then, through the cord, I feel the echo of others' pain. The pain of my soulmates as, confused, they feel my struggle as if it were their own.

Hand over hand, I pull myself to the edge of the lake and stare.

I'm bound as much to the lake as I am to my soulmates far above the surface of it.

Which side will win?

Which side will rule?

With a roar fueled by pure, blinding terror, I lurch myself with the last of my energy from the edge. The chains shatter and slip free.

As I lie there, panting on the shore, I wonder if it was all an illusion. They still look far too broken, too lifeless.

My heart rate calms, and I force myself to find the quiet dignity with which I do everything, and climb steadily to my feet.

This will not break me.

This will not ruin me.

I straighten my clothing, smoothing fingers over the tears and using tiny threads of power to mend them.

In seconds, I'm pristine again.

I back away to the entrance. There is no more laughter, and the chains are still.

The last thing I notice as I turn to climb is that the light, too, has gone.

12

HELENA

Lucifer's revelation wipes me out for the day, if I'm totally honest. As soon as we make it back to the palace, I slink off to my little suite and lock myself inside.

Don't worry about me, mate. Your prisoner ain't doing shit tonight.

To be honest, I'm not sure what I'm doing outside of tonight, either. This soulmate thing is a bit of a bombshell, and that's on top of me not being able to go ten feet without two shadows popping up to watch.

Well, thirty meters, but who's counting, hey?

Lucifer really meant business when he decided to take care of this.

I really am nothing but a problem.

Squeezing my eyes shut tightly against the unexpected warmth of tears, I take a second to lock my thoughts away. This is a minor setback, that's all. And hey, even the Devil is kind of shocked and confused, and that's fun, right? How many people can say they've seen that?

With a sigh, I pull myself off the corner of the bed, where I've been tucked into a tiny ball like the total badass I am, and check out the bookshelves. I need something light. Something distracting.

Something that won't remind me I'm banned from Heaven, a prisoner of the Devil, and I'm already failing my parents for the second time.

Two minutes into realizing I have to save them, and I suddenly become the soulmate of the man who's holding them captive.

Earthsea. Perfect. Could not be more removed from Hell if it tried.

I take my book to the window seat, grabbing the comforter along the way, and curl up in the corner. Hell's strange sun burns its orange light down through the windows, and if I don't look too closely, I can pretend it's sunset. The golden hour.

Strange how those golden rays seem to literally be in the room with me.

I turn back to my book, sinking effortlessly into the lines. A flicker of something, like a bug, covers my vision. I bat it away, barely paying attention.

It comes back.

Squinting in irritation, I lower the book and glare, cross-eyed, at the bug. It's like a firefly of some kind.

No... it's like a light. My jaw goes slack, lips parting as I stare at the dozen or so tiny glowing dots that bounce around my head.

"What the hell are you?" I murmur, reaching out carefully.

As my finger breaches the little dots' glowing aura, they buzz and pull back angrily.

Right then.

"Message received," I murmur, but I don't take my hand away. I leave it out, like I'm trying to entice a butterfly to land.

The dots swirl lazily around my fingers in an orbit. They're definitely sentient in some way.

"Can you talk?" I wonder out loud.

The buzzing increases, which I guess is code for both no and yes at the same time. I.e., we *are* talking, dumbass. You're not listening.

"Fair point," I say drily. "Sorry I don't speak Tinkerbell."

Annoyed buzzing.

Finally, I pull my hand back and rest it carefully on the open pages. After several seconds, it becomes clear the lights aren't going to do anything in particular. Just chill.

I wonder if these are the parts of my power that explode things. For a moment, I consider asking Lucifer, but there's probably no point. He'd tell me if he knew something.

He has to know I'd want him to, and he's made such a point of being kind even as he holds me here.

It would be, like, seriously unkind if he kept answers from me.

For a moment, I feel the strangest sensation in my chest. Like he's in trouble. Like he's... drowning... It hurts, and I clutch at my chest, wondering if this is a heart attack or something. But after a few minutes, it passes.

I blink, staring at the lights. They haven't moved, and nothing seems on fire. Okay, just indigestion, then.

"Can I read my book, or do you want something?" I ask the lights, clearing my throat hesitantly.

They buzz lazily, so I turn back to my escape. But my attention keeps drifting back to the strange little orbs. How could it not, right? Strange little orbs—they command a certain level of respect.

As I watch them, they settle down near my feet, falling like little stars to my skin. The effect reminds me of the shoes I used to wear on stage, the way they'd sparkle in the light as I kicked.

A memory pops into my head. A smiling man who'd just cheated his way through the gaming rooms downstairs. Rumors had spread through the staff, even though they hadn't managed to catch him yet.

"Like my shoes?" I murmured to him, tilting my head so that I looked up at him beneath long lashes.

"I like what they're attached to more," he said with a sharp-toothed smile, running his hands along the back of my thighs and under the edge of my skirt.

I'd pickpocketed his room key while he was busy copping a feel, and that night I pilfered a good ten percent of the chips he'd already cashed.

I never took more than ten percent, because any more would be noticed. But in the high of the win, less than ten was an easy steal.

I wiggle my feet, admiring the way the skin sparkles. There was a certain glamor to that life, even if most people would have turned their nose up at it, you know? It kept the rent paid. And it meant I could wire home some money every month.

Ease the guilt that ate away at me like acid.

I fold the book closed carefully and run my fingers over the cover, barely seeing it. Okay, so I'm stuck here. Wandering the Devil's palace while he hides away from me in his penthouse at the top and two guards follow my every move. I can't escape, and I can't find my parents.

But I'm not completely without resources. And while these three are pains in the ass, they aren't my enemies. They're just... my opposition. I've dealt with men like that plenty of times before.

I don't feel unsafe around them. I don't even feel like they don't like me.

Quite the opposite, in fact.

Maybe I'll, like, I don't know... make an effort.

I wriggle my toes. Or maybe I'll con them into giving me what I need.

A noise startles me, and I look up to find Logan shadowed in the doorway. His arms are folded, his hair falling across his face, but his eyes glow yellow.

A jolt of heat courses through me, beginning in my chest and curling to a delicious halt between my thighs. I nearly ask if he's off to howl at the moon, but something stops me. He would think I was teasing him, and not in a nice way.

I know what it's like to be teased like that, and I suspect Logan does, too.

"How are the others?" I ask cautiously, tucking my book down the back of the window seat so he can't catch me off guard again.

It's not like it's just me who took the whole soulmate thing with a side of panic attack. Lucifer disappeared the second we were safely back on home ground. Tobias wouldn't even look at me.

Strangely, Logan seemed fine with it. Although he did go silent for a long time. Then he just kind of... shrugged it off. Like it was nothing.

He lifts one shoulder now and steps into the room. "Beats me. They do their thing. I do mine."

"And what's your thing?" I ask, swinging my legs over the side of the window seat and angling my body so it's subtly unchallenging. Safe. Maybe he'll open up to me if he remembers I'm not a threat.

"Right now? It's checking on you. You've been missing all day."

That makes me pause. He's checking on me?

I look behind me at the sun; shit, he's right. It's far lower than I realized.

I run a hand over my hair and wince at the tangles. I haven't even showered since Mystic's Peak. I'm still covered in sweat and dirt... what the hell?

I must really have been out of it.

Standing up, I move over to the ensuite in a silent invitation for him to follow, instead of standing on the precipice like he is now.

He follows. I hear the soft pad of his footsteps, followed by a pause as he stops to examine the items on the top of my dresser.

"They aren't mine," I point out, flicking on the bathroom light and beginning to undo my plait. "So you won't learn anything by being nosy."

"I know," he says in a low voice. "I brought them here, remember?" He pauses, and then says in a strange, too-casual tone, "I saw you reading that fantasy trilogy."

That fantasy trilogy... Lord of the Rings?! I blink up at him, startled enough that I barely even feel the slow curl of unease that someone saw me without my guards up.

"You haven't heard of it before?" I ask, pausing and turning back to face him.

"I hadn't, no," he says, picking up another perfume bottle and examining it. "But I've read it now. It's really good."

My hands fall to my side. "You've read it. Now." I'm too confused to even form the question, but somehow he gets it.

Logan grins at me. "I read it because you were reading it."

He shrugs, oblivious to the shattering inside me.

Logan takes a step closer, into the bathroom now. He's taller than me by a long shot. I have to tilt my head up a little to catch his gaze, same as Lucifer. But Logan seems to notice, and he makes a point of leaning down when he murmurs, "I do a *great* Gollum impression. Want to hear?"

Oh, boy. This'll be good. Everyone thinks they can do a great Gollum impression until they actually go to do it.

The corner of my mouth curls, despite my attempts to stay serious, and I pretend to consider it.

But then reality kicks in. "You read an entire trilogy just because you saw it on my nightstand?"

"No, I read an entire trilogy because I saw the look on your face when you had it on your nightstand."

My stomach flips, some feeling in it churning too fast to ignore. I think it's unease; I'm sure it's unease. But before I can take control of the situation and get him to leave, his hands come to my shoulders and he gently turns me to face the mirror again.

I see the look in his eyes, and everything else falls away. The feeling twists, and it isn't unease at all.

In this light, his hair is a deep, earthy brown. Rich, like the soil of a fertile garden. The highlights of red glint as he moves, but they're only teasers, a reminder of how he looks in the sun. Tonight, he's all night and shadow.

I watch as Logan reaches out and takes over undoing my plait. His eyes catch mine in the mirror, holding my gaze as he undoes the braid with slow, deliberate movements.

It's a side of him I haven't seen before. One hidden behind the joking and the smiles. I don't know what to make of it.

I feel like it should scare me, but it doesn't.

I wonder if what I'm picking up on is the fact that it scares him.

He runs his fingers through my hair, teasing apart the waves and letting them fall down my back.

"I'd brush it for you," he says idly, his fingers still trailing a path over my shoulder even though I'm sure he's no longer touching my hair. "But then I'd keep hitting knots and making you wince... it isn't as romantic as people think."

I burst out laughing, and the sound seems to jolt him out of some trance. He looks up at me and grins as I turn around to face him again.

"So you're trying to be romantic, now?" I ask him, biting back a smile.

His eyebrows jump in mock surprise. "Trying? Darling, I *am* romantic." He takes a step toward me, our hips brushing as I pull back and find I'm already against the counter. "But that isn't why I'm here."

"No?"

I look down as his hand finds mine, watching as he brings my palm up to examine it. Then he lifts my other palm, comparing the two.

They're covered in open cuts, and I wince as he lowers his head and blows gently against the skin.

Immediately after, I shiver in a curious mix of pain and burning desire. Holy cow, that's hot. Weirdly hot.

He gives me a wry smile, apparently not noticing my little freakout. "Had to check the nerves still worked. You never know with obsidian. Those rocks cut up skin like they're coated in poison. They can make the body do strange things down here, even though the wounds are fresh."

"They'll heal," I say, looking to the side so I don't have to see the cuts. I'd planned on dealing with them, I just...

I'm so sick of being injured. Chased. In danger.

Maybe that's why I've spent all day hiding in my room. It isn't the soulbond at all; it's everything else.

As much as I hated every second under Ronin's control, sometimes it was a relief—my body didn't feel like mine, and so the pain, the unease... that wasn't mine either.

Sometimes it's nice not to feel.

I take a breath, forcing my gaze back to the cuts. It isn't so bad. I'm used to this, thanks to him. Even though it's been a while, and even though the pain isn't usually so obvious.

"They'll heal better if they're treated," he says calmly, and he reaches over my shoulder to open the cabinet behind my head.

My breath catches as he leans into me, his hair falling against my face, his neck close enough to kiss. I have to bite my lip to make sure I don't, and when he straightens, I can see he's laughing. At me.

"That wasn't very nice," I mutter.

"On the contrary. I'm very nice," he insists. "You just happen to be making this more complicated than it needs to be."

"Oh?" I ask saltily, looking up at him as he dabs antiseptic onto the cuts. I don't even flinch, managing triumphantly to steel myself against the pain I knew was coming. "And what about this *isn't* complicated?"

Suddenly, it all comes pouring out. I don't even try to stop it.

"Was it the bond linking our emotions to the literal Devil and that other bozo?" I ask, staring furiously down at my cuts. Logan keeps treating them, calm and methodical. "Or was it the fact that I seem to be destroying Hell with this mysterious power, and our bond is the only thing keeping me from going off the rails? Which part of this ridiculous situation isn't complicated? Because I'm dying to know."

Logan glances at me, his face still tilted down toward my hand. Carefully, he lifts my palm, turns it, and kisses the back of my fingers. "The part where we're bonded. A soulbond is a soulbond, Helena. Forget about the rest. And this one isn't even the bad kind. This is a Ludus bond—we're chosen for a divine hookup, no strings attached. Well..." He smiles wryly. "One string. In three directions. But it's just Ludus. Flirty, harmless fun, with a soul we were destined to share this moment with." He turns my hand again and kisses my palm this time. "And I want to worship you for however long this moment is. It doesn't make it any less special for being short."

Something about the way he's phrasing this sounds off, but I can't work out why because what he's offering me sounds so damn good. I don't even know what Ludus means beyond Lucifer's one sentence explanation, but the way he's describing it is perfect.

He's right; it isn't complicated. It's just fun. A divine hookup. How good does that sound?

I don't owe them anything. Just a bit of fun.

But... "The Devil," I murmur, unable to break free of his gaze. "The other bozo. They don't share—you can just tell."

Logan grins, and suddenly it's wicked, the mood completely transformed into something full of heat and fire. "I do."

I don't understand this. How is he so chill about a soulmate bond with the freaking Devil? It's not just me in here, mate, it's a whole litter of cats tied together at the bum. You know how that shit's gonna go down, and it won't be pretty.

Logan lowers his head, pausing with his lips just brushing mine. "Is that okay with you?"

More than okay. Maybe if Logan takes the lead, we won't claw each other's eyes out. "I think I'll manage."

He laughs softly and then crosses the last of the distance between us.

The kiss is soft. Tender. Like he's drinking in the feel of me, unhurried.

Just as I'm getting into it, feeling the heat burn through me like a wildfire, he pulls away.

I stumble forward a little, and immediately glare at the smug grin he gives me.

"I've been wondering what that feels like," he says, voice rough.

He doesn't make me wait there long, stepping immediately

back in and circling his arms around my waist. Pulled in tight against him, I can feel the heat radiating from every part of his body.

He kisses me properly this time, mouth firm and deliberate. He's taking something as well as offering it, promising.

Begging.

Sharp claws prick into my waist, and I hiss in sudden pain. When my eyes snap open, I find his are glowing gold.

A thin line of fur coats his forearms, and his teeth are sharp when he smiles.

"Looks like the rut might have caught up to me," he says softly, eyes glinting. "Say yes, Helena. Let me distract you for the night."

My heart beats rapidly, the thought immediately consuming me. It's the distraction I'm searching for...

But it's also the complication I need to avoid.

I bite his lip sharply, relishing the low growl of want that drops from him. Then I pull myself out of his hold.

This time, he's the one to fall forward into the space, his hands flying out to slam into the sink and catch himself. He freezes like that, chest heaving, eyes heavy-lidded with desire as he looks down at me caged between his arms.

"Not tonight," I say sweetly, my lips quirking at the low snarl of protest that quickly becomes a whine.

Slowly, deliberately, he moves away. Two steps, three, until he hits the opposite wall. I can still see the rise and fall of his chest. Still see how badly he wants this.

"I guess I'd better head back to my room then," he says roughly. "By the way, Lucifer wants us all at dinner tonight."

I swallow, holding his gaze. "I'll see you there."

"I might be late," he says with a slow grin, leaving no illusions about what he'll be getting up to in the meantime.

Then, with a wink, he disappears.

I groan into the silent room and glance at the clock, weighing up the pros and cons of leaving now. Definitely more cons.

Looks like I'll be late too.

13

HELENA

Lucifer's dinner is a sit-down affair in the dining room I recently trashed.

I really can't get a read on this dude. One minute he's running as fast as he can, hoarding secrets like the apocalypse is coming, and the next, he's putting us all in one room and locking the door.

Even the staff look scared.

Although that might be my fault. My magic tingles at my fingertips, and like a true diva, it doesn't stop there.

The serving demon at Lucifer's side keeps putting out spot fires on the table cloth. Lucifer stares down at the once-pristine white cloth with a grim expression. After the fourth spontaneous pyrotechnic, the demon is shaking, Tobias and Logan are laughing into their wine glasses, and Lucifer is resolutely not looking at me.

"May I be excused?" Tobias asks, voice rich with amusement as he studies Lucifer's expression.

"No," Lucifer snarls, glaring at him.

Flame immediately roars into life over the doorway, but this time it isn't me. The serving demon makes an odd squeaking sound, mutters something about aperitifs, and disappears with a pop.

"No need to get sassy," Tobias says mildly, taking a long pull of his wine. "Just wondering what the meaning is behind this little display."

Lucifer grips his wine glass so tightly, I find I'm unconsciously waiting for cracks to appear.

"What display?" he grits out. "I thought we were having a nice dinner, so you could ask me all those burning questions you're choking on, but perhaps I'll go back to the first plan and leave you all to fucking rot." His voice turns to ice on the final words, and I choke for real.

A flicker of emotion appears in Tobias' eyes for a second, but it's gone as soon as it arrived. For a man who can read others' thoughts, he's well practiced at hiding his own, and the knowledge irks the crap out of me.

"You're offering us an open discussion," Tobias clarifies.

A light pop signals the arrival of the appetizers—an arrangement of dishes prepared in numerous succulent sauces and drizzled with herb concoctions that smell divine.

Up until this point, Logan has been lounging with his arm draped along the top of the chairs to his right, legs stretched casually in front of him as he watches the rest of us passive-aggressively face off like suburban housewives. Now, he draws three plates to him and begins eating with gusto.

I want to do the same. After the cave-in and the revelation that these three are somehow linked to me by Fate, I'm starving. Nothing like an unexpected marriage proposal to two demons and a shifter to make you work up an appetite, you know what I mean?

But instead, my brain latches hold of an opportunity, like it's so well trained to do.

If the Devil is telling the truth, and he's just as lost as we are... *and* he's trying to extend an olive branch...

This is the advantage I've been waiting for.

An unexpected, squirming sensation of guilt rises as I tune back into the conversation. Somehow, the topic has turned to formal dress wear, each comment from Lucifer and Tobias more barbed than the last, and I almost don't want to know how they got here.

Morbid curiosity has me in a chokehold, though. The kinky bastard.

"Don't we have more important things to discuss?" I butt in, taking a leaf from Logan's book and dragging two plates in front of me.

"Depends on your definition," Tobias says, all charm while Lucifer quietly but succinctly describes the way in which he'll disembowel Tobias if he says one more thing about Parisian silk.

Logan burps, pushes an empty plate away, and leans closer to me.

"He reckons it's a mark of respect to dress for the occasion, if you mean to really play your cards open," he says, pointing to Tobias. "And *he* says there's nothing to be gained by being a stuck up prig among friends." He points to Lucifer, grinning, then switches back to Tobias. "To which *he* was telling us a story about when Satan refused to meet a delegate from the Twisted Sands until they'd showered and soaked fresh clothing in perfume, even though they'd all gone out drinking together the night before."

I blink, looking between the two old friends currently debating each other's murder. If you throw the details aside, what Logan's saying is that Tobias is accusing Lucifer of being untruthful.

The thought niggles at me, but I can't put together anything stronger than that, so I have to let it go.

"If Lucifer wants to treat me like an old friend instead of a prisoner, I won't complain," I say lightly.

A tiny fire alights at my feet, betraying the rush of adrenaline as I choose my side and begin to lay my trap, but I stamp it out discreetly with my foot.

Tobias narrows his eyes.

Unfortunately, so does Lucifer.

"I would have hoped you already felt welcome here," he says tightly.

Oh. Lucifer doesn't suspect I'm playing him; he's offended at the idea I might feel like a prisoner.

Well. I'd been planning on buttering him up, but I can use guilt, too.

I hadn't realized he felt guilty.

Tobias' jaw tightens as he watches me react, my thoughts clearly compartmentalized away from even the trickiest of trickster demons.

"Why would you think that?" I ask neutrally.

His gaze turns piercing, and I get the impression he wants to whisk me away somewhere private, where Logan and Tobias can't hear. Instead, he speaks quieter, forcing them to lean forward.

"Because I have done everything in my power to make you comfortable."

My breath catches at the intensity in his gaze. It's true, isn't it? I'm having trouble thinking beyond that. He's done everything he can to look after me, and the way he's speaking now... I get the sense he's offering to do more.

To do whatever I want.

"Not everything," I say after a beat. It isn't part of my initial plan, but I want to know what he says.

I want to push this.

"What else would you like?" He isn't playing. He wants me to say it.

"This is a soulbond, isn't it?" I challenge him, my own eyes surely blazing. "Ludus? A bit of destined fun?"

I feel the atmosphere shift, heat pulsing from four corners of the long table.

Something flashes in Lucifer's eyes, and for a second he looks so hungry. So damn hungry. "Is that what you think Ludus means?"

Distantly, I sense Logan jolt beside me, but I don't move. I can't move—I'm captured by those blue eyes holding me in place.

"Isn't it what it means?"

I don't have a fucking clue what it means, beyond what he told us in the caves and Logan's earlier description. I just know I want Lucifer to kiss me. I want him to throw me down on this table and give me something to fucking live for down here.

I blink. That thought came out of nowhere.

"Not quite," he says. "They are fun"—Christ, he makes the word sound like a sin—"but they are still soulbonds."

Logan is so still, I can barely feel him breathe.

"They are forever," Lucifer finishes. "Do you want me forever, Helena?"

I can't move. Can't breathe.

Finally, Lucifer leans back. I feel like a spell has been lifted from me, and I barely keep from gasping in air. Holy shit.

When he puts it like that, I'm terrified. So I do the only thing I know how to do to control the fear; I seize hold of the situation and I take it back for myself.

What was I doing before? What was the whole point of this? Oh yeah, I want to use Lucifer's guilt against him.

I level Lucifer with a look, steadying myself and forgetting everything except what matters right now. I need to get outside the castle. I need to use him.

"Do I want you forever? I don't particular want you right now, mate. And no, I don't feel welcome. I'm physically tied to the Head Asshole of Hell, unable to walk three feet without him or his two bonus guards showing up to watch me breathe. Tell me—how am I meant to feel?"

His eyes flash with a different kind of heat. "Would you prefer I set you loose to destroy Hell the next time you stub your toe?" he asks politely.

"You could have more faith in me," I suggest, heart racing as I realize I'm going toe to toe with the ruler of Hell.

Logan leans forward in his seat, the spark of interest in his eyes looking weirdly heated. Is this turning him on?!

To my surprise, Lucifer doesn't laugh in my face. He studies me, expression almost closed off.

Finally, he says, "I doubt you could promise me any measure of control over these explosions." He leans back, considering me as he taps his fingers idly on the edge of the table. "So any faith I did or didn't have in you wouldn't matter."

I gape at him. I've never felt so... insignificant. "You could *ask*," I spit out, all thoughts of manipulating his sense of decency thrown out the window.

Lucifer shrugs. "And have you lie to me? Why bother?"

Tobias' eyes light up with a strange fervor. He flicks his hair back out of his eyes, the soft brown waves falling perfectly to the side. Then, he lifts one hand and clicks his fingers, the sound echoing like a gunshot.

Lucifer narrows his eyes. "What did you do?"

Wary now, I slam up my mental barriers even harder, protecting my thoughts from the demon opposite me.

Tobias smiles, slow and pleasant. "Nothing much. I only

thought, since you're so concerned with Helena lying to your face, we might level the playing field."

Lucifer flinches, fingers driving into the wood of the table hard enough to splinter.

"Undo it, you conniving little bastard," he spits out, but the words end on a strange sound, like a hiccup.

Lucifer clamps his lips shut, but it isn't fast enough to prevent a wine-red bubble from floating free.

It lifts above the table, unusually purposeful as it glides to the center. Reflections swirl on its shining surface.

My eyes widen. They aren't reflections. Sure, that's my face staring back at me, but those aren't my torn jeans and black tank top.

In the bubble's reflection, I'm wearing a long, silvery gown. I turn, glancing over my shoulder at someone out of sight, and the image reveals a lace back to the dress.

The lace is shaped like wings.

All up, the effect is ethereal, magical. I've always enjoyed making myself look nice, but my style is more understated— black on black with a cherry red accent on my lips.

Even on stage, I never wore anything as glamorous as this.

Tobias' grin widens. "So *that's* the real reason you didn't demand we change outfits. You're scared to face what you might find."

Logan bursts into surprised laughter, an expression like sudden, total understanding etched onto his features. I'm feeling a bit the same myself.

The Devil has faced down the armies of Heaven, but he's scared of me in an evening gown?

When I chance a look at him, his face is white with rage. A shiver of unease races through me.

And just like that, I know how to get what I want from him. I don't think it through, or question the likelihood of it working.

I just know, same as how I know when this bizarre power is about to light up like the sun.

Facing Tobias, I snap my fingers just as he did.

For a split second, there's a curious mixture of fear, shock, and respect on his face.

Then he coughs.

The bubble rises from his mouth, turning slowly in the light. None of us are reflected in it. Instead, there's a crowd of people, all jeering and pointing at something I can't see. They're dressed in an old style: long tunics, dull colors. Tobias pales. Then he abruptly stands, the motion sending his glass flying and shattering on the ground, and leaves the room.

Lucifer watches him, almost sad.

But also mollified. Like I wanted.

He faces me, and I make sure to keep my expression neutral —surprised and a little confused. Like I hadn't planned the whole thing down to the last detail.

"Looks like he can dish it, but he can't take it," I say mildly.

Lucifer drums his fingers on the table, watching me. "It is more complicated than that," he says finally.

But the glint of satisfaction in his eyes tells me that it might be complicated, but Tobias still crossed a line tonight.

And I paid him back for it.

That should earn me about sixty seconds of complacency, before Lucifer's logic takes over again.

Fifty-seven. Fifty-six.

"You may explore the city," Lucifer says, looking away. "And I won't follow. I'll even keep Tobias from meddling." He points at Logan. "But you'll have a guard, who will protect you and alert me in a heartbeat should something happen. Logan, I will give you something that will allow the bond to stretch that far."

Logan's head snaps up. "Protect her?" he questions, like he didn't hear anything past that.

Something passes between them, and it's like the weirdest alpha stand-off I've ever seen. I almost wish I were a shifter, so I could follow the undercurrents of the conversation via scent.

"Indeed," Lucifer says quietly. "She is your pack."

"It's a Ludus bond," Logan spits, and it doesn't sound so fun coming from his mouth anymore. "Let's not get too ahead of ourselves with all that forever stuff—it's only like that if you make it that way." He rolls his head back casually, eyes meeting mine as he reaches for my hand, brings it to his lips, and kisses it. "Don't get me wrong—you're beautiful, and I meant what I said about worshipping you while I can. But I know you don't want *me* forever, do you, Hel?"

The question surprises a laugh out of me. "Hardly," I snap, that same feeling from before, in the caves, rising back up in my throat.

I think it might be terror.

Logan lets my hand go with a soft trail of his fingers.

"See, boss?" he says, turning back to Lucifer. "You've got it wrong. Chill out and have some fun—it's written in the stars."

Lucifer snorts quietly before lifting his wine and taking a sip. "She is your pack, Logan," he says, but the words are almost vicious. "Protect her."

Silence falls, and a complicated expression slides onto the shifter's usually easy-going face. Then he grins and shrugs, as cocky and at ease as he always is, and just like that, I get what I wanted. Mostly.

But then I look at Lucifer's calm demeanor—the neat, deliberate way he sips his wine. I remember how hard he worked to lose us and get us off his back, and I wonder...

Am I the one who was conned in the end?

14

TOBIAS

IT TAKES ME FOUR HOURS UNTIL I CAN RE-CENTER MYSELF AFTER THAT mess. Four long hours.

It hasn't taken me that long since the queen of the Massagetae engaged me in revenge against her sister—but didn't realize her father was actually the one responsible. That was too many goats, even for me.

But this... this is different. My doubts were already blooming since Lucifer revealed that nugget of information about our soulbond. But they were only niggling concerns. Uncertain.

Until she did that.

How did Helena manage to tap into my power like that? It shouldn't have been possible, and yet I saw it with my own eyes.

I lean against the doorway that leads from my suite to the adjoining bathroom. It's strange being back in this wing; the musty, forgotten smell of it all reminds me how quickly Lucifer cast me aside when he thought I'd betrayed him with the others.

Even though my wing had been removed from the castle decades ago.

I sigh, trying not to think about all that ancient history. Reminding myself that I have more important things on my mind, I return my attention to the standing mirror across the room.

Helena's reflection stares back at me, but she has no idea I'm watching her. I enchanted the mirror in her suite. If she insists on closing her mind to me, I'll have to find other ways to uncover her secrets.

It's a sensation I'm not used to, and I can't say I like it.

She says something to herself as she unbraids her hair and shakes it out, but the mirror has no sound, and her arm obscures her mouth so I can't read her lips.

She moves her hands to the buttons on her shirt, and I turn around. The purpose of this isn't to be a peeping Tom. I have no desire to take advantage of women like that.

After a few minutes, I check again—she's fully dressed, but still not revealing anything that I want to know. No secretive powers. No secretive communications—unless she wasn't talking to herself after all. But with no one in sight, how can I be sure?

I don't have all day. I'm not used to feeling this agitated, and I fear it's making me slip.

The thought gives me pause; Fear. That could work.

"Fear exposes even the deepest of secrets," I say with deliberate care.

The words carry on threads of power, faster than usual because of how close we are to the kings and queen—the Devil's Court—and therefore the river mouth of all Hell's power.

In the mirror, Helena's hands grow still. I wonder what she sees, her eyes widening in fear and disbelief. But whatever truth my power has shown her, it's beyond the mirror's edge. I can't see it from here.

Which means it's time I took a closer look.

I step through the mirror and into chaos.

Fire licks at the walls, but this isn't Helena's power gone wild this time; it's mine. I lift my eyebrows politely and look around as Helena catches sight of me.

The fear in her gaze is mounting. Regret clouds my judgment for a moment, but it isn't strong enough to stop me, not with what I suspect she's hiding. How else could she have formed such a convenient soulbond?

Maybe now she'll be honest with me.

I glance around the room casually, as if we're out for a Sunday stroll, and barely manage not to blink in surprise when I see what illusion her fear has constructed.

"Who's the couple?" I ask, jerking my head toward the man and woman on the opposite wall.

Flame licks at their feet, covering the ties on their ankles and wrists that bind them to each other.

As soon as I saw the flame, I assumed Helena's fear must be the Devil's punishment. It makes sense. After a traumatic kidnapping where her memories and identity are toyed with, she's barred from Heaven. Even the most self-actualized person alive would have doubts.

But apparently not Helena. Or, at least, she fears something else more.

"Is this real?" she demands, voice rising over the crackling of the flame.

I reach out toward the flame and pull my fingers back with an affected hiss. Then I grin at her, keeping it lazy and relaxed in the face of her anger—needling her into a reaction. "You tell me."

Power slams into me, sending me flying across the room

and into the wall as the flames around the couple surge in response to Helena's rising panic. The fire is nowhere near me, but I can feel the heat. It's an exceptionally strong illusion.

Her fear must be immense.

These people matter to her, and the knowledge feels like a little crack in a door, opening before me.

Helena stalks across the room until we're nose to nose. The cool mask of her indifference is completely cracked. I'm not sure she even realizes her magic is keeping me pinned. I pull forward experimentally, but I can't budge.

My mouth curves into a smile; I can't help it. No matter who the supplicant is, I do love the moment they fully grasp the truth of what they're asking for.

The moment when they crack beneath the weight of it.

"Is. This. Real?" she demands, her voice shaking. "You fucking prick."

My heart twinges, regret flaring once more, but I don't break. What she's keeping from us is vital information, not just for our safety, but for the safety of all of Hell.

"They're your parents, aren't they?" The answer comes rushing in, filling the space between her fear. "They look like you. Are they in Hell already? Or are you afraid they will be?" My voice drops lower. "Or do you wish they were?"

Something complicated crosses her expression.

Across the room, the woman turns to us, her eyes so wide it's like they're pure white. Her gaze locks onto Helena, and recognition flickers there.

She says something to her, but it's swallowed by the flames. Still, I can see the distortion of her lip, twisting in anger. She struggles against her bonds, and her husband does the same, although his head is dropped in defeat.

Then, when his head lulls to the side, I see an unexpected

slackening of pleasure on his face, like he's somewhere far, far away from all of this.

These aren't really her parents, of course; it's an illusion constructed from Helena's mind. Which makes it interesting that Helena is choosing these expressions. Very interesting, indeed.

I turn back to her, waiting to see what she'll do.

Bizarrely, her face relaxes. "It's a trick," she says, voice clear and strong with certainty.

I allow her a shrug, wriggling my hands in the air—the only part of me I can move, pinned as I am against the wall. "Let me down, and I can tell you the answer."

She grimaces at me in disgust. "Doesn't mean you will, though."

I don't intend it to, but my smile turns a little mean. "Do you think you're the only one allowed to have secrets?"

She looks at me properly then, attention finally breaking away from the mirage of her parents' torture. "No, but I do think you couldn't handle the truth if it smacked you in the face, which I just might do if you keep this up, broken nails or no broken nails."

My jaw clenches, and I stare at her incredulously. "Can't handle the truth?" I repeat softly. "How very convenient for someone who doesn't want to share it."

She lifts her eyebrows and holds her hands up expressively. "Prove me wrong, buddy. Pretty convinced though that you're the kind of guy who'll go running to Satan the second you hear something you don't like."

I try to keep my usual jovial mien, I do, but white hot anger takes over. I open my mouth to retaliate, but then I get a flicker of something coming down a line of connection between us that, until now, we haven't shared.

She'd praying to me. She doesn't know it, but she is.

Just like she did the first time I met her, when she was running for the passageway down to the nine circles of Hell.

Vindication surges; I fucking knew she'd been praying to me, even though she had no idea who I was. She wants these answers as much as I do, despite the fact that she's already running away from them.

They always do, my supplicants. They beg even as they run.

I change my tactic. The truth is clearly what we need here after all.

With my tone deliberately nonchalant, bored even, I ask her, "You mean, I won't like hearing that you're an agent of God, sent to disrupt Hell?"

The flames disappear, her parents vanishing in a crack of displaced power as Helena stares at me in shock.

"I'm *what*?!"

"You deny it?" A faux-surprised smile graces my lips. "And which of us can't handle the truth, I wonder."

Her eyes flash. The paintings on the walls rattle, frames splintering under the pressure of whatever power she's harnessed. Now we're getting somewhere.

"You think I'm working for *God*?" she hisses.

"I think you have a very convenient soulbond and access to power you shouldn't," I tell her, holding up one finger and then a second. When I have her full attention, I hold up a third. "I think your power is ripping holes through Hell, and there are very few sources of magic that can do that." I hold up a fourth, eyes never straying from hers. Even now, she's so hard to read. Harder than any supplicant I've had before. "And I think there is no reason an angel would have their Heavenly passport revoked, unless someone wanted them down here."

She takes a step toward me, shoulders square on. Aggressive. If she wasn't five foot nothing, I'd be wary.

Fire licks the walls, giving me pause. I probably should be wary, nonetheless.

"I don't give a shit about your logic, mate," she says tightly. "Facts are just pretty details that can be spun into any story you fancy."

She takes another step, bringing us nose to nose, and jabs a finger into my sternum.

"You really want to stand there and tell me I'm working for *God*, when he let me rot down here for years?"

The flames ignite, tearing up the walls and sending the portraits to a fiery demise.

But the most interesting part of this isn't her power, even though it's tearing the Devil's palace apart, wards and all.

It's the fact that she's serious.

The anger burning in her gaze makes that clear. Without a word of a lie, she stands before me and calls God an asshole to my face.

No one has done that since Lucifer himself.

But I still can't read her mind, and it makes me cautious. I need to know for sure.

So, I reach out and lift one of the flaming photographs off the walls. It's a picture of the Eiffel Tower, taken circa 1901. One of Lucifer's little jokes for all his guest suites.

He's always hated Paris, ever since we were run out of there on a bar crawl in the 70s. Parisians don't do bar crawls; at least, not the ones we met. Maybe if they'd joined us instead of kicking us out, they'd have learned to relax a bit.

I hold out the burning photo to Helena. "Take it," I dare her.

She hesitates for barely a second. Then, she pinches the unlit portion of the frame between thumb and forefinger and plucks it free.

The room transforms. Vertigo rips through my brain—and

Helena's too, judging by how she clutches the wall—as the ground shoots hundreds of feet into the air.

We're atop the Eiffel Tower. A starry night expands in all directions, radiating as if we were the central point of all the world's vista while before us, the Heavens extend their reach into infinity.

Helena gapes at the view.

"Beautiful, isn't it?" I lean against the balcony. "Pity we got kicked out before we could climb it."

Her head snaps to mine,. "You got kicked out of the Eiffel Tower?"

"No—Paris." I sigh, rotating myself until I'm leaning back against the railing, head tipped upward.

"And 'we' means you and Lucifer, I'm guessing."

"What makes you say that?"

"Neither of you strike me as men with many friends."

Ouch.

"Lucifer holds a grudge against the entire decade, because of that," I say fondly. "Don't mention the 70s to him—or Paris. At least, not if you want the walls to remain firefighter friendly."

She snorts a soft laugh but doesn't say anything.

Lip twitching, I finally look at her. She hasn't moved from her spot, gaze fixed to the horizon.

Perfect.

"How's the view?" I ask mildly.

"Full of trickery," she answers equally calmly, making me laugh. "Why have you brought me here?"

"They say you can reach God himself from the top of the tower." I pluck the frame from her hands and rest it, still burning, on the metal of the bannister. I move carefully, so that it doesn't fall. "I wonder if you have anything to add."

She turns to me and raises one brow sardonically. From this vantage point, against the mundane yet ethereal trophies of

Earth, I can see her as the human she once was. Her file tells me she danced the Vegas showrooms, pilfering men's pockets as she served them drinks.

It took me a while to see it, but eventually I did. The subtle changes in her demeanor, depending on who she was speaking to. How she speaks far less than she listens. She's someone who knows the discreet art of manipulation, that's for sure.

I should know.

But up here, it's harder to maintain the walls. Fear and awe —the two quickest ways to drive straight to a human's heart. Whatever she feels when she looks at the stars is no longer locked tightly away; up here, you can catch hints of it breaking through.

"You want me to get God on speed-dial or something?" she asks finally.

"If you wouldn't mind."

Her eyes drop to the small smile on my lips. I wish I knew what she was thinking. I've never met someone whose mind was so completely closed to me.

"Do you really think God would be stupid enough to answer if he'd sent me down to spy on you?" She laughs, a soft huff of laughter that sounds oddly self deprecating. "The guy's a toad, but that doesn't mean he's dumb enough to fall for the old three-way phone call trick. This proves nothing."

Helena drums her fingers on the railing, staring out at the night.

She continues, "Which means this is yet another deception, because you'd know that," she says thoughtfully. "A deception within a deception, from a man who demands honesty."

She turns suddenly, picks up the frame of the Eiffel Tower that launched this illusion, and holds it over the side. "I wonder what would happen if I did this?"

My hands clench into fists, the reflex impossible to stop,

and her eyes drop to the movement. Her lips twitch; she's seen. She knows.

She listens far more than she speaks.

Almost in slow motion, she lets go of the frame and drops the photo over the side of the tower. I lurch for it, catching myself at the last second. It's all right; it shouldn't matter, because commandeering the Trickster Dream Bubbles I launched at dinner is one thing, but she'd never be able to twist my own reality into—

The world lurches sideways as the Eiffel tower tips onto its head. Blood races to my ears, the Heavens stretching into infinity above me.

"So, no," she continues. The long braid of her hair falls above her like a rope. It's a perverse facsimile of a noose, with Helena calm and unmoved beneath it. "I don't think I will play along. Not when your challenge is so rigged. You want to see how I look when faced with God, real or imagined, I'm guessing. You're somehow convinced that I won't be able to hide my devotion even if I only pretend to reach for him and fail."

She shouldn't be able to do this. I grip the rail tightly, my feet slipping from their surface on the balcony—the ceiling. This is impossible. Even if she somehow seized control of the illusion, she could never remove me from it. It's *mine*, my power, my control.

My foot slips, the sky lurching.

Helena watches me, feet fixed calmly to the floor. "Either you believe me or you don't," she says icily. "And I don't give a shit what you choose. I'm not playing your game."

My feet lose their grip, and I begin to plummet toward the ground. There's an odd sense of calm within me. It's been so many long years since I've faced Death's door, it's almost novel to feel the fear. And fitting that it should come at the hands of my soulmate.

Then a hand clasps around my wrist.

My descent breaks, and the world tips upright again.

Helena watches me, still gripping my wrist. We're back in the Devil's Palace now, the flames vanished and the photo a charred wreck at my feet.

Only, this time, we're in my wing—where I recharge best after expending so much energy, and therefore where my magic automatically returns.

I watch her take in the pale dust covers on the furniture. The lonely, forgotten rooms with doors that barely open anymore, their hinges are so lacking in grease. The stained glass in the windows full of cobwebs.

She blinks, confused. Intrigued.

Helena is intrigued by my secrets, just as I am by hers.

She could have killed me. I'm her only threat, if she really is God's weapon. But she didn't, and I intrigue her. It strokes my ego, shifting things between us once more. I do like a challenge, and Helena...

She's a challenge unlike any I've experienced.

"This isn't over," I tell her calmly. The words aren't a threat; they're a simple fact. "Not until you answer my question."

"What, about whether I'm God's pawn?" she throws back.

"Precisely." I lean back against the wall, arms folded. "Don't you want the answer, too?"

Her face crumples in confusion. "What the hell are you saying, now? Either you think I'm God's or not."

"Oh, I do," I tell her, smiling. "But I think it must be more of a sleeper agent situation, judging by your reaction."

She flinches, face blanching, and once more that cold thread of regret uncoils within me. Of course, this wouldn't be the first time she was played that way.

"So you want me to call on God to prove he doesn't like me," she says slowly. Already, she's shaking her head. "I'm not doing that."

I hold up my hand. "Not tonight, no." I can sense there's no point pushing her tonight. "But one day. Soon." I shrug lightly. "Or you risk us all."

"How can you just say that?" she asks, gaping. "How can you stand here with me when that's what you think?"

I let a little of the heat I'm feeling into my gaze. Her mouth snaps shut, and I see my own desire reflected back from her.

"You fascinate me," I tell her. "And I like you."

"But you think I'll betray you," she insists. "We're soulmates, but you think I'll betray you."

I smile wider and tell her cheerfully, "Yes, I think we're the doomed kind of soulmates." I shrug. "Such is life, sometimes. Even if you aren't a danger in the end, how could we be anything but doomed when we're tied equally to the Devil and he notoriously doesn't share?"

The horror on her face makes me want to reach for her, to offer her comfort, but that's not what I do. I offer the truth; and this is the truth.

Which makes one thing clear—she needs my help more than ever. After tonight, unexpectedly, I do trust *her*. But I can't trust what she will do, not until she proves to me that God doesn't own her.

However, since she did gain my trust for now, that begs a reward. She is my supplicant, after all.

"How about a new Game?" I propose, heart thudding with unexpected interest. "While we wait for you to prove your loyalty."

It's been years since I proposed a game with equal players, instead of only myself and a pawn. She stares at me blankly, suspicious.

Listening but not speaking.

I swallow thickly, studying her. "You tell me that secret you're keeping from the Devil, and I'll keep it for you. Not a word to anyone. And I'll still get you that key, no matter what the secret is. If I get you what you want, you confess all to Lucifer. If you win without my help... I'll protect you from his wrath when he finds out anyway."

Her eyes glint. This is what she wanted; why she prayed to me, even if she didn't mean to. She's toying with secrets and confessions, whether she knows it or not. Toying with the idea of trusting Lucifer or betraying him.

"Fine," she says after a beat, holding out her hand.

I take it, but all too soon, she draws free. The loss of her warmth cuts through me.

"I want to free my parents," she says abruptly, bringing me back to the present. "And I don't care if this lame power brings down Hell to do it."

It takes a second for me to process the implications, and when I do, I begin to smile.

"I'm impressed," I tell her. "Your secret makes the terms of my Game almost irrelevant."

She looks confused.

"No matter who wins, the Devil is going to turn on you."

15

HELENA

I keep waiting for Tobias to betray me, but after two days, it looks as though he's true to his word. He doesn't even interfere when I nick a couple of old guard uniforms, for future business.

I think he might even enjoy this—being the only one to know my secret. Even if he is demanding one of my own in return.

A secret I don't even have.

How can I possibly be God's chosen? It's ridiculous. And there's no way in Hell I'm calling up the Almighty on speed-dial just to have him look at me like I'm the scum on his shoe, to prove Tobias wrong. That just sounds... so damn painful.

I've had enough of people looking at me like that in my life, thanks.

Besides, if I face him, I'll have to face how mad I am at him for what he did by leaving me down here, and then I'll lose my shit. Like, proper lose it. And if I thought things were bad before, just wait until I tell God where to shove it.

Tobias is wrong, plain and simple. I know what it's like to be a sleeper agent; it feels nothing like this.

It feels...

Fuck, it feels like nothing. Like *nothing*. Like I'm worse than dead. Like I'm *empty*.

And I'm not putting myself through objective torture to prove that to him.

I take another turn on the garden path at random, trying to contain my agitation. I'd figured today was as good a day as any to test the new freedom Lucifer gave me. But, of course, Logan is nowhere to be found.

Ever since the dinner, Logan's been weird with me. He didn't even look me in the eye when he left the table.

We had that one, steamy kiss, where he promised me some no-strings fun while I was stuck here. Promised to worship me, actually. And then, just like that, he gets cold feet. Quickest turn around in the history of the male gender.

Something Lucifer said at the table got to him, and I'd pay good money to know what it was.

And the most aggravating part is that, thanks to the spell Lucifer cast on our soulbond, I know the prick is somewhere within thirty meters of me. And I still can't find him.

So here I am, roaming the Devil's private gardens like an idiot. Every now and then I see a flash of what looks suspiciously like spotted fur, but that's as close as I get.

The gardens are very beautiful, at least.

Purple butterflies flit past my face, reminding me of the Butterfly House at the zoo near where I grew up. There was a hole in the back fence of the zoo, behind the lemurs, and for years I'd sneak in and go straight to the Butterfly House. Nowhere else.

I'd let them land on me as long as possible, telling myself it was bad luck to startle them away. They had to leave on their own terms, and only then could I breathe again.

I stand in the center of the path, in front of a strange-looking rock that whirls into four main points, and watch them fly.

"I'm surprised to find you here," a voice says nearby, amused as ever.

I look up to find Tobias perched on a different rock—one without all the swirls.

"Great," I say flatly. "The one I'm *not* looking for. Isn't that typical?"

His eyebrows lift in interest. "You're looking for Lucy, too?"

"Technically, I'm looking for Logan. But I'd take Lucifer."

Just so I could yell at him.

Not really. But how am I meant to play by his "free under guard" rules if my guard fucks off the second he can?

Tobias makes a noncommittal noise at the back of his throat and props himself backward on his elbows. His dark eyes are intent as he watches me, but there's an unexpected warmth to his gaze.

"You're looking for Lucifer, I take it?" I hold out my hand to a passing butterfly, keeping very still as it inspects me with cautious interest.

I get it, little man. Trust no one.

"Yes. I want to know why this bond is getting itchier. And I especially want to know what is so important that he keeps disappearing on us and *making* it itchy." He casts me a wry glance. "I suspect it has something to do with your power, which means Lucifer knows something he isn't sharing."

I blink in surprise. I hadn't realized this new honesty thing went in both directions.

Maybe he was serious, after all. He does like me.

I consider what he's said about Lucifer. I believe it's possible that Lucifer knows more about my power than he's sharing, but I also don't think he would keep anything vital from me. Not about this.

He said he was going to help get me out of here, right? How would keeping secrets help me? I'm exploding power all over the place with no way to control it; any information would be helpful.

"What do you mean 'itchy'?" I ask Tobias, focusing instead on the other thing he said.

I'm compelled by the urge to rub my hand over the point where I think the bond enters my body, just above my chest, but the butterfly has landed, so I hold still.

Tobias watches it rest on my open palm, seemingly fascinated. "Can't you feel it?" he asks distantly.

I suppose, now that he mentions it, I can. I'd been trying not to pay attention to it, but now that I do, it almost burns.

I bite down on my lip to keep from flinching and startling the butterfly.

"Distracting," I say quietly, watching its wings beat slowly up and down. "So the itch appears when Lucifer vanishes on us? That's not so bad."

"For now," Tobias says ominously. "If it gets worse or happens more frequently, it could be devastating. Haven't you noticed what happens when the cord gets too agitated?"

"No..."

"It solidifies. Starts to become a real rope." His eyes bear into mine, intense like I've never seen them before. "No longer a soulbond, but just a thread."

"Isn't that a good thing?" I ask distantly.

Tobias laughs without humor. "To destroy a soulbond like that? Even you can't believe that, Helena."

He's right. It sounds... doomed.

Tobias drops lightly off the rock and moves toward me. His movements are lithe and graceful. Cat-like.

The butterfly doesn't even flinch at his approach, and I'm

stuck there, unable to move because then it *will* fly off, and that feels like a real bad omen given the cause.

"I'm just curious," Tobias says into my ear, his breath so soft it barely stirs the hair at the base of my skull. "Why haven't you asked Lucifer for help, instead of going to all this effort behind his back?"

I frown, a strange feeling settling low in my stomach, like rocks.

"What do you mean? I can't just walk up to him and ask him to set two of his prisoners free. He'd lock them up even tighter. I'd never find them again."

Tobias doesn't answer for a moment. The silence fills me with dread, though I can't work out why.

"He's done more for boons requested by people he loves less than you," Tobias says finally.

I startle, my hand flinching. The butterfly flutters in place, nervous. Holding my breath, I watch it settle back down.

"Lucifer doesn't love me," I say as calmly and quietly as I can. "What the hell are you talking about?"

"He's soulbound to you."

The words cut through the noise in my brain, leaving me speechless.

"He said it was just a Ludus bond," I say. "The least important of the lot. Like a fling."

I deliberately don't think about how he asked me if I wanted to keep him forever.

Besides, the way he asked me made it clear that *he* didn't want *me*.

"Mmm, it is," Tobias says, reaching his hand out slowly to rest in the air next to mine. I can't even stop him, or the butterfly will escape, frightened. I can only hold my breath and watch. "But that doesn't mean it isn't love."

"Does that mean you love me, then?" I ask before I can

think.

These men have a way of forcing my innermost thoughts to the surface, even without mind-reading. They knock me off balance just enough that my real self leaks through.

I didn't even know she was still around.

Tobias gives me a sideways glance, but neither of us move because the butterfly has begun to creep slowly toward him.

It walks lazily, wings drifting up and down, to the edge of my hand. It pauses, stretching one leg out and back, hesitant. Then it walks onto Tobias' palm.

I let out a breath slowly, lowering my hand back to my side.

"Would it surprise you if I did?" Tobias asks quietly, holding still while the butterfly settles.

"Of course," I say, the words barely a breath. "We've only just met."

"But we were destined to."

"Love doesn't work that quickly," I argue.

Tobias' lip quirks. "So you don't believe in love at first sight."

I pause. Our argument is happening in fierce whispers, the butterfly still unsure and ready to leave at any moment. We've barely moved, and I can feel the tension stiffening up my neck.

"No," I say slowly. "I don't think I do. You're my guards. Lucifer is my prison keeper. None of you are on my side, not really, because if the Devil clicked his fingers, that's who you'd fall in behind—not me. No matter how much you help me."

"Those are obstacles," Tobias says, voice distant. "They don't have anything to do with the love itself."

A strange feeling twists in my stomach. I can't name it. I almost don't want to. I can feel everything he isn't saying. It's pouring into the space between the words.

You fascinate me.

I like you.

I want you.

He hasn't said that last one, but I know it's true. I see how he looks at me when he thinks I'm not watching.

"Helena," he says quietly. "You're always watching."

He must have caught that last thought, my mind too scattered to keep it hidden. My breath catches, and the butterfly flutters nervously.

Tobias knows I've seen him looking. He wants me to see.

Bizarrely, I think back to the inner depths of his wing in the castle. There were so many secrets there, and I know he won't share even a whisper of them with me. Not if he can help it.

But he fascinates me, too, and I want to know how he can be the Devil's closest friend when he clearly hasn't stepped foot in those rooms for years.

I squeeze my eyes tightly shut, trying to remember the plan. This isn't about me and Tobias. This is about Lucifer—it's about whether he would give me what I ask for.

"It still doesn't mean Lucifer would help me with this," I insist. "He wouldn't."

"No," Tobias says, bringing his palm to his face and watching the butterfly closely. "But I didn't say that you *should* ask."

He gives his hand an irritated flick, and the butterfly flies off in shock. I can't hold back my gasp, the way my body lurches forward in protest even though it's already too late.

Tobias watches me, finishing his thought in a slow, meandering way. "I said it was interesting you hadn't thought to."

He drops his hand so suddenly, I jump. For a moment we're just staring at each other, so much unsaid, both knowing it doesn't need to be.

"Now, shall we follow this Devil?" Tobias breaks the silence finally, his voice as light and easy as ever. "Or do you not want to pickpocket his keys after all?"

16

HELENA

Tobias' words eat at me as we ransack the Devil's study, making me uneasy. Should I have just asked Lucifer for help? Surely it isn't that easy.

Even Tobias didn't try to persuade me, and I get the feeling he'd happily watch the fallout with popcorn.

"Best way to catch a Devil is in his trash," Tobias says idly, inspecting a slip of paper he's just pulled from Lucifer's desk and throwing it over his shoulder onto the floor. "He religiously guards his private schedule, but he's too arrogant to think someone might stoop to trash picking."

"So here we are. Stooping." I pick up the paper he dropped and read it out loud. "Whisper source—Lake Eildon?" The question mark isn't my own, but I do have a few hanging around my head right now. "What does that mean?"

"It means he's hunting down the lingering scourge of Ronin's rebellion," Tobias says idly, throwing another piece over his shoulder. The name lances my chest, like it always does, and I can't tell if the wound is healing or becoming numb. "But everyone knows that. This isn't where he's sneaking off to."

He pauses, casting an irritated glance toward the door. Reaching toward his own chest, he wraps his fingers around something I can't see and tugs it.

For a moment, one of the blue threads materializes. Like Tobias said, with Lucifer's absence and Tobias' own agitation of the cord, it's becoming solid. Like it's reacting to the stress and losing its magic—becoming just an ordinary rope.

But, fortunately, it glimmers again almost immediately. Tobias only gave it a quick tug after all, and within seconds it's a shimmering, ethereal cord of magic once more. I let out a slow breath of relief.

"Where is that brat?" Tobias mutters as he lets go of the thread.

Brat? Is he calling Lucifer a brat?!

Something slams into the door, making me jump. I look up, eyes wide, to see Logan leaning in the doorway with his hand splayed on the open door, as if he's just halted his own fast descent down the corridor.

He glares mutinously at Tobias. "Stop doing that," he warns in a low voice, eyes glinting.

I blink in surprise. I've never seen Logan angry before. But it fades quickly, and he strides into the room, running a hand affectionately over my hair and winking at me.

Oh—that's what Tobias did. He pulled on the soulbond like it was a bell cord.

And Logan came running.

"Well, stop sulking and I won't have to," Tobias says cheerily.

"I'm not sulking."

Tobias only grins wider, like Logan has said exactly what he wanted him to.

"Wait," I say, holding up one hand. "Can't we just do that to Lucifer?"

Tobias' expression darkens. "I have been. The man is too self controlled. Fuck knows I've been pulling it enough. Should have either fallen off or sent him running for my head on a plate by now."

My face flushes at the obvious, crude innuendo, but no one pays attention to me.

"So why weren't you with us, then?" I ask, turning my irritation on Logan. "I've been looking for you. I wanted to go out."

His face does something odd. Contrite but annoyed. Sheepish and mutinous all in one.

"I had things to take care of," he says finally.

Tobias snorts but says nothing.

I grit my teeth to keep from snapping and go back to checking Tobias' cast offs. It's not like I know what I'm looking for, but it's ingrained in me to find what others miss.

The notes are useless though, as far as I can tell. Meaningless scribbles scrawled on the back of napkins and receipts. They'd make sense only to Lucifer himself.

After a minute, I feel eyes burning into my back. I look up to see Logan watching me, his thumb running back and forth over his lower lip and his eyes so dark the iris is almost completely obscured.

It's only through years of training that I catch myself before I suck in a breath. Heat pools in my abdomen, an ache of want coursing through me.

I'd forgotten Logan was so close to the rut, but obviously he hasn't. But why hasn't he asked me again?

He catches me looking, winks, and turns away.

Fucking mercurial bastard.

I shake my head and turn back to the papers, but man, it's hard to focus after that. What was I doing again? Receipts. Yeah —that's it.

Anyway... who on earth is issuing the Devil receipts? I flip it over and squint at the faded writing. Ah—it isn't from a place in Hell. It's from Earth. Some restaurant in Portland. If my memory serves—and it may not, because it's been years since I was alive—it's a jazz bar.

Well, at least I don't have to wonder which poor, naïve sucker is giving the Dastardly Ruler and Chief Torturer a receipt for eight bucks fifty and twenty change. That kind of shit would keep me up at night, at this point.

Movement catches my eye, and I turn to see a mirror like the one in the throne room, complete with a stormy portal swirling gently inside. My heart skips a beat. Could I reach out to Ciera like this?

I've hardly dared to think about her. It hurts too much, knowing how close I was to having my best friend back, and then losing her completely.

I take a step closer to the mirror, Lucifer's warnings ringing in my head. *No contact.*

But will he even know?

The mirror swirls, and I whisper her name under my breath, just to see what happens.

Inside, the storm clouds flicker with lightning. A shadow darkens the center, beginning to take shape into something that looks like a body...

My senses flicker—something has shifted in the room—and I turn away abruptly. The silhouette melts back into the cloud, and I find Tobias staring, frozen, at a bit of paper. Slowly, he smiles.

"Got him." He holds up the paper so we can see.

Surge. Grave retraction. Pines.

Logan wrinkles his nose in irritation. "Are you gonna translate for us? We didn't all share a frat house, you know."

Images of Tobias and Lucifer letting loose in a frat house assault me. I know Logan was only joking, but the glint in

Tobias' eye tells me it might actually have happened. I refuse to ask.

"This isn't to do with the rebellion. It's to do with the Grave —Hell's power. For some reason, he's tracking a surge to the Pines." Tobias shrugs dramatically, clearly enjoying an audience. "Maybe he's hunting a prisoner there. Maybe one of the other kings has gone rogue. Let's find out."

Right—the Grave. Ciera told me about that. The jewel that sits in Lucifer's hilt and funnels the power currents of Hell to each of the kings and queen.

When Ronin tried to take over, Lucifer redistributed the power, and Hell's landscape adjusted with it. New strands. New Hell.

Fresh start, or so he thought.

If something is drawing the attention of the Grave, he would definitely keep it from us. It could mean a second rebellion, or the first regaining traction, if one of the other kings has crossed over.

Either way, he's clearly choosing This Problem over Our Problem and that's making Tobias pissed.

I wonder if there's a way I can use that to help me get this key.

It only takes a few minutes for us to restore Lucifer's study to how we found it and catch a carriage to the Pines. Of course, since Lucifer commands the entire ocean of power that constructs Hell—physically, geographically, and magically—he can get there in seconds. Which is part of why it's so hard to track him.

"Yes," Tobias says, not turning from where he rests with his chin propped on his hand, staring out the window. "And the other part is that he's so frustratingly solo in his endeavors, even when they involve other people."

"You're reading my thoughts," I accuse him, slamming up my walls again.

He smiles, eyes flicking to me. "You're relaxing around me."

Logan shifts in his seat. He's been watching us closely for the entire journey, and whatever he's just seen has made him relax.

"You can't read Hel's thoughts?" he asks Tobias.

"Not typically."

Logan turns to me. "Is that something you learned from Ronin?"

Tobias grows still, and I can't help the startled lift of my eyebrows. No one else had put it together. "I didn't learn it *from* Ronin," I correct him. "I learned it *because* of him."

Well, how to do it this perfectly, anyway. I was good at it on Earth, but I doubt it would have stood up to Tobias.

Logan nods. "Because you had to keep your mind separate from what was done to you. How he controlled you."

Okay, now this is getting uncomfortable. I shrug, facing the window and signaling the conversation is over.

Ronin may have controlled me, but he wasn't the first. Controlling someone and fixing them, it's all the same isn't it? That's how it felt to me at the time, anyway.

I thought when people had baggage it was meant to be clear. Like, you could point to it and say 'there's my baggage, isn't it a whopper?'. But it isn't like that. Instead, it's like I'm trapped in a spiral, twisting and twisting while the same things hit me from different directions.

That's why I need to keep the walls. Something tells me that the day I lose them—the day I *feel* more than I can contain—everything is going to fall apart.

The carriage rattles through the plains, long stretches of nothing filled with bone carcasses and the occasional trashed hot rod. There's a certain style to it all, but before I can appreciate it too much, the carriage arrives at the edge of an immense pine forest.

We get out, and it vanishes with a rattle.

"How the hell are we meant to find him in here?" Logan asks sourly.

He clearly doesn't want to be here, and I don't know what to make of it, especially after that look in his eyes back in Lucifer's study.

It's like he can't stay away, even if there wasn't a literal cord connecting us. But he's spending every ounce of his energy trying to.

"You forget, we have a trail of bread crumbs," Tobias says cheerfully, flicking his finger over the blue cord that emerges from his chest. "This bond he saddled you with works both ways."

This time, I feel it. It's like a soft, echoing vibration that sings through my body and curls my toes.

It's like the beginning of an orgasm, actually.

With that little tidbit fresh in my mind, we follow the trail of pleasure into the forest, where the Devil waits at the other end.

As soon as I step foot among the trees, I know we're not alone. The shadows are moving; they aren't shadows at all.

I open my mouth, but Tobias holds up a hand, stopping me.

"It's best if you choose ignorance," he says lightly, sending chills racing through me.

We follow the cord, and the shadows follow us. I can't be sure, but it looks as though the shadows have bright red eyes, glinting every time they move. My power fizzles at my fingertips, reacting to my fear. More than once, Tobias glances at me curiously.

Eventually, he says, "If you start a forest fire here, you could pickpocket the keys when Lucifer rescues you."

I cast a glance at Logan, but he isn't listening.

"Sure, unless he leaves me to die," I mutter back.

Tobias smirks—an infuriating twitch like he knows something I don't. "He won't."

"You don't know that. I've been a pain in the ass to him from day one, and this would be a very convenient solution."

"If you're God's chosen, it won't matter," he says smugly.

I come to an abrupt halt. *There it is*, I think. *The moment I've been waiting for.*

Outwardly, I say nothing—just watch him. He studies me curiously, and then with a twitch of frustration when he can't read my mind.

"What?" he snaps.

The answer unfurls slowly within me. Tobias is the kind of man who has to needle at people, to poke them until they stop lying and burst out with the truth. It's the only answer he'll accept.

He's dramatic, and he needs a dramatic answer.

"Is now really the time?" I ask, making sure I look annoyed as fuck.

"Oh, whenever you're ready," he says airily. "You know I like you regardless of if you're a traitor."

Irritation flares, mostly because there's not a damn word of a lie in that sentence. He does like me—wants me—and he'll continue to help me so long as it doesn't directly contradict Lucifer.

But he still thinks I'm a goddamn sleeper agent.

And I really, really don't want to contact God just to prove him wrong, even though I know he is.

So, I bottle up my feelings just like I bottle my thoughts. I know this power now, unpredictable though it is. I know it's just waiting for a reason to blow.

And there's only one way it can blow that will convince Tobias it isn't me doing it.

"Fine!" I yell, flinging my arms out like I just can't contain the anger. "You want me to prove I'm not some fucking traitor?!"

Logan watches us, a deep frown etched on his face. But he doesn't ask questions. It's like it doesn't even matter to him.

That pisses me off even more, and the power within me surges violently. It rages against the cage of my willpower, unused to me making a single attempt to control it. Sweat beads on my forehead as I funnel all my energy into this one, gigantic bit of focus.

I cup my hands around my mouth, knowing I've only got seconds before I blow, and yell up to the sky. "Do you hear that, God?! Your presence is wanted, oh enigmatic *asshole*—" I don't need to act out the horrified shriek that comes when I let my power free.

It explodes, igniting the one thing I'll let it touch.

Me.

Tobias and Logan yell as the flames consume my body, startling forward, panicked words filling the forest. But thank the fucking Heavens, my guess was correct; the flames don't hurt me. I drop to the ground, screaming—again, not entirely acting that one—as I roll on the earthy floor in desperation.

By the time they reach my side, the flames are mostly out, and I stare up into two horrified faces.

Horrified and scared.

They're scared for me. That one's a shock.

"There's your bloody answer," I wheeze, injecting pure fear into my voice as I brush my singed hair from my face. "I don't think the big guy likes being called an asshole."

"No," Tobias murmurs, eyes scanning me, checking me over

as he very tenderly pulls me to a sitting position. "It would appear that way. Unless..." He studies me carefully.

A jolt of uncertainty hits me; he's suspicious, of course. So, I make sure my voice holds nothing but contempt and indignation as I say, ice cold, "You think I would light myself on *fucking fire* just to spy on you assholes?"

There's a long pause, before he gives me a measured smile. "No, I don't."

Then, his face relaxes into a real smile, and I know I've done it. I've convinced him. He trusts me now.

A strange sensation hits me, like guilt, but I force it down.

"Well, if that's it, then," I say quietly, looking down under the pretense of brushing my trousers off. "Shall we keep going?"

Tobias doesn't answer.

I look up, fear hitting me. Has he seen through me already?

Then a different kind of fear washes over me like a wave. Tobias isn't there.

No one is there.

I'm alone.

The shadows around the clearing flicker strangely. I was right before; they're inset with glowing red eyes, and those eyes are now fixed on me.

They've done something—the shadows have separated us somehow, and I'm on my bloody own.

Swallowing thickly, I count down the seconds before panic sets in. At the last moment, I remember the bread crumbs. Slowly, carefully, I find the cords at my chest. I don't look at them, for fear of making them vanish, but I tug one. Very gently.

It holds, and I breathe a sigh of relief. It doesn't really matter whose cord I follow; I just want to find anyone at this point. The forest looms above me, and the shadows are the only thing preventing me from being completely alone. Which is *not* a good thing.

After several twists and turns, and long minutes that stretch into nothing, I hear a noise.

Singing.

Fear rises, sticking in my throat, until my body catches on. It responds instinctively, drawn toward the sound because it's just so beautiful. Like home.

That's when I recognize it.

This is the singing of a seraph.

Lucifer was a seraph.

I round the corner and find him in front of a strange little hut. He doesn't appear to have noticed me yet. I'm damn sure he wouldn't be singing still if he had.

I freeze as still as I can, not wanting to ruin this strange moment. He leans against the hut, his head tipped back so his attention is fixed on the forest canopy above.

With the slow sense of puzzle pieces clicking into place, I realize it's possible to see through the canopy to the night sky above. And I realize there are no stars. Hell has no stars.

Didn't Lucifer do something to the stars when he fell? My knowledge is hazy, but that little fact hammers itself over and over into my brain. Light bringer. The morning star falling to Earth, and when he fell, his light burned away from his body and became a thousand new stars in the sky.

He created the stars, but there are no stars in Hell.

I must make a sound of some kind, because he stops abruptly and looks in my direction. His blue eyes flash demon gold.

"Come out, Helena," he says in that smooth, caramel voice I don't trust at all.

I step into the small circle of light from the hut. My curiosity burns; I want to look inside the hut to discover the kind of person Lucifer is sneaking off to meet.

But the look in his eyes tells me it isn't worth asking. Whatever Tobias has thrown us into, it's big.

"How did you find me?" he asks.

There's something in his voice when he asks the question. A sense of knowing—almost dread.

Confused, I shake my head. "I didn't. Tobias brought us here, and then the forest separated us and led me to you."

Lucifer blinks. Then, he slowly uncurls from his lean against the wall, graceful like a cat, and stands upright. "Tobias. Of course." He goes silent, staring into the dark forest for a beat. "And what carrot did he dangle to get you to agree?"

Surprise rattles me, followed by a sinking feeling of understanding. Of course Lucifer would see right through this.

My mind speeds ahead, constructing an elaborate story about the soulbond itching—true—and how I feel trapped and alone—also true—and I want him to let me see Ciera—very fucking true—so we wanted to get blackmail fuel to make him agree—there's the lie.

Always bury the lie. Make it even deeper when you're dealing with people like Lucifer.

But before I can weave my story, Tobias' face pops into my head for some reason. I see the genuine smile he gave me. The unexpected trust in his eyes. My stomach squirms.

Why can't I just ask Lucifer?

Cat always speaks fondly of him, and, okay, I don't know her super well but it's well enough to trust her judgment. And he's apparently my soulmate, and surely freeing two little souls won't make anything explode?

"I want to free my parents," I say.

The honesty of it burns, and I immediately want to hide away and never come out. But there's also a sense of relief in asking. In dropping the con and just being upfront about what I want. I've never had that before.

But then Lucifer's expression darkens, and I take a reflexive step backward.

"Your parents," he repeats softly.

The words echo like thunder. The trees rustle in a sudden wind, creaking in protest. I watch, eyes wide, as threads of Hell's power whirl around Lucifer's face. They're barely visible —probably because I'm not a queen and can't access them, I guess—but they're so captivating, I can't look away.

His face blends into something different, and I realize with slowly dawning horror that he's called down hellfire.

His demonic soul bursts free. Bone and sinew twist his face into something from a nightmare. Piercing blue eyes darken to black inside hollow sockets, but half of his face is covered. Golden metal covers his left cheek and temple, welded somehow to the skull beneath, and it gives him a terrifying edge of aristocratic madness.

Power and chaos. Vitality and death. He's a mix of it all, and the worst part of it is that there is still something hidden. Some kind of dark, amorphous mass writhes beneath the bone, waiting to emerge.

This is the Devil.

Not the pretty man with the soft curls and the blue eyes. Not even the intimidating figure on the throne who commands Hell with ease. No, it's this man before me.

I'm seeing him for the first time, and it terrifies me.

What terrifies me more is knowing that this is only a glimpse. A whisper.

A deep sense of knowing sets into me: the day I see the Devil's true face will mean my death.

"Your parents will never see the light of day, Helena," Lucifer croons, sending icy shivers down my back. "Don't ever ask me that again."

The power vanishes, hellfire fading with a snap of darkness.

His soul vanishes too, but his face is cast in shadow now that the wind has blown out the lights from the hut.

I shiver in the sudden silence, scared and unnerved. Unsure what to say.

The Devil is just like the rest of them, and I struggle against the old, painful emotions rising like a tide inside me. He's like every adult who ever realized my situation in school. Every care worker.

Every boss who found out about my family. Every friend.

In the end, they were all the same. *Your parents are addicts, Helena.* They don't deserve to live.

Slowly, I realize I'm no longer afraid.

I'm shaking with rage. And the ground is shaking too; it's too close to my last outburst, when I fooled Tobias, and there's residual power inside me just begging for an outlet. Trees quake, bending beneath my wrath, wind howling. And in the flash of sudden lightning, I see Lucifer's face; it's white with fear.

Good.

The forest bursts into flame.

17

HELENA

OH, THIS IS GOING TO HAVE SOME SERIOUS REPERCUSSIONS. I GAPE AT the roaring flames, my stomach churning with fear and guilt as I try to suck the power back into me. But I can't. It's out, and it won't be stopped.

For the first time, I think Tobias might be right. Maybe this *is* the power of God. It would fit, that's for sure. Vengeful, brutal, and callous as all hell.

Although, you'd think the Big Guy would smite me for thinking that too loudly near his Flames of Death, so maybe not.

Lucifer grows still, eerily watchful amidst the chaos reigning alongside him. Surely there's no time to assess? And yet, that's what he does. He moves his hands in three careful motions, and each time the flames change color just a little.

Each color glints off the golden armor chiseled to his face. Blue, then green, then a chilling white that's like a naphtha flash in the night.

With the last, he explodes into movement again. I don't

realize Tobias and Logan have found us until Lucifer is yelling orders to them.

But of course they have. I lit a fucking beacon.

The shadows from earlier are still among the trees. They haven't fled the fire, and it sends shivers down my spine. Who the fuck is watching us? And what's worth risking a fiery death just to observe?

"Get her out of here," Lucifer yells at Logan.

A strange look crosses Logan's face, same as it did at dinner last night when Lucifer told him to guard me.

As if he can sense the hesitation, Lucifer glances over his shoulder, face twisting when he sees Logan pause. "Protect your pack, alpha!" he snarls, and then he twists his hand toward Tobias, making him stumble as if he'd been yanked forward. "You. With me."

For once Tobias doesn't argue, although his scowl speaks volumes.

No, it's Logan who hesitates. Because apparently whatever Lucifer just said was the wrong thing times a thousand, and saving my life is such a drag.

He stares into the flames, his face expressionless, body still.

I snap my fingers in front of him. "Hello? Let's do this. Not keen on dying here."

If there was any chance I could help, of course I'd stay, but Tobias and Lucifer are currently dead center of a roaring wall of fire that I can't penetrate, and if I wait any longer, I'm going to blister.

He looks at me, moving so slowly it's like he's in a trance. And there's a minute, there—one long, terrifying, painful minute—where I'm hit with the certainty that he's going to leave me here and run.

Then Lucifer's voice coils from the trees, like a snake. In a low, furious whisper, he says, "Logan. That's an order."

I move as if in slow motion, compelled to search out the man who belongs to a voice like that, so fierce, so... terrified.

Why is he afraid?

Our eyes meet, his expression twisted in a grimace of wide-eyed agony as he watches the flames descend upon me—and it hits me. He wants me to be safe.

He can't fight this until he knows I'm safe.

Logan grabs my arm, reaches into his pocket for one of those one-way teleport things linked to the palace, and we vanish.

I barely talk to him when we return. He's made it clear he has nothing to say, and I'm still reeling from Lucifer's change. The way he twisted into the enemy, as though those were his true colors all along.

And then the way he looked at me when I was in danger. Like he wasn't the enemy at all. Like he'd fight a thousand enemies to keep me safe. It leaves me conflicted and aching and... fucking lonely.

It hurts. I expected nothing, and it still hurts.

When our bond flickers, hours later, to signal their return, I don't go looking for either of them. And just in case Tobias is perving from my mirror again, I stick my finger up at it. Fuck him and his plans. His manipulations.

Fuck Lucifer.

Tomorrow, I'm going to make Logan take me into the city, and I'm going to hunt until I find a torturer I recognize.

Then I'm going to flip the tables on Lucifer's little power game and find my parents.

The sour streets of Hell's downtown remind me of Ronin. He stunk like this, and I wonder if it's because this is where the rebellion rose from.

I tap my fingers on my thigh, checking that I'm still here. Still inside my body.

Yep—this is me. Hot and sticky and kind of pissed off.

You know, when I died, I thought I'd faced enough of the shit life had to offer. If anyone were to hear my sorry life story, they'd pull one of those damn faces and then drag me onto daytime telly or something.

But then Ronin happened. And that was like... an entire lifetime's worth of torture.

How many lifetimes of torture can one girl have?

"You've got that look on your face," Logan says, his low voice startling me.

I slide a glance toward him, prowling beside me. His shifter vitality has never been more apparent than now. He's restless— a caged jaguar, even though Hell stretches for miles and he's free to roam all of them.

"What look?" I smooth my hands over my thighs once more. Still there.

Logan gives me that slow curve of a smile, filled with heat. "Like you want me to piss off and leave you alone in your window seat."

My stomach dips. Dammit, I really shouldn't have let so much of myself free in front of him. I'd just been so distracted by the books.

"Don't know what you're talking about," I say vaguely.

Logan's eyes drop to my mouth, and I swear they glint from something other than magic. He still wants me, but he hasn't offered again. Not since that night.

"I can do that, if you want," he says. "Take you back and give you time alone—your wish is my command."

He gives me a slightly mocking little bow. His smile is soft enough that some of the sting is removed, but his eyes are still so sharp. I don't know where I stand with him anymore.

I snort. "You mean Lucifer's wish."

Logan shrugs. "It's not so bad, is it? A cage doesn't have to be a prison."

Wow. That's a new one.

Something slices through me—an unfamiliar emotion. "You mean I can find something fun to pass the time?" I throw at him, feeling cruelly triumphant when I see his expression shutter closed.

He shoves his hands in his pockets and turns back to the front.

"What did Lucifer give you that makes the bond stretch this far?" I ask the wall of his back.

He glances over his shoulder, lip quirked in a wry smile, but doesn't answer or turn around. Figures.

Honestly, I want to know what his damn problem is. But I get the feeling that if I ask, he'll run and never look back. No matter how much our bond protests.

He's been ready to run since the fire. Earlier than that, even.

Gritting my teeth, I stop beside a small vendor, pretending I'm immersed in his wares instead of listening for voices I recognize.

My time with Ronin told me that this area of the city is where the real bastards go to play. The sadistic torturers who don't care about the crime; they'd do it to an innocent just as surely. And since I was rarely in charge of my body, it's their voices I know most of all.

It doesn't take long. What can I say? I got used to waiting and listening.

"Another five," the demon croaks. "Don't get cheap."

I pretend to be captivated by the tacky—and probably

stolen—jewelry on display, and listen in carefully. Logan leans against the tent pole and stares moodily into the distance, fingers flexing.

His knuckles keep rippling with spotted fur, which I pretend not to notice.

Every so often, he glances over at me, his eyes flicking from the jewelry to my face, an odd expression on his own.

"Are you accusing me of undercutting the scales?" the sales demon growls, lips rippling over sharpened teeth.

Summoning Demon, then. Without a witch, clearly, so his power is low. Raw and useless.

"Depends," the torturer answers, leaning in menacingly. "Are you accusing me of lying?"

What a standoff. The dull, reddened sun blares down on the market. We're nestled between two tall, brick buildings, but the heat still penetrates.

It never made sense to me why Hell only has one major city, but I think I get it now.

The city is its own torture chamber. It stretches on and on into the desert, the downtown running for miles upon miles. And everywhere you look, you see the rattle of chains as tortured souls shuffle past.

Even demons recognize the bleak, barren wasteland of modern high rise living is its own hell.

I guess that's why they prefer smaller communes and townships among the ever changing geography, and leave the city to the trade and torture.

A scuffle breaks free—finally—but it's no surprise who wins. The seller is on his back in seconds, squealing, while the torturer clamps a vice around his neck.

"Say it again," he hisses, and then presses a button that makes the demon light up.

Literally.

He screams silently, as if he's too far gone to even make noise, while blue light courses through him. Logan watches with a disgusted sneer, but I'm used to steeling my expression here. I keep it cold, and when the torturer makes eye contact with me, he nods in approval, as if we're somehow in solidarity.

I force myself to nod back, because this way he won't suspect anything.

But my stomach churns, and I feel flame licking at my fingertips, begging to leap free. I swallow thickly, counting the seconds for something to focus on, and finally I push the power back down.

I think the forest fire is still too near in my memory; it makes it easier to resist before I burn anything else.

At last, the light stops. The demon twitches on the ground, while the torturer steps over him and picks up his bag of commerce from the table.

He drops coins onto the demon's chest, spits on him, and leaves.

"Are we following him?" Logan asks in a quiet, bored voice.

Surprised, I glance at him sideways. He's paying attention after all.

"Yes," I say quietly. "In a second."

I turn to the demon again, who's now back on his feet. He rubs his horns tenderly, still half doubled over, and watches me approach with a wary eye.

I hear Logan say something behind me, but I ignore it.

"No more sales, today," he spits, tugging the cloth over his wares.

"What about if I were to offer *you* something instead?"

He laughs bitterly. "Don't want it. Piss off."

"You don't want revenge against that torturer?"

He pauses, eyes glinting with pain and fear.

And greed.

"What kind of revenge?"

My heart flutters in anticipation. I've got him.

"You tell me where his house is, and I'll sic the Queen of Hell on him."

The demon's eyes widen. I've no idea if Cat will agree to this, but she has a strong justice streak, and from what I remember of this torturer, there's nothing just about him. Honestly, I'll be doing Hell's admin a favor.

He might even be in the rebellion. Who knows?

"Hel," Logan says quietly. "The shadows are back."

I bat him away, barely listening.

"Soulstone," the demon demands, wetting his lips in anticipation. "Soulstone or nothing. No deal."

My eyebrows shoot up. "You want me to soulstone him? Shit that's nasty."

Cat might not go for it either. One was used on her for years.

He shrugs and half turns away.

"Soulstone or nothing," he repeats.

Anger snaps inside me. "I'll even let you watch," I lie.

The demon's eyes shine with desire. No one would let him watch, but he doesn't need to know that.

If I can get the address off him, I can get *everything*. My parents' location, keys to the cages, everything.

"Hel," Logan insists, grabbing my shoulder. "The shadows from the forest are here."

He spins me around, forcing me to look.

I freeze, staring into the familiar red eyes coated in shadow. Three sets of them. Watching us.

Except this time the light from the sun reveals just enough for me to know who they are. The engraved V of the rebellion— the *Rising bloody Snakes*—swings from their neck.

Which means the Rising Snakes were watching us in the forest. They saw my power explode, and they followed me here.

I don't wait to find out why. I grab Logan's wrist and hurtle down the strip.

The cord between our chests vibrates, agitated. My grasp on his arm is fragile, and I can feel him squirming in my grip. Agitated, too.

It clicks.

"You were going to leave me," I hiss, turning to glare at him as we run. "Just like in the forest."

Barrels go flying as we tear past. The shadows flit in and out of the stalls, never quite visible enough to catch. They're using some kind of spell; demons hiding behind witchcraft.

A cart of fruit appears to our right, and Logan beelines for it, laughing in delight as he tips the whole thing over.

He's like a different man. Saving me, like a damsel in distress, puts him into a trance. But running, like this is all some kind of game... He's somehow okay with that.

I don't pretend to understand it. I just dodge oranges and keep running. We take corner after corner, gaining ground, slowing them down by leaving chaos in our wake.

And then we hit a dead end. Broken cars litter the street; it's some kind of dumping ground.

Logan pulls up, skidding to a halt.

"Shit," I hiss. "Pull out your little teleport thingie."

"It's not recharged," he says flatly.

Oh no. Here we go again. He's eyeing off the brick wall, gauging the height in a way that makes it obvious what he's thinking.

He wants to shift and leave me behind.

"You have got to be kidding me," I snarl, feeling murderous. "What is your *problem*?! Why do you keep wanting to leave me to die?"

He snaps out of it. "I'm not leaving you to die!"

"Then what would you call it?"

He opens his mouth and shuts it again. His long, reddish brown hair has become tangled by the wind, giving him the impression of a mane.

A very large, strong man with a mane.

A flicker of heat stirs in me, choosing the exact wrong time to make me start thinking about everything our soulbond implies.

"You can't rely on me to save you," he says suddenly, voice rough.

My face twists into a grimace—part confusion, part rage. "I can't rely on you for anything, clearly," I snarl. "I wish it was Tobias guarding me, because at least he'd give me a fighting chance before he stabbed me in the back."

Logan's eyes narrow before landing on something over my shoulder.

"Come on," he growls.

Then, suddenly, there's an arm around my waist and I'm flying through the air.

I yelp, startled and on edge. A lick of flame tears up the wall, but it vanishes in a shocked puff when all sound is drowned out by the roar of an engine.

Logan drops me on the back of the bike, slides on, and pulls the throttle.

"Hold on."

I have just enough time to do that, and then we're racing back through the way we came, past the flickering shadows with the red eyes and up the street.

18

HELENA

As we skim past the shadows, I see them for what they are. The sun slides in at the right angle, glinting off reddened skin and horns.

They're Summoning Demons, but I don't know any more than that.

Downtown fades around us in a vicious blur. I dig my fingers into Logan's waist, hugging myself to the solid press of his back. He's warm, and large enough to hide behind, not that he'd let me.

You can't rely on me to save you.

I might have the emotional resonance of a fish, but even I can read between the lines on that one. So the question is: who couldn't you save?

We tear through Hell, only stopping when downtown is far behind us. We're on the outskirts of the palace gardens, but Logan doesn't take us all the way. He stops outside a sweeping mansion. As soon as I'm on my feet, he rolls the bike into a ditch decorated with vines.

They twist and writhe with interest, consuming the bike in seconds.

"What did you do that for?" I ask dumbly, staring at the place the bike disappeared.

It's still like four miles to the palace.

"Don't know if they're using us to get inside," he says, shrugging. "Want to give it twenty minutes for any tracking or hitchhiking spells to fade." He checks his watch. "But then we're out of here, okay?"

He's nervous; there must be a time limit for this bond loophole. I file the thought away for future.

"So, what do we do in the meantime?"

To my surprise, Logan grins and turns to the mansion. "You wanted to go shopping? Let me show you something better."

Frowning, I follow as he leads me up the drive. We keep to the edge of the path, but it soon becomes clear no one is home.

Apparently, Logan can pick empty homes.

"What are we doing?" I ask quietly as Logan breaks the lock with a twist of his hand and slides open the back door.

"All the fun, and none of the problems," he answers, which tells me absolutely nothing.

The hallways are dead silent. I'm surprised at how tastefully it's decorated, but then, I probably shouldn't be. There's no reason demons can't also be pretentious twats.

I pause at a painting I faintly recognize. A woman with a monobrow stares intently at me from a jungle of green. No doubt it's an original.

I sigh, unconsciously leaning into the painting. There's something to be said for being a pretentious twat. Always has been. Why else did I spend so many years conning them out of their bum change?

Turning away, I find Logan watching me knowingly.

"This way," he says and leads me down the hallway.

I creep silently, holding my breath as I focus on each footfall and listen out for unexpected noises.

There's a strange familiarity to this that has nothing to do with conning Vegas businessmen. Each footstep feels personal, somehow. The hair on the back of my neck lifts, and my heart races.

Mustn't get caught.

Mustn't wake them up.

I shake my head, frowning as the thoughts come out of nowhere. What the hell was that about? No one's asleep here, and no one's waking up pissed. All these car chases have fried my brain.

Logan glances over his shoulder at me, a strange look on his face as he sniffs the air. His eyes glint, and for a moment he seems to see right through me. But he looks away, and the moment passes.

He opens a door at the end of the hallway, and I step through after him into the master bedroom.

"Whoa," I breathe, spinning in a slow circle and forgetting my little brain blip. "So much for minimalism."

The dark green walls are covered in artwork, like the hallways, but this time it's more personal. Portraits of the same couple surround me, over and over. Two women, side by side.

Often naked.

I stare, transfixed, at the sensuously painted bodies, wrapped around each other in opulent passion.

Logan gapes. "Shit, man. Talk about a power couple."

Literally, I think. I'm fairly certain one is a demon and the other her witch, gauging by the deep black eyes and sharp fangs that are present in only one of the women, and only in half the paintings.

"Please tell me we aren't robbing them," I say faintly, unable to look away.

Did those eyes just move?

Logan laughs, the sound coming from nearer than I expect. The soft jingle of jewelry has me turning, and I wince as he holds out a necklace full of diamonds from the bureau.

"Hell no," I breathe. "Do you have a death wish, mate?"

"We're only borrowing," he says soothingly, moving behind me. "All the fun, and none of the problems."

I don't stop him, even though my heart races as the cold stone settles against my collar. He fastens the clasp and lifts my hair free. Somehow, in the motion, he undoes it, and long brown waves fall over my shoulders.

The diamonds sparkle in the mirror of the bureau.

"What the hell are we doing?" I breathe, but I can't look away from the shine.

I've never owned anything like this, but God I've wanted to.

Logan must have seen the way I looked at the jewelry in the market, even though it was all cheap stuff.

"This way, it can't be stolen," he says, his voice oddly mesmerizing. "Can't be taken. Can't be ruined." He sweeps the hair free from one side of my neck. His breath caresses my skin. "But you still get all the fun of wearing it."

"It doesn't last though," I murmur, transfixed as I watch him in the mirror. He seems to be holding back, eyes closed, barely an inch of space between us. "We can't keep it."

He laughs. "We can't keep anything. Not truly. Nothing lasts."

My breath hitches. "Why are you so afraid of this soul-bond?" I ask, already knowing the answer.

Logan's eyes open. "Because soulbonds are forever," he says simply.

He's so afraid to lose something, he won't even try to keep

it. To hold on to it. The idea of having it and losing it is worse than never having it at all.

My breath catches, but before I can speak, he kisses me.

His fingers thread through my hair, tugging gently as he pulls me to him. Heat ripples through me, making my knees weak—but he holds me upright, his hands almost desperate. And through it all, the cold, heavy weight of the most beautiful necklace I've ever seen rests against my skin.

Logan walks me backward until my legs bump the bureau, bringing us to a halt. His lips curve wickedly against mine as he lifts my thighs and brings me to a seat.

Bizarrely, the bureau barely rattles. He's unusually good at leaving no trace, even among the dozens of perfume bottles.

He lifts my hand—still kissing me, pressing me back against the mirror—and slides something cold onto my finger.

I look down and begin to laugh. It's a matching ring.

Logan grins at me and holds up a bracelet.

"Aren't you meant to be taking those things off me?" I ask, tipping my head back to raise an eyebrow at him.

"Nah," he says easily, fastening the bracelet without looking away. "It's everything else I'm going to take off."

Desire pulses through me, and his eyes darken as he very slowly and deliberately presses between my thighs. I feel him plainly, hard and straining.

He pulls back a little, and then thrusts slowly in again.

Holding his gaze, I pull off my shirt and drop it on the floor.

Logan stutters, his hands gripping my hips painfully as he stares down at my bare chest.

"No bra," he says in a voice I barely recognize.

"I'm small enough," I say, arching my back.

He lowers his mouth immediately to my breast, moaning as he sucks lightly on my nipple. "The perfect size," he says with a grin.

My mouth falls open as he thrusts against me once more, but before he can undo his fly, a noise interrupts him.

It's a door, softly closing at the other end of the house.

"Time's up," Logan says ruefully, but his eyes gleam with fire. He's more alive than I've ever seen him.

I don't want to lose this.

I hook my finger into his shirt and tug him back between my thighs. "Or the timer has just started," I say quietly. His breath catches on a low moan. I lean in to whisper in his ear. "How long do you think we have before they find us? How quickly can you make me come?"

A growl rumbles in his chest, and when he pulls back to face me, his eyes are glowing shifter gold. More than that—there's something else golden.

His claws are out.

This time, I'm the one who loses their breath. I'd forgotten he was so close to the rut.

If I'm honest, I hadn't fully grasped the meaning of him being an alpha.

An alpha shifter's golden claws exist no matter their vitality, marking their position on the shifter hierarchy without any doubt. That way, even non-shifters, who lack the superior sense of smell to be able to navigate this fraught world, know what they're facing.

Logan's eyes glint in the dark room, and this time when he kisses me, it doesn't feel like a game.

It's hard and possessive. Nothing about this man is recognizable, and a flicker of fear makes my desire burn stronger.

He fumbles with his fly, shoving his jeans away easily and sliding my pants over my ass before I've even caught up. He presses against me, slick and hard, but his eyes burn with a question. He pauses, thumb tracing over my clit with slow deliberate movements as he watches me.

"Are you sure you want me to be the first?" he asks in a low voice.

I scoff, stunned. "I'm not a virgin."

His eyes glint, and his smile widens. "I didn't mean that. I meant out of the three of us. Are you sure you want me to fuck you first?"

First. He says it like it's inevitable that I'll be with them all. Like he wants that.

But more importantly—this question matters to him. The realization sucks the air out of me, and I gape at him.

I think of them all—my jailer, my guard, and an ancient demon who's convinced that we're doomed but wants me anyway.

If we are inevitable, which one of them do I want to give into first?

Then I remember the man who brought me books, who watched me set them up with calm, deliberate interest. Who revealed his own love for escaping into those stories, surprising as it may have been.

And now, his own fear of having anything he might lose.

"Yes," I tell him, tugging him back into a fierce, desperate kiss. "I want you to be the first one to touch me."

His growl has a hint of animal in it as he drops his hands to my hips and sheathes his cock in me. I bite down on his shoulder to keep from howling, but he doesn't wait for me to adjust. He slides back, sending shivers racing through me as my body locks around him, and slams in again.

Then, with a wicked grin, he begins pounding into me. I let my head fall back, surrendering to his relentless rhythm.

Already, we can hear the noises in the house getting closer. Soft voices and laughter.

"I'm gonna do far more than touch you," he murmurs, and I get the impression he's claiming me.

Leaning back, his gaze locks on my breasts, his eyes flashing as he watches them bounce. The diamonds shimmer on top, catching the light and throwing it over our faces.

"You look good in diamonds," he murmurs.

His thumb finds my clit again, circling over me. A feral grin crosses his face; I've never seen him like this. This sharp edge of anger. Of danger. The hair around his temples is slick with sweat, and his black Henley is damp to touch. He's burning hot, the rut coming in close, and it suddenly hits me how batshit this is—he's going to knot me.

We're going to be caught in the home of two powerful women, and we're going to be found with his knot inside me.

We're so dead.

My head drops back as a rush of heat and fear washes through me. It's crazy, but the knowledge of how close we are to danger makes me feel alive again. Like maybe I'm not a ghost after all.

Like maybe Ronin didn't kill me, because how can I be afraid of dying if I'm already dead?

Logan's rhythm begins to stutter. The voices are closer now; I can make out the words.

"Where did you last see it?"

"By the sink in the ensuite!"

Oh God; they're coming this way.

Logan falls against my body, his teeth biting into my breast as he fucks into me with shaky, rough movements. His thumb speeds faster, and I can't think, can't breathe as my climax hits me.

I clutch him to me, shuddering as wave after wave of pleasure courses through me.

His cock swells, and I think—this is it. We're busted. But, God, he feels so good. I can't move, can't do anything while my body pulses over his hard knot, the pressure building and building as my orgasm finally crests and begins to fade.

"Oh oh," he breathes into my ear, shaky and amused.

Loving it.

The door handle rattles, turning, just as Logan picks me up beneath my thighs, spins us around, and backs up two steps into the closet.

The bedroom door opens just as the closet shuts, and the voices carry inside. Meanwhile, I cling to Logan's shoulders, my heart pounding in my chest. My back rests against the wall while my legs wrap tightly around his waist.

Logan's breath is unsteady in my ear, his own heart racing against mine.

My shirt is still out there on the floor. I'm wearing this woman's diamonds, for fuck's sake.

And Logan's cock is trapped inside me.

He lowers his head so our cheeks are pressed together and whispers into my ear.

"Are you okay?"

"Peachy," I breathe back.

He huffs a laugh. "So you don't care if I do this?"

He tilts his hips, rocking his knot inside me. An explosion of pleasure hits me, and my head tips back against the wall with a thunk.

The voices outside pause, but then resume. Whatever they're looking for, they can't find it.

And my shifter soulmate is playing on the edge of the rut, so he doesn't care. He just wants me.

"Oh," he says in a faux surprised voice. "You *do* care." He does it again, harder this time, and my body begins to respond. "You want me to do it."

"Logan," I warn him in a hiss. "You're going to get us caught."

"Only if you scream," he says casually, rocking faster now. "Reckon I can make you scream?"

At this rate? I'll fucking howl.

I bite down on my lip, dropping my forehead to his shoulder and clutching at him. I can't move, can't do anything except sit here and take it as he rocks inside me.

And that's when I see it: a bright red jewel glimmering at Logan's waist.

My world shifts sideways. So *that's* how Lucifer has stretched the bond. I don't know the specifics of the magic, but I know there's no way Logan would be holding the Grave for any other reason.

Well, it hardly helps me right now. There's no way I'm stealing that without things going seriously wrong. Even I know my limits.

Logan's breathing quickens, turning rougher. "Scream, Helena. Get us caught." His voice is louder than before.

Fucking hell.

He's losing his common sense; the rut is too close.

What's my excuse?

I lean back and clamp my hand over his mouth. His eyes flash with heat, but he mercifully stops talking.

He doesn't stop moving though.

As the voices outside move closer, calling out something about checking under the bed, he begins fucking me just like he had outside. My body soars, humming with pleasure as his knot presses at all the right angles. My eyes fall close, and I focus on keeping my hand on my idiot soulmate's mouth, and trying not to scream.

The voice outside is triumphant. "Got it! Let's go, before I lose you to another torture shift again."

A torture shift.

These women are torturers. They'll have what I need.

The voice fades, the front door slams, and I drop my hand from Logan's mouth. He kisses me instantly, growling as his cock begins to pulse, coming again.

"Fucking scream, Helena."

I scream.

19
LOGAN

I stride through the Devil's palace, winding my way up the staircases and hidden little passageways to Lucifer's penthouse. Very few people are given the privilege of meeting the big guy here, but I'm one of the lucky few.

That luck has me feeling some kind of way, these days. But right now, it's the anchor to stability that I need. I need a job.

And there's only one man who can give me one.

I knock on the door to his suite. His penthouse. It looks plain out of place now, with the ancient ruins resurrected and lit up like a medieval castle. Tapestries and glowing orange wall sconces sit right next to this—an elevator.

I shift uncomfortably in the tiny little foyer that sits just outside the golden elevator doors. Lucifer keeps a potted plant out here: a sharp, spiky cactus of a thing that's especially good at giving people hay fever, even if they never get it. It's one of his nasty little jokes.

I sneeze into my sleeve, wipe my nose and glare at the cactus. As if it knows what it's doing to me, a neat little white flower blooms on the side of it.

Bastard of a thing.

And he's a bastard of a man.

Which is exactly what I need right now. I need to forget the feeling of Helena under my skin. In my hands. I need to forget about the sounds she made, the sweet little noises as she tried to stay silent.

Because if I keep thinking about this, I'll go mad.

It isn't just the memory of her desire, either. It's how I reacted to her—not to her desire but to her fear.

Something in that house had her afraid, and she couldn't even fucking say it out loud. She barely even knew it, but I could smell it on her. I could hear the stuttering breath, the racing of her heart—how she was seconds from bolting like a rabbit caught in headlights.

Why else did I kiss her like that? Even before the rut kicked in, I still took her too fast and hard. We had Hell's damn rebellion nipping at our heels, and no time to play. But I had to distract her, didn't I? Had to rip her mind away from wherever it had gone.

I wanted to protect her. To chase away the things that haunted her. And I've never wanted that. It's dangerous to want that.

Man, though... the sight of her. Shirtless. Breasts pressed upward into the light.

And that shining, shining necklace glinting above them.

That's dangerous in a different way, because I'd do it all again just for a glimpse.

The door swings open, and Lucifer leans against the architrave, one hand sliding sensuously up the wood.

I don't think even means to. I think this man just oozes sexuality.

It's never bothered me before. It's just been a perk of the job. But now that there's that little blue cord driving from my chest to his, right beside the one linking me to Helena and the one for Tobias, it sparks a different sort of question.

And it occurs to me that maybe I'm in the wrong place for the distraction I'm after.

Lucifer's eyes glint. I think he might know what I'm thinking. I think he might feel enough little tweaks of it down the bond that he can guess and fill in the gaps.

"Come in, Logan," he says, his voice just a little deeper and rougher than normal.

I adjust myself in my jeans and follow him through, shutting the door behind me.

"I need a job," I say, not waiting for small talk. "I'm going stir crazy here. What have you got for me?"

Lucifer raises an eyebrow and sits down on the designer chair in the corner.

I follow his lead, dropping into the one opposite. Two crystal tumblers of an amber liquid rest on the coffee table between us. I take it he peeked through the peephole when he was making me wait out there.

"You need a job," Lucifer parrots, eyeing me up and down. "And yet you can't go more than a block from the palace without the Grave."

"You gave it to me yesterday," I point out.

The wry grin curves onto his lips. "When you were taking care of a task for me."

The pause turns expectant; he's waiting for me to ask why he wanted to give Helena the freedom she asked for. Why it wasn't simply a man giving into a repeated request.

And he knows I won't ask.

The corner of his mouth deepens as the silence stretches— he's satisfied. He knows that he's talking to the one person who won't press for answers, even though Tobias and Helena seem hell bent on finding them.

"Say no if you don't want to," I tell him with a shrug. "But since it's coated in spells that return it to the palm of your hand after an hour, I don't see the danger."

Lucifer relaxes back into the chair, picks up his glass, and takes a long sip. I follow his lead once more.

He watches as he always does, taking in every movement, every subtle decision behind my actions.

I think I've always fascinated him. An alpha who refuses to lead.

But he's never said anything, never questioned it.

So I suppose that makes two of us. That's why we're such good company.

"You're correct; there is no danger," he tells me, voice lilting. "I'm merely adjusting some theories." He taps his fingers on the glass. "So you say there were no power explosions while you were out?"

"None at all."

"And the Grave returned on the hour, as predicted?" He pauses. "Without any interference from the Joker?"

"Nope." I take another swig and refill with the bottle resting beside our chairs.

Anyone else would have their ears pricking up, taking notes, because he's clearly revealing some sort of inner workings here. But I really don't give a shit.

Lucifer gives a soft laugh, dangling his arm over his chair with the glass clasped loosely in his fingers. He uncrosses his legs and folds them the other way, in the process giving me an eyeful of the not insignificant bulge at the front of his trousers.

I don't think he's hard or anything. It's just how he is.

I wet my lips and take another sip, slower this time.

"Then I see no issue," he says, lips forming with a sense of amusement around the words. "If you really do need a job."

"I really do," I tell him. "Or I'm gonna lose it and inflict a little torture of my own."

Lucifer laughs properly this time. "That's not like you, Logan," he says, so sure, so certain that it sends a shiver of heat through me. "You wouldn't inflict that on anyone else. Trust me, I know the type."

I make a noncommittal noise, taking another sip. "Yeah, but I wasn't talking about anyone else."

Lucifer's expression turns oddly sober. "Ah," he says "Now that I do believe you would do."

He sets his tumbler on the table and leans forward, elbows propped on his knees. His typically half-buttoned shirt gapes over his expansive, smooth chest.

"I can't give you any job of significance," he says carefully. "It will be shit kicker work, nothing more."

So, it seems I'm no longer in the Devil's confidence. But from the way he's talking, it sounds like nobody is.

"That's fine," I tell him. "I just need something."

"Well," he says slowly. "It is difficult to be in two places at once at the moment, and the ah... the Rising Snakes"—he pulls a face at the phrase—"have apparently set up a stronghold in the lower east side of the lake district. I haven't been able to work out where yet though. Think you can rough a few people up for me and get some answers?"

I grin at him, and I see the glint of yellow flicker across his face as my eyes flash shifter gold. "I reckon I could do that."

He studies me for a minute, and in the silence and the relief of knowing that I'll be out of here soon, if only for a few hours, I look at him properly for the first time. I frown.

"Your hands are shaking," I say.

Lucifer looks down, surprised, and there's a flash of something like betrayal across his face.

Of course there is; I've broken our unwritten rule. I've

acknowledged that something lives below the surface. Secrets. Problems.

"So they are," he says, a hint of warning in his voice.

I let it slide, but an unfamiliar sensation settles low in my gut at the thought.

I've never seen the Devil show weakness. I don't know what this weakness might mean, for any of us, and for the first time there's a question on my lips.

I want to ask him what's wrong.

I know it isn't welcome, but the feeling bubbles inside me, rising, compelling me. I bite my tongue to keep it inside, where it belongs.

Draining my glass, I set it on the table and rise to my feet.

"I'll get you your answers, boss," I tell him.

Relaxing once more, he tips his head back against the chair and looks up at me through half-lidded eyes. Again, he doesn't mean to, but the expression and the position send a jolt of heat through me, making my dick harden instantly.

"I know you will," he says in a low, seductive voice.

After a beat, he reaches behind him, plucks something free, and tosses it to me.

I catch it one handed, taking a second to study the glittering facets of the red jewel. A flicker of something appears in my chest; Lucifer trusts me with this.

He doesn't trust anyone with it, not since Ronin stole it and warped it.

He swore never to part with it again.

But it's covered in a thousand spells that would mutilate and destroy me for even thinking about stealing it. Not to mention that it's locked to him in some way, and it returns to his hilt after an hour.

So it can't mean that much, after all.

I make for the door, but just before I reach it, he stops me with a word.

"Logan," he says.

I shiver. He doesn't say my name very often, and certainly not like that.

"Yeah?" I ask, half turning but not enough so that I can see him.

"What did you do with Helena yesterday?"

I stiffen, knowing instantly that this is payback. Payback for the question I didn't ask but left hovering in the room between us.

He knows that's why I'm running, and here he is, digging the knife in just a little. For once, I decide to do exactly the same.

Without even thinking about it, I smile, seeing the glint of yellow on the wall before me, and say, "I fucked her."

There's silence.

Assuming the conversation to be over, I keep walking. It's only as I'm through the door, just before it shuts behind me, that Lucifer says, "I bet you looked good together."

I stop just as the door slams, a shiver racing through my whole body.

I bet we did, too. I bet we'd look even better with Lucifer there.

I've been wondering why the hell all four of us have been bonded together—why it isn't just two of us. I've always known I was greedy, but I didn't think Helena was. And Lucifer and Tobias seem like they'd rather tear someone limb from limb than share their toys.

But it's beginning to make more sense now.

All four of us crave that deeper itch. I can feel it; we couldn't possibly be satisfied with one person.

And all four of us like to scratch.

It isn't a sensible answer, but it's the one that calls to me. It leaves me with visions of Lucifer and Helena in that couple's bedroom.

Maybe I could persuade him to wear some diamonds, too. Trailing down that beautiful chest while I was on my knees in front of him, sucking that gorgeous—

I break off the thought. I'm meant to be having a rest from this madness, not giving into it.

"Fucking Lucifer."

I mutter it quietly, but I swear I hear a soft chuckle behind the door as I escape into the elevator and go to deliver the Devil's message.

I tear through the streets of Hell, winding my way past the usual bars and dives that I gather information from, and further, to the rough side of town.

I barely know what kind of beasties live here. I only know I don't want to fuck with them.

A sentiment that is enforced the second I walk through the door and roughly ten sets of eyes fix on me and blaze with white-hot power.

Well. I had planned to do this my usual way... Buy a few rounds, dig a little deeper with each new drink.

But sometimes it's better to just go for the throat.

I let the lazy, arrogant grin spread across my face, and even as a distant part of me arcs up, agitated, begging my shifter soul to stay hidden...

Another part of me—a stronger part of me—loves this. Loves what I'm about to do.

"So," I say lazily. "Which one of you ugly bastards can tell me where the *Rising Snakes*'"—I make sure to twist the words like a grimace in my mouth—"stronghold is?" I pause for emphasis, and then I bark. "*Well?*"

Several demons snap to attention, responding automatically to an alpha's bark.

The rest rise up in fury, and it's on. No bouncer's gonna throw me out this time. No one gives a flying fuck what we do here, and it's exhilarating.

I give as good as I get, taking down demons around me, and even though I end up on my back a few times, pinned beneath the weight of an impossibly sized monster, it's clear who's coming out on top.

It's clear who's the alpha.

It's a fucking terrifying thought, and I don't know what's come over me.

That's not true. I know exactly what's come over me, and her name is Helena.

She has beautiful, deep brown eyes that make me think of Creedence Clearwater. And she makes the most exquisite sounds when you take her apart.

She's my soulmate, my lover, and it's my duty to protect her.

A duty I swore I would never fall hostage to again.

It seems Fate had other plans.

I flip the nearest demon over with my thighs and catch him in a stronghold, my arm twisting around his neck.

"This will all be over, buddy," I tell him, "If you just tell me what I want to know."

"River's Mouth," he chokes out. "Near River's Mouth, that's all I know. Please."

I let him go, and the force of his desperate attempts to escape mean he thumps his head straight down on the floor and passes out.

Oops.

I stand up, dusting my hands off, and punch an approaching demon right in the face.

"I'm off then, lads," I say, and I escape back to my bike before they can catch me.

My heart feels somewhat lighter with the exhilaration of the fight still thrumming in my veins.

Even if perhaps I have no answers for myself, yet, I have the ones I came looking for. And that will do for now.

20

HELENA

T‍HEY DON'T MAKE THESE GUARD UNIFORMS LIKE THEY USED TO, clearly. I've already torn a seam.

Gritting my teeth, I glare down at the gaping hole above my knee. It used to be so easy on Earth. I'd have a costume change down in under thirty seconds, and a new personality on show in forty.

Now, I just keep hitting problem after problem. And their name is Tobias or Lucifer.

Even with my thorough reading up on how to fake a guard uniform, and the fact that I used to freaking wear these for Ronin, it's still all going to shit.

I smooth down the fabric as best I can and edge further behind the decorative suit of armor. Rule number one of a successful con: act like you belong.

Unless a mind-reading trickster god shows up. Then, you hide.

"How much longer are you going to be, you trumped up relic of a bygone era?" I mutter to myself.

"Until it stops being funny, I guess," Tobias answers from down the hallway. He doesn't bother to look up from his book.

Dammit.

He's known I was here all along. I've been waiting behind this armor for ten bloody minutes!

I shuffle out from behind my cover. "You mean I ripped those stupid leggings for nothing?"

Tobias smiles. "See? Hilarious."

"You're into some really sick shit, you know that?"

He uncurls from the wall, still laughing, and prowls toward me. "Says the woman who's currently masquerading as her own torture device."

I shiver, sickened by the memories of what Ronin made me do in this outfit. "Screw you," I hiss.

Tobias comes to a halt before me. Like always, his expression flickers with amusement, like nothing really matters enough to be serious. But there's an edge to it; his eyes burn.

"I thought we had a deal," he says, studying the rings on his hand like they're brand new.

"I said I'd tell you the truth. Not that I'd let you keep tabs on every time I eat or shit," I snap, enjoying how he flinches at the crude jab.

"And yet, you aren't telling the truth," he insists, tugging lightly on my collar in a semi affectionate touch. His palm lingers a moment before he lets it fall. "What's with the disguise?"

"Sneaking out of the palace without Logan."

Tobias' eyes glint—amused, but still with that unexpected sharpness. "And how were you going to handle the pain of the proximity bond?"

"Grin and bear it," I snarl. "Hadn't quite got that far. But you know what they say—bungee me once, shame on you..."

He laughs softly. "And where are you going?"

"Stealing records from a torturer's house."

"How did you find the house?"

It's like a bloody tennis match, back and forth.

"Logan led us there three days ago."

Tobias' eyes darken, his expression abruptly stormy. It's the first time I've seen him without any amusement at all, even when he threw us onto the Eiffel tower and then plummeted over the side.

"And what did you do in that house?" he asks, each word carefully placed between us.

Oh.

I blink at him. He knows what I did with Logan. Of course he knows. My thoughts might be hidden, but Logan's aren't.

Logan's been thinking about it.

My cheeks begin to heat, and Tobias' lips curl in triumph.

"There it is," he says, lip twitching in amusement once more.

But I know him now. I know the laughter is a cover—it always is, with these types. So, he isn't amused. He's upset.

Which is, you know, absolute bullshit.

"I don't actually owe you a blow by blow of every little thing I do," I snap, ignoring the heat in my cheeks. "It isn't lying to keep my private life private."

"But is it private when we're all bound together as one?" Tobias asks thoughtfully.

Noise echoes down the corridor. The guard shift is changing, and I'm losing my chance to leave. My chest tightens, fists clenching as I glare into Tobias' arrogant, godlike bloody face.

He's a god, isn't he? That's what Logan called him. I'm arguing with a bloody *god*.

And I'm not about to stop.

"Ah, yeah," I throw at him. "I'm still entitled to closed doors, no matter how much of a dick you want to be about it."

"Just fucking kiss already," a new voice interrupts.

We startle in unison, looking over to find Logan leaning against a wall, eating an apple and looking like he's having the time of his life watching us.

For once, Tobias is lost for words. He runs his thumb over the rings on his fingers, watching Logan silently.

"I couldn't find you," he says abruptly.

I blink at him, confused by the sudden turn. "What?"

Tobias reaches out, adjusting my collar once more. Only, this time, it's clearly an affectionate move; there's no sarcasm in sight. It's almost thoughtless, like a man adjusts their lover's clothing before they leave. My heart stutters unexpectedly, and I fight to keep it from showing on my face.

"I couldn't find you after the forest," he says in a low voice. "I wanted to make sure you weren't... burnt."

Oh.

He's still reeling from my alleged altercation with God.

Too slow, I realize that something has shifted with Tobias. I should have noticed—should have been prepared for this. But I've had so many things to track, I missed it, and now I'm racing to catch up.

"I wasn't," I say, a touch breathless.

His eyes flick to mine as he smooths the seam over my arm. "But you could have been."

There's a small furrow in his brow. I think I'm catching up.

I'm no longer a threat to him, but he doesn't have answers for what I am, and Tobias is a man who hates not having the answers.

It's making him possessive.

Abruptly, he straightens.

"Enough of this," he says, lifting his chin. "We've more important things on our hands."

My eyebrows shoot up. "Excuse me? I already had plans, and you're not invited."

"Am I invited?" Logan asks with a grin.

"No," I snap, flushing. "You'll just distract me."

Tobias' eyes darken again. This is all going to Hell in a hand basket.

Although... my mind begins to whirr. Tobias is acting like a jealous teenager, whether he realizes it or not. Which means that right now, he's susceptible to getting caught in stupid arguments and losing sight of his goal.

That's pretty rare for him, from what I've seen. I'd be a fool not to take advantage.

"You realize," Tobias says stiffly, "that you can't pickpocket Lucifer's keys if you're never in the same damn room as him?"

I shake my head, jabbing him in the sternum with my finger. "That's your plan. This is mine, and I don't need the keys."

"My plan is better," he insists, eyes fierce.

I barely hold back a grin, already sidling past him. "Nope. You had last go. Now it's my turn. That's the rules of the Game, yeah? I get a chance to win without you."

Logan steps forward, shoving his apple core beneath the suit of armor's visor. "I've got a question," he says in a low voice. "Why are you tracking down torturer's records, and who are you trying to find?"

Tobias' lip curls, and the bastard practically purrs. "Yes, Helena," he says. "Who are you trying to find?"

The asshole thinks I'm going to lie. I look him in the eye and say, "I'm rescuing my parents."

His gaze flickers, but I can't read it.

Logan gives a low whistle. "Your folks are in Hell? Shit."

His voice sounds strange. Like pity. I hate it. He doesn't know anything about us. Before I can speak, he continues.

"Why are you breaking them out?"

That stops me. I stare at him, dumbfounded. "Why am I breaking my *parents* out of *Hell*?"

I mean, isn't it obvious? All ghosts have unfinished business tying them to the realms they're meant to leave. Logan already knows I think of myself as a ghost, despite his reassurances.

What could my unfinished business be but this?

"Yes," Tobias agrees, snapping his fingers. "Especially when the core tenet of your predicament is the fact that you're still systematically decimating Hell piece by piece. Stalking Lucifer would give us key insights to what he knows about your power, bringing you one step closer to ultimate freedom. So, why are you searching for your parents *now* instead of cracking Lucifer like a nut?"

Logan frowns, looking between the two of us sharply. "That's not what I meant, you psychopath. I meant why are you breaking them out if they're bad enough to be down here?"

I gape at him, distantly aware that something curious is twisting onto Tobias' face.

Someone reaches for me, a distracted movement, and I pull away without thinking. Logan. It was Logan. I shake my head, blinking back into focus in time to see them both studying me with matching, unreadable expressions.

Cold presses into my back; I've shoved myself back into the corner.

"How dare you say my parents are bad people!" The phrase rings in my ears. Bad people. Bad. People. "Of course I'm going to bust them out of here."

Logan lifts his hands in defense, but his eyes still study me, watching how I'm crowded into the corner.

Maybe if they backed off, I wouldn't be in the corner!

"They're in Hell, Helena. The question had to be asked," he says in a soothing voice.

He and Tobias share a look. Once more, I can't read it. Why can't I read it? I can read anyone, dammit.

Tobias clears his throat. "Technically, we're all sinners," he says with a grin, his voice much lighter. "Coming down to Hell simply means you never repented and chose the Lord as your light and Savior."

I snort, irritated beyond words. "Oh yeah? Well there should be a place for me then, considering how many damn people I stole from and how little I gave a shit about any of this religious crap."

Another strange look crosses Tobias' face, but I don't have time for this. I don't have time for any of it.

"My parents are down here because the system sucks, and I'm getting them out. End of story. I don't even know why you're sticking around, Tobias. Surely you've got some loophole you can work to run away from us."

The fake smile on Tobias' face snaps, and his upper lip pulls back in a snarl. For a moment, I see a glimpse of the demon he is below the god.

"Trust me, pet, it would be far easier to let you all rot in your own mess and go back to my world." His smile turns bitter for a moment. "We're doomed, remember?" He closes his eyes for a second, and when he opens them again, they're sharp. "But I'd like to see any of you break this bond and last a single day on your own. We can't. Not until it's ready to let us go."

Vaguely, I notice he said it would be easier—not that he wants to.

Doomed or not, I fascinate him.

This time, Logan succeeds in distracting us, but instead of speaking, he gives an exaggerated yawn, covering his mouth.

"What do you want?" Tobias snaps.

Then, oddly, he flinches. It takes me a second to realize Logan must be thinking something quite heavily.

And another to realize what he must be thinking.

"I want to see you admit why you're really staying," Logan says, an unmistakable challenge in his voice. "Instead of hiding behind all of us, like a coward."

The air shifts. Something he's said has cut through Tobias' attitude, tearing it to shreds.

"Like a coward," Tobias echoes, and all trace of anger vanishes in place of this eerie, arrogant, drawl.

His eyes cut to mine, and I note how dark they've become, the pupil obscuring the light brown of the iris. A darkness that I thought was shadow... isn't.

It's desire.

He reaches for me, and I half expect the kiss to be brutal. Urgent and needy, like it was with Logan, because that's what he's competing against, isn't it?

But even if it is, it's not how he's chosen to compete. This is Tobias—trickster god, powerful demon, and oldest friend to the fucking Devil.

He cradles the back of my neck, and the kiss he presses to my lips is so soft, I'm barely certain it's there. My hands come to rest against his chest.

After a few dazed seconds, I decide to give as good as I get. I wasn't a Vegas show girl for nothing.

I lean my hips into his, deepening the kiss and parting my lips to allow him entrance. His breath stutters, and the hand on my neck grows possessive.

"That's more like it," Logan says from somewhere beside us.

His voice sounds thick, raspy.

He's getting turned on by watching us, and the realization sends shivers racing through me. A hungry sound pulls from deep in Tobias' chest.

"You don't scare me, Helena," he whispers against my

mouth. "You couldn't, not even if you were God's weapon. Not even if you're something worse."

"What about if all I am is your soulmate?" I breathe.

I realize, abruptly, that what I've been witnessing up until now is Tobias in perfect control.

I realize that because now the control snaps.

He groans, an untethered, agonized sound that's only half desire, and crushes me against the wall. The suit of armor goes toppling over, landing in pieces with a crash.

He doesn't notice. His hands fall to the stupid ties on my stolen uniform, and he undoes them in rough, economic movements.

Okay, so I'm under no delusions that what's about to happen will be as sensual as his first kiss.

And I don't care.

I spread my legs as he slides his fingers down the front of my pants, not wasting time with foreplay.

His kiss doesn't end this time. His fingers find my core, flicking over me, tracing the slick folds until he finds a rhythm that makes me gasp into his open mouth.

Finally, he draws back, staring down at me with dark eyes as I slowly lose the ability to think.

"You're definitely more than that," he says quietly, but the tone doesn't fit the original question, the accusation. He's saying something else, and I've no idea what it could be— what's possibly *more* than a soulmate, and more important than God's weapon?

What would turn an ancient trickster demon into a coward?

He slides his fingers inside me, thumb circling my clit, and I begin to crest. My head tips back, whimpers dropping from my lips. A hand covers my mouth—Logan—and I look up into two sets of hungry eyes.

Noise comes from down the corridor, making me startle,

but Tobias keeps stroking, dragging my final moans free as I shudder beneath his touch.

I grab at my clothing, straightening it just in time.

Two demons round the corner, glancing curiously at the fallen armor. But there's nothing odd about a guard and two of Lucifer's men, so they keep walking, clueless.

Tobias tucks a strand of my hair behind my ear when they're gone, eyes still glinting, while Logan leans in to press a slow, lingering kiss to my jaw. "When Lucifer relinquishes the hold he has on your power, you will find your parents in a heartbeat," he says softly. "It's Lucifer who is the priority. Lucifer and his secrets."

He's right.

His plan is better, goddammit.

But I need to do this on my own, without his help.

However, before I can argue, Logan reaches out and plucks something from my shoulder with a sharp rip.

Startling, I turn to look. It's the uniform's insignia.

He's damaged my disguise.

People will take a second look at me now, and that's all I need to be caught.

I gape at him, taking in the sheepish smile. "Sorry, Hel," he says lightly. "Devil's orders. Don't want anything blowing up out there."

He—

I can't believe he—

I turn to Tobias, who looks unfairly smug.

"You're meant to be helping me," I snap.

He shrugs. "I told you, I'm a man of my word. You're not allowed outside the castle walls."

Then, with nothing but a wink, Tobias leaves, with Logan trailing casually behind him.

Those bastards. I knew this, knew they would choose Lucifer over me, but those *bastards*.

I'm just about to sag against the wall when movement catches my eye. A shimmer, opposite our alcove.

A veiling spell drops, and I see him. Lucifer. Piercing blue eyes fix to mine, dark with desire.

For a while, we simply stare at each other, neither of us speaking or moving.

I wet my lips; Lucifer watches the motion.

"Could've knocked," I say, my voice raspy.

"On the armor?" he throws back immediately, his own voice just as low. He gestures elegantly to the wide open corridor, without looking away from me. "Or perhaps the floor?"

"Maybe on your own head," I snap, heart racing. "It'd be hollow enough."

What the hell is wrong with me? I don't just say shit like this. Think it, yes. But I never say it.

Lucifer's eyes flash golden, like Logan's. But he's nothing like Logan. This power is demonic, and something in me hums in recognition.

"Sleeping with your guards," he says quietly. "How very complicated."

"It doesn't have to be," I tell him, Logan's words echoing in my ears. "Call them off. Remove the bond."

"Soulbonds are forever," he answers, deliberately misunderstanding which part of the bond I mean.

And he takes a step toward me.

My stomach jolts. This isn't forever; this is just fun.

What part about this is fun? There's something in me that calls to them, all of them. I don't know how I didn't realize they were calling back just as loudly.

"Stop holding me here," I try again. "Let me free."

I'm desperately searching my mind for what I can say that will affect Lucifer the most. It shouldn't take me this long. I should be able to just become the person that he needs me to be—that *I* need to be—but I can't. And standing here in this stupid guard uniform, I don't feel like I'm in disguise. I feel like a damn fraud.

"I can't, Helena," he says, taking another step closer, and his voice sounds so. Bloody. Sad. "If I could, I would set you free in a heartbeat, my love, but there are so many things at stake."

He means it. He wishes he could let me go, and he fucking means it—all that kindness is just bleeding through him, impossible to misunderstand. Just seeping out, and I can't take it. The Devil isn't meant to be kind.

No one is meant to be kind unless I make them do it.

He comes to a halt right before me. His eyes have returned to that piercing blue, and I don't know what to say. I feel like he's asked me a question, but I don't know what it is.

I think of the last question he asked me.

Do you want me forever, Helena?

It doesn't matter what I want, because I can't have him. No one person could ever have Lucifer.

But we aren't one person, are we?

I open my mouth, trying to find the words that will turn me into someone else, someone more than this quivering mess of a thing who can't look Lucifer in the eye. But I can't find them, and he knows it.

He leans in, his breath ghosting over my lips, but he doesn't kiss me. He lifts his hand and holds it above me, an inch away, not touching me. Slowly, he moves it over my body, following some path that feels familiar, still without ever crossing the distance.

It hits me: he's tracing Tobias' movements.

He's tracing Logan's kiss.

His hand moves lower and lower, pausing just before my

thighs. I can feel the heat burning from his palm. If he relaxed his hand, his fingers would curl and brush against me.

A small whimper escapes me, cut off just in time.

Lucifer smiles.

Backs away.

"Better get back to your biggest priority," he says, right before the veiling spell hides him again. "Lucifer and his secrets."

The words echo into the seemingly empty corridor, but I feel very far from alone this time.

I swallow, heart racing, heat burning through me at the echo of a touch that didn't even land.

Then I run.

Tobias' plan is better, but I can't stay here like this, with them. I don't care what these men say to me, what they think. Feel. I only know one thing.

It's time I got the fuck out of here. And this time, the Devil won't catch me.

21

HELENA

IN THE END, I DON'T DO ANYTHING HALF AS FANCY AS MIMIC THE guards. The thought leaves a sour taste in my mouth, and visions of crying men and rivers of blood keep taking over my mind whenever I try.

I just break in when the torturers leave.

Crass but efficient.

It's fun seeing how the other half lives while rummaging through their shit, and it brings a nice wave of nostalgia as I remember the hotel rooms I pilfered while I was alive. Rich bastards on "work trips", completely expensed while they screwed their way through the hotel staff. I never felt bad about a single thing I took. Not off them.

Besides, the number of Rolexes I nicked... Honestly, you'd think being rich would give you better taste.

These ladies do have taste though. Their work office is incredibly lush, the walls covered in more of the same artwork as the rest of the house. Only this time, the subject is torture.

They also have a Mac. For the modern torturer who also loves a digital filing system.

I swear, half of Hell is covered in ancient ledgers inscribed in blood, and the other half is decked out with sweet tech.

Listening out with one ear for movement from the rest of the house, I search the desk drawer for a note stuck at the top.

"Bingo," I mutter, peeling the paper free and entering the password.

The computer pings gently to signal I'm in, and I start sweeping through folders systematically. Rows and rows of torture files scroll past, most of them with video extensions that I do not click.

Pain ripples through my chest, and I rub the area where my soulbonds enter absently. It's beginning to blister and peel... I'm not sure how much longer I have before that bungee cord rips me through time and space to Lucifer's smug feet.

I wasn't completely honest with Tobias; I did have a plan to void the proximity bond. I just didn't need him to start thinking about loopholes.

Besides, it was a bit gross, and very dishonest, and I didn't want to see the look on his face when he found out.

I check the tiny pouch around my neck. There are three locks of hair inside and...

A number of toenails.

Look, I wasn't taking any chances, and there was no way I could safely steal the Grave.

My research told me that proximity bonds could be temporarily overridden if you remained in the presence of a *piece* of the other half of the bond, and the Grave had already proven that proxies could be used. I'd raided their hairbrushes and managed to get a few distinct strands. But it never hurt to be sure, and all those toenails were just sitting there.

We should all just be glad I didn't have to drink it.

The sun streams in the window, actually producing a bead of sweat on my forehead and making me squint. There's a plant by the glass, and I swear it shrivels in the heat, the leaves curling up at the tips.

A file name catches my eye. Spiral fifteen. I hesitate for barely a second, and then I open it up.

It isn't a video, thank God. It's a report. I skim the words, my eyes glazing over at the bureaucratic mess of it all.

Fifteen percent entitlement.

Damages incurred.

Part share 'disgust'.

I frown, chewing my lip slightly as I piece together what the fuck I'm looking at. My eyes flick to the top of the document. Third Circle.

Third Circle.

Oh shit, of course. I sit back in the chair, blinking at the screen as my understanding of Hell mentally shifts. This layer, where the demons all live, is only the surface. I knew that; I just never thought about it.

It's like that Italian poet dreamt. There are nine circles of Hell, each one deeper than the one before, and that's where the torture is carried out.

It's also obviously where the rivers of power, the Hell currents, rise up from. The source of hellborn power, for those who have natural access to the rivers, comes from below.

All those streams of agony, terror, rage... they rise from the torture in the different circles.

And this report is dividing up the energy earned from this particular torture session and deciding how much goes to each demon. They apparently distribute extra power beyond the natural amount the demons and other hellborn can reach on their own, based on each torture session. No wonder being a torturer is such a sweet gig. It's not about status power; it's literal power. Magic.

This spiral torture my parents are recorded for appears to be something to do with the Third Circle, although it isn't actually down in the Third Circle.

It's by the Black Lake.

I stare at the screen silently, building up whatever backlog of strength I'm going to need to take care of this. And then I'm up, straightening the room in under thirty seconds, wiping my presence clean, and running toward the lake district.

As I run, I start to reach for the power. It's the first time I've ever properly called on it—the first time that something other than my apparently overactive emotions has brought it down.

A grumble of something like irritation ripples down the soulbond, which is impossible, of course. How could Lucifer feel my power surge all the way from the palace?

But then, maybe he's just feeling me. As in, my emotions. Because he's my soulmate.

Damn it, I should have thought of that. Of course, now that he's realized I'm gone, he can track me in a second. The toenails don't prevent that.

I throw finesse out the window and just grab for the power. It answers immediately. It's like a light, bubbling thing curling around my feet. Like the ground itself is sort of heaving, moving, waiting to erupt.

I think I might be running faster.

I think the ground might be shifting beneath me, helping each step grow longer, further.

Eyes wide with a sudden rush of vertigo, I reach my hands out beside me to steady myself, to find some sort of stability. It's not easy. The ground is definitely rumbling.

In fact, the trees beside me are shaking.

In fact, I might be up shit creek.

I run faster.

There's no time to mess with any of this; I've just got to get out of here. I'm already well down the rabbit hole of Stockholm Syndrome, and if I keep going down this route, I'll end up falling for Lucifer before the end of the week. And that's the last thing I need.

I need to remember he's my jailer. I need to remember that Logan and Tobias, no matter how sexy or affectionate they may be, aren't on my side.

Tobias thinks we're doomed.

Logan has some other shit going on.

And both of them agree with Lucifer: that I can't roam freely.

I don't need any of this. I need to bust my parents out of here and find my way back to Heaven. Tidy up my little ghost trail of unfinished business and return things to how they're meant to be. How they were meant to be from the beginning.

The dusty paths give way to more tropical, lush plants. I swear at least three of them have a poison dart in the center; there's just something about those bowl-shaped flowers that screams danger. It's one of nature's warning symbols, like bright yellow on an insect or people who wear sunglasses inside.

I shield my neck from unexpected darts and cut underneath a low hanging tree, into the shadows, so that Lucifer will struggle a little to find me. I don't want to hand myself to him on a platter or anything.

Then I burst free into orange sunlight and run toward the center of the lake.

Spiral, spiral, spiral. Where can I find a spiral?

What the fuck is a spiral torture? Why is it linked to the Third Circle if it's up by the lakes?

The answer becomes apparent quite quickly as I stumble to a halt and lay eyes on the aqueduct. I don't know what kind of engineering has gone into this monstrosity, but it's like no aqueduct I've ever seen.

Towering stone loops in faintly familiar arches, but that familiarity ends quickly and becomes—you guessed it—a spiral.

I'm relatively certain I know where that spiral goes.

Okay, so my parents have become part of the water system. Part of the plumbing. No big deal.

I grimace. I can handle that. I've just got to get them out.

I make my way down to the end of the lake, the wince on my face deepening as I hear the faint sounds of tortured moans coming from below the water.

I think the souls here might be moving the water around. Their presence is somehow connected to how the water traverses the layers of Hell instead of simply moving from the lake to the city.

I don't even want to think about it.

I stick my hands on my hips, straightening to my five-foot nothing stature, and gaze out into the water.

There must be a way I can find them in there. If I'm linked by a blue cord to Lucifer as my soulmate, there has to be something connecting me to my goddamn family. There has to be some way I can reach them.

I gaze down into the water. Faintly glowing green lights flicker beneath it, within the lines of faces contorted into agonized screams. These are the hellsouls.

They ride through the water, twisting along the pipes and channels of the aqueduct, servicing the hellborn for eternity.

And there is no thread connecting me to my parents. There is nothing.

Of course there's nothing; they made that so very clear when we were all alive.

I shake the thought away, furious at myself for even thinking it.

All right. Time for some power, baby, I tell myself.

The agitation along the cord connecting me to my men is vibrating at a frequency that suggests all three of them are pissed I've given them the slip.

I mean, fair enough.

The whole point of this bond was so that they could keep track of me, right? The whole purpose of Tobias and Logan's existence is to do everything the Devil says, even though they insist they're their own men or whatever.

I've given all of them the slip.

Instead of rejecting the agitation of their emotion, I latch onto it. I don't know how, but it's like I can feed on it and bring it into myself. And since this power of mine seems to go nuts for a little uncontrolled emotion, that's exactly what I need.

The surface of the lake at my feet begins to ripple and boil, bubbles surfacing and churning. The souls beneath it snap open their wide, sightless eyes. Their formless bodies retreat from the disturbance.

"Find my parents," I snap out through gritted teeth, commanding them.

Or someone, at least. Anyone.

My power, incredibly, surges. It flickers at my fingertips, rises, thrashes inside me, and for a moment there I feel like I'm the most powerful woman in Hell. I feel more powerful than the Devil.

I can find them and free them like this; I know I can.

It's almost like the sun above is reaching for me, responding to me. I'm drunk on it. High on it.

But then the power erupts. A giant geyser of liquid churns from the center of the lake. It's black, not clear or luminescent like the rest of the water. And it's sludgy like tar.

This liquid isn't the water.

And it isn't my parents' souls.

Something has gone wrong, and I have a split second of regret before the tar coats me and I fall to my knees, covering my eyes at the last second.

Wave after wave of black tar covers my body. I can feel it sticking, hardening.

What the fuck is going wrong? Is my power rebelling against me?

Is it the only one who can call the shots around here? Because that's hardly fair. It's using me as a conduit for whatever it wants, and it won't give me this—this one small thing.

And then I hear a voice.

I don't know how to describe it. It's a deep, rumbling, crying voice. It's in pain.

This thing is in pain, and whatever I'm doing is hurting it more.

"Not without the key," the thing rumbles, its voice impossibly deep, like the mountains themselves. "No cage opens without the key."

I freeze. Without even meaning to, I relinquish my hold on the power completely.

Instantly, the voice stops.

There's no question whether it's responding to me or not. When I called on the power, the voice protested. When I let the power go, the voice gave up.

What the fuck does that mean, though? What kind of beastie have I woken?

It sounds exactly like that thing in the passageway... The thing that had Lucifer running scared, even though he apparently couldn't even bloody hear it.

After several long seconds, I realize that the geyser of tar has stopped.

I lift my hand from my eyes, relieved that I can see clearly. I had enough foresight to save that much at least. The rest of me is coated in at least three inches of the stuff.

It's already hardening, sticking me to the ground, so I claw my way free while I still can and wade into the edge of the lake, hoping the water will at least slow the hardening process.

There's no sign of the geyser, but I can feel a throbbing, curious edge to my power. Like it's waiting. Begging me to do something—to finish what I started.

"I don't think so, buddy," I mutter. "I don't think that's a good idea."

I'm all for finding a loophole, especially when it comes to cages and keys, but I'm pretty damn sure that if I try that again without knowing what happened, it's going to be a bad fucking time for everyone involved.

"Not without the key," I say, my voice barely above a whisper.

That was what the voice said to me. Not without the key. Which must mean Lucifer's skeleton key.

There must be some kind of failsafe built into the torture systems. Without the appropriate authority—or without the key—you can't interfere. You can't break prisoners out and free them from their torture.

Drop by drop, like the tar spouting from the geyser, the heavy weight of realization sinks inside me.

I can't do it.

If I try to bust my parents free without Lucifer's approval, the thing behind that voice is just going to attack me again.

I've never felt anything like that. It's way beyond my power, way beyond anything I've felt down here. Some beastly guardian of Hell—some Cerberus that I can't see or fight.

It's useless.

Everything I've tried, everything I've fought for. It's useless.

I don't know who I'm meant to become to solve this. I don't know what to do.

As if on cue, the pouch at my chest gives a tired little fizzle, bursts into flame, and then disappears in a cloud of ash. I stare down for a single, horrified second, and then pain rips through me.

22

HELENA

I GRIT MY TEETH, SWALLOWING DOWN A SCREAM SO VIOLENT IT ALMOST makes me puke. I clap my hands over my mouth, refusing to give anyone watching the satisfaction of seeing me fall.

"No," I hiss, falling to my knees in the shallow water, thrashing around desperately.

The word comes out like a gurgle. Like a death rattle.

I choke it off, biting into my hand, back arching in agony. My body begins to tremble, the movement growing more violent by the second while the pain burns.

Water surges around me, and my hands scrabble reflexively at the shore. I think I'm drowning.

I know I'm dying.

What the fuck kind of proximity bond is this? This is torture. Real, actual torture. It's like I've gotten past the bungee point so it won't even bother; it's just going to kill me.

Then, just as suddenly as it began, the pain vanishes.

I've barely had time to process what that means when voices reach my ears.

"There she is," Logan shouts, and I turn slowly, through

thickening tar and a body that still sings with pain, to see my three soulmates hurtling down the side of the slope.

I force myself to take slow, deep breaths. Obviously the pain didn't reach them. They don't know what just happened.

I'll keep it that way, thanks.

By the time they reach me, the trembling has stopped and my heart rate is almost back to normal.

Tobias comes to a staggering halt and begins to laugh. "What the hell did you do?" he calls out, amusement coloring his voice as he bursts into laughter.

For all that he never takes anything seriously, I've never seen him delirious with laughter like this. His cheeks flush pleasantly, his eyes bright and almost boyish. He threads his fingers through the soft waves of his brown hair and falls back against Logan, burying his face in Logan's leather jacket as he cackles.

Logan stumbles to a halt beside him and covers his mouth with his hand immediately.

It's still too late. I can see the laughter at the edge of his eyes.

Lucifer doesn't say anything. He sticks his hands in his pockets and very slowly descends the slope toward me. Every movement is graceful, with not even a hint of unbalance.

I take a second to check myself over, cataloging everything, making sure that when I speak it won't sound hoarse.

Then I jerk my chin towards Lucifer. "Why don't you ask him?" I call out bitterly. "It's whatever beastly guardian he set up."

He quirks a brow, and I suddenly, adamantly, don't want to deal with this shit.

"It's fine," I snap. "It doesn't matter. I'm okay." I try to punctuate my words with stroppy gestures, but I can barely move through the thickening tar.

I don't want to admit it, but I think I'm going to need help getting out of this.

Lucifer comes to a halt in front of me. "This is quite a pickle," he says, his eyes caressing my body as he runs his gaze slowly over my figure and up again. "We're going to need a little heat to break you out of there, I think."

A shiver of desire runs through me. Bastard.

"Well, I need something," I say flatly. "Unless you just want to stand there like a wally."

His lip twitches, but he doesn't answer as he holds out his hand above my shoulders and murmurs a few quiet words under his breath. Gentle heat spreads through me, and the tar begins to melt away.

Lucifer opens his mouth to say something, but I pause, distracted. I don't catch the words.

I tilt my head up, staring at the sun. "What is that?"

"Helena," Lucifer says, not for the first time, I don't think. Maybe the third or fourth. "What is it?"

The other two have reached us. I didn't even notice.

"I can feel the sun calling to me," I say, my voice faint as I stare up to the right of the glowing sphere. "Can any of you feel that?"

Lucifer freezes, pulling his hand away slightly. The warmth from his power fades, and the sun sings louder.

Tobias glances at me oddly. "You shouldn't be able to feel that, darling."

I do, though. The strange, twisting mountains of Hell reach for the sun like desperate arms. And the sun is reaching back. I feel like I'm part of the mountains, part of the solid rock and earth that anchors the life above it.

Something flickers inside me, like a miniature sun of my own. The tar left on my body abruptly hardens and cracks; then it flakes off piece by piece until it's all dropped into the water and sunk to our feet.

A warm hand caresses my neck, and I look up into Tobias' eyes, my own wide with shock. His sparkle in the sun, his brow furrowed as he traces his fingers around my front, to my collar. His hair falls forward, shadowing his eyes.

"Something's happening," he murmurs. "What are you hiding in there?"

He drops his hand to my chest, his palm pressed between my breasts. At first I think he's seeking the talisman of toenails, and I open my mouth to explain.

But then some secret within me catches fire—a secret I don't know. I feel it burning, blazing beneath his touch.

Something else catches alight, too.

I turn to see Lucifer doubled over, his eyes glazed and wide, while his nostrils flare. I can't see them, but I swear I can feel the power currents ignite around us. This is bigger than any explosion I've created before—bigger and yet different, too.

This time it feels like an implosion. It feels *right*.

My power is leveling up.

But then Lucifer falls to his knees, the whites of his eyes visible as his head tips back, and I realize what else this new surge of power is doing. The knowledge crashes into me and turns everything on its head.

My power is killing Lucifer.

I think it's always been killing him.

He's hidden it well before now, but with this new shift, he can't conceal the truth. Whatever my power is, it's doing something to him. Something bad.

"No," I whisper, the sound coming out far more broken than I could have imagined it would be. Not for him.

My heart is racing so hard, I feel sick.

Tobias looks at me strangely, then follows my gaze to Lucifer. The expression on his face twists into a grimace, his brow furrowing as he drops to Lucifer's side and steadies him. Lucifer's hands clutch into Tobias' arms, almost frantic.

"What is it?" Tobias snaps. "Lucifer—what's wrong?"

"Shut... up..." Lucifer snarls, heaving in great lungfuls of air. "It will pass. One. Minute."

Our bond ripples with uncertainty, the emotion all mixed up and muddled. When I glance at Logan, he looks afraid. Unsure.

I know the feeling, mate.

But after a few agonizing minutes, Lucifer softens his hold on Tobias' shoulder—the gesture bizarrely vulnerable—and pulls himself up straight.

They stare at each other for several long seconds, and I've no idea what passes between them. I do know, though, that it's Tobias who looks away.

Lucifer's mouth twists in a weird, fierce sort of triumph, and he finally stands on his own.

My breath escapes me in a rush; I hadn't realized I was holding it.

"Look at the aqueduct," Lucifer hisses, a bitter twist of amusement coloring his words.

I look.

And freeze.

It shifted. While I was distracted by the voice in my head and the tar sinking me below the surface, I missed what Hell was doing around me.

The landscape has shifted, as it tends to do. I can hear demons shouting orders, racing all up and down the shattered rocks that were once perfectly placed spirals and channels.

I think back to the groaning, aching sound that echoed below the beastie's words. Was that the aqueduct falling? I thought it was the monster, but now I'm not so sure.

"Did I do this?" I whisper, knowing the answer already. Of

course I did. I keep doing this, over and over, and it's getting worse.

But surprisingly, Lucifer shakes his head. "This was Hell," he says quietly, a little breathless, like the episode hasn't quite passed. "It transforms on its own, sometimes. I've never known why."

There's something strange about his tone, but it takes me several confusing seconds to work out what it is.

He isn't angry.

Why isn't he angry? He's my prison guard, my enemy, and I busted out. I tried to free my parents after he explicitly told me they would never be free. I caused all—this.

If he's trying to punish me, why isn't he angry?

And why is he so insistent on keeping me close to him if my power is *killing* him?

The pieces shift slowly around in my mind to form a new picture. I thought this whole mess was about me being Lucifer's prisoner until he can sort my naughty magic out, and me calling on all my childhood street brat wiles to escape him and bust my parents free. But I don't think it is.

Because, apparently, he isn't trying to punish me at all. And since my power is apparently bloody killing him, he must have a really damn good reason for keeping me at his side. Because I'm toxic to him. My presence and magic are toxic, but he won't let me go.

The question is: why?

23

HELENA

WE ESCAPE THE SHIFTING, TUMBLING STONES OF THE AQUEDUCT. I think for a moment that Lucifer will stay to oversee the repairs, but he seems just as keen to get out of there as I am. And he doesn't even have tar filling up his ears.

Logan runs a hand over my hair, grimacing at the crustiness of the strands, and keeps me close by his side as we wind our way through Hell and back to the palace. Lacking a working teleporter, we have to take a coach.

I've never heard a silence as eerie as the one that fills that carriage.

Lucifer won't talk, Logan won't look at any of us—staring out the window with a frown on his face. And Tobias won't stop staring at Lucifer. He seems to be studying him with the same fear that is rippling through me.

So, he sees it too.

I want to ask him what he makes of it all. Why is Lucifer so insistent on keeping me a prisoner if my presence is so toxic to him, and if he doesn't actually want to punish me?

I'm not buying that whole "keep Hell safe" crap. To be

honest, I don't think I ever was. Hell changes all the time, and if he was really worried about me blowing things up, he could put me in a little valley of my own while he sorted it out. But he didn't. He kept me here.

So, why do that if I don't want to be here and you don't want me here?

Why is my power killing you?

All these questions run through my head, and I want to get Tobias alone, because of all the people here, he's the one most likely to both know and tell me the truth.

But when we arrive at the palace, it's like Tobias and Lucifer are made of water. They slither out of reach before I can grab hold of them.

Logan is the only one who lingers a few moments, his expression sharp with amusement. But he, too, seems bothered by what we saw today.

Maybe he knows something.

"The Devil," I say slowly, folding my arms and shivering a little in the cool hallway we've found ourselves in. Mosaic tiles decorate the walls, and subtly patterned curtains line the alcoves. "Do you know what he's hiding?"

Logan snorts, crossing his own arms and leaning against a pillar. "Now that's a loaded question," he says, "I'd say the Devil has a lot of secrets."

"You know what I mean though," I push. "You saw him today. He wasn't right."

The amusement wipes off Logan's face, and he frowns into the distance. "No," he finally agrees, "he wasn't. I've never seen him..."

He hesitates here, and for a second something like concern crosses his face. I remember that for all his problems, Logan is still Lucifer's right-hand man. Still his chosen confidant, as much as the man has one at all.

"I've never seen him so vulnerable," Logan finally says.

The sliver of unease cracks inside me like ice; that's exactly what I was thinking.

Today Lucifer was vulnerable, and from what I understand about the machinations of Hell and its rebellion, that's the last thing he wants to be, especially now.

"Well then," I begin, intending to probe Logan, but he's already gone.

He disappears down the hallway, vanishing into a room that I'm fairly sure wasn't there a moment ago. Errand boy privileges, I suppose.

So we're all concerned about Lucifer, but none of us are going to do anything about it. Isn't that wonderful?

Isn't that what we call a nice healthy relationship?

Are we a relationship?

I frown, shaking off the sudden shiver of cold that rushes through me. I really need to get to a hot bath and a hot meal.

But, like, seriously: are we a relationship?

I mull the thought over, hurrying down the corridor towards my suite. I think it's technically a polycule or something, isn't it? But is it even a polycule if none of us really want to be involved?

Well, I suppose that's not true.

I think of Logan's hands on me, of everything we did together. I think of Tobias—his unexpected jealousy and the softness of his touch. We worked well together, the three of us, but there's one person missing.

And besides, they're still my jailers, still my prison guards. It doesn't matter how well I get along with them, I'm not free. I'm under Lucifer's thumb for reasons that I'm even more confused about than I was at the beginning, and whether they like me or not, whether they want me or not, Tobias and Logan uphold the Devil's will.

But then... it's only a Ludus bond, isn't it? Why can't I enjoy it while it's here? It's not like I have forever with these men, and maybe I'm being an idiot not to take what I can. Who cares if they hold the key to my freedom? They're also trying to help me fix this wayward power enough that I can leave safely.

I flood the bath with hot, scented water, sinking beneath the bubbles and throwing my ruined clothing into a basket that I hope will be delivered to the laundry room with the implication that it needs to be burnt.

I never want to see that clothing again, or smell the thick, sludgy scent of tar. I think it's permanently stuck up my nostrils. Sinking below the water, I thread my fingers through my hair, easing out the caked-in substance from the strands.

I spend an hour in the tub, until my fingers and toes are pruney and there isn't a speck of dirt left on me. Then I climb free and dress very carefully, that frown still etched into my forehead.

Even the delicious soak in the tub hasn't fixed that.

I need answers, but I don't even know the questions. Can I just march up to the Devil and ask him: what the hell's your problem, buddy?

If I'm so dangerous to you, why do you keep me around?

If you're not trying to punish me, why are you locking me away like this and keeping me from everyone I know and love?

I swallow thickly, ignoring the tiny voice at the back of my mind that tells me it isn't *everyone* I may love. There are three people who I'm very much not locked away from, and they maybe, kind of, fall into the category of...

Okay, love's a pretty strong word, but there's potential there; I feel it.

And it confuses the shit out of me when I still look at them and feel nothing but anger at the way they're controlling me.

The thoughts ebb and flow as I braid my hair, each strand

twisting around like a new thought. Pros and cons wrapping neatly around each other. I lose myself a little in the mesmerizing flow of it. When I reach the end, I come to a conclusion.

I've been fighting against Lucifer like a toddler kicking the walls. It's stupid of me, because it means I'm missing things, and I should know above all else that what you need in situations like this is information.

Information can be turned on people. Information can twist reality into something new. And I've been so busy kicking the walls that I've no doubt missed something vital.

So, this time, I don't frantically follow Lucifer like we have been doing. This time, I watch him. I want to know what happened by the lake, today. I want to know what's wrong.

He seems normal enough at dinner. Normal enough in the sense that his pathological need for control rules his every movement, but this time I notice the undercurrents of something beneath it.

I notice the twitch in his left cheek.

I notice the way his eyes fix for too long on one area of the room.

The motion isn't distracted. He isn't at ease. It's intent. Fixated.

I notice the calm, methodical way that he twitches his knee, rising and falling on the ball of his foot beneath the table.

It's a tick.

Lucifer has ticks.

I should have known the control was a front for something, but is it concealing some kind of temporary stress I never noticed, or is this his permanent state?

That's the first question I need an answer to.

There's something he isn't telling me about this power. Something he knows and won't share, and that doesn't feel fair, because it's my power, isn't it?

I drop my spoon into my bowl, sending an accidental arc of soup onto the pristine white tablecloth.

Lucifer stares at it as intently as he's been staring at everything. It's such an unusually sharp gaze... There's something just slightly off about it. Something familiar, if I'm honest, but I can't place it. Not in this context. It's too far removed.

"Did you have something to say, Helena?" he asks sharply.

"Oh, no," I say, smiling and dropping my chin into my hands. "But I thought you might."

"When I desire to speak, I speak."

"Are you sure about that, though?" I push, giving him a fake smile. "Because I'm getting a really distinct impression that you've got things you need to say, and you're not saying them."

Tobias pipes up. "I'm on her side," he says happily. "Anything you want to share, old boy?"

A low snarl echoes through the chamber, even though Lucifer hasn't opened his mouth. It's like the sound echoes from his body with just a thought.

"I'd advise you to rethink your attitude," Lucifer says quietly, each word very carefully enunciated.

"Oh, piss off," Tobias says, throwing his own fork down onto his plate. "We're not your little circle of princes." His voice ends on a rough snarl. "We're more than that, whether you admit it or not. You made us more. Now you have to deal with the consequences." He jabs a finger down in the center of the table. "We're your mates." The finger then jabs at Logan. "His pack. You get that, don't you? You get what that means. It means you don't run off on your own anymore. It means you don't hide things."

His eyes are piercing as he glares at Lucifer across the table.

Surprisingly, the answer comes from Logan. "Back off," he snarls, his eyes glowing golden.

"Oh, and what are you going to do about it, kitty cat?"

The snarl turns into a growl. Fur erupts over the back of Logan's hands, and suddenly his long red hair looks like a mane, even though jaguars don't have manes.

Tobias grins in delight, standing up and bracing his hands on the table.

Logan follows, and Lucifer smacks his palm down on the wood, making everyone jump.

"Enough." The cold distance of the word sends a shiver down my spine. It's controlled; too controlled. "End of discussion," he says, very simply, and then he leaves.

Logan waits a beat and then stalks out after him. I'm left face to face with Tobias, both of us riding the sharp edge of our own fury.

"He's hiding something," I snap.

"He always has," Tobias agrees. He picks up his fork and taps it, irritated, on the table. "And he's far too good at concealing his thoughts."

I huff a laugh. For once, I wish Tobias was better at his little eavesdropping power.

"What else can we do?" I ask.

Tobias leans back in his chair, spreads his fingers wide in a shrug, and gives me a surprisingly defeated look. "For now, nothing. We can only wait. All secrets come to the surface one day."

Color me surprised that some day turns out to be three hours later.

I don't know what wakes me. Some kind of distant sound or movement.

I rise out of bed, compelled by something I can't name, and step out into the corridor outside my room.

There it is again, familiar and lilting.

The sound of music draws me closer. It's a strange melody, almost like jazz, but deeper in resonance than the jazz I'm used to. Every so often it makes me think of angels—specifically, the choir of seraphim I used to hear above Heaven.

I'm not sure there are such things as coincidences.

Brushing my hair back over my shoulder, I pull my silk robe tighter and pad down the hall. The pattern of baby's breath on my robe seems horribly out of place compared to the enormous dread that's rising in my throat.

Why did I wake up? It's clear no one else can hear this music, so why can I?

The hall opens to the penthouse elevator, lit surreally by giant candles that flicker their light onto ancient stone walls. I pause on the threshold, accepting what I've been trying to ignore. Somehow, Lucifer is calling to me.

I could turn away. I could ignore the sinking feeling in my stomach that tells me I know what's coming, because I do. I can feel it down the bond. It's every sign I've been trying to ignore, every excuse I've made up in my head. But the truth always finds a way, and I've been here too many times before to miss it.

Swallowing, I step into the elevator. I follow the pull to the foyer upstairs, and then I walk inside Lucifer's private quarters until my eyes land on the smooth marble of a vase on the bookshelf.

I'm beyond questioning how I know. Whether it's the bond telling me or my own power, I don't care. I pull the fake vase down and walk into the secret passageway behind it.

Somewhere in the palace, I can sense the other two wake up. They're not following Lucifer's call; they're following mine. If I were in a better state of mind, I'd stop sending out distress signals, but I can't help it. I'm distressed.

I come to a halt at the end of the short passageway and stare at the sight before me.

Lucifer lounges on a pile of silken cushions, the open ceiling revealing a multitude of beautiful stars and swirling galaxies that aren't usually visible from Hell. He stares up at the Heavens and breathes slowly, one hand resting on the jewel in the hilt of his sword, the other on his own chest, as if he's measuring the pulse of each steady breath.

He's relaxed, at ease, perfectly as one with the universe above him.

He's high as a kite.

Behind me, I sense rather than see Tobias and Logan come to a halt. One of them is breathing rapidly. I suspect Logan, because Tobias surely knew about this. It can't have been a surprise to Lucifer's oldest friend.

Then I turn and see the expression on his face. The shock turns his brown skin a sickly pale white, and when he turns to me, I barely even recognize him. The layers of subterfuge and trickery are gone.

"I heard whispers," he says quietly, and I realize with an odd sort of detachment how far away we all are from each other. It's a broad passage, and there's at least three feet between us all. "But I thought they were rumors. Lucifer is too controlled to dip into Euphoria like some of the other kings."

"I don't think it's just Euphoria," I murmur. "Can't you feel it?"

Tobias closes his eyes, and after a second where his wide, frantic gaze flicks to mine, Logan does too. They breathe into the silence. Without being kings or queens on the Devil's Court, we can't physically see the strands of power as they flow through Hell. We can't see the emotions that drift above the tortured hellsouls, screams of fear transformed into pure energy.

But with our soulbond, we are connected to Lucifer. And so, with a little effort, we can sense what he senses.

Power brushes up against my skin. It feels similar to the power that takes over me, that wreaks destruction through Hell's landscape. But there's something raw about my own power, like I'm trying to grasp a hurricane with my hands.

This power... it's like I *am* the hurricane.

A sigh escapes me, and the sound must startle Tobias because his eyes snap open. His gaze is too bright, too wide, and a shiver races down my spine, chasing away the pleasure I'd fallen into.

"It's insidious," I whisper. "It feels like it isn't that strong, but that's how it gets you, isn't it?"

A memory from my past shoves its way into the front of my mind: cold, pale skin. Unseeing eyes. A girl crying out for a mom who will never wake up.

Suddenly, anger overwhelms me. "He should be smarter than this," I hiss, speaking louder than I mean to. "He should know the dangers."

Tobias looks at me properly then, his face softening as his expression finally loses that haunted tinge. "Of course he does," he says, leaning back against the wall. "Addiction has nothing to do with intelligence."

"What are you three doing skulking in the shadows?" Lucifer's voice makes me freeze up, but then my brain translates and I realize he isn't angry.

He should be angry.

We turn around, Logan unusually quiet as he squeezes my shoulder in brief comfort. The Devil lifts one hand—the hand on his chest, not the sword—and smiles lazily. "Come to witness my downfall, have you?"

His eyes are too bright. And not with worry, like Tobias's.

Lucifer's eyes are glazed and excessively happy. His expressions are lazy, but he's speaking too fast.

"No, we haven't, old friend," Tobias murmurs, stepping into the room. "Is there something we should know?"

Lucifer laughs, the sound low and easy. Too easy. He shouldn't sound like that.

"You already know it now. Well done. You're part of..." He frowns and holds up his hands, counting down the fingers. "A select seven who know my secret. Congratulations."

"And yet I feel no triumph," Tobias says, coming to a careful seat on the cushions beside him.

He half turns to me and holds out his hand. Moving on autopilot, I take his palm and let him guide me beside him.

Logan doesn't move. He stays by the door, and I don't think he even realizes what he's doing. Guarding us.

Guarding our vulnerability.

Smiling, Lucifer lets his hand fall again, and his eyes flutter closed. "You should feel triumph," he says. "My enemies would."

"We are not your enemies," Tobias says, a touch forcefully.

Lucifer doesn't answer that.

After a moment, he says—quietly, as if only to Tobias: "Watch out for the Devil."

Tobias frowns. "Lucifer... you are the Devil."

Lucifer laughs, bright and easy. "Sure, sure. And the doctor controls Mr Hyde. Watch him, Tobias. The power... feeds... him."

So that's why the drug hurts him, even at its highest points, even before the dark sinks in. It feeds the Devil in him.

Jesus fucking Christ.

No one speaks for a long time, and my world shifts into something new. By the time dawn arrives, nothing will be the same.

I know Lucifer's secret now. I understand why he can't be

near my power surges. Why they're hurting him—killing him—and yet he can't let me leave.

He's an addict, just like my parents, only Lucifer's addiction is magic. All forms of magic, by the look of it. Which, down here in Hell, must be a powerful addiction indeed.

The knowledge drifts lazily through my mind, and I find I'm trying to lock it away, like I do with all the thoughts I don't want. But it won't go. It's too big. Heat tingles at the end of my fingertips, waiting to ignite.

He's a power addict, tempted and burned by the magic I wield, but unable to let me go. Because his devastating addiction doesn't change the fact that I'm *still* exploding things wherever I go.

If Hell's rebellion got hold of me, they could light fires all up and down this world, and he'd be powerless to subdue them. Shit, man, I could destroy him just by existing. Just by—what was it that he said?—stubbing my toe.

I'm hurting him by staying, and I'd hurt him just the same by leaving.

It's the thought of leaving that snaps me out of it. Something shifts inside me, and I sit up a little taller. A little straighter. This time, I'll do better. This time, I won't abandon the person who needs me—I'll accept responsibility for what I've done. What I'm doing.

I won't leave him, like I left my parents.

This time, I'll be better.

24

HELENA

WHAT DID I MISS? THE QUESTION HAUNTS ME ALL NIGHT, SO I LAY beside Lucifer on the cushions, staring up at the sky.

He barely stirs for the rest of the night, but we don't even suggest leaving. We caught him right at the end, right as the high leaves him but before the dark sets in. And no one deserves to be alone in the dark.

Near dawn, Tobias whispers to me. "You should ask the question out loud."

"What question?" I ask, startling.

I hadn't realized how silent it was until he broke it.

"The question that I keep hearing echoing inside your brain," he grits out through clenched teeth, "but that I can't quite catch the words for."

Logan huffs a laugh. "You should just keep thinking at Hel," he says quietly.

I glance back to see him still in his position by the door, but this time he's sitting down—leaning against it, with his arm propped on one knee and the other leg stretched out before him.

"Just let him suffer." There's an edge to Logan's voice, a bitterness that isn't directed outward.

Even he didn't see this coming. None of us did, and we should have.

"How did we miss this?" I ask. Lucifer sleeps pleasantly beside us, his breath shallow, curls of hair falling across his face.

"No, not that question," Tobias says, shoving his fringe back and glaring up at the sky. "I can hear that one. No, something about darkness. Why do you keep thinking about darkness? Or dark setting in..."

Oh, he's right actually, that wasn't the question.

"Do you think we only know him when he's on a comedown?"

Tobias stiffens. "What makes you say that?"

"Because he's so different now," I say. "So I know I've never seen him high."

"So you think the Lucifer that we see day in day out," Tobias asks, his words oddly forced, "is a Lucifer that's in withdrawal. A Lucifer who is merely waiting for his next hit."

I glance over at him, confused at the anger in his voice until I realize what's going on.

"No," I say softly. "I don't think the Lucifer that you have always known is an addict."

He turns to me, abrupt. Very slowly, the stiffness in his shoulders eases and he relaxes back into the cushions. A wry smirk plays on his lips.

"Touché. Might make a protégé out of you after all."

"Do I have a choice in the matter?" I ask him.

"Not with the way you're going," he says flatly, turning back to his sky gazing. "I agree with you, as it happens. I'm sure I've known him in between addiction, shall we say, but..." He winces here. "You're right, there isn't much difference between

Lucifer as he normally is and this withdrawal version that I think we're seeing. The anger, the quickness to react, the isolation, the silences, the secrets and lies... It's all making sense, and I wish it weren't."

I tip my head to study Lucifer. He's still breathing just as soundly, passed out. He could be passed out for days, but I've no reason to think he's in danger from it at the moment.

For all I know, this happens every night.

"Should we roll him onto his side anyway?" I ask.

Tobias doesn't speak. It's Logan who, after a tense moment of silence, stands up and crosses the room.

He's surprisingly gentle as he moves Lucifer's unconscious body, rolling him to the side and propping pillows behind his back.

"There," he says gruffly, and there's a wealth of pain in that expression. "Seems all right." But then he backs away, as if afraid. "I've got to—" he starts, but he doesn't finish.

He shakes his head, turns, and disappears down the corridor.

Tobias frowns after him and glances back at Lucifer. "You know what? I'm going to stay here," he says, "but I think you should go."

I study him, trying to read between the lines, trying to read his thoughts for once. But nothing reveals itself. He's as much of an enigma as ever.

And I need to get out of here.

The same bubbling energy that propelled Logan out the door is coursing through me, even if it's for a different reason.

With a silent nod, I escape out the door.

Tobias watches me as I go, and the last thing I see is his gaze burning into me from the dark room, just before he rolls over and circles an arm over Lucifer's waist.

I stare at the locked door for a long time. It didn't call me here, like Lucifer last night. But I remember it from my earlier look around the castle. I remember the missing wall that opened into the Heavens.

I still haven't slept. The noon sun is high in the sky, and for the first time since that damn portal spat me out, I want to see the stars again. I want to pretend that twilight place above is still my home.

But as soon as I step inside, I realize the flaw in my plans. No amount of Lucifer doting on me via my wardrobe could have prepared me for this party.

Elaborate ballgowns whirl in dazzling loops around the floor. Slinky dresses, suits with embroidery I couldn't hope to replicate in a million years... This is a proper ball, and I stand out like a sore thumb.

"Huh," I mutter to myself. "So it seems I need a dress."

I walk quickly along the outer edge, struggling not to stare at all the ostentatious detailing that marks the corners and edges of the room. It's like a ballroom out of Versailles. Bright colors, gilt with gold, and a cavernous space filled with dancers.

And, of course, the missing wall that opens straight out into the night sky.

Although, now that I look at it... I think this might be a different party. A different room, even though it was behind the same door. Either I just have an extreme affinity for the cosmos, or Lucifer really likes punching holes in the building.

You know, if this is the cage that I'm stuck in, it really could be worse. It's not like Lucifer ever banned me from any of this. Maybe that's how he expected me to spend my time—dramatically lamenting that I'm banned from Heaven while he sorts it out, and I just party the night away.

God, maybe he saw how I lived on Earth and thought he was giving me a gift.

A shiver runs through me, bringing with it some kind of emotion that I can't really place. Can't identify. Heat pulses from the wall I'm sidling against, and I glance over my shoulder in alarm, expecting to see fire flickering at the edges.

But it isn't.

I can feel the power, though.

I feel it burning, wanting something more. Maybe this power of mine isn't just a fire power. Maybe it does something else.

That could be cool.

Carefully, cautiously, I force my body to relax. Instead of trying to direct the power, I just... feel it.

A whisper starts up, a bodiless voice that I can't place.

At first it doesn't sound like it's saying anything in partic-ular—just meaningless noises and syllables. But then I start to make out words.

Shouldn't have done that.

Just like your mother always said.

Stop it. Stop it!

The voices are different. It isn't just one person I'm listening to. It's three, five, eighteen.

The voices pile over and over, sometimes obscuring each other. Sometimes coming through crystal clear.

You're a fucking embarrassment.

Look at this dress.

Look at yourself in the mirror, you fucking loser.

Jesus, these voices are horribly unkind. I turn around, spin-ning in a slow circle, searching to see what it is that I'm hearing.

I know my power is bringing the whispers to me, but where are they coming from? Are there people standing at the side of the room, arguing? Is someone talking to themselves in the bathroom?

Then I catch sight of a woman standing near the mirrored alcove by the buffet table. She's wearing a beautiful dress that looks like the midnight sky. Tiny pinpricks of light sparkle from it, and I know it isn't just reflective material catching the light. It's something deeper.

She looks like moonlight, commanding but quiet. She takes up space with her presence, and everyone who passes her gives her a subtle once-over, drawn to her power.

The last whisper comes again.

Shouldn't have worn a fucking dress like this. You look just like your mother always said you did. Useless tart. Slut.

My eyes widen. These are her thoughts. I'm hearing her thoughts, just like Tobias does. Jesus.

And then, critically, shamefully, I realize that I can take advantage of this.

I hesitate, knowing that the people I used to take advantage of were ones I could justify. Creepy men who'd slipped their hands up waitresses' skirts at the card tables. People who were hiding wedding rings at the bottom of their suitcases.

I haven't seen anything about this woman that makes me want to con her.

To my left, a demon with horns running along the ridge of his nose turns to me and frowns.

"Where's your sword?" he snaps, eyes narrowing in suspicion.

"I'm not a guard," I say, affecting a casually powerful expression on my face. There's a slight flicker of fear on his face; he's intimidated by power, so I drive the knife in a bit further, reckless though it may be. "Are you really as stupid as you look?"

He snarls in shock and anger and—whoops!—looks like I went a bit far. He lunges for me.

I dodge out of his grasp.

"Listen, mate." Time to walk it back. "We can't all just trot down here from our rooms in perfect formal dress. Some of us need to have that shit delivered."

The thing is, I know I don't pass as upper crust right now, so it's best to lean into the other half. I'll pretend I'm here on whatever passes as some kind of charity for these guys.

His face crumples, confusion overriding any sort of thought. He doesn't know what to make of me, which is exactly where I need him.

I slip away as two of his friends turn to look at me, and cross the ballroom to where the woman shrinks further into the shadows.

The really shitty way to do this would be to prey on her insecurities.

I'd call her those words I can hear echoing in her mind, the words her mother threw at her.

And then she'd storm out and I'd follow, and when she stripped off the dress in her room and collapsed in a puddle of tears, I'd nick it and sweep back down to the floor.

I could do that, but I don't especially want to. She hasn't given me a reason to.

And there's a whisper in my mind that feels almost like intuition. It's telling me there's a better way.

So I decide to go for it.

"I can light their dresses on fire for you, if you like," I murmur to her.

She turns to me, eyebrows leaping skyward, before her face clouds with suspicion.

"And why would I want that?"

I steal a flute of champagne from behind me and take a slow

sip, leaning against the wall, affecting a casual air of nonchalance.

"Because you hate them," I tell her.

Something flickers in her expression, but she's too good at concealing it.

Far too good. No one else in this room would suspect that her demeanor conceals an air of complete self-loathing. Doesn't she know that every eye in the room is on her?

"I have no idea what you're talking about," she says airily. "Did Castrano send you? He always did like to fuck with my head."

"No, but it's quite thanks to your head that I'm here," I tell her. Before she can execute me on the spot for that, I say, "I can hear your thoughts, madam. I can hear you begging me to ease the pain of your own mind."

Shockingly, I realize it's true.

Is this how Tobias works?

He listens for the threads in our mind that beg for some kind of answer to the messy, horrible confusion of everyday life, and then he steps in to give us that answer in the worst way possible.

Am I becoming a bloody trickster demon?

Her expression turns shrewd as a faint moue of under-standing appears.

"You're a new god, then," she says, eyeing me up and down. "You don't look older than a century."

I splutter into my glass and hide it as a cough.

"Spot on," I tell her.

"Alright then," she says, studying me in consideration. "What's your price?"

"I want that dress," I tell her, knowing that in her mind it will be an absolute bargain.

Because I know, as soon as I say the words, that while I

might not be able to fashion a dress for myself with this power, I can fashion one for her. Just as Tobias can create illusions of the truth out of thin air.

An expression akin to relief settles across her features, and I feel a flash of something akin to pride. Pride that I can offer her this when she's sitting there collapsing inside a prison of her own making.

"Your terms are accepted, so long as you don't leave me standing here naked."

"You know I wouldn't," I give her a sharp smile. "That's not what we do."

And then, before either of us can change our mind, I extend my hand to her.

She clasps it after a beat, her own palm warm and dry.

Old instinct tells me to use the distraction to slip my hand into the pockets of the dress and withdraw whatever I find inside. But I don't. I'm playing a bigger game now, and I want to see it through to the end.

The second our hands part, fire rips through the ballroom.

When I said I'd light their dresses on fire, I'd only really meant the three gossiping women nearest to us. The ones who had so thrown my supplicant off her game.

But it seems her ego was more wounded than that.

Every dress in the ballroom catches alight. Screams fill the space, and fire flickers across the night sky that stretches across one wall.

Beside me, the woman laughs in delight at every shred of sadness and shame.

Every old hurt that had been brought to the surface fades away in pure, evil delight. It's a little bit wicked, and I'm a little bit thrilled.

I'm not sure how to do the next part, but this power coursing through me seems to know exactly what I want. Little orbs of light buzz around my head, appearing for the first time since they danced around my window.

Then, with barely a thought, her dress fades and re-materializes on me. In its place, the power crafts something different.

I carefully hide my expression of shock.

Rather than giving her the kind of dress she wanted in its place, it's given her one that is ten times as seductive as what she was already wearing.

Just like Tobias's trickster power, the price for this magic burns.

The woman looks down at her dress. Her face contorts, and suddenly I'm buffeted backward by the strength of the power surging through me.

I don't understand.

This firepower is now some kind of mind-reading thing that gets off on... what? On tricking people, like Tobias does?

What the hell does this mean?

The tap on my shoulder has me whirling around, and I come to an abrupt halt, freezing still at the sight of Tobias and Logan, dressed in formal wear, standing behind me.

Tobias smiles, an eerie triumph in his gaze that, even though we're definitely friends now—definitely more than friends now—still sends a slight shiver of apprehension running through me.

"What?" I snap defensively.

"Oh, nothing," he says, sharing a glance with Logan, who looks equally amused. "Only that it smells like me in here."

The observation is almost crass. I wrinkle my nose. "Ew," I say pointedly. "Maybe you should have a shower."

He only laughs in delight, which proves how screwed I really am. If Tobias is delighted, we're all in trouble.

"I'm just saying, it looks like your power's evolving." He

holds out his arm, elbow crooked, "And I think we should celebrate."

Pointedly, Logan holds out his arm to the other side of me, smiling. I pause for only a moment, and then I take both their arms, so they're on either side of me.

A vicious cough comes from behind me, and my men whirl me around like a giddy little four-year-old, steeling their amusement behind carefully constructed veneers.

The woman glares at me, her face split with rage. "What have you done to me?" she hisses. "This wasn't what we agreed on."

I open my mouth, and part of me wants to apologize because, truly, I didn't mean to upset her. But instead what comes out is a very nonchalant, "All you said was that you didn't want to be naked."

She shrieks in outrage. Behind us, in the ballroom, the flames are only now dwindling. Of course, with this many demons, they can put out a little fire quite easily, leaving only some scorched fabric behind them.

Everyone is clamoring, talking over each other—half of them in pure delight at the interruption.

They haven't yet realized that we're the only ones unburnt, and I'd like to keep it that way.

"I paid your price," she hisses.

Before I can answer, Tobias smoothly interjects. "You paid her price, and she gave you what you want." His smile widens. "Exactly what you want."

It hits me then: the dress shows her most secret desire.

My power listens to her thoughts, and it listened to her thoughts when it extracted her price, too. These are the truths that Tobias loves to expose us to.

The truth of what we say we want, what we feel we *should* want... and what truly lies beneath.

Before she can argue anymore, my two men whisk me into the center of the ballroom.

The dancing has almost resumed now, with the excitement of the fire becoming simply a passing extravagance, like any other pyrotechnic show.

Half the surrounding demons are wearing singed clothing that falls off them in strips, but it seems to just enhance the allure. It's all very avant garde.

I expect one of my men to fade off to the side as the other dances with me. Like they'll, I don't know, trade off positions as they go. But instead, Tobias spins me to face him, while Logan rests his hands on my hips and mirrors our movements from behind.

I'm trapped between them, and it sends shivers of delight coursing through me.

"When were you going to tell me about your new evolution?" Tobias murmurs.

Logan's hot breath reaches my neck. He's lowered himself so there are barely inches between us, not caring who's looking.

"It's only just happened," I say drily. "I should be asking you how you knew."

Tobias's nostrils flare as he breathes in a low, luxurious inhale.

"You couldn't hide this, Helena," he says, rapturous, "not from someone who shares the same sort of power."

"So this is what my power was all along?" I ask him, heart thudding at the thought that I've found the answer.

But Tobias shakes his head. "Trickster power is something that happens to you," he says fondly. "It takes your existing power and alters it for... a number of complex reasons."

Huh. So this isn't an answer. It's just another giant question mark. Great, I really needed more of them.

Tobias presses a kiss to my palm. "Some day, I'll tell you all about it."

My heart flutters. He loves this—loves the power surrounding us.

A deep, bone-weary sadness floods me then, as I compare the difference between Tobias and Lucifer.

Tobias is drunk on power to be sure, but he's a stable drunk, a happy drunk, loving the power that swims in his veins. And then there's Lucifer, bent beneath the crushing weight of it.

This is what Lucifer should be, and instead he's far, far away, falling into the darkness that lies beyond. I swallow thickly and let a little of my thoughts creep beyond the wall I usually keep them behind.

Tobias flinches, and some of the triumph fades.

"Yes, well," he says in a low voice, "that was really what we were coming to talk to you about." His lip quirks wryly, "This was just a delicious diversion."

"What is there to say?" I ask him, a little too harshly.

I'm not mad at him, not really. I'm mad that I came here for answers and comfort, and so far all I've found is the joy of humiliating a woman who probably didn't deserve it.

Tobias glances at Logan over the top of my head, and before I know what's happened, the two of them have switched.

I'm surprised. Usually, Logan wouldn't take such a forward position on something like this. He never likes to lead, never likes to be in charge.

But then I realize they've only changed so that Tobias can lean forward and whisper in my ear.

No one can hear him like this, and no one can read his lips when they're buried in my hair.

Another shiver races through me as his hands land where Logan's were, and I'm forced to look up into Logan's piercing, dark gaze as he guides me in this pretense of a dance that's really just thinly veiled espionage in the middle of a snake-pit of demons.

"I know how we can follow him," Tobias whispers in my ear. "I know how we can find him, and I think you will agree that, now more than ever, it is vital that we do so."

"Or we could just leave him to it," I breathe out, the words shaky. "He seems to know what he's doing."

He doesn't; I know he doesn't. But I want to hear what they say.

Tobias laughs bitterly in my ear. Logan's expression doesn't change, but his hands in mine tighten, and he whirls us a little faster.

"Lucifer hasn't a clue what he's doing," Tobias says harshly, "and he'll never admit it. You need him to get your parents out. You need him to help you control this power before it..." He pauses. "Evolves again and becomes something that you can't control. And Lucifer—" The word sounds broken as it comes out. Tobias swallows, hands clenching my waist, and tries again. "Lucifer needs to understand that he needs us just as much. He can't do this on his own, and if he keeps trying, he's going to..."

This time, when he breaks off, he doesn't try to finish the sentence.

My heart just stutters in my chest. I can't find anything worth arguing with. Everything Tobias said is true.

For a moment, it feels as though a light wind flutters my hair, but the strands don't move. It's an internal wind, a powerful force that's hitting my soul rather than my body, and I recognize it: my power is on the move again.

I hold my breath, and just like before, the whispers begin. Only this time, it's only one voice.

Lucifer's.

Weak.

Fucking weak piece of shit.

You said you'd stop, and you didn't.

Fucking weak, weak, WEAK!

Then, quieter, so quiet it's almost chilling:

I can't take much more of this.

Jesus bloody Christ. What is this power doing? Why is it bringing me Lucifer's voice from all the way across the castle?

I swallow thickly and force my mind back to the present.

"Sure, I need Lucifer. Lucifer needs us. But why are you both still here?" I force out. "You're just collateral damage in this equation, aren't you? It's me and Lucifer that are messed up, so why don't you find a way to break free? I'd let the two of us rot in our own mess, if I were you. Didn't you already say it would be easier?"

Even as I say it, I recall Tobias' expression as his arm curled around Lucifer's waist; that wasn't the face of a man who wants to let us rot.

Still. Lucifer and I both have what the other wants, in one way or another. But these two, they're just trapped with us, locked in the palace, unable to leave without causing themselves immense pain. Why don't they just break free?

Logan's expression tightens. I see a flash of something unexpected in his gaze, something like anger, even though all he's ever tried to do is run, either physically or mentally.

But he doesn't answer. Maybe he doesn't know.

Tobias, however, murmurs in my ear. "You don't get that truth from me, Helena. Not yet."

I close my eyes as the two of them hold me tighter. I can sense the looks from the other demons, sense their interest and faint confusion.

They're probably wondering what's going on between the three of us, what our relationship is. Who plays what role.

I'm wondering that myself.

If anyone were to ask me right now, as I know they want to, my answer would be: we're friends. But we aren't, are we? We're barely friends at all, and yet we're so much more. We're soulmates.

Maybe that's what keeps them here, plain and simple. Not the proximity bond that Lucifer wove into the thread, but the thread itself. Maybe that's what keeps me here too.

"All right," I say, still with my eyes closed. "Let's do it. Let's find him."

25

HELENA

THE EASIEST WAY TO CATCH THE DEVIL AT HIS OWN GAME IS TO shadow him—literally.

It takes me three witches and a lot of funny looks before I find someone who can do what I'm asking. You'd think there'd be more of a market for amateur theatrics down here, but maybe when you're a demon you don't need to be as creative. I don't know.

"You want to become someone's shadow?" the witch Gallafreya asks me thoughtfully. "If they're a high-level demon, they'll sense you. Are they?"

I cover my snort with a wheezing cough. "Yeah, pretty high."

She clicks her tongue.

Logan casts me a curious look from the opposite side of the Starbucks, but holds his guard position. Which is impressive, really, considering there are literal chained hellsouls moaning from the walls.

And yet the decor is somehow aesthetically unblemished.

The chains just blend right in like they were meant to be there. Remarkable, honestly.

Tobias, meanwhile, has prowled the perimeter three times and seems to currently be translating the menu into Japanese.

Lucifer, of course, is nowhere to be found.

"Then you'd be better off shadowing their shadow," Gallafreya continues after a pensive silence broken only by the gentle wailing of tortured souls. "Gives you more distance, and they'll only notice you if they are particularly adept at seeing the things that haunt them out of the corner of their eyes."

Her own eyes glint alarmingly at that factoid, like she knows things I don't.

I think about the stubborn expression on the Devil's face 24/7 these days. Oh, he has plenty haunting him. But I'd bet cold hard cash that he's trained himself not to look.

"Sounds perfect."

Gallafreya sits back, pleased. "All I need then is their name and a stone from their shadow. Just one that's rested in it for a few seconds, nothing fancy."

I swallow, forcing a light smile. Here we go. "Lucifer?"

Gallafreya pales. "Oh, hell no." She slaps her hands on the table and stands up. "Absolutely not."

Tobias appears out of nowhere, a hand placed gently on her wrist.

"Sit down," he suggests, making the idea sound warm and nourishing.

Slowly, Gallafreya sits.

Tobias produces the menu he's been scribbling on. "Can you read this for me?"

It's half Japanese, half some kind of rune spread. He's definitely doing some kind of calculation on it, and if I'm not mistaken...

I tilt my head sideways, but he slides his thumb further over the corner.

Not quickly enough, though.

Yep, that's a Venn Diagram. The trickster god who launched Hell's sun is sitting in Starbucks making Venn Diagrams.

"No," she says after a moment, frowning. "What is it?"

"Doesn't matter," Tobias says, disappearing the menu with a flourish of his wrist. "My point is that that is my specialty, and this—" He taps the business card we called her on. "Is yours."

Her eyes flicker with suspicion. "Yeah, no shit. Doesn't mean I'm stupid enough to take on the Devil."

"But you could," he says persuasively. "How many people would be able to say that?"

She shifts, uncertain now.

I realize with a jolt that he's got her. He knows what makes her tick, and with one small suggestion, she's hooked.

"How will you guarantee my safety if he finds out?" she asks after a beat.

I notice she says if, not when. Which means she really does think she can fool the Devil. And the urge to try is strong.

"Burn your maker's mark off the spell," Tobias suggests.

Uncertainty rises within me. Maybe it's only because I think I can read him now, but he looks almost aggressive when he suggests that. Taunting.

Maybe I really *can* read him, because Gallafreya flinches and shakes her head.

"No, I want your sword if he comes for me," she says quickly.

So, she can't bear the thought of going uncredited, even if it risks her life.

Tobias raises an eyebrow. "You think I stand a chance against Lucifer?"

Gallafreya's expression turns shrewd. "You're Tobias of the Hills, aren't you?"

It's my turn to raise a brow. I haven't heard this name before.

There's no doubt about it now, Tobias' smile is definitely aggressive. "Where did you hear that?"

Moving slow with triumph, as though she's suddenly the one with the power, she drags a napkin to her with one finger and writes three characters on it in a language I don't recognize.

"The Devil's oldest friend. Co-lighter of the fires of Hell," she says slyly.

Tobias' eyes narrow. With a stilted, abrupt movement, he grabs the napkin and lights it on fire.

I bite down hard on my tongue to keep my shock from showing. I knew he launched the sun, but co-lighter of the fires of Hell?

Firstly, that sounds like he created Hell side by side with Lucifer.

Secondly, how fucking old are these men?

"If Lucifer uncovers your spell, I will assure him he goes through me before he reaches you," Tobias says in a smooth, persuasive voice.

Obviously, this is enough for Gallafreya. She holds out her hand, and without even blinking, Tobias deposits a small stone in it.

"What am I even doing here?" I mutter, sitting back in my chair with my arms folded.

Tobias smirks, but otherwise no one acknowledges me. Gallafreya holds her palm over the rock and chants softly under her breath.

The lights flicker, plunging the Starbucks into shadow. A fraction of a second later, they return, although the soft glow of the hellfire that lingers behind this facade of a coffee shop is burned into my brain.

"Here," she says, dropping the stone into Tobias' palm and folding his fingers over it.

A strange emotion stirs in my chest, spiky and warm. I clench my fingers into my forearm to keep from launching myself across the table.

"Hold the stone, and we'll be invisible to him?" Tobias confirms, rolling it back and forth over his knuckles, like a coin.

Gallafreya nods. "Should have twenty-four hours of charge, but that's only an estimate. Don't push your luck."

She rises, and an unexpected fire burns in her eyes as she looks between us. She makes a sharp, small gesture with her pointer finger and her thumb, concealing it against her chest. "Make him burn," she says.

And then she's gone.

I frown, turning to Tobias and expecting to find him as confused as I am. But he isn't. His brow is furrowed in uncharacteristic concern as he stares at the spot the witch just left.

"What is it?" I ask, trying to dull the rising sense that we just floated up shit creek.

"That witch was part of the rebellion against Lucifer," he says thoughtfully, still with that pinched look of concern. He turns to me. "And it seems we've convinced her that we are, too."

It should come as no surprise that moonlighting as a shadow is a dark experience, and yet here I am. Surprised.

I squint through the shifting mass of charcoal that surrounds us.

"There," I breathe, barely above a whisper.

Tobias' fingers tighten around mine, while Logan gives the palm of my hand a friendly tickle with his thumb.

See, Gallafreya was being literal when she said to hold the stone for the magic to work. So, here we all are, three grown-ass adults huddled around a rock, holding hands and shuffling together like we're Harry bloody Potter.

Logan hadn't wanted to come. Again. It had taken Tobias plucking the bond cord like a harp string and somehow using it to irritate Logan into leaping up with a snarl before he would follow us out the door.

Shame we couldn't have done that to Lucifer, or this would have been over a lot quicker. But Tobias has been trying all afternoon, and the man is made of stone.

Lucifer stares up at the moon, hands in his pockets. Then, after giving a big sigh, he reaches into the sky, plucks out a strand of Hell's power, and disappears.

This is why we haven't been able to follow him alone. Even the royal guardians of Hell's power, the kings and queen, can't manipulate the power strands like he can.

Although, after what I learned today, I'm wondering why Tobias can't either.

A light tug pulls at my abdomen, and I hold on tight to the stone. There wasn't even that much of a delay; only half a second at most.

And now, as the shadow of the Devil's shadow, we hurtle through space to follow him.

At first, I don't know where we've landed. The moon is out, but no stars—there are never any stars in Hell—and its low light only illuminates a few hills.

A light breeze tickles the hair at the base of my neck, and I nearly jump when a warm hand appears and gently smooths it down.

I look up into Logan's amused, smiling face and bite down

on my own grin.

He's been different, since our little B&E session. Still wary, still poised to run... but he isn't running yet. And it's kind of nice.

It surprises me how nice it is.

With a sharp jolt, Tobias tugs our joined hands and leads us after the figure moving by the base of the hill.

My eyes have adjusted enough now to see there are strange pillars lining the hills around us. We're in some kind of valley; the ground smells like a rainforest floor, but there are only shrubs within a fifty meter radius. No trees, except on the top of the hills, their sweeping canopies shimmering in the breeze.

The pillars are statues. We pass by a wizened creature with haunting eyes, frozen still in granite. But then Lucifer disappears into a hut that was almost concealed in the hill, and I have to follow without looking closer.

We lean against the wall inside the hut. There's barely room to move, especially when we're trying not to be noticed.

The hut looks abandoned. Furs lie strewn over the earthen floor, and an upturned cup spills liquid over the table. It's still steaming.

Lucifer is chasing someone.

I glance at Tobias, noting his tight expression. Logan's thumb traces my palm again, but the movement feels distracted —more of a soothing motion for him this time than for me. Like he's reminding himself I'm here.

Lucifer stands frozen still, like one of the statues outside. His eyes flick from the furs to the gently smoking embers in the fireplace, and finally to the cup. His right hand clenches into a fist. Eases. Clenches again.

Then he snaps.

He picks up the wooden chair with one hand and hurls it against the wall. I freeze, my heart racing, eyes wide. Logan's hand grips mine fiercely, painfully, as Lucifer starts tearing the hut apart.

The fur goes flying into the fireplace, the edges curling and blackening as a sickening smell wafts through the space. The table is smashed over and over into the wall, splinters flying.

Tobias' mouth twitches; he looks almost smug, triumphant. Rage—kindled by fear—burns inside me, and I just manage to hold back from yelling at him.

I'm getting really sick of his hot and cold attitude. He's either helping us or he isn't; we don't need this trickster crap.

Unfortunately, while I might have held back from yelling, there's another part of me that screams far louder—and I don't control that part at all.

Light flickers along the walls.

Tobias turns to me sharply, an admonishing look on his face even as his lips twitch in growing amusement. Logan looks ready to bolt.

Lucifer stills, his eyes narrowing as he studies the streak of lightning. Mercifully, it fades almost immediately—yay for mindfulness—but it isn't enough.

He turns unerringly to face us, drawn easily to the one patch of shadow that never moved, even as he decimated the hut and its contents in a whirlwind of anger.

"Which one of you is it?" Lucifer asks, deceptively calm. "My old friend? My *soulmate*?" The word sounds like an insult. "Or the man who swore he would never betray me?"

Logan swallows; he seems frozen in place. Unusually inert.

Tobias regards me, still smiling. For a moment, I think he's going to take the fall. Lucifer wouldn't hurt him, surely.

But then, with a pop, he disappears. I gape into the place he was standing, betrayal constricting my chest.

Lucifer's eyes narrow, "Shadow's still there," he says thoughtfully. "And Tobias has gone. New theory: all three of you are sneaking around behind my back, like filthy little *liars!*" The last word is yelled as he lunges toward us.

I act on instinct. I close Logan's fingers around the stone, throw him to the other side of the room, and run out the door.

Lucifer won't kill me, not when this weird power is still going nuts. It would be stupid.

I really hope the Devil isn't stupid.

With a bellow, he gives chase. I dive to the right, among the statues. The night swallows me whole, and I move as silently as I can as I wind through the labyrinth of silent guardians.

Ronin taught me a lot, but everything he learned is from Lucifer.

The man is silent as a cat. Until he speaks.

"What was worth the risk, Helena?" he asks, amusement lacing his tone like poison. "How many of my secrets are you desperate to unravel?"

I should make him think I already know one of them. Use it as a bargaining chip.

Instead, I yell, "Why? How many you got?"

Why the hell do these men make me lose all my careful planning?

He snarls, lunging for me, but I twist away—behind a rearing unicorn of obsidian.

"I don't like my privacy invaded," he snaps, moving quietly again.

The night air throws his voice, and he moves fast. I can't locate him.

"Well, you're the one who said it," I snap. "We're in this together, so maybe you should let us in a little before our ignorance gets us killed."

The words come from somewhere deep and bitter. I'm surprised to realize they're true.

I'm pissed because Lucifer isn't letting us in.

I take a step, and my foot lands on something hard, which cracks with a loud snap. Strong arms close around my waist, and Lucifer pulls me into him so my back is flush to his chest. I yelp, elbowing behind me, but he catches it with one hand.

"Killed," he repeats in a strange tone.

"Dead," I emphasize. "And don't say that won't happen. We know this is big." I grab the blue cord that's materialized between us—through us—and tug it sharply. Now, his head is almost level with mine, leaning over my shoulder. His eyes flash blue in the moonlight. "We can feel it."

Lucifer takes a deep breath and exhales slowly.

"It wasn't my intention to risk your life," he says carefully. A wry grin breaks onto his face. "It wasn't my intention to have any of you involved at all. But here we are."

Well, I know how that goes. I offer him a smile of my own. His expression warms, just a little, but he doesn't let me go.

I think I could break his hold on me. Between Ronin and my training in Heaven, I'd have a chance. But I don't mind being held for now. It's the closest I've been to Lucifer since that bond took over, and the irony isn't lost.

How long have I wanted him to hold me and refused to admit it? I locked the desire away with all my other thoughts and expected it to just stay there.

"You want to know what I'm doing when I leave the palace?" he asks.

His voice is low in the night, thumbs tracing up and down my bicep soothingly.

"I need to know," I correct him. "I'm involved in this whether any of us like it or not. We all are."

Lucifer inclines his head in silent acknowledgement. "I'm searching for a spirit," he says. "One from my earliest days of Hell. Before Judgment."

My eyebrows lift. He waits, probably for me to ask why. I

wait for him to tell me.

It's a subtle kind of mind game we play, and I couldn't tell you who's winning.

Lucifer's lip twitches. "Would you like to know why I need this spirit?" His voice drops into a dangerous, seductive croon.

"That would be appreciated," I say, fighting back a shiver.

"Because I'm losing my grip on Hell's power threads, which means I won't be able to rule much longer, whether the rebellion wins or not."

My heart plummets into my stomach. "You're not serious."

With a glint in his eye, he nods slowly. "Deadly serious." His thumb taps against my arm again. "And word on the street is that someone is siphoning it away. Drop by drop." He pauses, the silence loaded with meaning. "Explosion. By. Explosion."

My jaw drops.

He means me.

Lucifer is losing control of Hell's power, and I'm taking it.

Everything shifts once more, finally settling into its proper location: he isn't my jailer, not really. I'm his.

I have him trapped and broken at my feet, and neither of us have the power to stop it.

"Well," I say, swallowing thickly. "I was right."

Lucifer lifts a polite eyebrow in question.

"This does concern me."

A soft laugh escapes him, almost like he didn't mean to, and when he speaks, it sounds a little sad. "I suppose it does."

"How long have you known?" I ask him, my chest squeezing at the thought of how he must have reacted when he finally discovered what my power was.

He doesn't answer immediately, and in the darkness, I can't read his expression. "Two days," he says finally.

Since the aqueducts, then. Of course.

Lucifer's hands fall from my sides, and I shiver, suddenly

cold. "What now?" I ask, a bit stupidly, I'll admit.

"I couldn't tell you," Lucifer says.

He sounds almost lost.

I wonder what he needs right now. I can't tell; it's too dark, and he's too good at hiding. If it were Tobias, I'd offer him a little tidbit of something true. Something raw, to get him back on side. With Logan—well, shit, Logan's easy. I'd just flash him some skin and see what happened.

Lucifer... he's too much like me.

The thought rings in my head, over and over.

He's like me. Obtuse, careful, and in control. Not that I've made a good show of it, with the way these boys seem to drag my real thoughts out of me, but still.

So, if he's like me—what would I want right now?

I'd want a joke.

"You could..." I say hesitantly, the words sounding funny in my mouth, "handcuff me and drag me back to the castle now? If you want."

There's a split second of nothing, where I think I'm holding my breath, and then it works. It fucking works.

Lucifer cracks a smile.

"I thought the idea of handcuffing prisoners was meant to be because they *don't* like it," he says, a dark note of suggestion in his voice.

I shiver—this time in delight. "How do you know what I like?" I challenge him. I'm playing with fire now, and it's well against what I should be doing, but I don't care. I want this. I want something real. "You've barely looked me in the eyes since I got here."

A low sound erupts from his chest, like irritation, but he doesn't look irritated at all.

Before I can move, he pounces, arms wrapping around me, and the scenery whisks away in a flash.

26

HELENA

I BARELY MANAGE TO FIGHT THE URGE TO SWING MY LEGS LIKE A naughty child.

"I can't believe you actually handcuffed me to a chair," I mutter, tugging futilely on the shackles around my wrist. "And not even in a fun way."

There's a pause in the movement behind me. Then it starts up again, slower this time. I can hear the sound of clothing dropping onto the floor, piece by piece, and my heart begins to pound. Did he take that as an invitation?

Do I want him to?

Visions of the Devil lying me back on his bed and spreading my legs flood me, and I have to bite down a moan before I embarrass myself even further.

The sounds become slightly more distant, and then a shower-head turns on. Disappointment cuts through me. Of course he didn't take it as an invitation. He doesn't want anything to do with me, beyond our ridiculous Ludus bond, which he keeps dismissing as the kind of soulbond a slut forms.

He hasn't said it in those words, but I can hear it in his voice.

"If I let you free, you'll take the chance to look through all my possessions," Lucifer says lightly.

He's right; I would. "No I wouldn't."

Lucifer laughs. "It's been a long time since anyone lied like that to my face."

A shiver runs through me, and I'm suddenly glad he sat me on this chair facing away from him. Still, I don't know why he didn't just let me go back to my rooms. He summoned Logan and Tobias the second we blinked back into the palace, using our shadow magic against us, and sent them to their suites without even a shared word among us. He could have done the same to me.

Unless he feels like this conversation isn't over between us, too.

I'm taking the Devil's power. The thought echoes over and over in my head, mixing with the secrets I still haven't unpacked.

No wonder my power is killing him; it was already killing him, when it was his and he was in control of it. But I've shattered that desperate thread of control and now I'm just throwing his temptation in his face with all the finesse of a toddler. I've made it ten times worse, and it's bringing him to the brink.

I wet my lips, my stomach churning as I remember the whisper of his voice in the ballroom. His shame.

And even still, that's not everything. It gets worse—oh boy, does it get worse.

Not only am I stealing his power, but I'm taking it when he's already facing an insurrection. If the rebellion caught wind of this... they'd make me a symbol. I'd become Lucifer's enemy.

Given the danger of his addiction, technically, I'm already his enemy.

There are so many fucking layers to this. So many circles of Hell.

Maybe it's time I stopped trying to handle it on my own. One circle at a time—together.

"Last night," I say slowly, wondering how to ask the questions burning through my mind.

None of us have known how to broach the topic with him yet, but we can't keep running.

"Mmm?" he asks easily. "What about it?"

He doesn't know.

My eyes widen, heart racing as I stare at the black tiles before me. He doesn't remember that we saw him.

He doesn't know that we know his secret.

"Never mind," I say, my voice breaking only a little. Time to change the subject. "You know, I'm just as muddy as you are. Don't you think I might want a shower, too?"

His voice is slightly muffled by the water when he replies. "I must confess, I find it difficult to care very much about what you want, right now."

There's a note of amusement in his voice that suggests he doesn't truly mean it, but the unease from the forest is still there, too. Unease that I caused.

But to my surprise, the handcuffs click away from my wrists —undone with a thought—and fall to the ground with a clank of metal. I palm my wrists, rubbing away the pain, and rise to my feet.

And then I pause, because I don't know what he means by this. Am I meant to go have a shower in my own little suite?

Or...

"If you stand out there forever, I will be done by the time you undress," Lucifer says drily.

Heat courses through me. I don't think, don't question whether he means it or not.

I throw my clothing in the corner and step inside. My gaze falls immediately to his chest, the long lines of muscle mixing with scars and the odd burn or two. Something in me softens, just as another part of me flares into life.

This man has been around for centuries; I can't forget that. I can't even comprehend the life he's led before this.

But I can appreciate the man it's made him.

He doesn't protest, doesn't speak or make any effort to control us for once. He just stands there, leaning one hand against the tiles as the water sluices down upon him. Since he's feeling no shame watching me, I abandon any attempt at manners and simply drink him in.

My eyes drift lower, following the vee of his hips, the sharp jut of surprising muscle that blends into thick thighs. They're normally hidden by perfect dress trousers; I didn't expect this, and a wave of desire rushes through me at the contradiction in him.

It isn't the only contradiction.

He has no tattoos.

At least none on this side of him. I expected a hidden sleeve, or something elaborate on his thigh. But there's nothing.

I take another step inside and let the door fall shut behind me.

It's a big shower, made for two. Or three. Or four.

One step at a time. No need to be a keen bean, or you'll scare him out the door.

Mind you, he'd have to push past me to find it. Naked, sopping wet. I think I could convince him to stay.

My eyes find his, and I realize I don't need to. He isn't going anywhere.

The corner of his mouth twitches. "Have you drunk your fill?"

"Hardly."

Hunger flashes in his gaze, and he beckons for me to come closer. There are literally two shower heads; I don't need to be close to him at all.

I step into the cascade of water and take the soap he hands me. My breath catches. I wait for him to cross the threshold, to knock the soap from my hands as he presses me against the tiles and consumes me.

I don't need to be a mind reader like Tobias to know it's all he's been thinking of since he saw us together. It's written all across his face. He wants me. I think he's always wanted me.

Why doesn't he take me, then?

After a beat, I turn away, hiding the disappointment on my face. I hear the water shift as he moves behind me, and sense the motions of him washing himself. So, I do the same.

But unfortunately, I can't stop my big mouth from taking things further.

I swear, these men are turning me into someone else. Someone I can't control.

"I know you think I'm a slut for dragging you all into a Ludus soulbond," I say before I can stop myself. "And that's really not very fair of you. Slutshaming is so last decade."

The sounds of Lucifer soaping himself behind me pause, and then suddenly I can feel the heat radiating from his body. He still isn't touching me, but he's right there.

My breath catches, every nerve ending prickling as my body unconsciously reaches for him, reaches for more.

"The only bonds I ever form are Ludus," he murmurs, his voice low in my ear as he brushes my hair away from my neck. I grow very still. "So unless you're calling *me* a slut, I suggest you rethink your deductions."

"Oh," I say, far too breathless to pretend I'm unbothered.

He laughs. There's a strange edge to the sound, but I can't question that because he returns to the task of diligently soaping, only it isn't his own body he's working on this time.

He's finally touching me.

My chest rises and falls, faster than before. I can't quite believe he's here, his skin against mine, and like with a wild animal, I'm too scared to move in case he vanishes back into the forest.

His hands roam my shoulders, chaste at first, but as they get lower down my back, I can feel the seduction in them. I'm not sure he even means to. I think this man is just pure seduction.

"And I would never shame anyone for enjoying... copious... amounts of filthy sex," he continues.

This time, his words are said into the back of my neck. I can't contain my shiver.

"What happened to your other bonds?" I ask, steadying myself against the shower wall as he moves his hands to my front, beginning at my collarbone and working slowly down.

"I live a long life," he says simply. "And this is the nature of Ludus bonds." I can hear a wry smile in his voice. "I lied, a little, when I first explained them to you. They are no less meaningful, but they are simpler than the others." His hands cup my breasts, the soap making his fingers slide over my skin like silk. He traces the shape of them, pausing as my nipple peaks beneath his fingertip. When he speaks again, I can hear him smiling. "We carry their echo with us forever, but when new bonds form, stronger ones, Ludus are the bonds left behind."

"So you have a trail of lovers left behind you," I say, not even bothering to hide how I'm panting now. "Should I be jealous?"

"I don't believe love is ever something to be jealous of." He trails his hands lower, over my stomach. The water cascades onto his back, sending droplets bouncing onto my skin and cheek. "My bonds with them are treasured. As is my bond with you."

My breath catches. It's the first time he's said anything positive about this bond. About me.

"And yet, you don't share."

He stills, and I can sense the surprise in him. "You have a point," he says after a long moment, and I wonder how many times he's ever acceded as much. To anyone. I'm willing to bet I could count them on one hand. "How very outdated of me."

Then his words sink in, and the answer to my question hits me like a truck.

He isn't slutshaming me. He's sad.

"You want more than a Ludus bond," I whisper. "How many thousands of years have you been here, and the only bonds you ever form are the ones that never stay."

The water hits my back, steaming hot, but his sudden absence leaves me cold.

I won't let him go. Not like this. Not tonight.

We're bound together by fate, and since he isn't my jailer— not really, not in the way I thought—there's no reason I can't have him.

I catch hold of his wrist, and he pauses, going so very still. Waiting, I tighten my grip, refusing to give into his subtle demand to be freed.

If he wants to be free of us, he needs to let me go first.

Maybe that isn't fair of me, but I don't care. I've never played fair in my life, and I'm done waiting for my soulmates to work through their shit before they give into destiny.

If Ludus bonds are the ones that are left behind, then I want to collect the set before it disappears.

"Helena," Lucifer says softly, turning to regard me through heavy-lidded eyes. "You have to be certain you want this."

"Why wouldn't I want this?" I ask, breathless. "You saw me

with Tobias. You must know about Logan. Do I look like someone who doesn't take what I want?"

Lucifer's mouth twitches again, deeper this time. "You look like someone who gets what you want, yes," he says, which isn't exactly what I said, but I barely notice because he finally turns around.

I don't think I was prepared for this.

I don't think I fully appreciated what it would mean to be faced with the Devil in all his naked glory. Lucifer. Satan. Lord of Hell.

He comes to a halt in front of me, so close that my nipples brush his chest with each breath. He tips my chin up, guiding my head slightly away from the water so I don't drown standing up—even though I already kind of feel like I'm drowning.

"But what I meant was that this will change things between us," he says in a low voice, his eyes fixed to my lips as if he's committing the sight to memory.

"Of course it will."

That twitch again. "You'll no longer see me as the Devil," he says, voice softer now, barely above a murmur. "You'll see me as a man, and that will make it difficult for me to hold my distance from you."

I bite down on the embarrassing sound that wants to escape me. Like I didn't already see him as a man. Idiot. "You said you've had Ludus bonds before," I manage to get out. "So what's the big deal? You've done this with other people."

Lucifer pauses, his thumb swiping across my lower lip as his eyes flash. "Ah, but Helena," he says, "you're different. It's like you said—you're the one I want to stay."

He leans in, and my gasp of surprise is cut off as his lips press urgently to my neck.

I thought he was going for my mouth, but at the last

second, he turned away. His teeth trail along my skin as he mouths up to my jaw. Wet, slow. His hand falls to my neck, cupping me gently, and I steady myself against his chest, waiting for his lips on mine, waiting—

It doesn't come. He stays at my neck, my jaw. His mouth carves a line behind my ear, taking my lobe between his teeth and flicking his tongue across it in a slow and languid promise.

"Kiss me," I tell him.

"I am," he says, his laughter coating the skin of my collarbone. His voice is filled with lies—he knows what I'm asking for, and despite the urgency building between us, he won't give it.

Instead, he tastes every other piece of me. Everything he can get his hands on, his free palm roaming my back, my ass. Lucifer slides a finger down the center of my ass, barely dipping into the crack, just a hint of what he might like to do to me there.

I jump, startled, and he kisses the other side of my jaw, my cheek. His lips brush the very corner of my mouth, slowing, teasing.

I turn toward him, but he's too fast; he pulls away.

I've no time to miss him because he's on his knees.

Water sluices down his hair, leaving the curls in long, soaked ringlets by his face. He shakes them back, sharp jaw tilted up in what looks terrifyingly like ecstasy.

His pupils are blown wide, eyes half closed in lazy pleasure as he slides one hand between my thighs and raises an eyebrow in question.

I nod quickly, not trusting myself to speak.

He laughs again, a flash of surprised delight in the sound, and then lowers his attention from my face completely.

The first thing I feel is hot air, blown slowly and deliberately across my clit. It's followed by a brush of lips that has my head falling back against the wall behind me, the rush of water hitting my breasts and cascading down.

Lucifer laughs, but there's nothing amusing in the sound anymore. It's dark. Possessive.

He kisses me again, lingering, and the very hint of a tongue dips out.

It's like he's tasting me.

Like I'm a decadent kind of sweet at an expensive dinner.

"Lucifer," I moan, reaching out to thread my fingers through his hair. But then I pause. Can I do that? Am I allowed to touch him like that?

He swipes his tongue across me, and I decide that I'm going to mess the shit out of the Devil's hair.

I grip him with both hands and tangle the silky strands of his hair beneath my fingers.

In response, he nips the inside of my thigh, a low sound like a growl coming from his chest, and then he begins to lick me.

Slow, teasing licks that feel possessive. Perfectly controlled. I groan in protest, messing up his hair as I writhe up into his face.

He doesn't react this time, just keeps that same maddening pace. My toes curl, my eyes fluttering closed.

I want to mess him up. I want to ruin him.

But he's intent on ruining me.

Another warning nip on my thigh, even though I didn't do anything that time. A low rumble.

I twist his curls around my index finger and pull hard enough to hurt.

Lucifer responds by sliding two fingers deep inside me, making me scream.

Before I've recovered, he curls them, stroking inside me and flicking his tongue very deliberately over my clit.

"You're not playing fair," I complain, gasping.

His fingers keep stroking, but his mouth pauses enough for him to say, "No one can play fair with you, Helena, or we'd lose."

I grin in triumph, my eyes still closed. "What's that meant to mean?"

Lucifer twists his fingers, and I hear something strange in his voice. Something like affection. "You think I haven't noticed all that you're collecting in your suite of information? You think I don't know your talents on Earth?"

He licks a long, slow swipe along me, pausing to flutter his tongue. Pleasure rushes through me, making me shiver, making my hands clutch at him even harder.

"I've no idea what you mean," I breathe.

"I'm sure," he agrees in a low voice. "And neither do the missing guard uniforms, or the fingerprints lining the keyholes of all the interesting rooms in my palace."

He places a kiss on my hip, lingering there, so his next words are said against my skin. "You're drawn to the night sky."

"Any romantic fool likes the stars," I reply, barely aware of the words coming out of my mouth.

My grip on his hair has fallen slack, and instead I'm writhing beneath his touch, begging him for more as I ride his fingers and press up desperately in search of his mouth.

"Not all of them," Lucifer says so softly I barely hear him.

He kisses me, sucking gently as my pleasure rises in waves. I'm gone, completely destroyed, fucking up against him as he brings me off in an agonizingly meticulous rhythm.

Controlled.

Perfect.

It's nowhere near enough of what I want from him.

I crest, coming in waves. My head thunks painfully against the tiles, and by the time I can look up again, Lucifer is standing.

My heart stutters. He doesn't look like the Devil right now. His hair falls in long, wet ringlets by his face. His chest rises and falls faster than usual, matching the unreadable darkness to his gaze.

His cock hangs heavy between his thighs, softening, the evidence of his own pleasure already vanished down the drain.

He doesn't look like the Devil; he just looks like a man.

Lucifer regards me quietly, reaches out just enough to brush a strand of hair behind my ear, and then moves away.

27

HELENA

I SPEND THE NEXT TWO DAYS MOSTLY IN MY ROOM. I HAVE HUNDREDS of books I can curl up with, room service on demand, no reason to leave.

Only the slow ache of shame and guilt.

Knowing that not only is my presence harming Lucifer, but I'm the reason he's losing everything.

I'm not just damaging to him; I'm fucking usurping him. I can even see it happening in real time now, in the small details around the palace. The way the doors seem to swing open for me a second before I arrive. The way the suits of armor stand a little taller.

Even the freshly cooked meals seem warmer for me, while Lucifer grimaced into a freezing cold pie just this morning.

I assume the others know by now, judging by the shocked silence that greeted me at the breakfast table. The silent stares and the thick scent of apprehension on the air. I can't face them. I don't want this. I don't want any of it.

Nothing in my books is helping me, probably because the words keep buzzing around and I can't focus on them. But still, you'd think there'd be something in all these books on magic and power that would explain how someone who has not ascended to queen or inherited the role of princess can even access this power.

And why is my form of it coming out more like Tobias? It's like I'm taking Hell's power—Lucifer's power—and I'm transforming it into something else.

Maybe I'm just making a fun little scrapbook of all my soulmates together. A little bit of Lucifer's power here, a little bit of Tobias's power there. All I need now is to grow some golden claws and I'll have caught them all.

I snap the book shut after the fifth time reading the same sentence in a row and stare moodily up at the ceiling, dropping back into the pillows.

Even these beautiful first edition fantasy books won't distract me. All I can think about is everything I'm doing wrong.

I can't free my parents. I can't help Lucifer because he won't let me. And my presence is destroying everything.

It's destroying Lucifer, it's destroying the very political structures of Hell—because if the *Rising Snakes* see that I have Hell's power, that's going to throw everything out—and it's destroying the land beneath us.

I laugh bitterly as it suddenly occurs to me that what happened in the ballroom was Hell's power. Of course it was. That was a thread of the shame current that I tapped into.

All those little whispers I heard were shame.

And Lucifer, right at the end. Lucifer's shame, his deep, dark secret: the control that he loses every time he lets the power win.

I wasn't doing anything special in there. I was only accessing the same power that the kings and queen of Hell can access.

The only difference was that I was using it like a cheap con artist would. Using it to get what I want, which is exactly what the kings and queen vow not to do.

A faint noise outside my window alerts me, but when I look up, there's nothing there. It's probably just a little Hell beastie climbing the walls. We see them all the time—little lizards and strange furred creatures scuttling among the rocks.

I drop back down into the pillows, but then I hear it again. Frowning, I sit up slowly.

A faint sense of apprehension floods my body. That didn't sound like claws. It sounded like—

It comes again, and this time I see it: metal striking stone.

A grappling hook thrown high and landing on my window sill.

My eyes widen and I sit bolt upright, hurrying across the room. Maybe if I'm quick enough, I can pull the hook free and make whoever's climbing it plummet to the ground.

It's a demon, and he's nearly at me already, his snarling, smiling face riddled with hatred.

"Fuck," I hiss, and I turn to run from the room.

I yell for the guards the second I'm in the corridor, screaming something about Rising Snakes and grappling hooks in my window. Little licks of flame burst into life behind me.

No doubt this is the rage current. Makes sense—it was the first one I tapped into after all, judging by what happened at the portal.

After everything with Ronin, it probably hooked into my own rage and just combusted on the spot.

I take a turn and then another, ducking through a secret passageway so I can reach the elevators quicker. Lucifer must be in his penthouse; I have to warn him.

I slam straight into a hard, tall body.

Calm hands steady me and I look up into piercing blue eyes framed with dark curls.

"Lucifer," I breathe, "the rebellion's here. They've breached the walls."

First up in sentences I have now shared with a medieval peasant.

His face darkens, but he doesn't look shocked. "Damn them," he mutters, and then he carefully moves me to the side and strides forward.

I stare after him, stunned, and then give chase.

"What are you doing? We need to fight them! We need to get the guards on the battlements!"

Number two in sentences I've shared with a medieval peasant.

"It's no good," he says sharply. "And I've already prepared the battlements."

"Already? But didn't I just tell you about it?" I ask, incredulous.

Finally, he glances over his shoulder, his eyes meeting mine with a flash. "You did," he says, infuriatingly obtuse, and then he turns away.

"God damn him," I swear under my breath.

Tobias careens out of the corridor to the right.

He grabs me by the upper arm and whirls me to face him. "How many?" he snaps.

"I only saw one," I say quickly. "But he was prepared for a fight. It has to be an onslaught."

"They wouldn't come with less than twenty," he says distractedly, staring into the distance as if he's making mental arithmetic. "Come with me."

I glance back over my shoulder, but Lucifer's already at the end of the corridor, and he doesn't give a shit. He doesn't care what I do, even though it's all out in the open now.

Technically, I hold the power that he needs to defeat them.

We could be working together, but instead we're running in opposite directions like twats.

Furious, I turn away and follow Tobias. At least he'll let me help.

We wind our way through the palace. It's in full uproar now, with guards running to the battlements and those little wooden training swords replaced with cold, hard steel.

Tobias leads us to one of the smaller balconies, off a guest suite from somewhere on the middle levels.

"We can't do much from down there," Tobias says quickly, "but we can throw illusions from here, especially if you follow my lead." He winks at me, making reference to the power I have somehow stolen and then transformed into Tobias' image.

"Where's Logan?" I ask, mirroring him and standing with both hands resting on the balcony. "Is he down with the guards? Shifting?"

Tobias' expression tightens. "No," he says shortly, then: "I couldn't find him."

So, he's hiding then.

My stomach sinks in disappointment, even though I can't say I'm truly surprised. He's made it clear from the start: he doesn't want to be responsible for defending anyone.

He doesn't want to be responsible for anyone at all, or anything—not even himself.

"He's probably halfway across Hell on his bike," I say bitterly, my hands clenching into the marble. "Or at least thirty meters away, with the engine rumbling," I amend, deciding it's pretty unlikely that Logan nicked the Grave for a joy ride.

Even though I'm sure he wanted to.

Tobias reaches out a palm and pats me gently on the hand, but he's too distracted to look at me properly.

Right. Of course. Now is not the time.

Already, there's movement down below, and not just on the

ground. I can see figures scaling the wall. Dozens of them, their grappling hooks glinting in the moonlight.

My guy must have been a scout. Unluckily for him, he chose the one location that would end with a girl screaming her head off down the corridor.

But that hasn't deterred them. Like little cockroaches, they swarm across the palace, and there are far more than Tobias' estimate of twenty.

A strange feeling courses within me. It isn't dread or unease, like it has been for so long. For the first time since I learned my power was hurting Lucifer, killing him, I feel a sense of hope. This is something I can do.

I'm far enough away from him that surely whatever I do from here won't affect his addiction. He won't get high on the power, and it won't send him into sharp withdrawals when he gets a whiff of it—because he won't get a whiff of it, not from here.

So I can help. I can use this power, now that I know what it is, now that he's finally told me. And with Tobias at my side, he can help me craft it into a weapon.

Then I can defend us.

The hope burns into a fierce need to prove that I can be useful.

I can do this. I know who I'm meant to be now. Finally.

"I'm going to fill out the guard line with extra men," Tobias says, a small bead of sweat appearing on his brow. He's already weaving illusions, making it look as though there are waves and waves of us. He grins tightly, but the effort is still clear on his face. "Don't suppose you want to set something on fire, darling?"

"I'd love to," I tell him with a grin.

But that isn't all I want to do. I think of that thread of shame and how it immediately transformed me into a far more efficient con artist than I'd ever been in life.

It wasn't exactly my most shining moment, but what if I could do that here?

What if I could make the rebels run before they even saw Tobias' guards?

Closing my eyes, I feel out in the same way that I did when I was in the ballroom, searching for something. I let my desperation for an answer flood me, consume me.

It isn't long before the whispers start. But it isn't shame. It's fear.

My eyes snap open in shock. They're afraid.

Not because they're attacking the castle. They're attacking the castle *because* they're afraid.

I open my mouth, hesitant. "Tobias, do we know anything about why the Rising Snakes are trying to usurp Lucifer?"

He turns to me, incredulous.

"Helena, I'm holding about thirteen different complex illusions right now. I really don't have time for a philosophical discussion."

"Right. Okay. Fine. Got it."

He's right, of course. But this isn't what I expected. I expected anger and bitterness and some sense of entitlement. I assumed they wanted the power that Lucifer had always held until now.

But that isn't what I'm feeling from them. I'm feeling fear and desperation.

These are people with their backs against a wall, who have no other choice. And those people are much harder to defeat than anyone else.

I never try to con people like that because they have nothing to lose.

Still, I reach for them again, and I grab hold of the first whisper I can hear properly.

Gonna die, the whisper comes, and then over and over again, *gonna die, gonna die.*

Gonna die screaming. Gonna die bleeding.

God, they're frantic. And yet, a coldness sweeps through me as I realize exactly how I can use this, and more importantly— that I will.

Gonna die screaming. Gonna die bleeding.

God, fuck, am I really doing this? I remember the hatred contorting the face of the rebel below my window. I didn't need to read his thoughts to know what he would do to me if he caught me.

An enemy is an enemy; I have to remember that.

"All right," I say to myself, ignoring Tobias's glance of confusion.

Then I take that thread of fear, grasping it with my mind. Suddenly, it's like I can physically hold it. It's no longer a snazzy ethereal metaphor—some river floating in the air below me.

It's there, in front of me.

It's water, running from beneath the earth and twisting up, up into Hell. And so I reach out my hands, looking like an absolute ninny, I'm sure, and I dip them below the current.

Power courses against me, like waves on a shore. I grasp it, twist it, and shape it into an illusion—a trickery of truth. A fear illusion crafted from the power of fear itself.

He *will* die screaming and bleeding, but only if he believes it first.

I hear the screams with my ears this time, and down on the bridge that connects the gardens to the palace entryway, I see there are more of them. They're hiding in the bushes, and one of them is screaming their head off as they look down on themselves and see rivulets of blood pouring free.

Their nerve endings translate the visual illusion into pain and agony, because that's what they'd always known would happen. They were ready to believe.

More screams rise, and I feel sick to the core, but I'd do it again in a heartbeat. Otherwise this attack will be an onslaught. We don't have enough guards, or else Tobias wouldn't be wasting his time on an illusion to make more of them.

"Nice," Tobias says, a rare, genuine grin on his face.

They're retreating.

No, they're not retreating; they're unsure. They're hesitant. They don't know what spell we've hit them with.

Triumph fills Tobias' voice as he crows, and as I look over the battlements, I see wave upon wave of guards swarming the bridge, the paths. They aren't real, of course. Can't possibly be real.

But then I see something that is real among them. A dark head of hair. A body with a permanent moat of space around him—no one willing to get too close—and a blazing sword held high.

Lucifer is at the forefront, unlike me and Tobias, hiding back, throwing illusions. He's down there, fighting.

And the bodies he's fighting are no illusion.

Rebel after rebel falls beneath his sword, and this time the blood is real. It coats the flagstones, and I watch in amazement as he breaks through the line and emerges into the gardens near where I cast my illusion.

The danger doesn't hit me until it's already happened.

My illusion is still spreading. My power is still rising, and this time Lucifer is *right there.*

I see him pause, feel my heart stutter.

He stumbles. I can almost see his struggle from here. Can almost feel how the power is twisting inside him, consuming him, controlling him as he fights to tear himself free.

"I have to get down there," I hiss.

I don't know how to bridge this gap. Can I jump? Will my power catch me? Can it do something like that?

I don't know how to use it. I don't know how to terraform Hell into a mountain I can run down, but Tobias is already there.

He doesn't ask why. He just sees the fear on my face, hooks an arm around my waist, and suddenly we're on the bridge.

I steady myself, my mind swimming with vertigo. For a moment, Tobias looks at me, and it's the strangest sensation—like he's seeing me for the first time. Seeing who I am. But that's bonkers because in this moment I'm no one. In this moment, I'm just... afraid. I'm terrified, and all I could think up there was that I had to get *here* and *now*. It was Tobias who was incredible, knowing my mind in a second and getting me here, like we had no need for words.

I don't deserve to have anyone look at me the way Tobias is right now—with that strange, impossible expression on his face, his eyes bright and his lips parted in shock.

I don't deserve it, and I have no time to think about it because Lucifer is in danger, and it's all because of me.

So I turn and run.

I run toward where I saw the Devil fall, and I pray I'm not too late. That the rebels don't realize his vulnerability before I can get there and save him.

Three rebels huddle beneath a stone parapet lining the palace garden. Their hands clutch at their heads, but already the illusory blood I crafted is fading from their bodies. Any moment now, they'll open their eyes and see.

As I lurch towards the Devil, with Tobias close behind, that's exactly what they do.

They blink, stare in confusion, astonishment... and then

rage. Their eyes find Lucifer and they hurtle toward him, seeing the moment for what it is: an opportunity to win.

Fear like I've never known it before takes hold in my chest, and I don't even need to think the power into existence; it happens in the blink of an eye.

Hellfire rises.

It splits the earth between me and the rebels. They're cut off from Lucifer, howling in fear and surprise as they stumble away. Tobias and Lucifer shift, their demonic faces emerging amidst the hellfire flames.

The Rising Snakes take one look upon the true face of the Devil, turn tail, and run.

I leap through the fire, landing at Lucifer's side just in time to catch him around the waist as he stumbles and falls to his knees.

His face wavers like an illusion itself. Terrifying bone twists into a skeletal visage plated with golden metal. But it flickers and fades, like fire itself, becoming the beautiful lines of his angel face.

The faces flicker, back and forth, but each one, beautiful or terrifying, is contorted in a grimace of agony as Lucifer struggles to resist the pull of this power.

I wonder for a moment what it would be like if he gave in to it. If he just let go for a moment. Maybe it wouldn't be so bad. Maybe he could even use it for his advantage.

And then I remember, no, that's exactly how addicts think. You don't control the drug; it controls you. No matter how much you swear it's the other way around.

In that moment, I'm disgusted with myself for thinking it— thinking it would be easier to let him use the power that this addiction gives him.

He falls against me. I don't think he even knows it's me; his eyes are wide and unseeing, his mouth twisted with the effort of straining against the power's call. The drug.

I rein it all in, pull the hellfire back, relinquish it all with a violent snap of the air. The smoke, the flames, the fire—it all goes out, and I bring my power with it, just like the thoughts I keep tucked behind walls in my mind.

Lucifer blinks, gasps, and looks for a moment like a drowning man surging above the water.

"Helena," he rasps, leaning heavily on my shoulders and glancing down at me through sweat-soaked hair.

All around us, I can hear the sounds of fighting, but no one has realized we're alone yet. Tobias is nowhere to be seen, and I imagine he's out in the thick of it, coordinating his illusions.

So I take the opportunity to lead Lucifer behind one of the statues of his garden, tucking him into the crook so that I don't have to hold him quite as much.

He doesn't lean on the statue though; he leans on me. I expected him to pull away the second he realized what was going on, but he doesn't. He stays there, his breath heaving in deep gasps of air, one hand pressed to his forehead as he shoves his hair away from his eyes and stares out into the garden with a frantic expression.

I've never seen him so uncomposed, so uncontrolled.

"What was that?" he rasps.

That was an oopsie, I think, but it isn't the time for my usual brand of understatement.

"That was me fucking up," I say, "and I'm sorry. I didn't think you'd be close enough for the power to affect you."

He frowns down at me, confused, and then I see the slow, sick thread of awareness cross his expression.

"You know," he says, and it isn't a question.

I knew he hadn't remembered that night we found him, but the proof still hurts.

"We all know," I say quietly.

There are so many things I want to say after that.

We want to help you.

I know what you're going through.

You're doing so well.

I'm sorry that my presence hurts you.

But none of them come free. In times like these, there really is nothing that you can say, and every single thing that you want to.

He closes his eyes, and the heaving of his chest quickens, becomes almost frantic.

I tell him, like I'm soothing a child, "It's gone now. There's no extra power here; only what you want to draw from Hell yourself."

"That," he grits out through clenched teeth, "is precisely the problem."

Fuck, of course it is. My wild untamed power triggers him, but it isn't the source of his addiction. His addiction is all around him. It's in the power he draws on every day, the power he must seize and use to maintain control of Hell, and the power that he is losing to the detriment of everything he's worked to gain.

He has to keep his addiction in balance.

He has to keep his addiction in the palm of his hand, or he loses everything. Every day, he is forced to resist it.

It takes me a long moment to realize that Lucifer is watching me. There's a thin sheen of sweat across his forehead, and his eyes are shiny with some kind of emotion. I think for a moment that it's the high of the drug, and then I realize, no, this is simply Lucifer without his masks.

The shock of it leaves me reeling. I steady myself against the statue, and Lucifer, mistaking my movement for falling, reaches out to grasp me by the wrist and keep me upright.

I don't correct him.

I let my hand come to his waist, and together we help each other stand.

"How did they get in so quickly?" I murmur, searching for something to say that isn't about the two of us, that isn't going to end with me saying something I can't take back.

"They didn't," he rasps out, his eyes searching my face. I don't know what he's searching for. "They've been trying for weeks."

I frown at him.

"Trying for weeks... But I haven't seen any sign of them."

He gives me a bitter smile. "I've been holding them at bay."

It hits me then, just how much I've missed. Christ, I'm so stupid. It wasn't just the addiction; it's a giant ass battle, and Lucifer's right in the middle of it.

I thought this whole time that we were fighting off the dying remnants of a rebellion. Some skirmishes on the outside and a couple of weak attempts to break through. But we aren't. We're dealing with the fucking middle of it, man.

Lucifer has been fighting them this whole time.

Alone.

This is his world. He's been holding them back single-handedly, and I only noticed when he crumbled.

Something flickers in his gaze, and he reaches for me. After a brief pause that seems to last for hours, he crosses the last of the distance between us, slides his fingers through my hair, and cups the back of my head.

My breath catches, and I realize that for all we shared in the shower that night, he still hasn't kissed me.

Not like this, not like he so very clearly wants to.

God, the heat in his gaze... but it's more than that. I can feel it flickering down the bond. I can feel just how much he wants this.

The strength of his longing almost makes me feel ill. It's too much to bear—aching, terrifying. It's a rising tide held back through sheer force of will, just as he holds back everything that he feels.

He lowers his head and pauses an inch above me. My heart races.

"Maybe I should swear fealty to you after all, Helena," he says softly. I'm not sure he even realizes what he's saying, or that I'm here to hear the words. "It wouldn't be such a bad way to fall."

I don't know what to say. I open my mouth to speak, but the words catch, tumbling over each other.

He lowers, further still, our lips just barely brushing, the merest hint of a touch—

—and then a loud crash shatters the night. Lucifer's head whips up, and any expression, any emotion, that had escaped from beneath the mask vanishes. He's a perfect statue of control.

In that frozen moment, I think of a dozen paths laid out before me. A dozen things I could do, or people I could be, that would carry me through this mess. But really, there's only one path that will take me to the other side. Everything else has been a fantasy.

I've always been able to escape; I've just never actually tried because I wanted to stay.

Still holding his gaze, so he suspects nothing, I reach forward with one hidden palm and pick the Devil's pocket. He doesn't see.

With one final inscrutable look back at me, lost among his own demons, he pulls his hand free and runs back into the fray.

28

HELENA

I STARE AFTER HIM FOR A FEW MINUTES. FOR SOME REASON, PART OF ME really thinks he'll turn around. He'll come back. But of course he doesn't.

There's literally a battle going on right now, Helena, get your shit together.

I shake my head and look down at the Grave in my palm. It slid free from the hilt surprisingly easily, like it wanted to be with me. It will return to Lucifer in under an hour, no matter where I am, I'm certain of that. Otherwise there was no reason for Logan to be so strict on our time limit in the market. But an hour is plenty of time to get far enough away.

The Devil has only bound me to him in Hell, after all. I noted that little loophole at the beginning. And I've proven without a doubt that I can't stay here.

It wouldn't be such a bad way to fall.

I stare at the shouting, fighting figures—too close for comfort—and feel like I'm spinning out of control. I don't belong here.

It doesn't matter if I can't free my parents or return to

Heaven; I need to get out. I need to get out of here before I destroy everything.

Before Lucifer lets me.

I barely know what I'm doing, but suddenly I'm running. I'm running from the garden, I'm running from everything that's happening behind me.

It's still not fast enough.

The ground shudders beneath my feet, and I remember how the earth carried me away when I ran to the aqueducts. It was obviously Hell terraforming in response to my screaming emotions; I know that now.

If there was ever a time where that moment would repeat, it's now. And bonus—I even sort of know what I'm doing.

Scrubbing away tears, I search for the power that hovers just beyond my reach. It's with a bitter sort of satisfaction that I find the strongest, closest river is grief. It pours, rushing, buffeting me, and I choke out a sob as I seize hold of the power and funnel it into the ground at my feet.

The earth rumbles, caves... erupts.

A cascade of dirt and broken shrubs launches me forward, like a wave, and we're past the gates, past the battle. Far from even the noise of it. It's eerily silent out here, with the forest stretching above me and the highway ahead.

The cord at my chest burns white-hot, fumbling and confused as it acknowledges we've reached the thirty meter mark. I give it a second. Two seconds.

The Grave in my palm shimmers, and a gentle, steady warmth flows into my skin. The bond settles.

I wonder if it's a similar sort of magic to the gems in Mystic's Peak. Logan's words from days ago echo in my mind.

"How do they fit whole worlds in there?"

"I'm told that, to them, we're the ones inside the gem. If you want answers, become a mystic for the next few thousand years."

Maybe this gem contains worlds, too. Maybe it somehow contains Hell. It would mean that I'm nowhere near the thirty meter mark of our proximity bond; the entirety of Hell rests in the palm of my hand.

Shaking my head, I bury the metaphysical thought exercise for another day. Maybe one where I'm not on a time limit.

I look around carefully. There are no convenient motorbikes around here, no carriages I can hail. Fortunately, though, I also don't see any scavengers who might attack a traveler on foot, and the rebellion certainly aren't here. They're all occupied at the palace.

In fact, a disturbing number of the outlying population here are occupied at the palace.

I don't want to think about that too much, so I just keep running, using a little of Hell's power every few minutes to propel me forward.

Before long, I'm weaving through the market streets and skirting the fringes of the forest. When I'm finally at the edge, I find a carriage, abandoned on the outskirts. It probably escorted half the bloody rebellion to our gates, but I won't think about that either.

I won't think about Lucifer's confession—how long this has been going on, how close he is to failing completely.

I climb inside, give my order to the skeleton driving, and lean back. I'm going to the portal into Death.

I can't be above, I can't be below, and I can't be in the middle, so I'll have to be sideways. I'll find Cat in there, and she can help me sort out a new life.

The coach rattles over the rocks and hills, making my teeth chatter. I keep tensing, waiting for the bond to suddenly burn and bring me to my knees, but it doesn't. It's a dull kind of ache. I'm conscious of it, but not conscious enough to worry.

After a particularly violent bump, I end up twitching the

curtain and pressing my face to the glass, watching the scenery come and go. The land is volatile around the coach, even though I'm not consciously funneling the power anymore. It's almost like a river, the earth surging like waves. I clutch at the window and stare down at it, wondering if the turbulence might be caused by something else.

But I know it isn't.

I don't dare try to stop the movement, in case I wake up another beastie and end up covered in tar again. Instead, I ride the earthen waves, jolting about in the carriage and accepting every knock of my head against the wood like penance.

The landscape shifts intentionally, marking the more barren cliffs and crags that line the border to death. The portal is around here somewhere; I can remember it faintly from my time under Ronin's thumb.

I just need to get this over with before I change my mind.

I still want to change my mind.

But this is the only solution that makes sense. I can't roam Hell freely, or I'll usurp Lucifer. I can't go back to Heaven. And I can't stay with them in the castle, because I'm fucking killing him.

But I don't want to leave them.

It isn't just a cord that draws me back. It's more. It will always be more. Like Lucifer, I crave so much more than Ludus.

But I'm fucking terrified of it, because like Tobias, I know we're doomed.

I stumble from the carriage and run up the hill, casting aside memories like forgotten stones until I land on the one I need, from Ronin's time: down the slope, by the twisted tree. Bones litter the exit.

I can find that.

My heart races. With every step I take, I expect to hear a

shout behind me—someone calling me back, begging me to take the path I desperately want to take.

I don't think I'll have the strength to resist a second time.

I end up humming the Spice Girls under my breath, just to keep me going. It's ludicrous, and possibly unhinged, but a sparkling rendition of Wannabe gets me all the way to the portal.

The shimmering light is like a beacon, and I could weep with relief. On the other side of this, I'll find Cat, and she'll get me set up in Death. She can take a message to Lucifer and let him know that I've left.

"You won't have to worry anymore about why I'm taking Hell's power," I mutter to myself, panting from the descent. "I don't fucking want it, mate. It's all yours."

I fall down a crack in the valley, scraping my hands, and have to haul myself out again. My words are becoming frantic, even though I'm only talking to myself.

"You don't have to help me get back to Heaven, Lucifer, and you don't have to worry that I'm going to accidentally take Hell. I'll live out my days in Death if I have to. Become a hermit, living on the edges of life."

I skid to the bottom, landing among the bones, and pause. For a few seconds, I simply study the shimmering swirls of power within the portal, sensing the cold, dark nothingness that lies beyond.

Death is such a strange place, so empty of color. Maybe it will even dull the sensations of our soulbond, so there won't be anything calling me back to them.

I take a deep breath, ignore the inner protest, and step through the portal.

Pain courses through me, and I hurtle back, my body slamming against the mountainside. Something shatters. I feel the bone twist, and when I fall to my feet and my hands, my wrist collapses beneath me.

I look down to find it bent at a strange angle.

"What the fuck?" I yell, staring in sickened shock at the damage.

I can't feel it yet, but it's only going to be a few seconds before the pain hits. The adrenaline is keeping it at bay, but I can feel just how crumpled my body is, how strong the force was that threw me from that portal.

Seriously, another portal has blocked me? But it doesn't make sense! I wasn't blocked from coming into Hell, and I wasn't blocked from Earth. I should be able to go to Death.

Why would I only be blocked from Heaven and Death? No one gives a shit about Death. It doesn't make sense.

The earth rumbles, and the mountain behind me gives a giant heave as rock spews forth and a giant foot steps beside my head.

I scream, hauling myself backward with my good hand, scrambling, trying to find my feet. But I just end up doing some weird kind of three-legged crab walk into the crevice.

The foot shifts, groans. It's made of rock, like some kind of giant. What the fuck lives in this mountain? I know Hell is full of beasties, but this is no beastie. This is some ancient being.

A voice rings out from way, way above my head.

I know that voice.

Memories take over my mind—Lucifer's arms wrapping around me as he pulled me from the passageway in Hell's palace. And that voice, calling: "Tell him."

I look up, but before I can see the face of this beast, the foot crumbles into dust. I gape at the space it once filled, clouds of ash pluming from it while a shriek builds at the back of my throat.

It was definitely a foot. I didn't imagine it. Is the thing behind the foot still alive, or did the whole body crumble?

What kind of stone giant lives inside of a mountain and then dies the second it bursts free?

There's another groan and a rumble, and the rockslide sends me plummeting forward. Another foot emerges, stepping so close to my head it nearly kills me in one stomp, and then it too crumbles.

For a moment I swear I see a giant stretching toward the sun, tall and silhouetted against the light, a vicious smile on its face. But then there are only plumes of dust and a swirling, howling wind that creates tornadoes from the sand the second it hits.

"Christ on a stick," I mutter, falling back on the ground and staring up at the howling winds above me in defeat.

Is this how I go then? In an utterly batshit fight against rock and sand, with a broken wrist, and the memory of the Devil's lips brushing mine. You lived an interesting life, Helena.

Pour one out for me, boys.

But then something else descends over me. It isn't salvation —no, not even close, but it does stop the tornadoes from reaching me, even though it shouldn't.

Giant golden bars descend, so that in a few seconds I go from sitting in the middle of a desert to being trapped in a four by four room—a gilded cage that grew from the earth.

I blink, covering my eyes as the dust settles, squinting. With tears pouring free, I try to see through the sand storm. How can a cage grow from the earth?

I reach out to touch the nearest bar, wondering if it's an illusion. But no, golden metal meets my hand. A gilt cage.

I turn slowly, the pain from my wrist making tears swell in my eyes. It could still be an illusion, but I don't think it is.

There's a synesthetic flavor to this kind of trickery—I know from Tobias' illusions. They smell rainforest rich with a metallic air, or something, and this has nothing of the sort. Plus, when I shake the bars with my good hand, it feels too real.

There's an almost... squishiness... to Tobias's illusions. Poke them too hard and they'll crumble. This cage is real, and it sprouted from the ground to keep me here the second I tried to leave.

Understanding sweeps through me.

This is real.

I'm not only barred from Heaven now, I'm banished to Hell. I'm stuck here, and the only man who's on my side, who can help me, is destroyed by my presence. Tobias and Logan support me, sure, but they can't actually help me. They can't do anything to fix this.

They can only fuck me stupid while I wait for it to end.

I sink slowly to my knees, my fist reaching out to prop myself against the bar as my forehead falls against it.

I'm fucked. I'm deeply, irrevocably fucked. Can't free my parents. Can't return to Heaven. Can't leave Hell.

Can't stay with the Devil.

Don't want to stay away from him.

Fucked.

I don't know how long I sit there, my forehead pressed to the cold metal, my gaze unseeing as I stare down at the ground. Even though the earthquakes have stopped, Hell isn't static. This part has decided to terraform, for God only knows what reason.

There's a space about two meters in front of me that's constantly changing, rippling through beautiful stretches of grass, a field of flowers, a pond... It changes over and over like some kind of strange screensaver.

It holds my attention, and that's how Cat finds me when

she bursts through the portal from Death, drawn by the unexpected terraforming I assume, and rushes to my side.

"Helena, what the fuck?" she says eloquently, gripping two bars and falling to her knees before me. "What the hell have we missed?"

I begin to laugh—loud, bitter peals of laughter—as I stare up at her. Her men aren't far behind, approaching slower as they scout the area for danger. Warriors to a fault.

Not like me. No, I ran from battle, but it's apparently the only place I belong.

"I don't know," I tell her simply, my smile widening as her hesitation grows. "I really, really don't know. If you've got any ideas, I am..." I gesture vaguely to my head. "All ears, babe."

She blinks at me, and then her expression softens. "Well," she says carefully, "I'm going to start by getting you out of here, and then... I think I'm going to talk to Lucifer about letting Ciera back through."

My heart stutters, and I stare up at her, barely able to hope. "Ciera? Why though?"

Cat's face does something complicated. "Because I think you need a friend."

A friend. Huh. Yeah, that tracks.

She strokes my hair gently. "She contacted me while I was in Death and told me that Lucifer had banned all Heaven contact with the palace—and banned her from Hell entirely." For a moment, Cat's expression flickers, and I remember that she has a fierce side to her despite the softness she seems to choose instead. "But she heard you, Helena, when you tried to call out to her. She's looking for another way in."

I remember the portal in Lucifer's office—the figure among the clouds. Maybe I did some good after all, even if I didn't know it at the time.

"Come on," Cat says gently. "It's time to get you back to the palace, where Tobias is waiting."

"Tobias?" I frown slowly. "What do you mean? And anyway, they're fighting at the palace. The rebels tried to get in." I pull the customary face and wave jazz hands in the air, as I say, "The *Rising Snakes*."

Cat huffs a laugh. "Well, the fighting is over, and Tobias reached out to me. He couldn't escape the palace—something about your bond keeping him there. But he knew you'd come here."

I stare at her, uncomprehending. Of course he couldn't leave the palace. None of them can without the Grave.

"But how did he know I would come here?" I ask her.

I can't keep the incredulity from my voice. It makes me sound weak.

Cat's expression softens even more. She whispers something beneath her breath. In a heartbeat, the cage vanishes, and I fall forward into her arms.

"They always know," she says quietly into my ear. "Don't bother questioning it."

They always know. Who's they?

But my gaze falls to her men approaching, each of their gazes fixed on Cat, like a magnet. Like they're just simply drawn to her.

Like they just know.

Instead of answering, I close my eyes and bury my face in her neck, relishing the one chance of human contact that feels anywhere close to simple.

Even if it is just an illusion.

29

HELENA

TOBIAS IS WAITING FOR ME WHEN I ARRIVE.

"It's okay, darling," Tobias says.

I don't protest. I let him lead me to my bed and guide me down onto the mattress, where I sit huddled on the edge.

I'm still shocked at everything that happened, still trying to process.

Even coming back here was like walking through a nightmare. The halls might not be lined with bodies, but that's only because they've obviously had a cleaning crew run through already. And the crew haven't yet come back for the blood.

There were literal streaks of it, covering the floors, the outside walls. Inside, there's evidence of explosives hurled through the windows—charred walls, burned tapestries.

I couldn't even look in the moat as we crossed the bridge; there was still *something* floating in there, and I didn't want to know what it was. Cat's somber expression was enough for me.

Tobias sits beside me, running a hand over my hair, and gently presses a kiss to my forehead. "What do you need, love?" he asks.

Isn't that the million dollar question?

I needed to get back to Heaven and I couldn't. I needed to free my parents and I couldn't.

I needed to get the fuck out of here, and I couldn't. I needed to help Lucifer and I *just. Fucking. Couldn't.*

"I think I need to be alone," I say quietly.

I'm not sure that's actually true, but I can't process this with him looking at me like that. Unfortunately, he doesn't seem to agree. His brow furrows, and he studies me for a very long time, gently brushing the hair from my eyes and picking flecks of gravel from my clothing.

"Here's the deal," he says softly. "I'm going to give you twenty minutes. You're going to have a nice bath, get into some fresh clothing, and then I'm going to come back."

"What if I'm not here?" I say tartly.

His mouth twitches. "Then I'll find you. Are my terms acceptable?"

I look at him properly then, seeing the concern on his face. The horror that lingers just behind his eyes. He's probably still processing the damn battle.

The blood hasn't even cooled on the stones outside; what the hell was I thinking, adding to their distress like this?

And he hasn't asked me where I went, hasn't asked me anything.

He isn't pushing, but he also won't leave me.

My face must do something strange, because all of a sudden he softens and pulls me into a hug. He presses a kiss to my forehead and whispers in my ear, "You can cry if you need to, Helena. I won't judge you."

A sob breaks free, but I only allow it for a second before I push him away and stand up.

"No," I say forcefully. "It's fine. Twenty minutes. I'll be down in the gardens. Will you find me there?"

He nods.

"And you won't ask questions?" I ask, pushing a little.

He doesn't answer so quickly this time. His steady, thoughtful gaze roams my body, as if he's searching for an answer, taking in every scrape and bruise.

The gravel that's strewn across me, the dirt over my face.

His gaze lands on my broken wrist, and his expression darkens. "You're asking a lot of me, Helena," he says.

I swallow thickly. "I'll let you point me straight in the direction of whatever serves as a hospital room in this place, if you just don't ask me where I went tonight."

He gives me a funny look. "I know where you went," he says carefully. "I sent Cat after you, remember?"

Oh yeah.

"Well don't ask why I went there," I snap, clutching my wrist closer to my chest.

It's beginning to really hurt now, and I honestly would like someone to set it or whatever they do down here for broken bones.

Tobias stands and crosses the room. "You mean, don't ask you to tell me that you ran from us because you're terrified of how your power hurts Lucifer," he says slowly, but with an undeniable force behind the words.

He reaches for my wrist, and I suck in a breath at the pain even behind his gentle touch as he takes my arm in his hands.

Tobias continues, quieter still, "And don't ask you to tell me that you were escaping into Death, because there's nowhere else for you to run."

The gasp escapes me this time, at the crystal truth of his words—at his unerring gaze as he fixes his eyes to mine. His hands move gently over my wrist, and he mutters something beneath his breath.

Warmth spreads through me, and the pain fades a little.

"Yes," I hiss. "Don't ask me any of that."

He laughs under his breath. "Then I suppose you won't want me to tell you that I'm glad you came back, even though I suspect you had no choice."

I freeze, unable to look away from him. His hands move steadily back and forth over my wrist.

"And you won't want me to say that you're my missing piece." He pauses and adds, "That all of you are. And that I'm just waiting for you fucking morons to catch up."

That surprises a laugh out of me.

I wince, waiting for the pain to set in as I jolt my wrist, but nothing happens. I look down in shock.

It's straight again.

Tobias pulls his hands away casually and rests them by his side.

He healed me.

Is it an illusion?

I turn my wrist over, studying for signs that it won't last, that it's just a painkiller.

"It's no illusion," he says. "Just a simple spell I keep on me."

He gives me a real smile, then. A true one. I don't think I've ever seen it before.

"I'm rather clumsy, as it were," he confesses.

I don't think that's the whole truth, but I don't ask.

"Twenty minutes," he repeats. "I'll find you."

"I'll be waiting," I tell him.

———

I end up waiting for Tobias in the conservatory, with a giant bowl of popcorn I pinched from the kitchens and a stupidly expensive throw rug over my feet. I don't know why; this place was just calling to me. And I'm desperate to follow any kind of joy after my disaster of a day.

Unfortunately, though, being out in the gardens at night brings up the same burning question I keep running into.

Why does Hell have no stars? And more importantly, why didn't Lucifer *make* stars? He did once, intentionally or not, unless I have my mythology all wrong.

I cram another handful of popcorn into my mouth and stare up at the starless sky. I guess it's still pretty. Bursts of magic drift upward from various parts of the city. And there's a moon.

I wonder if Tobias hung that, too.

As soon as my thoughts turn to Tobias, I'm fucked. All I can think of are his hands caressing my wrist, healing me, telling me I'm his missing piece.

All I can feel are his fingers inside me while Logan watched. His tongue down my throat.

And that makes me think of all of them. Of Logan—and then Lucifer. His lips brushing mine. How long ago was it now? Barely hours, but it feels like days, after all that's happened.

I hadn't realized how much I was clinging to the possibility of running away as my only hope on the horizon. Not until the possibility was taken from me.

Now I'm stuck here, with a power that terrifies me and three men that terrify me more.

Not because they're dangerous, but because I am.

Despite that, shivery need races through me whenever I'm near them. A hot ache starts between my thighs, begging me to throw the bowl of popcorn aside and go find them, for Christ's sake.

But if I find them, something will go wrong. It always does.

In some kind of desperate self sabotage, I close my eyes and call on the wild inferno that's hooked itself onto my emotions.

A cold shiver travels down my spine, and my hands shake in

sympathy. Sweat breaks out on my brow, but I hold on. I try to tame it, even though Hell can't be tamed.

What is my power doing? There's no fire in here, I don't think, but it feels wild. Angry. It's definitely manifesting into something.

Is it burning the conservatory to the ground with me still in it? It doesn't feel hot enough for that.

Maybe that would be a good solution though.

Tobias' voice comes from my right. "Any particular reason you're showering the garden in fireworks?"

My eyes snap open. I stare at the sparkling rain that drifts down into the gardens.

"They're not fireworks," I say quietly. "They're stars."

Tobias' face tightens. "Don't let Lucifer hear you say that. And maybe rein it in a little. I don't mind, of course, but you're singeing some of the plants, and Lucy's in enough of a temper as it is, after all that."

I glance up at him, but he doesn't elaborate.

"You didn't tell Lucifer where I went, did you?" I ask quietly.

"No," Tobias answers lightly, coming to a halt with his hands in his pockets. He studies the night sky out the broad stretch of glass. "But I imagine he knows. He has called off the proximity bond, after all, to ensure that no one is severely injured if there are any more foolhardy attempts at escape." He pauses, glancing at me. "Can't you feel it?"

A spark of shock zips through me; I search internally for a sign of that familiar restriction, the binding. But it's gone. Only the soulbond remains—a cord that connects but doesn't tether.

Not that it matters anymore.

Still, that small hint of freedom loosens something inside me. Unfortunately, the emotion that rushes to fill that new space isn't relief.

I wipe away a tear with my thumb. "So that's why he's angry," I murmur.

Tobias shakes his head. "No, he's not angry over that. Never that. Don't fret, sweetheart. He's in a temper over other things."

"I suppose the fight with the rebels would take up most of his energy," I agree flatly. "There are some advantages to running away mid battle." I pull a face, squashing the guilt of my failed flight and trying to distract us both with mission talk. "You'd think he'd be able to relax for a day or two though. They aren't going to launch anything new immediately."

"Yes and no," Tobias turns away from the glass and sprawls out beside me, arm propped behind his head. "Firstly, Lucifer never relaxes. And secondly, I don't think it's the fighting that's on his mind. There's always fighting in Hell; he's remarkably stoic about it. In fact, I think he kind of gets off on it, and it's when there *isn't* fighting that he's properly pissed, because then he has to deal with everything else on his mind."

He sighs dramatically, making me wonder what 'everything else' is. What could possibly be bothering the Devil more than the recent insurgence or my near escape?

Then Tobias tells me, and I almost wish he hadn't.

"He's probably agonizing over what it will mean now we're all fucking." He laughs as he speaks, clearly answering my unsaid thought as he plucks it from my head, the rude bastard.

I choke on air. "Is that what we're doing?" I spit out.

My brain shoves an instantaneous thought into my mind: if Lucifer is agonizing over that, it means he's just as affected by our near-kiss as I am.

How the hell are we both reeling from an almost-kiss when he's literally eaten me out in the fucking shower?

Tobias smiles at me, eyes bright. "Would you prefer I call it making love?"

His shit-eating grin snaps me out of it. "Mate, if you think fingering a girl for thirty seconds is making love, you can cut that blue cord right now."

When I look at him, though, he isn't offended. His eyes sparkle, and his voice is low and heated when he says, "No, Helena. You'll know when I'm making love to you."

A flush rises in my cheeks, and I'm glad we're seated in the dark. Still, Tobias is perceptive, and something in my face must show even as I turn away.

He sits up with a frown. "You haven't created these stars out of pleasure," he says, cutting straight to the point in the strangest way, like he always does.

"No," I say flatly. Then, "leave it. You said you wouldn't ask questions."

He tsks me softly. "I don't think that was our agreement, Hel."

It's the use of Logan's nickname for me that stops me from retaliating in blind anger. Tobias has never called me that before. Never given any hint that I'm more to him than an attractive distraction.

"I promised you the truth, not unbridled access to my every thought," I argue, but it's a weak argument, even to my own ears.

"If you can't say the truth out loud, even to yourself," he says slowly, "Then it isn't private; it's a lie. You're lying to yourself." He pauses, and then softly adds. "Why did you run, tonight?"

Lying to myself.

He already knows why I ran, but he wants more. He wants my deepest, darkest secrets. He wants the confession I won't give, even in my own head.

I swallow, head swimming so fast it sounds like I'm screaming, over and over. "There was no unfinished business," I say breathlessly.

The stars disappear in a rush, plunging us into darkness.

Tobias doesn't speak. I want to let the silence drag, but the words bubble out of me anyway.

"I thought being stuck in Hell was like a ghost thing. I had the chance to finish what I'd left behind, because it was like I died twice, you know? But it wasn't like that at all. It's just a giant mess of *shit,* and I'm destroying Hell just by existing here. And now I've dragged all of you into it, trapping you to this disgusting, tainted mess of a woman who can't even touch anything without it going up in flames. Figuratively or literally."

I laugh wetly, the words pouring faster.

"Like, what is so wrong with me that I make people do this? Lucifer was right—I'm just a problem to be solved. I make Hell bloody combust just to get away from me. I make people drink or worse because they can't stand the sight of me, and then I fail them, right when they need me *most.*"

I choke off a sob as the images flood my mind. I always wanted too much, I know this. So when they stopped trying to fix me... when they told me to get out and never come back...

I did.

And I wasn't there when they needed me the most.

My body begins to shake. I try to lock it down, but I've spent too long trying to feel it again—the pain doesn't go easily. I'm teetering on the edge of something, and I think the only way forward is down.

"I feel like wounds are at least meant to be clean," I say flatly. "Pain is meant to be clean, isn't it? It's just... pain. But I've got so much of it. So many slices in my body." My words sound distant; I can barely understand what I'm saying. "If I just knew what kind of person could fix this, I could *do* it. Become it. Con my way through to safe ground. But there are so many... so many slices, and they each need someone different." I laugh—

loudly and bitterly. "And what does it matter, anyway? Because conning someone never solves a problem. It just covers the bloody thing in wallpaper."

A hand on my shoulder launches me violently back into the present. I flinch, yanking away from Tobias' wide-eyed expression.

"No," I say, too harsh but I don't care. "Don't touch me. You're all always *touching* me, but nobody *wants* me. I don't want that. I don't want that now."

Tobias' expression does something strange. "Is that what you think? That we touch you because we *don't* want you?"

"When you want something, you devour it," I say, the words burning in my throat. "You taste it and savor it and can't get enough of it. When you just need something, you'll touch whatever's in front of you that fits that need-shaped hole. Isn't that what a Ludus bond is? A fun fling? Something to touch and then forget?"

"No," Tobias says in a raspy voice. "That's not what a Ludus bond is. If you needed space, Helena, I'd give you that in a heartbeat, sweetheart. But I can't let you keep thinking this nonsense."

He reaches for me very slowly, giving me a chance to pull away. His fingers brush my cheek and cup my jaw. "Your old hurts have blinded you, and I think the last thing you need is space. You need to be touched." I suck in a breath at the fire in his eyes. "And, Helena, if you let me touch you, I will devour you."

30

TOBIAS

A T FIRST GLANCE, YOU MIGHT MISTAKE HER PAUSE FOR HESITATION. BUT the heat in her eyes tells a different story.

I hold out the slip of fabric and watch her pupils dilate.

"I thought you said I was already blinded." She wets her lips. "A blindfold seems counter productive."

"Not at all." I smile. "We need to filter out everything that doesn't matter. If you can't see how much I want you, then I'm going to make you feel it."

She can't hide the shiver that spreads through her body at my words, and I can't hide how much it affects me.

I no longer want to.

Carefully, Helena takes the blindfold from my hands and then pauses, watching me with a glint of amusement in her eye.

"And you think I'm just going to slip this on because you told me to."

My heart stutters, an unexpected warmth rushing through me.

"Of course not," I tell her, a slight grin on my lips. "And I am not Lucifer; I do not demand your absolute submission."

Helena lifts an eyebrow. "What are you demanding then?" She rests back on her hands, and a hint of the overwhelming sadness, the weight of it, returns. "You want to touch me when I said not to. You want to cover my eyes so I can't see. And you want to convince me of what I'm certain is a lie." She shakes her head in mock disappointment. "It's all very unlike you, Tobias."

Well, a challenge has been laid down if ever I saw one.

I snap my fingers, and the conservatory blurs a little around the edges. It doesn't fade, but it's as though it's out of time. Caught somewhere on the fringe.

Helena's eyes widen, and she turns to study the edges of the glass. They shimmer as she reaches her fingertips carefully toward it. And then, when she touches it, they fade.

A different conservatory takes its place.

My conservatory.

"What is this?" she breathes.

"You accused me of acting out of form," I say politely. "So I thought I'd bring it back to home base."

Her eyes widen, gratifyingly large. "This is your home."

"This is my castle," I say wryly.

She gets to her feet and walks to the far edge of the domed window. She peers through and grows still as she lays eyes upon my fortress.

There are perks to being friends with the Devil, and my home is one of them. I trust that even in my unusual absence, my castle is exactly as I left it.

I rise to my feet and come to stand behind her. She doesn't flinch, although I sense the change that comes over her body as she becomes aware of my presence.

Moving slowly, I reach out to take the blindfold from her again. "How about a game?"

She laughs, the sound unreasonably affectionate. "And what are the rules this time?"

"Well," I say, pretending to think it over, like I haven't already planned this out to the last detail. "If you keep the blindfold on for the entire time, and you don't beg me to touch you, then I'll let you take whatever you want from my library."

She sucks in a breath, and I see the hungry look in her eyes, even if she doesn't realize it. She craves knowledge. And more than that, I think.

I think she craves the companionship that books provide.

She gets what she needs to con people from her books and her research. But she also gets something else.

The strength to keep going.

I'm not sure even she realizes that.

Her lip curls, smug. She thinks she can withstand me. She thinks I won't have her begging by the end of the night.

"And if you take the blindfold off and beg me to touch you, then I win," I tell her quietly. "And I get to touch you however I please."

Something must reveal itself in my expression, because I see the shiver run through her. The sudden edge of thrilling fear.

"Game on," she says and closes her eyes.

I bring the blindfold up and rest the satin material against her face.

She sucks in a breath but doesn't speak while I tie the bow. She's planning to win, and I love that about her.

But she doesn't stand a chance.

"Turn around," I tell her softly, stepping away.

I still haven't touched her, and I won't, not until she begs me to.

I know Helena well, already, and she'd call me a cheat if I did anything less. Despite the fact that, in my shoes, I'm sure she'd cheat her way to victory.

She turns around and leans back against the glass. The

dome of it curves up over her head, encouraging only the slightest lean, since she's so short.

For me, I'd have to stoop if I came any closer.

I pause, and then I lean down so that my lips are only a few inches from her neck. Then I blow very carefully against her skin.

She shivers, lips parting.

"Is that all you've got?" she taunts me in a breathless voice.

"Darling, I haven't even started."

Button by button, I take off my shirt, making sure she hears as it slithers down my body and falls to the floor.

She stiffens as she hears the sound of the fabric dropping, and then freezes even more as I slide my belt buckle free and let my trousers follow.

"Are you—" she asks and then shakes her head. "Cheap tricks," she accuses me. "It isn't going to work."

I didn't expect it to.

I don't bother holding back my smile. She can't see it anyway. She can't see how filled with joy I am to watch her like this. To see her practically unguarded as the disorientation of the blindfold makes her forget about her defenses.

I come to lean on the window beside her, the glass cold against my skin.

Her body tenses and unconsciously leans closer to me.

"Do you know what it means to make love to someone?" I ask her quietly, thinking back to her earlier comment.

A soft hitch of air meets my question, but her reply is tart. "If you go all '*Merriam Webster dictionary defines...*' on me, I'll kick you in the teeth," she says. "Only wankers do that shit."

"I assure you, I don't need a dictionary definition to explain it to you."

I lean in again, and instead of breathing on her skin I simply let my words fall there, trusting that the rush of air from my mouth will tickle her senses.

"Merriam Webster dictionary defines," I begin, barely holding the laughter from my voice.

She makes an irritated sound and groans in disgust. Then, she raises her hand to smack me roughly where my shoulder would be—but pauses at the last second and slowly lowers her hand beside her again.

Smart girl. That would have been a technicality.

"Try again, wanker," she says affectionately.

"It means my hands are made for holding you," I tell her, and I watch the laughter drain from her face, replaced instantly by a deep, yearning ache that she never would have let me see if she didn't have her own eyes covered. "It means my body knows the feel of yours whether we're together or not. It means I breathe for you, Helena."

She whimpers, but I don't stop.

"It means I'll take any excuse just to look at you, to see you as you are now when you can't stop me looking."

I rise, coming slowly to stand before her, leaning my arms on either side of the window so that I'm braced above her, framing her.

"It means I'll construct the flimsy excuse of a game to blind-fold you, just so that I can see you as you are now, the truth of you, the rawness of your soul laid bare."

I lower my head until I'm breathing the words into her ear, "Because now, you can't see me. You can't place your projections onto me. You can't assume motivations that I don't have. You can't twist this into a lie of your own making."

Her breath catches.

"I am free to look at you, Helena. I'm free to drink my fill, but it will never be enough. This bond that connects us, it may be Ludus for the other two, but I know that ours is not bound to stay there. Ours will grow if you let it. If you let me love you, Helena. If you let me give you all of me."

I move so that my lips are above hers, the words a caress of breath against her skin.

"If you let me touch you."

"Please," she whispers.

I don't think she meant to speak, but even as she startles at the sound, she doesn't take it back.

My chest fills with warmth; it's one of the many things I love about her. Whether she's afraid, whether she's unsure, she never backs down. Never turns from a fight.

Five-foot nothing and far more bark than bite, but she never runs. Even though she thinks that's all she does.

"Please what, Helena?"

"Please," she repeats, stronger now. More desperate, urgent.

"You have to say it."

Her hands lift to her face, but she pauses, shakes her head, and forces them visibly down.

"Please touch me," she begs.

It's only half of the stakes; I haven't won yet.

Smiling, I do as she bids. I pull her shirt over her head and let my hands roam across her skin—once more drinking my fill without the interruption of her own gaze.

Her chest rises and falls quicker, her heartbeat fluttering like a butterfly.

I know she can feel me watching her.

I take my time, unhurried, as I kneel on one leg and then the other. And then I slide her pants over her hips until they fall with a slither of fabric onto the floor.

She's naked before me, and I've never seen a more beautiful sight.

"You're beautiful, do you know that?" I tell her.

She shivers. I press a kiss to her hip, letting it linger.

"But more than that, you're beautiful inside."

This time her body grows very still, and I know that I need to tread carefully here because I'm dealing with a wound. An old, old wound.

"You are golden inside, Helena." I kiss her thigh. "You are light."

I let my lips trail across her skin as I move from one hip to the other and lower down her other thigh.

"I worship you, Helena. More than your body, more than your mind, more than your soul. All of it. My life was empty before you. Cold, lonely and alone."

I press a soft, barely there kiss to the apex of her thighs. She shudders, her hands clasping futilely at the glass.

"You have brought me light, Helena. You do not bring the darkness that you fear, and if you could only see my face, you'd know it for the truth."

She shudders again, deeper this time. I see a shining trail of wetness on her cheek—a tear that's escaped below the blindfold.

I'm playing with fire here, and not the fun kind, but she needs to hear it.

She needs, more than anything, to know that the lies her soul tells her are nothing but dirt.

"Tobias," she says in a broken voice. "I don't know how you can say this."

"Very easily," I tell her, kissing her again. Longer this time, lingering—trailing my tongue over her as I pull away. "I say them with my mouth."

I kiss her again.

"With my tongue."

I swipe over her, lingering at the sweet apex as she shivers.

"And with my heart."

I kiss her on the abdomen, just below her belly button, and

one last, giant shudder racks her body. I hear a sob, and then her hands fly upward, tearing the blindfold free.

She looks down on me, her expression twisted in accusation. "You cheated."

"I only told the truth," I insist.

As she looks down at me, I know she sees it in my face.

I grab her hand and pull her down on top of me as I stretch out on the conservatory floor.

She kisses me. I don't know if she realizes, but she's devouring me, giving away far more in this moment than she probably intends to.

It doesn't matter.

My heart swells, my body surging toward her. I've never needed her more than in this moment.

She lifts her hips, guides me toward her, and sheathes me inside her. Then, very slowly, she begins to rock.

Our movements are small, with our hands and our mouths doing most of the expression. We clutch at each other, grasping, reaching for every sliver of skin we can find.

Every piece of us.

I barely take my mouth from hers, kissing her deeper. Showing her with my lips and my tongue what this means to me.

Against all odds.

Her lips part as she cries out, her hips writhing over me, becoming frantic.

I brace my feet against the floor and thrust up into her, watching as she arches—her back a pretty bow and her breasts lifted toward the sky.

"Come for me, beautiful," I tell her. "Come for me, Helena."

She does, crying out into the night and taking me with her.

After, we curl up beside each other with blankets pulled

from the chest. I've spent many a long night here observing the Heavens.

Or the makeshift ones, at least.

It's cozy and dark in our corner, alight with something new.

"I lost," she says, not sounding like she minds at all. "And you got to touch me wherever you wanted."

"Not wherever," I tell her, lips twitching. "But it will do for now." I kiss her softly on the neck. "It may take me days to claim my prize."

She shivers beneath me, but it's different to the shattering sobs from earlier. "I think I can work with that," she says.

"But we aren't one-nil, like you think," I tell her, watching the languid pleasure shift into slight confusion. "It's one all."

She stares at me, not comprehending.

"You won our first game," I tell her.

Now she grows still. "No, I didn't," she says.

"Ah, but you did, by the terms laid out. It happened in the wrong order, it's true. But you see, the terms were that if you succeeded with my help, you would tell Lucifer what you were doing." I let my lips form a smile, even though my heart is aching. "A loophole is a loophole, no matter which end it appears at. You told Lucifer before I had a chance to help. Which means I owe you my assistance."

Her eyes widen. "What are you saying?" she breathes.

I reach behind me for the pocket of my trousers and produce a small, ornate key. "I know that you can't leave Hell now," I tell her. "But you can set them free."

She stares at the key for a long time, and I don't have to read her mind to know what is going through it. The conflict, the knowledge of what it will mean if she frees her parents from beneath Lucifer's nose.

The repercussions such an act could cause.

I don't have any regrets; I'm bound by the terms of our

agreement, after all. And seeing her like this tonight, I'd do it anyway.

"But this could change everything," she says hesitantly.

I force the smile to my lips, trying to keep it from being bitter. "Doomed, remember? This balance between the four of us will never last, Helena. Something will happen to change it one day; it may as well be this."

Her expression wavers, and we stare at each other for a moment. I can't read her thoughts; I can't even read my own.

Her hand closes over the key, her fingers warm against mine, but she doesn't get up and leave.

She lies down, her head pillowed by my arm, and settles.

That surge of warmth floods my chest again, and I lie down beside her, my other arm over her waist.

"I'll go in the morning," she says, distant, distracted.

I kiss her softly, slowly, until she melts into me, all conflict wiped from her expression. "Then I'll continue to claim my prize."

31

HELENA

As soon as dawn breaks, I head for the aqueduct.

It doesn't take me long to make my way back to the lake, and Tobias was true to his word—there's no sign of a bungee cord *or* agonizing pain. The proximity bond is gone, although I barely have the energy to enjoy the freedom.

The path seems more treacherous in the cold rays of the early morning sun. Hell's sunrise is nothing like Earth's. Hell's sunrise is like a reminder that we're all trapped down here, doomed. One day I'll have to ask Tobias why the fuck he created a sun that brings no warmth, only heat, and how he managed to do that. But not today.

Today I free my parents.

The edge of the lake is eroded, the water beginning several meters back from where it was the other day. Whatever that tar creature did to me, it's had lasting effects.

And the aqueduct, of course, is gone. Crumbled.

In its place, a gigantic mountain rises, reaching almost desperately toward the sky.

Maybe it, too, feels the lack of warmth. It, too, is desperate for a real sun.

Ugh, Helena, you're getting so morbid.

I push through the underbrush surrounding the lake, through thick swampy reeds, and through shallow water that no longer contains the faces it once did.

The torture that was conducted here doesn't appear to be in operation anymore. But there'll be a trace of where they've gone, I'm sure.

For the first time, I'm confident I'm going to win.

I'm confident that this is it—the end.

I can't do much down here in Hell, with my power tied to Lucifer and that cage waiting for me whenever I attempt to leave, but I can do this.

I kneel beside the fallen rocks and bricks, the remnants of what was a fairly magnificent structure, if I give credit where it's due. Towering spirals that once stretched skyward now crumble sideways on the ground. The gargoyles that sat atop them, completely unnecessary in such a practical construction, leer at me, their faces squinting in the growing light.

Ugh, they're alive. Or at least they're not dead. They've just been left here.

I reach my hand towards the nearest gargoyle, and he snarls, snaps at my fingers, and then leaps free from his tower and scurries away.

Okay, so they're choosing to be here for some unknown reason, like cockroaches among decay.

I climb to the top of the pile and search. I don't know what I'm searching for, but I'll know it when I see it. A sign of where they might have gone, where they once were. Anything.

Movement catches my eye: a lone demon peeking through the rubble, a set of keys swinging from his belt.

That's it. That's what I'm looking for. A man with a key.

They always know where shit is. They bloody pride themselves on it.

I straighten myself, fix my expression into an arrogant leer, and stroll across the rubble toward him.

"Oi!" I yell, inwardly wincing as my accent rides free. "What are you still doing here?"

The demon jumps, startled, then immediately goes on the aggressive.

"You're not meant to be here," he hisses, his voice a strange rasping grunt of a thing. "We've been evacuated."

"Yeah, I know. On my orders," I tell him tartly.

And then I let just a little of this horrifying, controlling, terrible power leak free.

The earth shifts, quakes, and the demon suddenly looks at me with fresh fear. I can practically see the thoughts running through his head.

When did Lucifer share any of his power? Were the rumors true? Is she usurping him? Or is she supporting him?

Finally, he swallows thickly and does the only thing that it is safe for him to do. You can always trust a demon to look after their own skin.

"Got some missing prisoners," he says, jingling the keys at his belt and laughing hysterically. "Don't need the keys no more. But they do strike a nice bit of fear when they hear them."

"Right," I say, grimacing. "And which prisoners are missing?"

The demon pulls a face. "How should I know? Don't matter. We'll find 'em soon enough. Ain't nowhere for them to go now, is there?" He laughs again, ending in a snort.

Cream of the crop down here, that's for sure.

"Where's your ledger?" I ask, deliberately curling my lip into a sneer. "Or did your administration fall down in a heap when the aqueduct did?"

He seems to abruptly realize I'm serious, and he scrambles to an upright position.

He's taller than me, though he doesn't act like it.

"Got the papers back in me coach," he says, jabbing his finger toward a dilapidated carriage being pulled by a giant worm. "Everything's in order. Nothing to see there, love. I mean, sir, I mean, queen," he says hesitantly.

I bite back a laugh, although it's tinged slightly with hysteria. Is that how they're seeing me? Some kind of new Hell queen?

Or do they mean I'm Lucifer's queen?

God, I'm not helping the rumors by being here, but what choice do I have? I have to do *something*. I can't just give up.

I give a dismissive wave and climb over the rocks toward his carriage. Then, before he can put two brain cells together and work out that something's wrong with my presence here, I riffle through the papers, silently thanking the universe that even demons keep things in alphabetical order.

I find my parents' names. Lou and Stacy.

My hands pause, fingers tracing over the familiar letters. There are two marks beside them, and I frown. It's some kind of footnote.

I flip through and find the note in the appendix.

Solitary confinement.

The date reads the day I arrived in Hell.

I look up, staring into the distance, frowning as the pieces rearrange themselves. My parents were never at the aqueduct.

They were never actively on any torture, not since I arrived here. Maybe Lucifer doesn't hate them as much as he pretends to.

Then why won't he free them?

Why was he so angry when I asked?

I shove the papers back and run, hailing down a carriage

and directing it to the location of the cells my parents are kept in.

For all the weeks that have passed in blinding fear and uncertainty, this final leg of the journey is over in seconds. The cages are right nearby.

I drop some coins into the tin behind the driver and leave the carriage, unsteady on the rocky ground beneath me. But even more unsettled by the sight before me.

They're right there. I can see them.

The cages around them are broken and rusted, but I don't know that they can even see those. Their Hell is private. Haunted eyes pass right over me, leaving me behind as they huddle on the ground.

My parents have been kept on the brink of terror for years.

For fuck's sake, their whole life they were on the brink of terror, running from unknown fears into the arms of a drug that slowly killed them. They've never escaped it, even down here.

For a moment, rage fills me. So much rage that the sun itself blacks out, if only for a moment.

"Why would he do this?" I ask, my words dropping into the silence too harshly.

My mom looks up. "Who's there?" she asks.

I freeze, my breath catching in my throat, and suddenly I'm eleven years old again, tiptoeing through the house while my parents sleep off their high in the front room.

Mustn't get caught.

Mustn't wake them up.

Don't know what their mood will be when they wake up.

I look at the lock on the cage, and then I look at the key in my hand, and for one weird, fucked up moment... I hesitate. I don't even know why, but the thought of putting the key into that lock hurts me. Scares me.

My mom's eyes lock onto mine, and she goes very still.

"Mom?" I say quietly.

"Helena," she says. The word is a quiet, shocked whisper. "You're here."

Guilt twists my stomach. For how many years wasn't I here, though?

"Yeah, I'm here."

I wait for her to say... well, anything. To thank God I came. To beg me for help. To yell at me for taking so long. I'm open to anything, expecting anything, but then she...

She laughs and drops her head back down. "Your father's still getting his beauty sleep, but there are eggs in the fridge if you want to cook us all up some breakfast."

"If I want to... what?"

Her brow furrows. "Oh, it's too early for this, Helena. Just—eggs. Fridge. You'll work it out."

She's acting so normal. Like she isn't lying on the dirt floor of a cage. It's like any other morning when they've woken up late.

I tilt my head to the side and force myself to look at the cage. It's a perfectly ordinary cage, with steel bars and a giant ass lock.

But then, maybe it isn't.

"Where are you, Mom?" I ask hesitantly.

She barks a laugh, loud and obnoxious, and then stretches luxuriously in the dirt. "Where am I? What kind of question is that? I'm in my lovely, fluffy bed, Helena and I'm *not* getting out of it, so you can quit looking at me like that." She yawns and closes her eyes.

Mom thinks they're at home.

She thinks they're safe. And, through a weird technicality, they are. They're in solitary confinement with no active torture.

If I let them out of here, I'll be bringing them into Hell.

My hands clench into fists, and I force myself not to lose it.

Stepping forward, I begin to walk the perimeter of the cage, just studying it at this point without really thinking about what I'll do.

There are no guards here, and I've been here a full ten minutes now, so it isn't a rotational thing either.

Where the hell are the guards?

Instinctively, I pull back from the edge of fury and duck into the crevasse of the mountain, just as the rock before me shudders. If I hadn't been looking right at it, I never would have seen it.

I'm willing to bet my own freedom that these are the guards. But I don't think they're guarding in the usual way. A prison guard doesn't need to hide itself, especially not down here.

Unless it's trying to lull you into a false sense of security and catch you in the act.

I look at the scene again, and this time I see it for what it is.

Bait.

Several of the rocks are too shiny, barely coated in the ash that covers the rest of the mountain. And the longer I stare, the more I see of those ripples, like the rocks are shuddering from the effort of holding their form.

It was too easy to get here. The way that guard didn't turn back at the noise... I knew something was off. I thought it was luck, but it's the opposite.

It's no secret that I want Lucifer to free my parents. Not since the Rising Snakes shadowed us—literally—in the forest. Now, it seems that someone is waiting for me to give up asking and just *take*.

And if I were an idiot, I might just appreciate the support. But this isn't a selfless act. This is politics.

They want me to free my parents because it undermines

everything Lucifer is trying to achieve. It undermines his power, his strength, and his authority.

If I do this, I give the tatty remnants of the rebellion fuel to be reborn.

Is that really what I want to do?

I look down at the cage for a very long time. If I'd been handed this key the second I arrived in Hell, I wouldn't have even thought twice. I wouldn't question it at all; I'd just open the door and run.

But so much has changed.

I don't want my parents to be hurt, but I don't want to hurt Lucifer either. And... my parents aren't hurting right now.

They're happier than they'd be if I let them out and they realized where they really were.

"It's not forever," I murmur, staring vacantly at the bars. "Just until the snakes are gone. I'm not going to give up on you."

This isn't like last time.

I'm not walking away when you need me most.

I squeeze my eyes shut, trying to ignore the twisting, writhing discomfort in my gut. It's more insistent than it's ever been. But when I look down at the key in my hand, I know I've already made my choice.

The demon at the aqueduct showed me the truth of it; they see me as a queen. They see me as Lucifer's equal.

And shit, maybe this messed up power means I am. I don't know. Lucifer doesn't know.

And Lucifer... I hold my breath, pain coursing through me as I remember seeing him stretched out on the floor, gazing up at the starless sky.

He's weak and getting weaker.

If I betray him publicly and make my opposition to him a truth, then Hell as we know it will fall, and Lucifer will fall with it.

I don't know if he has the strength to rise again.

I take a deep breath and let it out slowly, palming the key so I can no longer see it.

But I can't look at them. I'm not strong enough for that. Not when I'm turning away from them. Again.

Silently, I vow to free them one day.

First, I have to secure Lucifer's reign and see him in full possession of the power that is rightfully his. It's not like I want it. I never wanted it.

So if I'm going to do that, it's time he stopped being a blithering idiot and doing everything on his own. I glare fiercely into the distance, turning so the cages are behind me.

I'm going to help him, and he's going to let me.

32

HELENA

I CHARGE BACK TO THE PALACE, CAREENING LIKE A TORNADO THROUGH the rooms as I search for Lucifer. But of course he's hiding up in his little penthouse at the top.

The thought infuriates me. After everything I've gone through, everything I've worked for, and what I'm giving up to help him, the least he could do is have a fucking open door policy.

Tobias catches me halfway through the dining room, heading toward the elevators. He catches me by the elbow, whirls me around, and quirks a lip.

"Now there's something I need to know about."

"You don't need to know shit, mate," I snap at him, which only makes him laugh.

"No, I think I really do. I think this is about to have... What do we call it? A ripple effect."

I take a breath and let it out through pursed lips. "I'm going to find Lucifer, and I'm going to demand he lets me help him, because he's being a dickhead."

"Well, you're right on that one," Tobias says, and then he gives a low whistle.

Logan steps through one of the doors, munching down on a packet of crisps.

"Is this where you went?" he asks Tobias, mouth full. "I thought you were heading to the jacuzzi."

I lift my eyebrows, glancing between the two of them. "You two were off to the jacuzzi."

We have a jacuzzi?

"Well, you'd fucked off on us," Logan says, grinning to soften the accusation.

"It was either find you and deal with your wrath, not find you and deal with Lucifer's wrath, or go have a soak in the hot tub," Tobias says.

Something in me softens. I don't know whether they realize it, but just the idea that they were willing to let me have a morning of escape means that they trust me.

After everything, they finally trust me.

And each other too, if they were willing to go have a soak together.

"Well, I'm back," I point out, resting a palm on Tobias' hand, which is still curled around my elbow. "And I'm on a mission. And if you interrupt me on a mission, then I'm going to lose steam and I'm not going to complete it."

Logan laughs. "That's impossible," he says, glancing over at me. "I don't think anything could put you off a task you've got your mind on."

Well, apparently some things can. I very carefully remove Tobias' hand from my arm and give myself a quick shake.

"Look, it's all good, I just need to do this now, before I change my mind."

An interested look passes between Tobias and Logan. That

one got through. They realize now it's not about me having the courage to go and face off against Lucifer.

It's about me making a choice that I don't necessarily want to make.

Tobias, of course, must know what that choice is. And when he turns back to me with a soft expression, it's almost too much.

I turn away and leave them behind me.

Perhaps if it all goes well, I'll join them in the hot tub soon.

The elevator music is obnoxious as I ride up toward the penthouse. I think that's precisely why Lucifer designed it this way. He likes to unsettle his opponents. And even the fact that anyone who is invited up to his penthouse clearly isn't a real opponent doesn't stop him from using every weapon in his arsenal to shift the power balance in his favor.

It ticks me off even more, and by the time I arrive at the top, I'm livid.

I debate kicking the door down for emphasis, but decide it would probably tickle the edges of Lucifer's temper a little too much.

I knock.

A shuffle of footsteps behind me makes me turn as the door swings silently open, propelled by magic. Logan grins at me, and Tobias gives an affected little finger wave.

Unexpected warmth surges through me. I said I would speak to Lucifer before I lost my nerve; I didn't realize they'd come with me.

The door thuds softly against the stop, revealing Lucifer's study is mostly in shadow. Jesus, how can he see in here? Mountains of paperwork litter the desk, compared to last time we were here, and there must be half a dozen little espresso cups serving as paperweights.

He's still sitting at the desk, having used power to open the door rather than get up.

"Yes, Helena?" Lucifer blinks, gaze shifting—slightly unfocused—to Logan and Tobias. "You're all here."

Only a little nervous—okay, shitting bricks—I step into the room. "We thought it was time to try a different approach."

Lucifer's eyebrows disappear into his hair. "And so you march into my study as if you were off to battle?"

"I don't want to fight you. I want to help."

Silence.

Very slowly, Lucifer comes around to the front of the desk. Folding his arms, he leans back against it.

"Help," he repeats.

In the light, his eyes are incredibly bloodshot. Is he even sleeping right now?

"Yeah. You said this spirit you're chasing is one of the first creations when Hell was birthed. One of the first demons. But you can't track her because your power is too out of reach." I spread my arms. "So use mine. Honestly, I don't know why you haven't tried it sooner."

Something flickers in his expression, but when he speaks, his voice is almost empty. "You think your usurped power will be the answer to my problem."

Taken aback, I shrug. "Why not try?"

Tobias steps in between us. "Go on, Lucy. Stop making it difficult on yourself. What's the harm in trying?"

"There could be immense harm in using untamed power to find an ancient demon spirit just barely clinging to the fringes of life," he says in a measured voice. "We could destroy her, for one."

My stomach sinks, guilt and shame twisting together. I hadn't thought of that.

But Tobias makes a rude noise. There's too much emotion in

his expression, too much fire. He's latched onto this fight and is turning it into one of his own.

Something tells me that none of us are safe when Tobias does that.

"And losing your position as Hell's Big Bad to an angel has nothing to do with it, I'm sure," he says.

Lucifer's eyes flash, and a strange feeling slams into me. Tobias is right. That's why he won't do it. He's threatened by me.

The flames in the candles surge two feet high, illuminating our faces in an eerie flicker.

"Is this true?" I ask coldly, taking a step forward.

Tobias looks between us with delight. "It's why he won't fuck you properly, either."

Ignoring my hitch of breath, he steps in close, leaning over my shoulder to whisper in my ear, eyes locked with Lucifer.

"You're an anomaly, and there's nothing Lucy hates more than something he can't control."

Lucifer's eyes darken, but Tobias only gets more into it, ignoring how the rest of us are frozen with fear. He's loving this, all his cruel edges lighting up with joy as he twists our truths around us like a noose.

"You probably don't even want to fuck him," he says, making a rude noise. "Can you imagine him ever letting go? *Him?* He's probably missionary all night, and he won't even let you see his face when he comes."

"You know how I fuck, Tobias," Lucifer grits out, his voice undeniably rough. "And you know it's certainly not missionary."

Tobias' shit-eating grin widens. "Are you sure though? Or do you think he's lying?"

"I— I don't know."

"Liar," he says fondly. "You know you can't imagine this

restrained, uptight Devil prick ever bending you over the breakfast table like you want him to."

Lucifer makes a rough noise at the back of his throat.

Tobias' lip curls in triumph, and the next words are delivered mercilessly slow, like weapons. "He'll never make you call him Daddy while he fucks your tits."

The crude image assaults me, leaving me gasping and my core tightening with heat. He's right, I can never imagine Lucifer doing that.

But now that I have, I want to. I want to see him come undone.

Lucifer's jaw tightens. "I fail to see how this is relevant," he says, but his voice sounds broken. Raw.

Tobias finally pulls away from me and steps in to face Lucifer. "Just pointing out that you'll never be able to give her what she wants." He reaches out and undoes another button from Lucifer's already draping shirt. "You might try to look casual, but you can't even let her *help you* in case she threatens. Your. Precious. Control."

The last words are delivered with three subtle steps closer, bringing them nose to nose, and Tobias punctuates his point with a brutal kiss.

Even with the power clashing around us, Lucifer doesn't melt, doesn't bow. His lips curve into a sneer, his hand finding Tobias' throat and holding him there as he kisses brutally. Achingly.

Then he rips away with a snarl, picks up a candle, and throws it at the curtains.

I shriek, and the blazing inferno roars higher, competing with the low sound of chanting as Lucifer's eyes bear into mine.

And then the room vanishes.

We're outside another hut, and I know that this time, we've found her.

"The rebellion watches these parts," Lucifer says tightly, pointing out a faint mark on a tree. He jerks his chin at Logan. "Stay on guard."

Logan stiffens, that now familiar terror plastered on his face, but he nods.

Without waiting for anyone else, Lucifer strides into the hut and lunges at the far wall. Eyes wide, I hurry in after him, with Tobias strolling curiously behind.

Utensils go flying from the small table as Lucifer grapples with someone. Which begs the question, do spirits eat? Or is she couch surfing from abandoned hut to abandoned hut?

I should probably think about that later, not now.

I duck as a lit candle flies at my head, and then Lucifer slams the spirit on the table, his fist around her neck in a choke hold.

My shock fades fast. This spirit is something else. Wide, deeply sunken eyes stare out of a translucent face that seems both young and ancient at the same time. They skip around the room so fast it looks more like a seizure, but a low rasping laugh tells me she's still watching us, still taking in the scene.

Just very quickly.

"Oh, Lucifer, it's been too long," she cackles.

"Don't give me that," he says coldly. "You've been outrunning me for weeks."

"Precisely; you should have caught me in hours. You're losing your touch."

She taps on his wrists, gnarled fingers smoothing into a maiden's with each tap. "And your touch is turning cruel."

Lucifer snarls but lets her go, stepping back as if she'd burnt him. Tobias immediately blocks the door. But, like, can't a spirit escape through walls?

"My touch was always cruel," he says.

"Not so." She straightens, seemingly unbothered by the ordeal. "You've come to ask why Hell is running from you."

"I've come to ask why my power is shifting to Helena," he corrects her tightly.

She smiles. "Still asking the wrong questions. How about we make a deal—I'll give you the *right* question, and you promise me you'll find the answer this time?"

"Or you could just give me the answer."

"Ah, but I can't." Her eyes flicker with a strange light, and my hands begin to shake, sickness turning my stomach over like my body knows something I don't. When she continues, her voice is almost a croon. "See—the question is: do you rule or do you serve?"

As the last word leaves her lips, silence fills the room. It's an unusual silence—complete. Like we're in a void. An abyss of nothingness.

I suck in a breath, but I can't hear it. A ringing starts up in my ears, and I stumble back, away from this strange spirit who seems to be growing stronger by the second.

She isn't even see-through anymore.

Lucifer says something to her, his lips twisting in a sneer, but I can't hear it. She laughs, the sound completely gone, like I'm watching a movie on mute.

Then the sound comes back with a roar as she lunges at Lucifer.

Wind howls through the hut, a miniature tornado that sends the furniture shattering against the walls. She grapples Lucifer to the ground, reversing their earlier position as she clasps her hands around his throat. His eyes blaze, cheeks purpling as he clutches at her hands. He can't get free, and none of us can reach them.

"It's a simple question, Lucifer," she says, still laughing. "So what's the answer?"

"Rule," he snarls, choking on the word. He snatches one of her hands away from his neck and bends it sharply; I hear a snap. "You know I rule."

Her laughter grows louder, and she pulls her other hand back, freeing him. Her second hand snaps, too, and my stomach lurches as I realize she's done it herself.

"Find the answer," she tells him, leaping free before he can hold her. She traces a path with her broken hands over her neck, almost thoughtful. Distant. "And don't forsake your only asset for his command."

Then, she vanishes.

Whose command? Ronin's? Has Lucifer lost an asset in his fight to reclaim the control Ronin seized?

The wind keeps howling, louder now. Noise from outside penetrates the sound, but I can't make out what it is. Whispers? Is the spirit's power spreading outside?

The door bursts open. In the flickering light, I see enough to recognize Logan passed out on the ground. Figures pour into the room. Figures that have been lying in wait until we were distracted—weak.

Strong, unfamiliar arms engulf me, and then I'm whisked away into nothingness.

33

LOGAN

I come back awake just as she vanishes. Just as a flash of white and blue flame engulfs her and the bastard holding her, taking her from me.

I nearly lose consciousness immediately, again, when a solid fist slams into my head, knocking me straight back down onto the ground. I groan, clutching my jaw, wincing as the bright stars sparkle across my vision.

Rolling away on instinct, I hear something slam into the ground and scramble to my feet, shifting with a snarl so that I can at least fight with my best weapon.

Through heightened jaguar senses, I see the Devil stalking me. His face is split open with rage, his sword drawn. He's covered in blood, but it's not his blood.

It's the blood of the bodies that litter the ground behind him. The Rising Snakes.

"What have you done?" he hisses at me.

Tobias steps between us. Lucifer's eyes blaze, and I've never felt true fear from the Devil, but—fuck—I feel it now.

My traitor dick hardens as he slams me into the wall of the

hut, unable to tell the difference between fear and desire; the emotion is too strong.

"You let her down," he hisses.

"They got behind me!" I protest, but it's weak. He's right. I let my guard down, too unnerved to focus. I close my eyes, fighting the urge to flee.

I let them get past me.

Lucifer sneers. "You forget, I pass the final Judgment here," he croons. "I can spot a liar."

Fur ripples over my knuckles, receding as I shift back into a man. A naked man, held against the wall by Lucifer.

My shifter vitality is freaking the fuck out. Lucifer's seraphim blade is out, the metal at my neck as he prepares to execute me for my mistakes.

But then a thunder clap rips us apart.

For a second, I'm blinded by the sight of this fierce, glowing demon. Horns twist back from a face that's gnarled with age. Burning white eyes cast a glowing light down a fawn-like body.

He doesn't have a weapon; he stops Lucifer's blade with his forearms. They snarl, the sound echoing like thunder, coming at each other again and again. The ripple of hellfire distorts their bodies, man and demon twisting as one. Man in shadow, demon in flame.

"Don't forget, Devil," Tobias snarls. "You failed me worse than he failed you."

They freeze, chests heaving, the fire dulled so they're just two men. Lucifer grits his teeth.

"*I* failed *you*?!" Lucifer hisses, incredulous.

Tobias ignores the accusation. Maybe he just wanted to distract him. Maybe he's too pissed to argue about that right now, but thank fuck, for whatever reason he stays on task.

"He's one of us," Tobias says. "He's *ours*. Don't do this."

I won't lie, hearing Tobias say that does more than make my

dick hard. I can't even explain what hearing that shit does to me.

With a final grunt, Lucifer throws him off and stalks away. "Two hours," he says. "Find her in two hours or I'll change my mind."

Lucifer vanishes into the forest, the shadows engulfing him, consuming him.

The hut falls into an eerie silence. The bodies on the floor are still warm, blood pooling in rivulets beneath them. I sink slowly to the ground, bringing my knees up in front of me and resting my forehead on my arms.

A soft thump of fabric hitting the floor greets me and I look up to see Tobias has thrown my clothing back in front of me.

"Don't know how you shifters do it," he says thoughtfully, sliding his hands into his pockets and staring out the window. "All that ripped clothing. There's no point even having a wardrobe."

I huff a laugh and reach for my jeans, pulling them on. "You get used to it," I mutter. "You learn how to shift without ruining everything, or you bring a spare with magic."

I pause, staring up at him.

"What did you mean he failed you worse than I failed him?"

Tobias doesn't speak, doesn't move. "It's ancient history," he says after a beat. "I don't think Lucifer even realizes what he did." He laughs bitterly. "Which is why he can't see the bitter irony of his inability to accept other people's mistakes." Tobias shrugs. "I forgave him for his. He could learn to forgive you for yours."

I frown at him. "You don't look like you've forgiven him."

A tiny furrow appears in Tobias' brow, and his lip twitches in thought. "Perhaps I haven't," he says distantly. He shakes his head and turns to me. "We have two hours, or all hell breaks loose." He grins broadly—a threat. "Pun intended."

I shudder and pull my shirt on, feeling unusually vulnerable. "Two hours to find Helena. Alright. How do we do it?"

Tobias shakes his head slowly. "I've been hunting for whispers of where the, er..." He grimaces. "*Rising Snakes* set up headquarters, but I can't find it. They're good at covering their tracks, even if they aren't good at naming things."

He leans forward on the table, drumming his fingers in a slow, thoughtful rhythm.

"We could try chasing the magic they used to teleport her out of here," he suggests. "But it probably won't reveal much. They could have hopped to somewhere else immediately after. If they were smart, they could have done a dozen hops."

"Maybe they weren't smart," I suggest, my voice a low snarl. "It's worth trying."

Tobias shakes his head. "Lucifer's serious, Logan. If we don't find her in two hours..." He looks up at me through unusually thick lashes. "You're dead."

Fuck.

"Alright. What about the soulbond cord?" I reach out and pluck the string like a guitar.

Tobias shudders. Interestingly, it doesn't look like it's in pain. I file that thought away for a happier time.

"You've used it to irritate the fuck out of all of us. Surely you can use it for something useful now."

Tobias shoots me a warning glance, and my lips curve into a grin. Shaking his head, he reaches for the cords at his chest and strums them thoughtfully.

"I can't feel her," he says slowly. "The Snakes may be amateurs, but they do their research. They know about the bond, and they've put some kind of shield around their location. Unless she burns the building down..." He shrugs.

But that isn't everything. I've been around Tobias enough now to know when he's holding something back.

"What else?"

He meets my gaze, and I see the warring indecision in his face.

"She has to want to come back to us, too. And while enough has changed that she doesn't want to leave, now that she *has* left..." He pulls a face.

It surprises me that this demon, who's so full of trickery and agitation, could have something so serious beneath the surface.

"I don't think that she wants to return," he finally finishes.

"How can she not want to?" I protest. "She's been captured. Stolen. Who knows what they're doing to her?"

Tobias gives a bitter laugh. "But has she? Remember, Logan, they want her to be their queen."

His words send a strange chill through me. I'm not even sure who I'm afraid for. I adore Helena, would do anything for her.

But I'd do anything for Lucifer as well.

Who do I actually want to win?

"She thinks she's chosen Lucifer," Tobias says, driving the knife in further, in that way he's only too good at. "But he doesn't make it easy to do that. He's not an easy man to choose. And these rebels..." He waves a hand dismissively. "If they're good at anything, it's lying through their teeth well enough to convince people to follow them."

Understanding hits me. I feel suddenly sick, like I might keel over and vom all over my boots.

"You think she's going to drink the Kool-Aid?"

"I think that's exactly what she's going to do."

"How can you say that?" I snarl. "She's smarter than that. She's not going to fall for it."

"Fall for what?" Tobias says, laughing properly now. "Fall for the promise of possessing all the power in Hell? It's not a lie, Logan. She can do it. She's already doing it, and none of us know why. Even Lucifer can't fight it. You heard what that spirit said. *Do you rule or do you serve?* Maybe she's telling Lucifer he's fighting a losing battle and it's time to serve a new master."

"And maybe she's full of shit," I snap.

I pledged my allegiance to Lucifer long ago, and I've always known that meant something to him. As much as I tried to pretend I never own anything, never have anything to lose, I've always had that. I've always had the Devil's trust.

I'm only now realizing what it would mean to lose it.

"Look, he's not the most stable boss in the world, I'll give you that," I tell Tobias. "But he's been good to me. Until he tried to kill me, of course, but everyone's allowed a fuck-up or two. So we can't let this happen. We've got to trace her and get her out of there before she joins them."

The words land heavily in the room.

Tobias nods, and he seems almost apologetic. He crosses the room, fishing through the pockets of his trousers to find a single, final teleport device.

"For a rainy day," he says with a wide grin. "Let's go back to the palace. There are resources in Helena's library that we can use. She's been learning all she can about the rebellion, after all. Maybe it will come in handy."

I snort at the irony but don't complain. I reach out to rest my hand on Tobias's shoulder, waiting for the whirl of the teleport. But he pauses. Shakes his head thoughtfully, almost as if he's unaware that he's doing it.

Then he reaches out to grasp me by the back of the neck.

"Not like that," he says casually. "Not this time."

Then he pulls me into a bruising kiss.

The world vanishes away.

34

HELENA

I WAKE ABRUPTLY WITH THE BURNING SMELL OF SULFUR IN MY NOSE. I snap my eyes open, sitting up and searching for a way out. I don't find any. It's a simple room, roughly five by five, and I'm lying on the floor.

There's very little furniture—only a half-broken desk in the corner and a shelving unit with jars filled with squishy things I don't want to examine too closely. There's a cupboard on one wall, but that's it.

If this is the stronghold of the Rising Snakes, it's not exactly impressive.

"Little bastards," I mutter under my breath.

I bring myself slowly to my feet and assess my body for any damage.

It takes a second or two sometimes, connecting back to my body and knowing how it actually feels. Sometimes I don't notice when I'm hurt.

But no, it appears that they haven't mishandled me.

You know, I kind of think that might be worse.

A key scratches in the lock and my body sags, resigned as I turn to face the demon who brought me here.

"Your Majesty," he simpers with a sly little smile.

There it is. I fucking knew it.

"You know you don't have to call me that," I say with a grimace. "On account of the fact that I'm not a queen. Seems a pretty obvious conclusion in my book."

"Not a queen yet," he corrects me, stepping into the room and shutting the door behind him. "We apologize it took so long to find you. Our sources told us there was *something* on our side of liberation, but at first we thought it was an *it*." He laughs horribly. "Not an it—a she. You."

He's slimy enough, but not in the literal sense, like the other demons I've encountered so far on this side of the rebellion.

I guess what I've been encountering are minions. Do demons have minions? Seems a bit rude in this day and age.

Whoever this guy is, I wouldn't say he's at the top or anything, but he definitely has middle management vibes. It's in the way he keeps clasping his hands together in front of him, and in the slight tilt of his head, like he's had to grasp for any sense of authority in his life.

Oh yeah, definitely middle management material.

"Are you ready to join us in your quarters?" he asks me, his chin jutting out with every third word.

On anyone else, it would be endearingly human. But on a guy who's brought me to a random secondary location, locked me on a cold floor, and then asked me if I wanted to join him in my quarters, I'm really not endeared.

Sorry, mate, try harder next time. Maybe the next girl you kidnap will be impressed with you.

On the bright side, if he's convinced I'm his queen, he'll probably be susceptible to shows of power.

I can't let him see I'm afraid.

"I don't think so," I tell him sweetly. "But if I am your majesty, then maybe you could show me the door."

The demon's smile widens in a way I just want to punch off his face, and I'm not normally the violent type.

He shakes his head slowly. "Not until you've absorbed all we have to tell you."

He has a way of making the word absorbed sound dirty, and not the fun kind of dirty. I shudder.

"How about you just give me the Cliffs Notes?"

He laughs obsequiously. My eyes slide past him, and I begin to study the space. Since he isn't going to be forthcoming, I guess I'll have to find my own way out of here.

The lock on the door is only an office lock. It can be picked from the inside. If I keep him talking, maybe he won't notice when I liberate the pin from the cupboard door hinge behind me and use it as a pick.

"Do you have like a pamphlet or something?" I ask sarcastically. "All the good revolutions have reading material."

"Cliffs Notes... pamphlet..." He laughs again, touching his fingers together and jutting his chin out. "You're quite the joker, aren't you? It will be nice to have a ruler with a sense of humor."

"Now, now," I correct him. "Go easy there. Lucifer has a sense of humor. He's just often the only one laughing."

I pause as the words come out of my mouth. Funny. I remember Cat telling me that. I never fully understood it until now. I don't think I even agreed with it.

Undeterred, the demon smiles a sharp-toothed smile at me. "We have no reading material. But if you do not want to listen to our heartfelt pleas, perhaps a visual display will be more in order."

I can't help wrinkling my nose. "What kind of visual display?"

I swear this sounds like the worst kind of come on.

Bile rises in my throat at just how triumphant the guy looks. What's he done? What's he going to do?

The demon waves his hands in a complicated gesture, and a familiar book appears in his hand.

Correction: it's not the actual book, but a mirage. The kind of copy that administration demons forge when they need access to one of the registers.

Not the Register; the lower registers that you can view outside of the room.

I don't do him the satisfaction of asking what it is. I wait, looking annoyed and impatient. Unfortunately, this seems to ignite some sort of glee in him. Probably because this is exactly what a queen would do, dammit, and instead of being intimidated into following orders like I'd hoped, he's just thrilled to bits that he chose well.

I can't win with these pricks.

"Her Majesty has been most invested in the history books," the demon says, opening the book to a page and stepping through leaf by leaf. "But she has not requested the record of her own Judgment."

"That's because I wasn't judged here, dummy," I tell him. I'm not sure I even have an agenda anymore, with how I'm talking to him. I think I'm just pissed off. "I went upstairs, remember?"

And then *I* remember. I realize what he means—not my first Judgment, when I died, but my second. Down here.

But Lucifer said there was no Judgment. He said nothing happened—it was the whole reason why he bound me to him in the end, because he didn't know what was going on and he needed to keep me close.

Why would there be a record of my Judgment if the Judgment hadn't existed?

I don't realize I said the last bit aloud until the demon

chuckles. "Why indeed, Your Majesty? Would you like to see for yourself?"

You know what? I would. And that's the bloody problem, isn't it? They've played me like a harp, and I don't even try to deny it.

I step forward, eyes scanning the words on the page until I find my own name.

Helena.

Images burst free: a visual record of the Judgment Lucifer passed down upon me. I see myself quivering on the throne room floor. See the Devil laid back in his throne, laconic and at ease, knees spread wide, chin propped on one hand, seconds before he lays the sword against me.

Light pours from it. From the sword, from me. And from this angle, I can see what I couldn't at the time. There was Judgment, all right.

And in all the centuries of Judgment that Lucifer has passed, I don't think he'd have ever seen one like this.

If I were to take a wild stab at describing the kind of Judgment that usually happens down here, it wouldn't be a pass or fail situation. It's a 'fucked' or 'really fucked', you know? If you've made it all the way down here, then you're no longer a question mark, right?

The question mark happens the second you die. If you've come down this far, the Judgment is simply where in the nine circles of Hell you're going to reside.

But this Judgment...

Lucifer reels back, his eyes wide with shock and fear, and I realize then that this is when he knew. This is how long he's known for.

He knew my power was his power. He knew that Hell wanted me here—not to serve, but to rule.

And he chained me to him. He didn't tell me. He didn't warn me. He didn't prepare me. He just tried to control me.

He's meant to love me, and he tried to control me.

Anger like I've never known flares inside me. It's been a long, long time since anyone tried to control me.

I look up from the pages and see the demon laughing. Silent peals of laughter that are my only introduction to the fact that my ears are ringing with sound.

I can't hear anything from inside the room. I can't feel anything. And that's because a bubble of power has erupted from me.

Lucifer lied to me. He lied to me and he tried to squash me without me even realizing, without giving me a chance to fight back. Or to fight on his side, dammit, because it's not like I ever wanted this power either.

What else has he lied about?

I think of my parents moving from cage to cage. He promised me they weren't being tortured, but they're still in Hell. They're still afraid.

How does the King of Torture define torture? What lines does he draw and what lines does he cross?

The power begins to fade away slowly, but it doesn't vanish. It's still within reach. I know I could draw on it in seconds. I could bring this fucking world to its knees.

A deep, echoing voice cries out. It isn't in the room with me; it isn't anywhere nearby at all. And yet, it's everywhere. Everywhere that I am.

"Tell him, Helena," the voice cries. "Tell him where I am."

It's the voice from the castle. From the lake with the tar.

From the mountainous foot that appeared when I ran, and the cage it slammed down upon me before I could escape into Death.

It's been so long since I heard it, I'd almost forgotten it. But now that it's here again, I wonder how I missed the obvious for so long.

I know who this voice is.

It's Hell. Hell as a living, breathing, *beast*.

And it's calling to me, not Lucifer.

It roars, and everything in me wants to roar back, like a fucking beast myself.

"That's it," the demon says, his words just barely penetrating the fog that surrounds me.

I look up and see him giving me a slimy grin.

"Don't you want to take back what he stole from you? The Ludus bonds are the token bonds of the soulmate world. You owe him nothing."

Fire courses in my veins. I owe Lucifer nothing, and I'm damn sure he won't give me anything either. He's had more than enough chances.

Maybe I should just do this. Seize this power and run.

The demon laughs properly now. "Take the Devil down, darling. Make him burn. Let him bleed out."

The hate on his face sharpens as he drops the Rising Snakes' catch cry for something more personal—his true desires. I hear them echo on the currents of Hell's power. The rivers.

Let him bleed out.

Bleed out.

Memories assault me. Blood on my hands—innocent blood. My body out of my control.

"No," I breathe, seeing the demon for what he is: another Ronin trying to use me.

I watch him silently, relishing the moment that he realizes he's in danger.

His eyes widen, his breath suddenly catching in his throat. He begins to bow, disgustingly simpering. "Your Majesty, I meant no disrespect. We won't share the details of your bond with anyone. Won't tell the other demons, the other hellborn, what it might mean. It'll be our secret—we'll keep it with honor."

"Mate, I wasn't even thinking about the bond," I tell him, my lips curling in a sneer. "I was thinking about you, and how, when it comes down to it, I really don't like you."

He whimpers, cowering, expecting me to level him with a blow, to crush him at my feet, like I suppose the ruler of Hell is meant to do.

Like the ruler of Hell apparently tried to do to me in a far more subtle but no less real sense.

But I'm not going to do that, because I'm not the ruler of Hell. I'm just one pissed off angel who's sick of being treated like crap, who's sick of being controlled by the people who are meant to love her. "Get out of my sight," I tell him.

He begins to run, tripping over his own feet.

As if in slow motion, I sense a shift.

I might have wanted the demon to live, but someone else is unwilling to let him go.

The voice of Hell howls again, filling the room, growing louder and louder, and this time I can feel what it's doing.

It's feeding me the power—the power I just decided not to take from Lucifer. It wants me to take. It *wants* this.

But I don't.

"No," I breathe, my eyes widening. With everything in me, I reject the offering, send it hurtling back into this fierce, hidden beast. "Don't—"

Hell doesn't accept.

"NO!" the voice of Hell roars.

The building shatters. Stone and dust rise as a monstrous giant forms itself from the earth itself.

Its face is made of stone, whitened by the clouds of ash that swallow the volcanoes whole in the distant mountains. But shrubs grow from the crevasses—from its cheekbones and the ridge of its nose.

Hell itself stands before me, and I stare, frozen, as the little ripples of movement from its body extend into the landscape itself.

It lifts an arm; the mountains ripple. It sighs and the lakes flood. Fear eclipses me, sending waves of hellfire rising at my feet.

And from within the fire, Hell's face... shifts. Like the demons do, the face of Hell's soul reveals itself from within the hellfire.

I know this face.

It's the face of the Devil.

What the actual fuck? I reel back, my heart stuttering, brain whirring as I try to make sense of this. It's definitely the Devil—the same stretches of sinew, of golden metal bolted into the bone. The same leering, skeletal smile. And then, as I watch, it shifts.

That dark, amorphous mass beneath the bone simmers, rises. Changes. The bones of the skull reshape, elongating like a goat's.

Two sweeping horns emerge, and they single-handedly put every black metal album in existence to shame.

It truly is the Devil's face, there's no mistake, but it's also... more... It's like this is the real face of the Devil, and the one Lucifer wears is only an illusion. This is the real thing. This is what the illusion is based on.

How is this even possible? How can two beings share one soul?

Maybe I'm asking the wrong questions here, since a sentient version of the land I'm bloody standing on is currently throwing a hissy fit in front of me.

"Make him burn," Hell cries, and in a sickening parody of the Rising Snakes' catch cry for the Devil, the demon burns.

His screams echo in my mind, and I swear it takes years for him to die. Years where I stand there, transfixed—horrified.

Hell laughs, a horrible, beastly laugh that rings across the mountains and valleys. And then it... crumbles.

Becomes ash before my eyes, leaving me standing in a plume of smoke.

There's a second of silence.

A pause.

A breath of anticipation.

And then the landscape erupts. Stones rush by me, swirling, heaving.

One knocks into my head, and everything goes dark.

35

TOBIAS

LOGAN PACES HELENA'S ROOM LIKE A CAT CAUGHT IN A CAGE, WHICH I suppose is exactly what he is. I sympathize, feeling much the urge to do the same thing myself.

But instead, I force my restlessness down to one foot, my toe tapping incessantly while Logan shoots me daggers every time he turns.

"Pot, kettle," I tell him sharply.

He snarls at me in response.

He's been skittish ever since I kissed him. Good. I need that energy.

That'll keep him distracted from what he really wants to do, which is run.

It's time he learned to stop running. It's time he became the man he was always meant to be.

"Good kitty," I tell him, deliberately stoking the fire that simmers just below the surface. "Use your brain and your brawn."

I take a moment to consider whether it's really wise to stoke him this far when I need him to act and not to crumble. But I decide quickly that if he crumbles now, he wasn't worth it.

He wasn't what I thought he was.

"Be the alpha you were born to be," I tell him.

I've always heard the truth of how he hates that label on the whisper of his thoughts... and now I turn it back on him as a weapon.

Logan stops. Swivels. Long golden metal claws extend from his fingers, and his eyes flash shifter gold.

He growls a low steady rumble, and I know I'm not speaking to Logan the man right now, I'm speaking to his beast.

Good; it's his beast I need.

"You're Lucifer's right-hand man," I tell him, very carefully, very slowly. "You've been helping him on this for longer than you know. Where is the hideout?"

Come on, Logan, stop running.

His face twists in a grimace, complex emotions hurtling across it. I make a mental note to come back to this later. It looks intriguing, but even I know it's suicide to get distracted now.

He resumes his pacing, more frantic now, as if he's three seconds from pouncing at all times.

"Dead man's bar," he says suddenly, and his voice is almost as though it has two voices in it.

His shifter soul is blazing, writhing. He still isn't unified with his beast, but they're both here, and that's what counts.

"The Rising Snakes there... their cloaks were wet." He comes to a halt and grips the back of Helena's desk chair, fingers driving into the wood, snapping it into splinters beneath his palms. "There was no rain. And that demon said it was near River's Mouth."

I can see the thoughts whirring as he finally pays attention to details he has only ever blindly reported to his master.

"Lucifer took note of that," he continues in a distracted voice. "Took note of the damp. Took note of the algae at the edge—the red algae." His voice trails off, and then his head snaps up, eyes fixing to mine. "They're in the Ashketon swamps —their cloaks were still damp from the passage. That's where they're holding her."

"Very good," I tell him.

I watch with interest as he preens at the praise. So, he's an alpha that likes to be stroked.

Well, that's hardly new.

I take a step forward, unable to keep myself from moving into his aura.

"What else can you do?" I ask him, holding his gaze.

He watches me silently, but I can see the shift in his body language. The subtle way he holds himself as I approach.

He's still at war, internally.

Part of him wants to dominate, and he hates that part because it's let him down in the past. But because of that hatred another part of him—a much stronger part that will never truly die, no matter if his alpha-self surfaces—wants to submit.

To surrender.

To be told he's a good boy.

"Can you take me there?" I ask him, reaching out to trail a finger across the skin above his collar. Along the rim of his jaw. "Could you pull the carriage with me inside it? Would you let me steer you, like a common beast?"

His eyes blaze, and the war burning within him shines brighter.

He doesn't know what he wants. He both hates and loves what I'm offering him, and I regret that there's no time to explore it further. If we want to get Helena back unharmed, we really do have to leave now.

I step backward, but he reaches out and snatches hold of my

wrist, his claws digging in. I can't help the sharp intake of breath at his touch. There's a hint of domination within it, just as I predicted. His claws drive into my skin hard enough to hurt.

I keep myself very still, careful not to move. Not to blink. My heart stammers in my chest.

I've underestimated him.

I thought if I pushed him too far he would crumble, but I was wrong.

"Easy now," I tell him, speaking entirely to the beast and not the man.

Logan growls.

The skin at his forehead begins to produce a light fuzz of fur, the shape of his face shifting with it. Long, angular, sharpened teeth poke from his lips.

He doesn't crumble at all.

Interesting.

If I can keep him from running, it seems he turns into the proverbial caged beast and attacks.

We could do with that.

"Alphas aren't ridden," he tells me.

A shiver races through my body and I work very hard to keep from showing on my face. Yes, this is exactly what we need. We need to charge into the Rising Snake's stronghold with this sort of energy behind us.

With this and the Devil riding shotgun, we might actually have a chance.

The thought surprises me, shocking me out of the seduced daze I'd fallen into.

Why am I imagining Lucifer riding shotgun to this? It should be the other way around.

One of the claws digs in enough that a droplet of blood oozes free.

"You follow behind, pretty boy," he tells me, voice sharp.

"Gladly," I say, my eyes flashing.

Very subtly, I tilt my chin up, bearing my throat. Logan's nostrils widen, and his gaze turns hungrily to my neck.

He wants to mark me, to claim me.

But then something shifts in his expression and the hunger turns haunted.

He staggers backward, and internally I'm screaming, *no, fuck, we were so close.*

He won't crumble; he'll run. I have perhaps seconds to stop him. Seconds to salvage this mess I've created by wanting too much, always too much.

And then, I freeze. I drag myself from the incessant cloud of Logan's guilt and rising fear, and realize it's too quiet in here. I can't feel power humming at all. Any of it. And I should. I was there when it was written, at least into the shape of Hell we have now.

There's a seal on the door. I don't know how long it's been there, its shimmering, runic form undulating above the wood. I stare at it, eyes wide. We've been locked inside.

But more importantly, something has been locked out.

I cross the room, ignoring the shifter poised seconds from bolting, and destroy the seal with my bare hands. Light bursts free, and when I throw open the door, I step headfirst into an assault of power.

"Helena," I whisper.

She's calling for us. Screaming. And Lucifer made it so we wouldn't hear.

I turn to see the same shock and anger on Logan's face— finally, something has broken through. Snapped him back from the precipice of failure.

Rage fills me, wiping clean every agitated contradiction I've felt since this bond appeared.

Wanting her; wanting to leave. Hating Lucifer; loving him

again. Dismissing Logan's childish fears; and seeing far too much of myself in them. It all wipes clean.

"He's going to take her from us," I tell Logan, watching as the same fury sweeps across his face.

"Use the bond cord," he growls at me, stepping up to fill the doorway at my side. "She isn't shielded anymore; that's what he was hiding from us. Pull them in like you kept doing to Lucifer."

"Kept trying and failing, you mean," I correct him.

But my hand comes to toy with the cord at my chest. I've worried it so often, these last few weeks, playing with it, testing it. But I've never really tried to use it.

I was only ever teasing him. Taunting him. And annoying the others.

But Logan's suggestion has burnt an idea into my mind that won't let go. Lucifer can ignore my claim to him well enough—that much is clear—but he can't escape it. He's bound to us as much as we are to him. It doesn't go one way, as much as he's tried to have us believe that these past few days.

He used this bond to bind us; perhaps it's time I showed him the binding is equal. We are equal.

"What's going through that pretty head of yours?" Logan asks, a wry smile on his face.

I glance up at him, noting the glint in his eyes. "Calculations," I murmur.

The theory is all well and good, but the strength it would take to actually reel Lucifer in with this cord, like the proverbial fish I accused him of when this began... It's too much. The cord isn't strong enough. It only solidifies when it's agitated.

"But I could rip it free," I say slowly, distantly. "Then it would be as strong as steel."

I lift my hand to my chest and pause, my palm pressed to

the familiar warmth of the thread that links me to Lucifer. I could undo everything in this moment.

Everything that, if I'm truly honest, I've always wanted.

Logan glances at me, frowning. Then his eyes widen in abrupt understanding. He steadies me with a hand on my shoulder, and the cord that connects the two of us burns.

"You'll still be connected through me," he says gruffly. "You're not losing him."

I look up in shock, stunned by the wry, humorless smile on Logan's face. How much does he see? Ludus, my ass. We're far more than Ludus; Fate has simply been waiting for us to catch up.

I rip the cord free from my body. It solidifies in an instant, as though reacting to some sort of impossible pain. An ethereal magic transformed into mass through the crucible of trauma.

Then, I wrap it around my hand, pass it to Logan so he can grip it, too, and together we heave.

Helena's power screams. Burns. She's careening out of control, and Lucifer with her. He wants so badly to take her and leave us behind. If I pulled on her cord, Lucifer would simply dig his heels in and pull back, and we'd lose ourselves to the stupidest tug of war in the history of Hell.

It's Lucifer I need to reel in. He'll fight less if it's over himself.

The rope in my hand burns and flickers. Through the encroaching darkness, I see a room; this is what lies on the other end of the rope. Somehow, the bond is showing me.

Bare walls, simple furniture. Helena lies in the center, passed out, power rippling from her like water from a geyser as Lucifer kneels by her side and gathers her carefully in his arms.

The building has fallen to pieces, and jagged, new mountains rise in the distance.

Hell is shifting; something has gone terribly, terribly wrong.

The image ebbs and flows, difficult to catch. I can hardly see them. Can only feel them on the other end of our connection.

A shimmering thread of blue light appears, piercing Lucifer's collar. There's a split second of hesitation, where Lucifer frowns and even Helena's magic stutters, as if it's somehow sentient enough to know something is happening.

But then resistance appears through the cord, and I can feel the weight of Lucifer at the other end. Logan's hand folds over mine as we pull on the rope and bring them back to us.

The room shimmers and sways, and when it finally grows still, I find I'm speechless.

Lucifer stands in the center of the room, holding Helena in his arms like she's precious. Like she's his.

A vision of his thoughts appears in my mind, and I see what he craves in this moment: the two of them standing together, hand in hand as power ignites the air with every breath they draw.

A king and his queen.

Who are we, by comparison? A measly shifter and an old friend betrayed three times over. A shattered soulbond I destroyed just to drag them back to me.

This was always doomed; I knew that from the beginning.

But then my soul kicks in and demands its birthright. They're mine. They're all mine, and damn all the demon lords in Hell, I will fight for them.

"No," I breathe, eyes burning into Lucifer's. "You don't get to take her from us. You don't get to *leave* like that. You're. Both. Ours."

Lucifer's face contorts. He grips our lady tighter and turns on me.

"Give me one reason to stay," he says coldly. "When you have so diligently proven yourself inept."

Cold creeps into my heart. The icy threads of Lucifer's

hatred—so carefully cultivated, and brutally aimed—pierce me. Is it all over, then?

Has he turned from us at last?

Then a whisper of Lucifer's thoughts breaks free. A whisper so strong, he can no longer keep it from me.

I smile, relief washing over me and thawing my frozen heart. "Why should you stay? Because you want to."

The bond reforms, piercing my neck, and around the room the other threads break and reform alike.

They're no longer blue, but I can't tell what color they are. Maybe gold. Maybe a brilliant emerald green.

Colorless, for now.

Lucifer glares at me, eyes blazing, but he doesn't walk away.

For the first time, he stays.

36

HELENA

I WAKE ALONE, IN MY SUITE, BUT I CAN SENSE THAT ALL THREE OF THEM were here recently.

As soon as I can move, I look out the window. Hell looks the same as it did before. Normal. Safe.

I know it's a lie.

Somewhere out there, that beast has broken free. And he's linked to me, to my power.

His soul shares the face of the Devil, and he's linked to me.

I don't know what it's going to mean—for any of us—and for once I'm at a complete loss for where to search for answers. But I do know one thing: I'm pissed as hell at Lucifer.

I wanted to wait until we'd saved Hell before I demanded answers, but I'm beginning think we won't be able to save Hell unless I get those answers first. This problem needs all of us, and right now... I don't want anything to do with them.

So, I escape to find Catrina. I need someone sensible, who can talk me through what to do. I need an adult. A more adulty adult.

I've got questions. From one poly princess to another.

Okay, I'm never calling it that again.

Cat swings the door open to her private suite and blinks at me. "Helena," she says, frowning. "Where's the fire?"

"Attached to the pole up Lucifer's ass," I snarl.

Her eyes widen and she bursts into surprised laughter. "You'd better come in, then." She steps back from the door, making room. "The boys are out."

Good. I can't take more alpha crap right now.

Cat leads me further into the suite, making straight for the rustic, cottage style kitchen and pouring two large glasses of wine.

"There's vodka when we run out," she says drily.

I collapse on the stool and drain half my glass in relief. "Thank God."

We fall into an easy silence for a few minutes as Cat obviously wakes up, ruffling her hair and smoothing out the folds in her silky dressing gown. She's stylish and cool in a way I've always wanted to be. My heart aches for everything she has.

And then I remember the reasons why I'm holding back from taking the exact same thing, and my heart aches for a different reason entirely.

"Have you managed to reach Ciera?" I ask, skirting the edge of the issue that has me so mad and running for Cat's door.

I feel like if I could just talk to Ciera, I could handle this crap.

Cat winces. "Lucy still has her blocked. She's trying to get in via Death, last I heard."

Funnily enough, this turns out to be the last straw.

I explode. "How do you take it?" I demand, slamming my hands down on the counter and sending my wine glass wobbling dangerously.

Cat's eyes widen, and she holds up her hands, palms face out. "Whoa, take it easy. No hellfire in here, please. I'm fond of the curtains."

I try to keep it in, but it's hard.

I think I could create hellfire on purpose, now. I think I could do a lot of things.

"I know your guys sucked ass when you first met, so how did you do it?" I grit out. "How did you make it work when you didn't even want to?"

She wrinkles her nose. "If you don't want to, then don't. Jesus. That one's easy."

That stops me. I open my mouth and shut it, imagining if I never had them again.

I think of Tobias, coaxing the truth from all of us and holding it as precious, even when we won't. Logan, trying to give me the least amount of pain, when he's convinced that's all he has to offer.

And Lucifer... trapped in a cycle I'm all too familiar with. I feel betrayed by him, but I don't want to walk away. I want answers.

Because how can it feel like fate when he's still keeping my parents and best friend from me?

"I need to talk to them," I decide.

"Talking is good," Cat agrees. "Do you know what you want to say?"

No. Are you fucking kidding me? I'm not like Cat, who always seems to know what she's thinking or feeling.

I never know who I am. I only know who other people want me to be.

I close my eyes and force myself to look at the thoughts swirling in my brain.

Why did you keep this from me? Why are you trying to control me?

Especially—*why are you trying to control me when you can't even control yourself?*

I definitely can't ask any of that.

"I want him to let me in," I say slowly. "He's always keeping things from me, and it only makes everything worse. He's—"

I break off, visions of my parents flooding my head. Weak excuses. Promises. Their constant insistence that they had everything covered.

Coming home after school to find them missing. Fridge empty.

Late night returns, giggling and yelling.

We're fine, Helena. It's all fine.

A darker, deeper voice. Rich, with tendrils of seduction.

It's fine, Helena. I'm handling it. I don't know what your power is, but it's under control.

"He's lying to me," I say quietly. "And that's a deal-breaker."

An unreadable expression crosses Cat's face. She pulls on her lip for a second, and then says, "What about the thing with your parents? And Ciera? Those aren't deal-breakers?"

I grimace. "Obviously I fucking hate that. But he's the kind of man that never does things without a reason. If he would just talk to me instead of cursing and walking off, maybe I'd be able to understand—I might even agree with him, if it's a matter of life or death, or whatever. Instead, he just lies to my face. He thinks he's in bloody control of everything, but he isn't. He's falling apart."

Cat watches me shrewdly. After a beat, she says, "We went through the same thing with Ronin in our heads, but we came out the other side so differently. I know you still have shit to work through with what he did to you, but you've never blamed yourself, have you? You blame him."

I blink at her, startled at the thought that I might blame myself for what someone else did to me. It sits weirdly in my mind, like a hideous painting I don't want to look at.

Her final words sink in—you blame him—and I shake my head. "No, I blame God."

She chokes on air, eyes wide. The discomfort that had been building in the air shifts and fades away, and I bite down on my lip to keep from smiling. I don't even know why she's laughing.

"Well, you and Lucy are a pair, aren't you?"

Ah. That is pretty funny actually.

Cat wipes her eyes, still looking faintly incredulous, and gulps more wine. She pauses, staring down into the golden liquid before finally speaking in a different sort of tone altogether. Like she's finally talking to me seriously.

"Mistrust makes us hurt people we shouldn't," she says, looking up at me. "So, either Lucifer's a controlling asshole..." She pauses again. "Or... you need to uncover why he doesn't trust you. Because you don't deserve to be hurt. Not from someone who loves you. Not from someone you love."

I reel backward.

Love.

Right now, it's a four letter word, to be perfectly honest. I nearly throw it aside, dismiss it, and then I remember what Catrina is the queen of.

My eyes slide sideways, taking in the crimson circlet that rests on the cushion by the door. That thin strand of power, so different to all the other power currents down here. A stream instead of a river, but no less powerful.

If anyone would know what we were really dealing with, it would be her. And she's right: love isn't always enough. I need more from them—from Lucifer.

"Controlling prick... or he has a reason not to trust me," I mutter, swirling my wine and sipping it with a grimace. "Probably a little of both, yeah?"

"The truth usually is, in the end," Cat says, appearing to lose some inner battle as she reaches for the vodka.

I snort. "You should meet Tobias some time." I pause,

frowning. "Although I'm not sure he's really got that particular memo, yet."

A trickster demon obsessed with truth, who only sees the world as black and white. An alpha who won't lead or protect. And a ruler of Hell without his power... There are so many ways to describe us, and they all sound like turds rolled in glitter.

Warm, fuzzy feeling spreads through me as the alcohol kicks in. I grin, running a hand over the loose strands of hair by my face, and turn to her. "We're all a fucking mess, if you hadn't figured that out."

Cat grins widely, pouring the vodka into my glass and topping it with something that looks raspberry flavored. "Welcome to the club," she says cheerfully. "Now, while you're totally welcome to stay and get shitfaced with me here, I think you might secretly want to be somewhere else. Am I right?"

I groan, dropping my head onto my arms. "I want to talk to them now. I hate waiting. It just makes you feel icky."

Not knowing. Needing answers. I can't stand it. I think it's why I've been on edge this entire time—it's like I'm stuck in Limbo, technically above the nine circles but eternally part of them.

Cat pats my hair gently. "No one likes feeling icky, Helena. Go fix it."

"Right," I mumble. "Going."

I pause a little longer, leaning into the feeling of her patting my hair. She doesn't rush me.

I slam my hands on the counter, making us both jump, and stand up. "Going!" I insist.

Cat cheers behind me. "Go get 'em, girl!"

37

HELENA

I MARCH STRAIGHT TO THE ELEVATOR AND PING MYSELF UP TO HIS Majesty's golden coward box.

If he's going to run away from me and lie to me, I'm going to call it as it is. Cowardly.

Flickers of emotion trickle down the threads in my chest—I can feel the others in ways I haven't felt them for days. They've come back to me.

We've come back to each other.

But it's not enough—not yet.

I knock on Lucifer's door, pounding insistently against the wood. Three sneezes hit me in a row, and I glare at his stupid hay fever plant in the corner.

"I should shrivel you into ash," I hiss at it, and I nearly do, my blooming power coursing inside me.

But I hold still, control myself—unlike *some* people—and settle my power over it delicately instead. There's a slight pop of misplaced air, and then the terrarium-like bubble rests over the plant.

"Better." I smile. "Very 70s. That should piss him off."

At least, if Tobias' comments about Paris were accurate.

The door opens just as the elevator doors ping wide behind me. Lucifer stares at me, then at Logan and Tobias stepping casually through... and then at the bubbled plant in the corner. He narrows his eyes.

"Problem?" I ask sweetly.

He mutters something under his breath that sounds an awful lot like *fuck the 70s*, and turns away.

"Come in, then," he says over his shoulder. "If you must."

I glare at his retreating back and follow him inside. "Are you really going to pretend none of that happened?"

He drops into a comfy-looking armchair and rests his head back against the head. "None of what happened?" he asks with a provocative smile.

Tobias laughs bitterly, shutting the door behind him as he and Logan enter the room. Even Logan looks like he might be about to growl at Lucifer for that. I kind of wish he would.

Before I can say anything, Lucifer drops the smile. "What would you have me do?" He spreads his hands wide. "Everything is back to how it should be, no? Balance is restored."

"Fuck your balance."

His eyebrows lift politely. "I could throw it all into chaos instead, if you like?" His voice turns cold. "I'm sure the Rising Snakes"—Logan coughs something that sounds like *losers* under his breath—"had some very persuasive arguments for you. Maybe you should take them up on their offer and see just how much you enjoy it when the balance is fucked."

The way he says the word 'fucked' sends heat rippling through my entire body.

"That's what I wanted to talk to you about, actually." I fold my arms and lean back against his writing desk.

For a moment, something that looks like genuine fear crosses his face.

"Oh?"

"Yeah. I get that you've got bigger fish to fry, and all that, but the *Rising Snakes*"—Tobias mimics the words in a high-pitched voice—"told me something interesting. They said you knew I was stealing Hell's power from the beginning." My voice lowers, becoming cold. Angry. "And you never told me. We have a soulmate bond, and you never told me. You used that bond to trap me here, instead, and, honestly, mate? This bond means nothing if you're going to treat me like that."

Lucifer stares at me open-mouthed, while Tobias and Logan are clearly seconds away from getting the popcorn. Silence fills the room; I can practically hear the gears grinding in Lucifer's head as he processes what I'm saying.

"Helena," he finally grits out. "There are things you don't understand. To rule Hell... it's more than just holding and using power. There is a price, and that price is mine to pay. Not yours."

He's talking in riddles. "What price?" I snap.

"I was cast down here by Heaven, Helena," he snarls, neatly avoiding saying God's name. "Take a guess."

"What?!" My head feels all turned in on itself. "That's not an answer! Are you say—" I break off. "That's why I'm cast out of Heaven. Because *you're* cast out of Heaven. And this is Hell's power. Holy shit."

Tobias' eyes widen, and Logan's jaw slackens in shock.

"Certainly not God's chosen, then," Tobias says faintly.

Lucifer rubs his temple, suddenly looking precisely as old as he is. "That's one of the costs, yes," he says tiredly. "I was trying to save you that particular curse by nipping the power in the bud. Before it could deeply root itself in you." He smiles tightly. "I failed."

"So then... Ciera?" I ask slowly, the pieces rearranging themselves. "Is it that I can't be near an angel right now, or because you don't trust me to be?"

His expression darkens. "I swear it is not you I mistrust." He shrugs lightly. "I wasn't sure what would happen, and thought it not worth the risk."

Wasn't sure. Failed.

Anger spikes once more, red hot.

"So you decided to keep everything from me just in case. Isn't the choice mine?" I snap. "Let me in. Tell me what I don't understand."

"No," he snarls, fingers clenching into the arms of the chair. "It isn't yours to know. None of it is." He leaps to his feet, agitated, and crosses the room to the windows.

It's like a storm chases at his feet, power crackling, igniting.

His eyes darken, not in anger or lust, but in something else. I remember distantly that we shouldn't let the power become untethered around him—it's too much for him—but I can't focus on the thought enough to take care of it.

"This has nothing to do with you," he snarls, staring out the window with one hand pressed to the glass. "Any of you. This is my world."

I huff a bitter kind of laugh, furious and confused. "So, you've chosen to stay with us, sure, but it's like you're not even here. You don't trust us enough to let us in—not to anything that matters."

I can't reach you.

"I'm as close as you'll ever get me," he throws back, but there's something in the words. An edge of... sadness.

It breaks through my anger.

I think about the way he acts around Logan—his right-hand man, not his errand boy, but you wouldn't think it from watching them. And then Tobias, his closest and oldest friend.

He doesn't trust anyone.

It isn't me; it's everyone.

It's just that I'm the only one pushing back.

I glance at Tobias, noting the steel glint in his eye, and the swirling, colorless nature of his soulbond cord. Changing. Evolving from Ludus to... something else. Even Logan holds himself differently, more willing to fight Lucifer and less willing to run an errand without asking.

Maybe I'm not the only one pushing back anymore.

Okay. This is... okay. This is a start.

I take a deep breath, my thoughts whirring.

"The price is yours to pay," I repeat, frowning, trying to understand. "So you didn't want to lump me with the baggage, is that what you're saying?"

"Precisely."

I sit on the idea, turning it over, weighing it.

Nope, I'm still fucking pissed.

He lied to me, controlled me, and isolated me because he *didn't* want me to have baggage?!

"So instead, you locked me in a castle and let me blow up everything I touched?! How can you not see what the problem is? You've locked Ciera away from me! My parents!" My words catch at the end, breaking on a sob. "You torture them," I spit out, finally acknowledging the truth I haven't been able to face.

The words make me sick.

Lucifer turns sharply, his face oddly stricken. When he speaks, it's exceedingly careful. Measured. "I promise you, I have never. I have never tortured them, and I called off all active torture the day you mentioned them to me."

Tobias speaks. "He's telling the truth."

I watch them both. All of them, actually. Three men who've captivated and infuriated me. Lies, secrets. Privacy. Trust.

A shattered mess.

Maybe it can't be repaired. Maybe the new cord at Tobias' neck will only turn gray and crumble to ash.

"Never?"

"I swear."

The confession looks like it pains him. Which at least matches how angry he was with me when I asked for their freedom, so I agree this is probably the truth.

But it means he wants to torture them.

"But you won't let them go," I say softly.

Something flashes in his eyes, something hard and cruel. "No," he says in a quiet, crooning voice as he turns properly to face me. "I will not let them go."

"Why?"

I need a reason. It doesn't matter if they're not being tortured, or if they're safe. I need to know why he hates them.

His eyes flash, and for some unknown reason, my heart stops, like it knows what's coming when it can't. It can't know.

Lucifer speaks, his voice obscenely gentle as he says, in a tone that will not be argued with, "Because. They. Hurt. You."

There's a flash in the air, and it tastes the same as when Tobias took over our dinner. It's his magic revealing the truth.

The room shatters into a thousand pieces and disappears. Before me, in the cold abyss of darkness, is a rug. A simple, tattered rug, lying on the floor in front of the fire.

There's a child on the rug. A toddler, curled in on herself.

The fire went out long ago.

"She's cold," I say, oddly detached. Emotionless.

My voice echoes strangely in the space. I can't see the others; it's like I'm alone, except that I can feel them. I can feel the weight of everything they aren't saying.

The toddler stirs. Lifts her head. Shivers and lies back down.

Something in my heart cracks. There's pain there, pain I can't feel. Pain I won't feel.

I'm achingly aware that I'm not alone in the room. Three other people stand with me, watching.

Witnessing.

"That's enough," I whisper, broken.

The rug and the toddler disappears. No one asks why her parents weren't there, or where they were instead. What they were doing.

No one speaks at all.

"Okay," I say, staring down at my feet. I can feel Lucifer's rage pulsing from across the room, no longer contained. I can hardly bear it. How does he live with that? With that anger? That righteousness? "Okay, I get it."

Tobias opens his mouth to speak, but I cut him off with one hand. "No," I say softly.

He falls silent.

I search my thoughts for a thread I can hold onto. I won't let this break me. I won't let it.

Something wet lands on my cheek. Fuck.

Tobias' arms circle me.

I close my eyes and let my head fall against his chest.

Is this the day? Am I finally feeling more than I can contain, and it's all going to fall apart?

No—I won't let this break me, but if I'm to keep everything together, I'm going to need to bend. I'm going to need to let them in.

"You knew," I whisper.

Lucifer answers, "I knew." He clears his throat, speaking softer still. "Even before I knew the details, I knew, because the Joker was drawn to your power."

The Joker. The wild card. All the unnamed, untamed emotion left behind after Hell's power currents have come through.

The unclean pain.

Damage that can't be put inside a neat little box.

I snort—wetly. There's too much of me. There's always too much of me. I'm stealing Hell's power; I'm the accidental figurehead of a rebellion; I'm triggering Lucifer's addiction; I'm traumatized by Ronin; I have mommy issues.

Nothing about me can be put in a box, and I've no fucking idea who I'm meant to become to fix this.

But for the first time I think that maybe I'm not only a problem to be solved. I'm someone who's been hurt. And there's, like, one tiny, teensy weensy chance that I'm not meant to become anyone else at all, right now.

Because conning people never solves a problem; it just wallpapers over it.

I want to actually fix this, and you can't fix what you can't see. I look around at the men standing beside me, witnessing this truth—helping me to witness it.

This isn't over. I know that. More has to come out. Bubble up. The thought terrifies me, and instinctively, I slam up my walls.

They won't hold forever this time, but they'll hold for now.

I take a deep breath, pause, let it go.

"Distract me," I murmur.

38

HELENA

"What was that, sweetheart?" Tobias whispers, tucking my hair behind my ear.

"I need you to distract me," I say, looking up at him.

His eyes burn, and I know he's thinking about our last night together.

That isn't the kind of distraction I mean, and he knows it.

His hand moves beneath my chin, thumb and forefinger holding me there as he leans down very gently and kisses me.

It's soft, sweet, and my body tenses in anticipation, waiting for the moment that it breaks.

"I'm not going to fuck you hard after what you just witnessed," he says against my mouth, and a sob breaks free.

"No," I cry out. "Please distract me. I need this."

He kisses me again, cutting off the words.

"I'll distract you," he says, "but not like that."

Someone's hand tugs gently on the back of my plait, and I whimper as Logan presses a kiss to my neck.

"And not here," he suggests.

I look up as he turns to Lucifer, just in time to see the expression on his face as Logan says, "in that bedroom."

Lucifer's expression doesn't change. He watches us, and there are so many conflicting emotions on his face.

I can still see the rage, still feel the anger, but it wasn't anger at me, like I thought—it was anger for me.

And he didn't even defend himself.

He let me keep thinking the worst of him, rather than put me through the pain of knowing what he knew, what I'd obviously forgotten.

Something fractures in my mind, memories slipping in and out—not forgotten, not exactly. Ignored.

Something.

I don't want to think about it. I want a distraction.

I tilt my face up to meet Tobias'.

"Then just distract me," I growl against his mouth. "Whatever you're going to do, do it now."

I shiver as someone else's palm slides across my cheek, and turn to see that Lucifer has silently crossed the room to join us.

He gazes down at me, his eyes falling to my lips, his palm holding my cheek in place. After what feels like an eternity, he bends forward, brushes his lips over mine and pauses.

"I don't think we're finished here," he says, just quietly enough for only me to hear. "Are we distracting you to forget? Or to help carry the load?"

"The second one," I say, knowing instinctively that there is no chance I will ever forget this, not again.

He kisses me once more, deeper this time, longer. It's as though he's exploring me, and I realize in a rush what my agony and distraction had hidden.

This is the first time he's kissed me, the first time his lips have met mine.

A noise escapes me from deep in my chest, and I sink into him, sink into the hands holding me upright.

Tobias and Logan surrounding me, Lucifer holding me.

"Then," he says, a little louder now, speaking to all of us, "we will return to this another day. For now..." He smiles against my mouth. "Let us distract you."

Hands pull me backward, tugging me closer to the bedroom. The door swings wide, bumping us, and I fall onto a bed covered in the most obnoxiously silky sheets you could imagine.

Palms caress me, guiding me backward, pulling me down among the pillows.

It's no surprise when Logan and Tobias stretch out on either side, and through wordless agreement, Lucifer kneels above me.

Even though they're doing this for me because I asked for it, demanded it, I can't help but get the feeling that Lucifer needs this.

That he's been holding onto that particular truth silently for a very long time.

When Tobias and Logan peel my clothing off, piece by piece, Lucifer braces himself with one hand by my head. His fingers slide between my thighs, stroking me, slipping into me as I arch against him. There's a light in his eyes I've never seen before.

"I've wanted just to hold you for so long, Helena," he says in a voice that sounds like an apology. "But I couldn't be this way with you while I knew your secrets. Secrets you'd forgotten and didn't want to remember."

His fingers slip away, and I feel the aching press of him there against me. I gasp a breath as he enters me, clutching at his shoulders.

"This isn't distracting me," I complain, my eyes fluttering closed as my head falls back into the pillows.

He laughs quietly. "Do you see what I mean? I could never have held you without confessing."

He tilts his hips, sliding his knee higher up the bed so the angle is deeper. Rougher. A moan escapes me, and finally my thoughts begin to shift from dread to ecstasy.

My back arches, the thick slide of him inside me now a deeper rhythm, caressing me. It's a distraction like no other, but it isn't enough.

I turn to the side, ignoring Lucifer's jealous snarl, and pull Logan into a kiss.

There's fire in Lucifer's eyes as he watches us together. He takes in the urgent slide of Logan's mouth against mine, the way Logan clutches at my hair as though he'd been waiting for permission, waiting to take what he wanted.

I bat my eyelids open, glancing sideways to see Lucifer, to see what he's doing.

He hasn't looked away.

The thrust of him between my thighs is a slow, delicious ache, almost taunting, as he fixes a hungry gaze to the two of us.

"She needs more than that," he says wickedly, when he notices me looking. His voice lowers to a whisper. "She needs to forget how to feel anything but this."

He's speaking from experience. A cold shiver of dread courses through me, but it mixes immediately with a heavy rush of desire—a touch of his thumb sliding over me, the ache of his cock.

It's almost too much, but he's right, it isn't enough.

I can still feel something, the edge of something, and I know it isn't healthy to run from it like this. I know that no matter how much we tell each other we've only put the conversation on pause, that we'll come back to it, that we're mature, healthy adults...

I know our actions say something different.

I can't feel it.

I won't feel it.

"Fuck me harder," I tell him.

His eyes flash, and he does as I ask, but it's not enough, and I remember Tobias's words from before.

He'll never make you call him Daddy while he fucks your tits.

A sharp intake of breath from my left has me turning to see Tobias, eyes wide, desire contorting his features.

"Is that what you need, sweetheart?" he says, "because I'm happy to fill that role."

I shiver with delight at the thought of Tobias standing over me like that.

He's already moving, standing by the side of the bed, and Lucifer seems to know exactly what's happening. His hungry gaze, like some kind of overseeing director, fixes us in place.

Lucifer scoops his arm beneath me, lifting me with one arm and repositioning us so that my head is hanging over the edge of the bed. But when Tobias moves to line up with my chest, Lucifer stops him with a word.

"Take her mouth," he demands, "but do it gently."

It's there again in his voice: a hint of what he's really feeling, of the need he's had to comfort me, to look after me...

And his absolute inability to do anything about it.

Tobias looks at him, pauses, and then does as asked. He flicks open his fly, takes out his hard cock, and feeds it carefully into my mouth.

It's a difficult angle—can't say it's one I've done before, not while there was also a man between my legs.

And another watching, taking his own pleasure with his hand.

Heat blooms within me, and Tobias finds a steady rhythm —not overwhelming me, but God, it's hard to feel anything but overwhelmed when I'm filled like this. My body finally begins to relax; there is finally too much for me to think about anything else.

Something wet covers my nipple, and I gasp, my back arching, unable to see what it is but working out by frantic mathematics that Logan appears to be sucking on my tit.

All three of them surround me, taking and giving pleasure, distracting me just as I asked.

I begin to shake. It's not from an orgasm; it's from something else, from some deeper emotion. The one that I'm running from.

Logan's hand traces soothing circles across my belly, and then he finds my other breast, cupping and squeezing, while his tongue laves at my nipple.

Lucifer's speed hasn't changed, but Tobias is quickening, unable to control himself.

The soft moans that fall from above tell me how much he's enjoying it, how much he wants this.

"Helena," he rasps, "please tell me that dirty talk will distract you right now, baby, because I don't know how much longer I can hold off when you look like that."

Of course, I can't tell him anything right now. Not with his dick shoved right to the back of my throat, and my hands clutching at his thighs, upside down. But he knows this.

I can almost feel him rummaging through my mind as he seizes hold of my ecstasy and brandishes it with delight.

"Good girl," he murmurs, his thrusts turning harder. Faster. "You should see yourself spread out like this, love, completely at our mercy."

The four letter word he keeps insisting on takes on a new meaning like this, and the last of my body's defenses crumble away. I sink into the bed, completely relaxed and spinning out.

I barely notice as he pulls free, his fist flying as he spills over my neck. I barely notice as Lucifer removes himself from my legs and they swap places.

Tobias kneels between me, his tongue laving a long, slow lick over the apex of my thighs, and Lucifer...

Lucifer stands above me, cradling the back of my head so my neck isn't strained and I can look up into those piercing blue eyes.

Thick black curls fall forward to frame his face as he towers over me.

"Hold those tits together for me, Helena," he says roughly, and a moan escapes me as I hurry to do what he says.

He doesn't waste time. He lines his slick cock up between my breasts and begins to thrust.

I can hear Logan off to the side, his hand whipping over himself, gasps of desire dropping, while Tobias' quickening tongue is undeniable evidence of his own enjoyment.

And I can feel it too, feel it in the threads joining us together.

Feel it in the power that fills the room—my power and Lucifer's, blending together.

Hell's power surging.

I can't stop it, and I can't remember in this moment why I should, even though a tiny flicker of unease hovers in the back of my mind. But I told them to distract me, and they have, and all I can think about is the fast, thick slide of Lucifer between my breasts.

His hands replace mine, holding me there for him, creating a perfect channel. I can feel him getting close, feel him thickening against me.

The harsh pants that come from his lips are almost uncontrolled. The power is building, rising, and it's taking Lucifer with it.

And through the rising tide of my own climax, something—a flicker of a thought—makes its way into my head.

Don't let the power surge; he can't take it.

The thought flutters away, and my body arches, cresting as Tobias' tongue flicks wickedly over me, as Lucifer's cock thrusts against my breasts.

He comes all over me, all over my body, bent above me as he braces himself beside my hips on the bed.

The power continues to flicker. It rises and rises and rises, like it's caught hold of our ecstasy and it no longer wants to be kept on the sidelines. It wants to be part of it. It wants to be the star of the show.

And just like that, it is.

I know a split second before it happens exactly what is coming. My body shudders, fear drowning out my desire, drowning out my pleasure. It's too much.

Power burns too hot, too fast, and when Lucifer looks up, his eyes blaze with hellfire.

Gold and bone flicker at the edge of his face—a face that, deep within the shadows, is the wrong shape. It's too long, and it's framed by two sweeping horns.

The shadows fade, leaving him human again, but there's something in his expression that I don't recognize. It's a high he's never reached before, even in all the long years of his addiction.

He's managed to hold back from that edge until now, but not anymore.

"Lucifer," Tobias says in a slow, warning voice.

I scramble to my elbows, pulling myself away from the edge of the bed and trying to get upright.

Tobias' face is wide open with fear, and Logan's too, his eyes burning shifter gold as he prepares for the change.

"Lucifer, old friend, you can fight it. You're stronger than this."

Lucifer snarls, a low animalistic snarl.

Oh this isn't good. I don't recognize this man. I don't know this man.

When he speaks, his voice echoes—thousands of voices, thousands of souls burning forth from his vocal cords.

"You are correct," the voices say, deep and echoing. "I am stronger than this."

I don't know what he means by this, but I can guess: this room, this palace, this harem. Us.

We've lost him, I think. *We've finally lost him.*

It wasn't enough that he came back to us, because it was never Lucifer we were fighting. It was this power, this addiction, and the addiction has just won.

Lucifer vanishes, and my heart disappears with him.

39

HELENA

A TERRIBLE, HOWLING WIND ECHOES FROM OUTSIDE THE WINDOWS. Hell is terraforming, changing, but it's not like the usual shift.

This is a single-minded decimation, and it has one very distinct source.

We don't waste time. We gather our clothing, staggering together, hearts racing and fear churning in our stomachs.

And then we follow the trail of destruction.

My heart sinks at every broken building, every mound of scorched earth. The roads outside the palace are already unrecognizable. The gardens destroyed.

Even the sun blazes differently—too bright. Too angry.

"What has he done?" I whisper.

It was so quick. So brutal.

Had it been building this whole time?

How else could he unleash so much destruction so quickly?

Tobias says nothing. Logan's hand finds mine, and I squeeze it tightly.

Screams echo in the distance, near the lake district. Stomach sick with dread, we follow the sound, flagging down a coach and paying the skeleton driver extra to drive it into the ground.

I close my eyes as we wind through the streets, not wanting to see the horrors that rampant hellfire reveal. I've seen enough of demons' true faces for now.

When we come to a halt in front of a tall building by the Black Lake, my heart fills with dread. Logan holds the door of the carriage open for us, and we step slowly inside the doorway.

The door hangs off its hinges, and scorch marks line the walls. The symbol carved into the architrave tells me the rebellion have been here.

They aren't here now.

Bodies litter the floor, blood streaking the walls. Through a haze of numbness, I register half recorded plans on the still smoldering table. My hands move of their own accord, riffling through the papers, analyzing.

It's easy to put together the picture—I've put together more complicated pictures with far less research.

They were going to take out a village. Send a message to the Devil that he can't fight their armies. Lucifer might have even saved innocent demons.

But the bodies. They can't all have been fighters.

Tobias shudders, bracing himself on the table. "He doesn't —" he begins, then breaks off and tries again. "This isn't—"

What? Him? This isn't him? He doesn't mean this?

I know, just as I know it doesn't matter, because it happened.

I don't know what makes me turn. A sixth sense? It doesn't matter.

As one, we shift to see him standing outside the building, in the street. Just a man. Not a speck of blood marring his clothes. Piercing blue eyes bright with energy.

With power.

"Don't follow," he tells us, his voice silky smooth. "This isn't your fight."

"Lucifer," Tobias says, his voice cracking. "This isn't *your* fight. Don't do this."

Lucifer laughs, and the sound chills me. I've never seen him like this. Never seen him as a conduit for the power he should so easily contain.

It swarms him, consumes him, and I realize we have never truly seen the Devil with all of Hell's power. He's always been holding back, always trying to keep his addiction at bay. But now he isn't. Now, he consumes it all.

All I can think is: how long before it consumes him?

"You don't tell me what to do," he says quietly. "But I do commend you for your courage in trying."

Then he's gone. This time, there is no easy trail to follow. No whisper on the rivers.

He's just gone.

Logan falls to his knees beside me, and inwardly I do the same.

I should have known. It's never this easy. I *know* it's never this easy, and I still didn't see the obvious when it was right in front of me.

It doesn't matter if he chose to stay with us. They always choose to stay.

At the end of the day, something else chooses for them.

THE END

The story continues in Hellion Forsaken, coming soon...
(Join Jade's Mailing List for updates)

AUTHOR'S NOTE

Lucifer's trilogy is finally here! It took a little longer to arrive than I initially planned, and there are a couple of reasons for that. (Head's up, the tone is turning heavy.)

The first is because, during the release of Hell's Fire Burning (and while I was still editing the damn thing), I was diagnosed with lupus. It was a bit of a bummer, to say the least, and a few curly parts of the diagnosis dragged on so long that I simply couldn't get a handle on a new work routine that accommodated my sudden, urgent need for peace and ease. They're still dragging on, to be honest, which is why I'm not rapid releasing this trilogy. But don't fret, book two isn't far away, and there'll be a release date coming soon.

The second (and probably more important) reason this took so long is because I always knew Lucifer's trilogy was going to be about his addiction to Hell's power, and addiction is a personal topic for me. Frankly, I didn't feel ready to write it.

I still don't feel ready, but here it is.

I'm not going to rehash the plot here—you've read it, you know what happens. (At least so far...) Sometimes, the addicts in this book are good people. Sometimes they aren't. Always, the fact that they are addicts makes no difference to whether they are kind or cruel.

We live in a society that stigmatises addiction, overlooking and dismissing the social and trauma-related causes behind it. We treat addicts as problems, instead of looking into and treating the social and systemic issues that result in addiction.

This series isn't intended to be didactic, and I don't believe in one for one metaphors when it comes to writing, anyway. This story is still fundamentally a story, and Lucifer's addiction is to power and not a drug, so there are differences in how it manifests.

But regardless of how the story arcs related to addiction play out, I want to say this here: you're seen and loved. Whatever you're going through, whether it's your own addiction, or whether you love someone who suffers from it (and carry your own suffering from this), I hope you find the compassion you need to heal. You're worthy as a human, no matter what challenges you're facing. Sometimes this world will make you forget that; the world is wrong.

Thank you to everyone who has supported me while I learn to write in a better way for my health. Thank you to an old friend whose refusal to hide in shame inspires me. And thank you to you, dear reader, for sticking around.

ABOUT THE AUTHOR

Jade Bones is a paranormal romance writer who loves writing about delicious demons, magical worlds, and steamy romps. She is the author of the Hell's Fire Burning trilogy, a dark fantasy RH series following an escaped hellsoul and the demons stuck by her side. When Jade isn't writing, you can find her drinking tea, cuddling her dog, or taking tarot far too seriously.

https://www.jadebonesauthor.com

Desperate to know what's next? There are lots of wonderful projects in the works over here, and your best spot for updates is to sign up to my mailing list, or join me in my facebook group.

I share everything about the books in the group, along with giveaways for signed paperbacks and swag that I won't run anywhere else. So it's the best place to be if you want to stay up to date and get all the goodies!

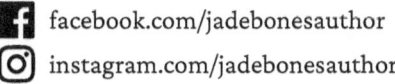

facebook.com/jadebonesauthor

instagram.com/jadebonesauthor

ALSO BY JADE BONES

Reverse Harem

HELL'S FIRE BURNING

Hellcat Escaping

Hellcat Fighting

Hellcat Ascending

STANDALONE

Viper's Fate

Ritual Bound

(available in the Booktober 2022 charity anthology)

Fated to the Fae

(available in the limited edition It's a Fated Match anthology)

One True Love Romance

MY DEMON BOUND

Lock & Portal

Heart & Soul

Rite & Fire

Dreams & Desires

MY DEMON BOUND SHORT

Infernal Fate